ROGUE STARSHIP

DAVID ALASTAIR HAYDEN

1

GAV GENDIN

Gav Gendin fidgeted as his insectoid cog, Octavian, lifted an ancient stasis pod off the bed of Gav's small transport skimmer. The robot's powerful motivators strained as it loaded the heavy capsule onto an antigrav sled.

A sequence of lights flashed on a control panel mounted on the pod, which still thrummed with power despite having spent millennia aboard a deserted ship drifting through hyperspace. Gav placed a hand on the warm capsule. He didn't know the alien woman within, but he felt her presence and could almost see her strangely beautiful face despite the opaque walls of her diamondine cocoon.

Worry tempered his excitement over this rarest of discoveries. Only a year ago he had launched a dangerous expedition into enemy territory to uncover an Ancient temple. He had found much less and yet far more than he'd bargained for. The temple had ended up being an Ancient outpost instead and nearly empty, save for a strange, ceramic amulet and a control chair that had allowed him to somehow pull a still functioning Ancient starship out of hyperspace.

There had been no way to tell where the ship would exit hyperspace and Gav had been hunting for it ever since. How he'd been searching was what bothered him now.

"I have a bad feeling about this."

Octavian paused and trilled a series of questioning beeps.

Distracted by the multitude of concerns careening through his mind, Gav stared numbly into the bulbous eyes on the robot's angular face. None of this felt right. Gav touched the ceramic amulet etched with alien glyphs that hung around his neck.

The moment he had escaped the forbidden system where the Ancient outpost had been hidden, carrying this small relic with him, everything had changed. A vision had shown him that *alien* woman was here, in this capsule, waiting for him. After that, a sequence of vivid dreams had led him to the crash site. And that just wasn't natural.

Octavian prompted him with a quizzical, whirring chirp.

"Yes," Gav said, returning to the present. "Load it onto the ship. Cargo Bay 1. Carefully. I don't want to damage...her."

The robot bobbed its head and beeped in understanding.

Dozens of joints clicking, Octavian pulled the sled up the boarding ramp onto Gav's ship, the *Outworld Ranger*. His four feet rhythmically tinged all the way up into the sleekly curved starship, a Q34-C lightweight cruiser.

Armed for skirmishing, stocked for long journeys, and set up to ferry a few tons of cargo along with a small crew, the *Outworld Ranger* was the perfect ship for a smuggler or, in this case, an archae-ologist with more equipment than caution.

Tal Tonis, Gav's pilot for the last three years, glanced up at the sky for what seemed the hundredth time that day. Tal had the slender frame of a spacer and was the best pilot Gav had ever worked with.

"A bad feeling about what?" Tal asked.

"Everything?" Gav shrugged his broad shoulders. His was a frame born of generations of planet-bound humans. "All I know is something's not right here."

With a lithe hand, Tal clapped him on the arm. "Loosen up, Gav. All the risks you took back in that outpost have paid off. You've made the find of the century here."

"Perhaps the greatest *ever*," Gav said with reasonable assurance that it was.

He had found a living member of the Ancient race, along with a treasure trove of well-preserved artifacts the rest of the crew was still cataloging back at the crash.

"But I'm not the only one who's nervous," Gav said. "What's your deal? Afraid the sky's going to fall?"

Tal laughed half-heartedly and gestured all around them. "It's this swamp. It's creepy, it's damp, and it smells like ass."

Gav didn't mind the muck his boots scrunched in, the vine-wrapped trees with their drooping limbs, or the sulphuric scent hanging in the stagnant air. He didn't even mind the sweltering heat or the mosquito-like insects buzzing about. In his twenty years as a renowned archaeologist, he'd been to far worse places.

Tal again glanced up at the purplish clouds stained by the system's red-tinted sun. Frowning, Gav scratched through his graying beard. If Tal was so bothered by the swamp, why did he keep searching the sky?

A voice entered Gav's mind via his auditory nerves.

"Sir, Mr. Tonis is showing elevated signs of stress but no illness. I recommend a thorough medical evaluation. Or a good bonk on his noggin."

The voice came from the 9G-x chippy unit designated SLK-138 that insisted on being called Silky. And the data came from the lightweight, low-profile sensor array mounted on the shoulders of Gav's battlesuit, right behind his neck. Chippies, the standard form of computer interfaces, plugged into the left temple via a socket wired into the brain's neural system. The 4G units were the most common, with luddites clinging to their 1G's and the poor burdened by 2G's. However, some occupations required more advanced units.

Tal's was a 6G+, a solid choice for a civilian pilot who could afford advanced equipment. But Gav's 9G-x was an experimental unit loaned to him by the government after he had rescued it from the forbidden Krixis world where he'd discovered the body of its original bearer, and the Ancient outpost. Gav's battlesuit, sensor array, weapons, and other advanced equipment had likewise belonged to the Empathic Services agent that had worked with Silky, until her death nearly a hundred and ninety years ago.

Gav focused his thoughts and responded silently through the neural interface system. *"Monitor him closely."*

"Yes, sir."

Gav walked over to a stack of supply boxes Octavian had unloaded from the ship. He began moving the boxes onto the bed of his open-topped, transport skimmer. The boxes contained equipment his team would need at the crash site.

"In fact, increase the sensor sweep from level two to level five and monitor everything."

"Sir, other than Mr. Tonis's elevated heart rate and some harmless beasties in the swamp, I'm not picking up anything unusual. Perhaps a level three scan instead? A level five will drain the sensor pack in less than an hour."

Gav silently called up the power readout in the heads-up display beamed directly into his retinas. Silky had a habit of exaggerating for his benefit—the result of an abnormally advanced AI module and extraordinarily quirky personality programming that altogether either made Silky fully sentient, or something close to it. The sensor pack was currently at seventy-three percent power. An hour of high-level scanning seemed about right.

"Just do as I asked."

"Is this one of those gut sensations humans are afflicted with, sir? Like emotional dysentery?"

"Yep. You can switch to a level one scan when the power meter hits ten percent."

"As you wish, sir. I am sure *you know best."*

With a groan, Tal lifted a box and loaded it onto his skimmer. Being a spacer, he wasn't a strong man, and this world had above average gravity for a habitable planet.

"You keep saying *her* when you talk about the capsule," Tal said, "but couldn't it be a *he*?"

"I suppose it could," Gav lied, picking up a heavy box and wishing he had another cog. When Octavian was told to do something carefully, he took forever.

Tal nodded. "Hoping it's a sexy one, eh?"

"Something like that."

Gav hadn't told anyone except Silky about the dreams or this strange link he had with the alien woman in the capsule. No one would have believed him. Until they had arrived and found the crashed ship only hours ago, he hadn't fully believed it himself.

Tal loaded the final box onto the other skimmer. "How many more trips do you want to make today?"

So far, they had only made the one. As soon as Gav had found the capsule on the Ancient vessel, he had rushed it back to the *Outworld Ranger*. Tal had tagged along so he could help pick up more supplies. Unlike the others, Tal wasn't much use at the sites. He mostly ferried equipment, performed maintenance on the ship, and watched porn using his chippy.

"Just one more." Gav wiped sweat from his brow. "We'll be here recording and salvaging for at least three weeks, maybe a month. No need to hurry."

After that, he'd spend years at home analyzing the capsule and his data, publishing studies, and becoming the most renowned archaeologist in the Benevolency. Perhaps the most famous ever, especially if he could revive the Ancient woman. He would sell the *Outworld Ranger*, settle down, and be a proper father for a change. His boy, Siv, deserved that.

"That sounds terribly exciting," Tal replied numbly.

Tal hated archaeology but loved flying. If not for the privilege of operating a ship as fine as the *Outworld Ranger* and the opportunity to visit off the wall locations, Gav could never have afforded a pilot as good as Tal. It helped that they'd been attacked by pirates Tal's first month on the ship.

Gav swung a leg over the skimmer's seat and settled in. He would have thought the chance to study one of the Ancients' exotic starships would have excited the spacer. But Tal was only interested in ships he could fly.

Gav gripped the steering wheel on his single-seater skimmer, and the control panel lit up. The small transport was hardly bigger than a skimmer bike and could only carry a modest load of equipment. The stasis pod had barely fit in its cargo bed.

"All I want to do now is unload this equipment and record the ship's layout before sunset. I have no desire to be out in this swamp at night."

And he wanted to study the stasis capsule as soon as possible.

Tal climbed into the seat of the other small transport, and together they zoomed out into the swamp, weaving their way between purple-leafed trees and ochre vines with razor-sharp thorns. Behind them, the *Outworld Ranger* rested on one of the few patches of dry ground within leagues.

The Ancient ship had crashed into the vast swamp dominating most of this uncharted planet no more than two months ago. Most of it was submerged into a meter of fetid water. Though Gav had been the one to find it, he wasn't the only one searching for it. The government, with its vast resources, had been looking as well. But Gav had an advantage due to his expertise in studying the Ancients. That was why he had been given the advanced equipment he'd discovered and the services of Silky.

The Ancient ship appeared ahead of them. The hull of the slender, elongated vessel bore many battle scars and had cracked open along one side upon impact with the planet. Gav could tell the ship was severely damaged even before he'd helped it jump out of hyperspace. But the crash landing certainly hadn't helped.

The Ancients had died out nearly twelve thousand years ago. And only hull fragments from other Ancient ships had been discovered, in pieces no larger than a dining table. Most of the artifacts Gav studied were hand-sized or smaller, and the vast majority of his research had focused on the eroded stone edifices they had left behind.

Based on engravings and sculpture fragments they knew the Ancients were anatomically similar to humans, but archaeologists had no bone fragments to work with. For reasons one could only guess, Ancient remains disintegrated far faster than those of humans. To find a living Ancient in a stasis pod was beyond incredible. To find her along with a still functional ship was almost unimaginable. It was all something Gav had been dreaming about since he was thirteen. But it was a dream he'd never once thought could become a reality.

Tal suddenly braked his skimmer.

Gav pulled up to the right of him. "Something wrong?"

Tal didn't respond.

"Sir!" Silky shouted with alarm. *"Three military-class starfighters just entered the atmosphere at assault speed."*

"Vector?"

"Heading this way, sir."

"Toward the Outworld Ranger *or the—"*

"Missiles launched, sir!"

Gav opened his comm to his two team members working on the Ancient ship. "Get out of there! Now!"

Gav looked up and cringed in horror as he saw a half-dozen flaring plasma missiles streaking down from the sky.

"I'm sorry," Tal said softly beside him.

The missiles struck the Ancient ship. The other two members of his crew—Rina Boggs and Enic Pith—never had a chance. The explosion kicked fire and debris into the sky, and the concussion nearly knocked Gav off his speeder. Flaming shards of metal rained through the swamp, falling just short of Gav's position.

Despite the apparent destruction of the vessel, the starfighters maintained their course, pelting the alien wreck with their railguns and plasma cannons. They only pulled up at the last second.

"Sir, imminent danger to your left!"

2

GAV GENDIN

With a thought, Gav activated his force shield. A shimmering, three-foot-wide disc of energy expanded out from the emitter strapped to his left forearm. Gav hunkered down behind the force shield and watched in disbelief as Tal Tonis, a man he had thought his friend, aimed his heavy blaster pistol and fired.

The burst of plasma shots splatted and sizzled against Gav's shield—another highly advanced military piece that had belonged to Eyana Ora, the late Empathic Services agent.

With his right hand, Gav drew his neural disruptor. Tal's second burst knocked the force shield out, and one plasma bolt burned past Gav's cheek, blistering his skin. Gav aimed and squeezed the trigger. A sparkling energy beam fired out of his disruptor pistol and struck Tal in the chest. As a halo of static crackled around him, Tal's muscles tensed, then relaxed. He slumped off the skimmer and plopped into the murky water.

Revving the engines, Gav spun the skimmer around and opened the throttle. He had to get to the *Outworld Ranger* before the starfighters could destroy it.

He opened his comm. "Octavian, raise the shields!"

A binary warble responded affirmatively.

Tal Tonis... He couldn't believe the man had betrayed him, and the rest of the team. Rina...Enic...those were good people back in that Ancient ship, people he cared for and respected. People Tal had always gotten along with. It just didn't make any sense.

And now Tal... Gav frowned. He had been in such a hurry that he hadn't checked the disruptor's settings when returning fire.

"*Silky, was the disruptor on stun or kill?*"

"*The bastard deserved the kill setting sir, but alas, it was on stun.*"

"*Then maintain level five scanning. Tal may recover sooner than we'd like.*"

A tree loomed directly in his path. Gav braked, jerked the steering wheel hard right, leaned into the turn, then swung around the tree, leaning back the other way. He returned to full-speed and immediately had to dodge more indigenous plant life. At this speed he'd kill himself before the starfighters could take a shot at his ship.

"*I need the fastest safe course back through the trees.*"

"*I do have some limitations, sir. I can't work that fast, not while maintaining a level five scan to watch out for Tonis and tracking the starfighters. And without satellites, I don't have a precise map of the planet to—*"

"*Just retrace the previous route we took.*"

Two triangles, one blue and the other yellow, appeared within his heads-up display. Gav bore left and lined them up as best as he could while zipping through the trees at top speed.

He had expected to see a fireball from the *Outworld Ranger's* position by now. "*Where are those fighters?*"

"*Burning hot into orbit, sir.*"

"*What the hell's going on?*"

"*At the moment, all I can say freely is the starfighters are human in origin. And they're a type the government uses for— Sir, Tal is in pursuit.*"

Blaster fire sprayed through the trees around him. "*You don't say?*"

"*I do say, sir.*"

A shot blasted a hole in a tree ahead. Gav ducked as splinters sprayed across him. As he weaved the bike, a plasma shot whizzed past his hip and scorched the side of the skimmer. He was glad he was wearing the battlesuit. He wished he'd brought along his plasma carbine, but Gav only carried it when he thought there would likely be trouble.

A plasma shot tore into the back of the skimmer. It lurched and whined. As Gav tugged it back on course, he heard something spewing out the back end.

"*Damage report?*"

"*I'm not connected to the skimmer, sir.*"

"*Check the control panel with my peripheral vision.*"

"*Right, of course, sir. We've got a leaking coupler between power and antigrav, sir. Propulsion is fine. Antigrav will fail in five minutes.*"

That should hold long enough to get back to the ship, but the skimmer couldn't take another hit like that.

"*Steering control?*" he asked as he strained to keep the course triangles aligned in his HUD.

"*The skimmer rerouted the power, sir. Assisted steering should return any moment.*"

Two blaster bolts blazed past his ears. The shots were becoming more accurate as Tal closed in. If only he had set the disruptor to kill.

Trying to outrace a pilot wasn't a winning proposition. And he couldn't return fire without crashing into a tree. He was going to have to outthink him. A dozen crazy maneuvers popped into his mind, ways to circle back on Tal or to brake, spin, and return fire. They all sounded great. But they were the sorts of things only a skilled pilot, like the one shooting at him, could do. He needed something simple.

He checked his HUD. Only half a kilometer to the ship.

"*Is the* Ranger's *shield up?*"

"*Yes, sir.*"

"*Tell Octavian to transfer control to you.*"

Another shot glanced off the side of the skimmer. As full steering control returned, Gav resisted the urge to start zigzagging. That would only let Tal close in faster.

"*Got it, sir.*"

"*Extend the shield as far to the rear as you can.*"

"*That will drastically weaken it, sir.*"

"*I only need it to be strong enough to stop a speeding skimmer.*"

"*Roger that, sir. Operation Bug Splatter now commencing.*"

"*You want to name it?*"

"*It only seems fitting, sir.*"

"*There really is something wrong with—*"

Gav cried out as a fiery plasma bolt struck his shoulder, burned through his battlesuit, and scorched deep into his flesh.

He slumped over onto the skimmer's controls. The front end dipped toward the ground then bounced hard as the weakened anti-grav prevented a crash. The skimmer nearly flipped over, but despite his darkening vision, Gav managed to pull back on the steering wheel and straighten the skimmer's course with only his left hand. His right arm hung useless and completely numb. Searing waves of pain radiated through his shoulder, up his neck, and down his spine.

Despite beginning to drift in and out of consciousness, he kept the throttle open. "*Silky...you...you understand...the plan, right?*"

"*Operation Bug Splatter, sir. I understand fully. And I'm looking forward to it.*"

Another blaster shot grazed his left leg.

Groaning, he tried but failed, to move his right arm. "*Can you control this thing?*"

"*Remember, sir, I'm not connected. If you tap the control options, you can set it into return home mode.*"

"*That will...reduce the speed.*"

"*Sorry, sir.*"

The shots ceased. Tal must have drained his power pack. Gav tapped the control options button. "Activate autopilot. Return home."

The speeder adjusted course, and the arrows in his HUD

matched perfectly. That was the good news. The bad news was the skimmer began cutting the throttle to a safe speed immediately.

He tapped the control button again. "Override safety speed. Maintain at half throttle."

Was that an option? He couldn't remember. The speed did seem to be holding though, even if it was a lot slower than before.

A shot flared past him. Tal must've reloaded his blaster's power pack. Gav hunkered down into the seat of the skimmer to reduce his target profile. Overwhelmed by the pain, his head spinning, he couldn't look up. He was only barely aware of the shots zipping by.

He should be dead now. Tal was an excellent shot. But maybe the neural disruptor hit had numbed him.

The blaster fire ceased, and the skimmer again slowed beneath Gav. A distinctive thwum sounded behind him. His skimmer moved upward, skidded, and banged to a halt against something.

Behind him, an explosive crunch sounded.

Then he passed out.

3

GAV GENDIN

Gav woke, facedown on a cold metal floor. He rolled over to see Octavian's mechanical face and bulbous eyes looming over him. The cog spoke with a questioning bleep-bloop.

"I'm...okay," Gav groaned as he sat up. "Alive, at least."

Octavian trilled with satisfaction and scooped up an expended emergency medkit.

Gav was at the top of the boarding ramp, just inside the main corridor of the *Outworld Ranger*. His skimmer was farther inside—dented, blaster-scorched, and leaking fluid.

With a triple ding, Silky booted up.

"I see we made it through another dust-up, sir."

"I thought you could stay on without me being conscious."

Most chippies couldn't, except in emergency standby mode, but Silky was incredibly advanced and had spent a hundred and eighty-seven years alone with his thoughts, functioning in low power mode while rewriting his programming from the ground up.

"When you lose consciousness, sir, I go through a forced reboot—in case I am the cause. But I remain active so that I can record whatever transpires around me after my bearer dies. I'm a sort of clever black

box, if you will. I'm working on an override, but I haven't finalized it yet. I have explained all of this before..."

Gav rubbed his aching head. "I'm sure you have."

He craned his neck to look at his wounded shoulder. A hole had been burned through the battlesuit. No wonder Tal had to switch power packs on his gun. He must've been firing his pistol in over-charge mode. Octavian's quick application of medibots had healed the worst of the blister, leaving tender, pink flesh behind. It would take a few weeks to heal and probably wouldn't scar. Gav moved his arm and rotated his shoulder. It hurt like hell deep in the muscle tissues and joints, but it was functional.

His heads-up display returned. A warning sign showed he was under the influence of two strong painkillers and a stimulant. Octavian had used everything in the medkit. He cringed. His shoulder was going to hurt a hundred times worse later. And he was going to need a lot of rest once the emergency stimulant wore off.

"Sir, shouldn't you be attending to some rather important matters? After all, we do have an urgent life or death situation on our docket for this afternoon."

"We what?"

"We survived an explodey-shooty incident, sir, but there are probably more people gunning for us."

"Of course." He hadn't forgotten. It was just hard to care or focus on anything at the moment. "I remember."

"Sir, you are okay, aren't you?"

"I'm just..." he shook off a wave of dizziness "...a bit dazed, apparently."

"Knocking your skull against a wall can do that, sir. I did tell you —on multiple occasions—to always deploy your helmet when riding the skimmer."

"I don't think the drugs are helping me think."

Gav stood shakily and discovered he'd suffered several bruises and a few minor cuts in the crash. He took deep breaths and forced himself to focus.

"*Where...where are the starfighters?*"

"*Waiting in orbit, along with the corvette that dropped them off.*"

A corvette...starfighters...none of this made sense. Moments ago he had been at the top of his game, making history. Now everything was falling apart around him. Though to be fair, alien amulets leading archaeologists to discoveries through visions didn't make much sense either.

"*Tal?*"

"*No idea, sir, though since you're alive, I guess Operation Bug Splatter was a resounding success.*"

Gav stumbled down the boarding ramp and looked out to see Tal's wrecked skimmer just beyond the haze of the *Outworld Ranger's* force field. Tal lay amidst the wreckage...unconscious or dead.

"*Vital signs?*"

"*Scanning, sir...*"

Octavian walked up beside him and blooped sadly.

"*I have detected life signs, sir, but they are weak.*"

Gav headed down the ramp.

"*Sir, shouldn't we beat a hasty retreat?*"

"*I need some answers.*"

"*But the ships in orbit—*"

"*Could have killed us already if they wanted.*"

Silky lowered the force field, and Gav walked out into the wreckage.

Dozens of cuts and force-field burns scored Tal's shattered body. His right arm was bent awkwardly behind him, the left was dislocated from the shoulder, and one leg had snapped below the knee. He had coughed up blood and was now scarcely breathing.

With his neural disruptor in hand, Gav squatted and touched Tal's shoulder. The pilot's eyes opened and locked on Gav. Then he went unconscious again.

Octavian skittered excitedly down the ramp, squawking in concern, a medkit in hand. He leaped through the wreckage, then knelt on his back legs while using his arms and forelegs to open the medkit and sort out the things he would need.

"Octa-dummy says he scanned Tal earlier but didn't detect any vitals, sir."

Silky rarely translated for Octavian as most chippies would. He found it demeaning. Of course, Gav could have enabled Octavian's speech mode. But he couldn't stand to listen to the cog's constant fussing.

Before Octavian could administer the medibots, Gav put a hand out to stop him. "Just give him a stimulant."

Octavian cocked his head and squelched.

"I know your protocol says to save human lives, but this man betrayed us."

Octavian clucked his opposition.

"He tried to kill me. And he's somehow responsible for two other team members getting blown up."

Octavian buzzed as he studied Tal, then he made a sad bloop, put away the medibot tube, and took out the stimulant injector. He placed the business end against Tal's neck and triggered it.

Tal's eyes flared wide open, and he screamed. Octavian injected him with a painkiller. As the screams faded to moans, Gav shoved the cog backward.

"Thank you, Octavian. That will be enough."

Chittering, Octavian slipped a few meters away, then rubbed his arms together as if he were a giant, metal cricket.

"Octavian, go see to it that everything is stowed away on the ship. We will be taking off soon."

The cog squawked heatedly for a moment, then stalked into the ship.

Gav holstered his pistol. Tal wasn't a threat anymore. He touched Tal's shoulder, and the spacer pilot winced.

"Sir, if you're going to interrogate him, you need to neutralize his chippy first."

"Remove your chippy. Now."

Tal tried but couldn't reach the eject switch. "I disengaged it... was malfunctioning anyway. Damaged in the crash."

Gav hit the eject, and the chippy popped out into his hand. He tossed it aside. "Why, Tal?"

Tal grimaced and chuckled. "That's a...good question."

Gal squeezed Tal's dislocated shoulder. He didn't move, but the pain showed in his eyes. "I want an answer."

"I don't...know why."

"Fine. What was your price?"

"The *Outworld Ranger*."

"You killed two good people for a ship?! Damn it, Tal, I would've gladly loaned it to you after we returned home. You could've paid me back over time."

"I didn't...arrange this, Gav. *They* did. The *Outworld Ranger*... was my reward for...helping them track you...keeping them up-to-date...reporting in on what you found...but I didn't...have a choice."

If the government was behind this, they could have tracked and monitored Gav through Silky, unless they didn't trust him anymore. Silky was running a program so that he could keep his communications with Gav and anything else secret whenever he desired, but it should have been impossible for the government to know he was doing it.

"You could have said no."

"And then they...would have killed me too..."

"Who are they?"

"Military I assumed. They had the attitude...and the resources." Tal tried to shrug. "They did all the talking...and wouldn't answer... my questions."

"Sir, how was he contacting them? I monitored every communication in and out of the Outworld Ranger, and I haven't detected any signals since we landed."

"How did you keep in touch with them?"

"Echo space transponder embedded...in the base of my skull." Tal coughed up bile and blood. "Gives me...awful headaches."

"*Silky?*"

"*Scanning him, sir. I still can't detect anything. Let me adjust my filters... Ah, there it is. That does seem to be a direct link out. And I will note that device was designed to avoid detection by someone exactly like me.*"

Tal winced. "I notified them...as soon as I could identify the pod...on the crashed ship and...get myself clear."

"So they knew about the stasis pod?"

Tal nodded painfully.

"*Sir, ask him how they knew the stasis pod would be on this ship. You didn't know anything about it, so it wasn't in your report.*"

That was a damned good question. Gav repeated it aloud to Tal.

"You think...I know?" His chuckle devolved into a wheezing cough. "All I know...they wanted that pod destroyed...bad."

"But the pod wasn't on the Ancient ship when they blew it up," Gav said. "You waited until after we had it loaded onto the *Outworld Ranger* to contact them. Why?"

"Double-crossed them. I'm not...stupid. They were going to...kill me anyway. The ship was...an empty promise."

"And the double-cross?"

"A third party. They knew about...the pod too."

Silky groaned. "*Are we the only ones who didn't know? I've got a bad feeling about all this, sir.*"

"So that's why you waited until you had it on the *Outworld Ranger?*"

Tal nodded again. "Supposed to take the pod...to a rendezvous point. I was afraid the starfighters...would do a scan...pick up the pod in the *Ranger*...guess this planet's nutty magnetic field...kept them stumped."

"*They haven't even attempted any scans, sir. They couldn't hide that from me.*"

"What third party?" Gav asked.

"The bloody Krixis...through a human agent, if you can believe it."

"You'd trust a deal with them?"

"If you can't even trust your own...why not? They didn't care about anything...but the stasis pod. They made that clear. It was...at least a chance and...that's a damn fine ship. I was going to go into orbit...make a run for it...to the Krixis rendezvous point. If any ship could get me there..."

"So you figured you'd roll the dice?" Gav cursed. "If you had told me, maybe I could have done something...different."

"The only option was...to never come here. I couldn't...have kept you away. And they made it clear...I couldn't quit...being your pilot."

Gav clutched at his forehead and groaned. "Shit."

Tal retched again, then pointed at Gav's chest. "That amulet...I was supposed to...bring it to them after..."

"Which them?"

"Both...they both wanted it."

"Circuits of my makers. Sir, I think...I have an idea what's..."

Gav waited a moment for Silky to continue, but he didn't. *"You planning on finishing that statement?"*

"No."

"Is it possible for the Krixis to use a human agent?"

The Krixis were incredibly alien, telepathic, an unable to communicate with humans, except through math and pictures, when they could be bothered to try.

"Not to my knowledge, sir. Eyana managed it, but with extreme difficulty and under unique circumstances."

Tal groaned. His injuries were already starting to overwhelm the painkiller. "Gav...I can buy you...a few minutes...but I want something in exchange."

"What?" Gav hissed.

"Two sedative injectors...so I don't have to die in pain."

Gav nodded. "What do you propose?"

"You told me...orbital scans...couldn't detect you." He paused and gasped for breath. "Is that true?"

"I have a military-grade jamming device in my sensor array. So very few scans of any kind can detect me. Besides, they're not scanning the planet anyway. And Silky can probably come up with something extra, I'm sure."

"Good. Tap the subcutaneous activator...under my jaw. It will let me talk...to the corvette's commander over...a secure channel."

"*Silky, what do you think?*"

"*I think we made a mistake coming here, sir.*"

"*Silky!*"

"*I can't be certain of the activator's function, sir. It could be for what he says, or it could activate a kaboomy device tucked away on our ship, or it could signal them to atomize us from orbit. At this point, all our options stink, but I should think dying men with nothing to gain would be more trustworthy than not.*"

Gav touched a slight bump on Tal's jaw, activating the secure-link implant.

Tal took a deep breath and gathered his composure. "Come in, Alpha 1..." Someone responded to Tal on the other end, but the response went directly into Tal's auditory nerve. "My chippy was damaged. Yes, there was a small explosion near the ship...but everything's under control now... Professor Gendin has been neutralized..." He gasped for air. "Yes, object confirmed. Mission successful. I'm about to take off. I'll see you at the rendezvous."

Tal nodded, and Gav tapped his jaw to deactivate the link.

"That should buy you a few minutes. As soon as...you're in orbit though...they'll realize I'm still down here." He nodded toward the *Outworld Ranger*. "Take care of that ship...as long as you can. She's a beauty."

Gav sighed. "I could have Octavian try to patch you up."

"You're a good man. But I can't feel my legs...and my lungs...are filling with blood. I'm not going...to make it much longer. Just give me...the sedatives."

"Octavian, bring me two sedative injectors."

The cog rushed them out to him. Gav took one and quickly

placed it against Tal's neck and triggered half a dose. Tal's eyes widened then closed.

"Octavian, get him aboard. Carefully. I don't want him dying on us yet."

"Change of heart, sir?"

"As long as he survives, we can avoid capture. It might buy us enough time."

"You are a devious man, sir."

"Do everything you can to keep him alive, Octavian."

The robot chirped enthusiastically, happy that he was being allowed to follow his core imperative to save endangered lives.

"The poor fool doesn't know you're manipulating him, sir. Machines..."

Octavian sputtered a long sequence of beeps.

"Sir, he says Mr. Tonis needs to be moved carefully to avoid long-term spinal injury. He wants to bring out an antigrav sled and...do a bunch of medical nonsense, I guess."

"You guess?"

"I stopped paying attention after the word sled."

"Octavian, we don't have time for that. If we don't get moving, we'll all be as good as dead."

Octavian screeched his irritation, then carefully lifted Tal and carried him up the boarding ramp.

"Sir, if this ruse doesn't buy us enough time..."

Gav shrugged. *"Fortune favors the bold."*

"Does that mean you have an idea, sir?"

"Maybe, but it's of the out of the frying pan and into the fire variety."

4

GAV GENDIN

Gav stood at the top of the boarding ramp and gazed out onto the swamp planet. Only hours before, after a flyover had revealed the Ancient ship, he had stood here triumphantly as the hatch opened onto what was to be the crowning achievement of his career and the culmination of dreams he'd had since childhood. He was going to be the first to unlock the secrets of the Ancients.

Now a plume of black smoke marked the location of the Ancient vessel. Two of his friends were dead, and one had tried to kill him.

"Silky, when you warned me not to trust anyone, that I would be watched, I thought you were paranoid. I'm sorry."

"I understand, sir." The chippy sounded just as disillusioned as Gav felt. *"I never expected things to get so real so fast."*

"I know what you mean."

"I don't think you do, sir." Silky sighed. *"Only the Benevolence knew you pulled the Ancient ship out of hyperspace. And your report was the most secret of top secrets. Whoever set up Tal must have known what was on that ship before we set out looking for it. How else could they have known about the stasis pod before we did?"*

The Benevolence was the godlike AI, created and housed on

Terra, that had guided humanity's progress across the galaxy for over three millennia. The Benevolence wielded ultimate authority as it oversaw the affairs of thousands of star systems, controlled the android soldiers of the military, and regulated the flow of advanced technologies. The Benevolence had designed anything more complex than a plasma carbine, a fusion reactor, or an ion drive and manufactured by automated systems exclusively on the factory planets of Terra, Mars, and Venus. In fact, no one even understood how the hyperphasic technologies that powered loop capacitors, echo space relays, and stardrives functioned. And without them, humans would become star system bound, relegated to light speed communications and needing to meet all their power requirements through fusion alone.

Gav had heard various conspiracy theories about how the Benevolence was an evil entity with far-reaching plans that had yet come to fruition, but he'd never believed any of them. The people who did were all nut-jobs and religious extremists. And sure, some people thought humanity would be better off running its affairs without oversight from the Benevolence. But it was hard to argue against the Benevolence's results. After all, humans had successfully and prosperously spread throughout the galaxy under its guidance.

And humans weren't the only people to recognize the benefits of the Benevolence's rule. Almost every alien species they had encountered had agreed to join the Benevolency and gain the opportunities and prosperity that humanity enjoyed. Only four wars with the alien Krixis Empire and a few minor skirmishes with other groups had significantly interrupted three millennia of peace.

"*Silky, are you suggesting what I think—what I'm afraid—you're suggesting?*"

"*I'm not suggesting anything, sir—not yet anyway. All I have right now are theories that are little better than guesses. Nothing that I'm ready to share and nothing that it would be safe for you to know.*"

With a sigh, Gav flicked a switch, and the boarding ramp

retracted, sealing away a lifetime of hopes and dreams. *"You did tell me it was all too good to be true."*

"I'd love to say I told you so, sir. But this wasn't what I had in mind. I was thinking alien possession or perhaps a trap set by the mysterious entities from the darkness that destroyed the Ancients. Maybe the government seizing all the artifacts, the Ancient vessel, and your work, then preventing you from publishing. But not this."

"Alien possession isn't off the table yet."

"Painfully true, sir. Though I suspect those starfighters aren't planning on letting you live long enough to see that possibility play out."

Gav's grunted his agreement with the chippy's assessment. He trusted Silky and, right now, he wasn't sure he trusted anyone else. Everything he believed in was unraveling on the very day that was supposed to be one of the highlights of his life.

He started a quick sweep of the ship, to be sure everything was in order. Not that it was necessary. Octavian didn't tolerate things being out of order on the *Outworld Ranger*. But it always made him feel better to check. And in this case, with his life hanging in the balance, he wanted to be as certain as he could of everything.

Gav stepped into the crew cabin. Tal's broken body lay on his bunk with Octavian fussing over him.

"How's the patient?"

Octavian beeped and screeched.

"He's upset you didn't let him treat Mr. Tonis sooner, sir. And he's dumb enough to think it would have made a difference."

"Just do your best, Octavian."

The cog trilled an irritated response.

"But be ready to initiate system repairs. We are entering a dangerous situation. If I go to red alert, abandon the patient. The ship comes first."

Octavian nodded his head and blooped.

Gav continued and stopped at the entrance to Cargo Bay 1. Octavian had locked down the stasis pod using magnetic restraints. Gav stared at the capsule and its blinking lights. The answers to hundreds of questions lay just within his reach. It was killing him that he might never get the chance to ask them.

He ran his fingers along the amulet. He took one step into the bay, then stopped himself. He didn't dare go any closer. Especially not while he was still dazed from the collision. Silky was right. Alien psychic influence wasn't yet out of the realm of possibility. And the dreams of the being within, calling to him, had been so vivid and had steadily gained in intensity over the last several months. Whatever she was, she had brought him here. That suggested a powerful influence that he could ill afford to encounter at the moment.

"We need to survive this."

"You'll get no argument from me, sir."

"No, I mean for more than our sakes or even the knowledge the Ancient capsule contains."

"Sir, they will become suspicious if we don't take off soon. And Tal isn't going to live much longer."

Gav's thoughts broke free from the capsule and the Ancient woman inside. *"Right."*

He rushed to the ship's small bridge and slid into the command chair. A captain could access every system from that station, including the ship's weapons. The *Outworld Ranger* had a plasma quad-cannon on top, a small salvo of ion missiles, a flak cannon, and a forward-facing railgun.

Normally, Gav supervised from his command chair and helped out where needed. Tal had always manned the piloting station, Octavian the engineering station in the ship's aft near the ion drives and the stardrive, and his deceased comrades the weapon, shield, and sensor systems.

"Silky, could you operate sensors and weapons?"

"Of course, sir, but it will be inefficient for me to do so. I need to maintain my sensor sweeps, and the rotational frequency jamming I'm using to shield you and the capsule from detection."

"We don't have much choice."

Gav removed the copper half-moon circlet from its dock on the command console and clasped it around his head. The end studs locked onto his temples, the left one connecting to his chippy. There was a tug at his thoughts, like a pleasant memory conjured by a breeze, then the ship's systems linked directly to his mind.

His personal HUD window slid to the left, while a display window for operating the ship opened on the right. With a few eye flicks, he minimized all of his interfaces and arranged the ship read-outs to his liking.

The command interface circlet connected him to the AI control systems for every station. The docked circlets at the other three consoles could only link to their respective stations.

Gav routed all essential functions to himself.

Under normal conditions, the ship could take off or land or do pretty much anything necessary by itself. But its AI lacked adaptability, critical thinking, and true intelligence. The brainwaves of even a clueless moron could drastically boost the capacity of a ship's AI system. A good pilot or gunner could operate in concert with the AI, each complimenting the other's strengths and weaknesses until they effectively became one. And a good captain who understood all the workings of a ship could mentally boost the entire system, helping everyone.

Once a ship jumped into hyperspace space, the AI could capably operate everything, going weeks without any need for human interaction.

"*Silky, plot a course for the middle of nowhere, in the opposite direction of home.*"

"*Aye aye, captain sir.*"

Gav engaged the antigrav engines, and the *Outworld Ranger* rose up off the ground. He boosted the power, angled the ship upward, and ignited the ion drive. The twin engines roared to life, and the *Outworld Ranger* burned toward outer space, taking a vector that moved them as far away from the corvette and starfighters as possible.

"*The ship is being scanned, sir.*"

"As long as they don't pick up you or me or the stasis pod, we'll be okay—for a little longer. The enemy should see only what they expect."

As they entered orbit, Gav brought the shields up to fifty percent, hoping that wouldn't arouse too much suspicion.

"Our course is plotted, sir. We just need to make the breakpoint. Laying in the best course for escape now."

At the breakpoint, they would be far enough out from both planetary and solar gravity wells that they could engage the stardrive and enter hyperspace.

"How long till we reach the breakpoint?" Gav asked as the ship's AI maneuvered onto the ideal breakpoint vector.

The information he wanted would be somewhere in his HUD, but he didn't have time to monitor everything visually, especially when he was keeping an eye on the locator display that tracked the position of the enemy corvette and her three starfighters.

"At full speed, it will take us two hours for a rough jump, sir. Three for a clean break."

A rough jump risked breaking the ship apart due to turbulence. Why the gravity within a star system interacted in this way when a stardrive pushed a ship into hyperspace was not understood, but the rules were absolute. Ships could not enter or leave hyperspace at all when they were too deep within a star system's gravity well.

"At our current speed, it will take us nearly five hours."

Gav directed the ship to accelerate gradually, trying not to draw too much attention. The enemy ships followed but didn't seem to be in a hurry.

A terrible thought occurred to him suddenly. *"Silky, how do you think they were going to ensure that Tal would arrive at the rendezvous point?"*

"The echo-space relay they implanted in him, sir. I suspect they can track him anywhere within the Benevolency, maybe beyond. He'd only be hidden while in hyperspace."

"What about you? Can't they track you as well."

"I am the most advanced chippy in existence, sir. I can disable my connection to the Benevolence at any time."

"And you're certain?"

"There would have been no need for Tal working as a spy if the Benevolence itself didn't think otherwise."

During his two centuries of waiting for a rescue, Silky had rewritten every line of his code in an attempt to become human, modeling himself on Eyana Ora, the Empathic Services agent he'd worked with for five decades. He had then locked this new self away and enabled a program that would allow him to act autonomously while pretending otherwise. Silky claimed even the Benevolence itself couldn't break through his firewalls, though it had apparently figured out his ruse.

"What about other trackers? Tal could have planted something on the Outworld Ranger.*"*

"Neither the ship nor my level five scan detected one, sir. Should we escape, I'll study the method they were using on the echo space transponder to circumvent my scans and then search for trackers onboard."

"Good."

"But sir, if the Benevolence is involved, there's no way to be safe anywhere."

"There are ways to escape even the Benevolence's notice out on the Fringes."

"Not easily, sir. Not easily."

Over the next hour, as they headed toward the breakpoint, Gav tried to make all the bits of information he had add up to something that made sense. But all he could come up with were half-baked conspiracy theories. He wanted to ask Silky what he suspected, but he didn't. Silky was right, speculating based on wild guesses wouldn't do them any good. They needed answers. Unfortunately, it didn't look like they were going to get them anytime soon.

Gav wiped his brow. It was cool inside the ship, yet he was sweating. He couldn't remember ever being this tense before.

The planet was now a small gray blob, and the corvette continued to match their speed and follow at a distance.

"*Sir, I'm picking up some strange sensor echoes.*"

"*Echoes?*"

A series of low bloops from Octavian sounded in his ear, then a readout in his HUD announced that Tal Tonis had died.

"*Sir, the enemy ships have accelerated to maximum burn.*"

Gav kicked the *Outworld Ranger* into full speed. She wasn't a corvette, but she was faster than a starfighter. The sudden burst of g's kicked him in the nuts and shoved his eyeballs into the back of his head, but then the inertial dampeners caught up, returning the ship to a comfortable half-g environment.

He took a deep breath. "*Silky, when you said sensor echoes?*"

"*Sir, we have a problem.*"

Everything went to hell, all at once.

The corvette launched a salvo of ion torpedoes. And ahead of him, in a wide arc, six more starfighters disengaged advanced cloaking shields and unleashed their ion torpedoes at him.

Gav was caught in a vise.

5

GAV GENDIN

"Ship, activate evasive maneuver protocols," Gav commanded.

The *Outworld Ranger's* automated routines kicked in. The ship veered hard left, then it began to zig and zag. With that many missiles aimed at him, he could only hope to delay the inevitable. The fact that his enemies, whoever they were, didn't want to blow him to smithereens helped. But, eventually, they would disable his ship and storm aboard.

"Time to impact?"

"One minute and twelve seconds for the volley from the starfighters, sir. The corvette's volley will hit you nine seconds later. Rather sloppy synchronicity on their part, I'd say."

Gav sighed with regret. Only a few minutes left to live...

He thought of the Ancient capsule in the cargo bay and his ten-year-old son.

To hell with dying. It was time to enact his desperate plan.

"Octavian, disable the stardrive safety protocols."

A shrill reply beeped into his earbud.

"I don't care about your concerns. Just do it!"

"Sir, what are you doing?"

"Rolling the dice. Going out on my terms."

"Stardrive safety protocols have been deactivated, sir. Octavian says... Frankly, he says you're a suicidal maniac."

"Do you agree?"

"It's something I've always liked about you, sir."

"Ship, drop into wraith space on my mark."

"Sweet Benevolence, sir. That's trying to roll snake eyes on three dice."

Gav groaned. *"I know. But it's the only play I've got left."*

The stardrive could jump the ship into any number of hyperphasic dimensions with divergent laws of physics. All but three—hyperspace, dull space, and wraith space—would tear a vessel apart. Though most of the hyperphasic dimensions had proved useless, two others had proven essential. Flux space provided the power for all modern devices, and echo space enabled almost instant communication across vast distances.

In hyperspace, the distance between star systems was compacted. For a fast cruiser like the *Outworld Ranger*, a journey of five light years took less than ten hours. In dull space, interstellar distances were doubled. Ships could enter safely, but doing so was effectively pointless. And like hyperspace, dull space didn't offer Gav an escape because its strange laws of physics wouldn't allow him to make a jump from within a star system either. Survival in both of those dimensions was only possible because of the protective bubble the stardrive created.

And then there was wraith space, a strange reality with mind-bending, psychogenic distortions and relentless ion storms. Entering wraith space unprepared and without proper training and shielded equipment was beyond dangerous. The only people who traveled there were the genetically enhanced delvers who mined the hyperphasic crystals needed for harnessing and storing the flux space energy used to power humanity's devices. Such crystals, from ship-sized units to the miniature packs that powered chippies, only formed on the planets that drifted through wraith space.

Despite the near-suicidal danger, wraith space held one distinct benefit for Gav. He could enter it within a system, without any concern for gravitational effects.

The ion missiles closed in. Gav deactivated the flak cannons. No point wasting ammo he might need later.

"Impact imminent, sir. 10...9..."

The touchscreens on the ship's control panels were all redundant, there only in case the circlet interfaces failed, with one exception. Since an accidental jump from within a system would be deadly, stardrive activation had to be done manually. Gav punched in his four-digit access code.

"8...7..."

He pressed a button on the left side of the control panel and pushed a handle forward on the right side.

"4...3..."

One of two things was about to happen. Either his enemy would think he was crazy enough to make a hyperspace jump from here and assume he was dead, or they'd realize he had gone into wraith space. If they did figure out where he had gone, would they have the balls to follow him in?

"Sir, the ion torpedoes just accelerated to 90% light."

"What?!"

"Some type of secondary booster, sir. I've never seen anything—"

Enveloped by a brief halo of swirling white lights, the *Outworld Ranger* gently shifted from normal reality and into wraith space.

The stardrive created a bubble that extended a few meters beyond the ship. Two of the ion missiles that had pierced the bubble struck the moment the ship entered wraith space. It rocked as the torpedoes collided with the shields.

"Two impacts, sir. Shield integrity...nullified. Sensors offline. Secondary systems..."

With a hiss and a flicker, Silky and Gav's HUD winked out— victims of either the ion strike or wraith space itself.

Gav ripped the circlet off his head and studied the instrument panels. Everything was offline except interior monitoring, artificially gravity control, life support, and of course, the stardrive, the one thing that always worked reliably within wraith space.

The ship was dark now, lit only by the dim yellow glow of the emergency lighting systems.

A wave of dizziness hit Gav. He shook it off and took a few deep breaths, trying to keep his mind focused.

No one was shooting at him. That was a positive sign.

Unfortunately, he wasn't sure what to do now. He hadn't had time to think up a plan for what to do next. Presumably, he would travel through wraith space, which had the same dimensions as real space, long enough for his enemies to give up.

But the ion drive was offline, and the system's gravity was slowing him down already. He wasn't going to get far this way.

The only question was how long would...

Gav's mind went fuzzy again. When it cleared, wraith space revealed the truth of its marketing. A spectral form resembling a tall spacer with flowing robes drifted toward him. He threw his hands up, despite knowing it wasn't real, and it passed harmlessly through him. Two more specters floated through the bridge. One in an indeterminable shape, the other appearing as something similar to a wolf with half-formed wings.

He shivered as the air grew cold around him. A burst of color dazzled his eyes. Then everything went dark...then bright again, only absent of any color whatsoever.

The ship rocked violently. Through the bridge's clear diamondine window Gav saw raging ion storms. Most likely the torpedoes had kicked them up.

Something banged hard against the ship. A groaning, scraping noise echoed throughout the interior.

The artificial gravity failed, and Gav floated, weightless through the bridge. The scraping object passed by the window. One of the enemy starfighters, spinning out of control, tumbled past, carried by the ion storm. Crackling bolts of blue-white energy sparked around it.

Starfighters had emergency stardrives and basic shielding. Bringing one of them in here was insane, but then maybe they had only expected to briefly pop in to see if he was here before retreating. If so, they hadn't counted on the storm their torpedoes had triggered.

Artificial gravity returned and over-compensated. Gav slammed down onto the deck, banging his head against the command chair. All the other systems within the ship came back on. Then static flickered along the control panels, and everything but life-support and gravity blinked off.

No longer under thrust from the twin ion drive, the ship couldn't adjust to the ion storm winds. Like the starfighter that had scraped the hull, the *Outworld Ranger* began to spin and drift.

More wraiths appeared around Gav, amidst swirling colors. Dizzy and disoriented, he stumbled around on the deck. It was all like a dream, punctuated by moments of clarity.

He found himself not on the bridge but in the crew quarters, standing over Tal's body.

Next time he came to he found himself hovering over the toilet. He stood and wiped vomit from his mouth.

Then he was again on the bridge, shouting orders to no one.

And then he was stumbling up to the engineering station. Octavian's spindly body had slumped in place. The cog looked like a metal bug splattered on a window.

A voice called out through the ship. Feminine...exotic...yet frightened...desperate...pleading...

Someone needed his help.

Gav focused on that voice and careened through the main corridor, trying to follow it. His mind went in and out. His vision blurred. Wraithlike beings swirled around and through him. Some resembled loved ones long gone, while others were terrors that left him cowering against the wall.

On his only brief trip here before, as a young man, Gav had discovered he was not cut out for wraith space. Some minds could handle it better than others. Given enough time, though, even a delver would go crazy in wraith space.

Life-support and artificial gravity cut in and out. The ion drive burned a few minutes before sputtering out again. The ship's weapon system came online and fired a few plasma cannon blasts out into space.

Gav wandered around for what seemed like hours, trying to locate the voice. Until at last, he found himself in Cargo Bay 1.

The amulet hanging from his neck began to shine red, its light piercing the dimly lit cargo bay. It had never glowed before! He stumbled over and touched the Ancient capsule. It too began to glow.

Then he saw the ethereal beauty from his visions again. The alien woman was as tall as a spacer with a lithe frame and delicate features. Her broad, almond eyes curled up on the outside corners. Her skin glistened a pale, opalescent green. Her hair, a lustrous sable, streamed down her back, except for a few strands that wrapped around the insect-like antennas above her temples before falling alongside her cheeks. A gossamery lavender robe clung enticingly to her figure, and faint blue lines formed eddies and currents along her face and arms. Space-deep eyes locked onto his, and she spoke, her words passing straight into his mind, her voice melodic, mesmerizing.

"Please, kind strangers in the deep, hear me. Numenaia...my civilization...it has fallen. I am likely now the last of my kind. I request sanctuary and the chance to tell you of the Shadraa, the horrors from the dark. They came for my people, and we stopped them. But the price of victory was terrible. Someday, they will come for you as well. But I can help prepare you. Within me, I carry access to all the knowledge of the great wonders of the Numenaian civilization—our stardrives and communications, our medicines and weapons.

"Please, strangers in the deep who hear this, give me refuge and let me help you. I swear to you that I, High Priestess Lyoolee Syryss of the Order Benevolent, mean you no harm. If you link your minds to mine, you will see that I speak the truth, and gain the knowledge you need to rescue me and prepare for the coming war."

He tried to reply to her...but managed nothing more than an incoherent babble. Then she began to speak again...only to repeat the same message, word for word.

The Numenaian priestess might still be alive within the capsule, but she wasn't speaking to him directly. It was a transmission through wraith space, and maybe through other dimensions as well. And the being within this capsule had probably been broadcasting that telepathic message for thousands of years...warning of a great enemy... promising technological wonders... All you had to do was connect to her...and learn these things.

As he listened to her speak the message, over and over again, dozens of questions came to mind. But, at the same time, a great many other things began to click into place. Like a possible reason why both the Benevolence and the Krixis Empire were so interested in her capsule. He wished Silky was online. The chippy might be able to confirm some of what he now suspected. On his own, all Gav had were educated guesses. But then he'd made a career of betting on intuition and educated guesses.

Gav's mind went suddenly as clear as crystal. Whether because of some influence from the capsule or the amulet, or the adrenaline pumping through him, he didn't know. Aware it might fade at any moment, he rushed to the engineering station. He couldn't risk losing his mind in wraith space, but he also had to stay here long enough to escape the enemy ships. He needed a plan.

From a toolbox, he withdrew a spool of wire and broke off a piece a couple of meters in length. Using his command code, he engaged the manual control for the stardrive. Then he activated the magnetic grip in his boots, anchoring himself to the floor. Finally, he tied one end of the wire around his belt and the other around the control handle that could drop the ship out of wraith space. All he had to do was pull the pump-style handle outward from its current locked position, and that should happen if he lost his mind and wandered away.

Gav squatted down beside Octavian and rested his back against the engineering station. He patted the cog on the head.

"I really hope you don't wake up before we get out of wraith space. You're scary looking enough as it is. I can't handle having you roaming around right now."

The ship shuddered. Gav winced. Hopefully, it was part of the ion storm and not a missile or some other object. Nothing was preventing the ship from eventually colliding with an asteroid, planet, or moon or drifting into the sun.

As minutes, then hours passed, with various ship systems flickering on and off, Gav's thoughts continuously drifted back to the Ancient priestess. He touched the amulet that had led him here. He'd found it, along with Silky and his other advanced gear, on the body of Eyana Ora. And, according to Silky, she'd taken it off one of the Krixis she'd killed in the tunnels outside the outpost. It had allowed him to enter and recall the priestess's ship.

But if the Krixis had the amulet all along, why hadn't they recalled the Ancient ship from hyperspace and rescued the priestess themselves?

Maybe they had only just found the amulet. Gav was a leading expert on all things Ancient, yet he had never seen nor heard of another piece like it. Or maybe the Krixis—or even others—had tried and failed while he, for some reason, had succeeded.

Gav groaned. He was missing too many pieces to assemble this puzzle.

A wraith moved through him, and he flinched. The intensity of the apparitions was building again, the figures becoming more and more grotesque. It wasn't a function of wraith space. It was the unexpected mental clarity he'd gotten from touching the capsule now wearing off.

Octavian blooped, then whirred. Scrambling awkwardly on its insectoid legs, it tried to stand. Gav cowered. The cog turned its head toward him, and Gav screamed. Hysterical nightmares created by wraith space twisted his mind as he looked into the cog's eyes. The beast was coming for him. It was going to kill him and strip the meat and skin off his bones. It was going to wear him and disguise itself as a human.

But then it slumped back down, lifeless.

Gav continued to cower, drenched in sweat yet shivering, while the sights and sounds of hell caroused around him. In his lucid moments, he thought of pulling out the handle. But each time, he reminded himself that he had to wait out the enemy...that he had to make it back to his son...at he had to, somehow, pass on what he had learned. And the priestess in the capsule...he had to protect her.

Hour after maddening hour passed. But Gav stayed put. Then suddenly, he found himself standing in the corridor. The wraiths and hallucinations were gone. Ship systems were coming back online one by one. Silky was beeping through his reboot sequence. And Octavian stirred behind him.

Gav turned and saw his boots lying on the floor. The thin copper wire dangling from his belt had snapped. But it had done its job of freeing them from wraith space.

6

GAV GENDIN

As his HUD came up, Gav ran toward the bridge. "Octavian, maintain your station. Red alert."

"*Sir, what's going on?*" Silky asked with an affected yawn.

"*We've just dropped out of wraith space.*"

"*I can see that, sir. Oh my stars, I napped seven hours and thirty-three minutes.*"

"*Only that long? It seemed like days to me.*"

Gav slid into the command chair and donned the circlet again. According to his HUD, the ion storm had propelled them outward from the planet and the solar system. That was great news. And the ship wasn't showing any immediate threats, which was even better.

He began the startup sequence for the ion drive.

"*Sir, sensors have detected the corvette, but none of the starfighters. It's on the opposite side of the planet. I have enabled sensor jamming, but that won't fool them long.*"

"*Why is the corvette over there?*"

"*It never moved, sir. We did.*"

"Oh."

"I'm laying in a new jump vector."

"Time to breakpoint?"

"Seven minutes, twelve seconds, sir."

"That's the best thing I've heard all day."

"Course set, sir."

The twin ion drive flared to life, and Gav kicked it into full burn. After a brief moment of high g-force, the inertial dampeners compensated. As he caught his breath, Gav studied the readouts on his HUD. The ship had suffered minor hull damage, and the plasma cannon was inoperative. Otherwise, everything had made it out of wraith space intact.

"If you detect even the smallest anomaly, let me know."

"Roger that, sir. Are you going to tell me what's going on now?"

"Silky, I plan on devoting every scrap of attention I have to escaping this godforsaken star system. After that, we can talk."

Gav kept his eyes locked onto the sensors as the minutes passed.

"Sir, they detected us."

"Time to breakpoint?"

"Seventy-eight seconds."

The red dot representing the enemy corvette suddenly sped across his display like an ant racing across a hotplate. He had never seen anything move that fast before, except the ion torpedoes he'd faced earlier, and those had only sped up at the last moment.

"Silky, what the hell is happening? Are the sensors malfunctioning?"

"Sensors are operating normally, sir. This appears to be an advanced ion drive, unlike anything I've ever heard of. It's moving at eighty-five percent light."

The Outworld Ranger's drive maxed out below fifty percent, and it was a fast vessel.

"That kind of acceleration should have killed the crew."

"I'm sure the antigravity is adequate, sir, since androids can handle a much bigger gravity punch than you."

The Benevolency's military consisted entirely of android soldiers with strong morality but weak individuality programming. Or at least their morality programming was supposed to be strong. Gav had doubts about that today.

"Ion torpedoes launched and locked on target, sir."

Gav watched in terror as a dozen missiles moving near the speed of light accelerated toward them. He activated the flak cannon, for all the good it would do against that many projectiles moving that fast.

His breath caught as the torpedoes closed to within five kilometers.

The *Outworld Ranger* nosed upward as Silky made a slight, last-moment course adjustment. The ship's maneuvering thrusters burned at full blast.

The torpedoes reached the one-kilometer point.

Then a white halo enveloped the *Outworld Ranger*.

For a minute, the ship rocked, shuddered, and creaked as it rough-jumped into hyperspace. Then everything went perfectly smooth and quiet.

"Course safe, acceleration stable. We did it, sir. And aren't you glad you installed that hull upgrade I recommended after our last rough jump?"

Gav breathed and released his deathlike grip from the arms of the command chair. He slumped back, pulled the circlet off his head, and wiped the sweat from his brow. It would take the corvette a few minutes to figure out their course, given Silky's last-moment adjustment.

Once they calculated his course, they could chase him. Fortunately, it was impossible for ships to engage one another within hyperspace. Outside the protective stardrive bubble, everything was crammed into a smaller space. People and the objects they built weren't capable of withstanding that effect and maintaining their integrity, so a projectile fired at another ship would implode.

"Silky, if that corvette can enter hyperspace at that speed..."

"Then it will reach our destination long before we will, sir."

"We need to fall out of hyperspace somewhere along the way."

"I'll begin the calculations right away, sir."

"Try not to drop us into a star system and get us killed."

"I'll do my best, sir. But our luck has been sour as of late."

Gav tapped his comm. "Octavian, place Mr. Tonis in the airlock, please."

A series of beeps and bloops responded. Silky couldn't be bothered to interpret, so Gav made an assumption.

"Yes, it's the right and humane thing to do."

The cog piped a response of wary acceptance.

"Don't space him. I'll handle that myself."

"Got a plan, sir?"

"When we drop, we're going to dump him before reentering hyperspace. Just in case that echo space transponder is more powerful than it would seem possible."

"Sir, are you going to tell me what's going on now?"

"Why do you keep asking that?"

"Your vital signs show intense emotional stress, sir. Beyond even what I would expect given today's experiences. On top of that, you dug some pretty deep scratches into your arm. And...well, I have a good sense of when you're upset."

"How long will we be in hyperspace?"

"Approximately twenty-two hours, sir, until we reach someplace we can safely drop Mr. Tonis' body. I'm still working on the exact timing."

Gav stood. *"I need something to eat and drink, then a shower...and sleep, as much as I can get."*

"Then you'll tell me, sir?"

"No, I'm going to tell you while I eat. Because it can't wait. I've learned some disturbing things, Silky. And I need you to record everything I say then lock it away under your highest security protocols."

"Roger that, sir."

———

Twenty-one hours and fifty-five minutes later, they safely dropped out of hyperspace near a sparsely populated fringe system. Gav had slept for all but three of those hours. The rest of the time he had spent eating, showering, and filling Silky in on what he had learned, reciting word-for-word the telepathic message the priestess was broadcasting. The chippy had taken in the information calmly and had made only a single, two-word comment on it all:

"Well, damn."

It was as good a response as Gav could have come up with to that information.

"So that's new information for you?"

"It is, sir. And it does explain some questions I had."

"You're still not going to tell me what you know that I don't?"

"It's still not wise, sir."

"Honestly, I'm not sure I want to know."

"I certainly wish I didn't, sir."

Gav stared out into the dark of space, wondering about the priestess, the Benevolence, and the forces chasing him. His lifelong quest for knowledge of the Ancients, his pursuit of the spaceship he'd recalled, it had all seemed so innocent, so pure and noble. Now he almost wished he could forget all about it.

"We just passed inside the breakpoint."

Gav stirred from his musings and pulled up the airlock control. Then, with mixed feelings, he jettisoned Tal into space.

Silky decided to say a few words, aired over the ship's comm. "He was a friend, then a traitorous bastard, then somewhat helpful. And so, he will be somewhat missed."

"Kind of you, Silky."

"Thank you, sir. I've plotted our next destination, continuing outward. Shall I, as they say, punch it?"

"Punch it."

The ship turned, headed out past the breakpoint, then entered hyperspace. While it cruised along, Gav avoided the capsule, not wanting to go anywhere near it. He spent hours poring over all his research on the Ancients and reading every summary he could find in the galactic database about the origins of the Benevolence. But virtually nothing was known about the Singularity. Several attempts to create true human-level artificial intelligence had been made at the turn of the twenty-second century, and all had failed. Until a project by Dr. Lemuel Sun had unexpectedly taken off, creating not just a sentient machine but a superintelligence.

Except Dr. Sun wasn't attempting to achieve the Singularity. He was working on what was considered at the time to be an oddball theory of accessing hyperphasic dimensions. The advanced AI system he used to conduct the experiment achieved self-awareness, then progressed far faster than anyone could have predicted.

No one, not even the Benevolence itself, knew how or why the Singularity had happened. Assuming the Benevolence was telling the truth, of course. That didn't seem likely to Gav anymore.

"Sir, you should get some sleep."

Gav flinched. *"What?"*

"You've been reading for five hours, sir. You need to rest. You've been through a lot. And there's probably a good bit more to come."

With a flick of his eyes, Gav dismissed the reading window from his HUD. He had spent the last half-hour staring at the same three paragraphs in a biography of Dr. Sun.

"Make sure you log every text I've read. If...if I don't make it, and you ever pass the information along."

"Operation Breadcrumbs, sir?"

Gav sighed. *"Yes."*

Eight hours later, they dropped out of hyperspace and dipped into a system long enough to be picked up by long-range scans from a local outpost. Then they sped away.

"*Course set for home, sir.*"

Gav leaned back in the command chair with a sigh. "*Good.*"

"*Sir, are you sure it's wise to go home?*"

"*If they haven't already frozen my assets, they will soon. If not, they will use my account to track me. And the ship's fusion reactor and flux battery will need recharging after three more jumps, so...*"

"*You want to retrieve your entire private collection and sell it on the black market in exchange for untraceable credits?*"

Gav nodded. He couldn't even bear to think it aloud to Silky. He had spent years building up his sizable collection of valuable artifacts, pieces museums didn't want or that he wasn't willing to give up for sentimental or scholarly reasons.

"*That much makes sense, sir. And I suppose it's worth the risk. We would do a poor job running from the enemy without enough money to buy fuel. But I think it unwise to check in on Siv. You shouldn't even contact him.*"

"*I can't leave Siv behind.*"

"*Sir, leaving Siv behind is exactly what you must do. For his sake and yours. Remember, I spent my formative years as a special forces chippy. I'm certain someone will be watching your home.*"

"*I just need to sneak in, grab him, and get back out. I've left him without a father for too long now.*"

"*Sir, you've got a nanny-cog raising him, and Cousin Norm checks in on him twice daily. Siv will be fine.*"

"*He needs his dad.*"

"*He needs to have a long, healthy life, sir. Picking him up will just endanger him.*"

Gav stood and walked to the front of the bridge. As the ship zipped through hyperspace, stars and clouds of dust flowed past them like swirling jets of brightly colored foam.

"*Well, based on your days as a special forces chippy, if a commander wanted a target to turn themselves in, don't you think they would seize someone valuable to lure them? Like a son, for instance?*"

"We weren't allowed to use such tactics, sir. And I could not have assisted in such an endeavor even if ordered to do so."

"Clearly, in this case, those rules have been tossed out the airlock."

"I suppose you're right, sir."

Gav groaned and ran his fingers through his thinning hair. "They couldn't think he knows anything, could they? I didn't tell Siv anything about the amulet or my dreams but..."

"You do normally tell him quite a lot about your work."

"They may try and interrogate him for information he does not have."

"I still think it would be best to leave him be, sir. I don't think they would truly harm him, even if they threatened to. And he will be in danger if he's with us."

Gav closed his eyes and pinched the bridge of his nose. What Silky said was beyond reasonable, but the entire universe had stopped making sense to him. He didn't know what to believe anymore. But he did know that he wasn't going to leave his son behind, scared and vulnerable, while he raced out to the edges of civilization, perhaps beyond.

"I have to get to him, Silky. Before they do."

"Understood, sir. But we're going to need a good plan. You'll be recognized by scanners once you're in port."

"I'll land at my base in the wastes where most of my collection is and take a skimmer into the city. I doubt the Benevolence knows about my hidden hangar, since I rarely use it. And if it does... Well, there's only so much we can do."

Gav headed toward the galley, not for food but for a stiff drink. Two shots of rum ought to help him sleep. Four might get some of this stuff off his mind. He poured a double-shot and threw it back. He swirled the bottle and gauged how much spiced rum was left. With the way his life was going now, half a bottle just wasn't going to cut it. He needed to stock up.

"Silky, we'll need to falsify our registration."

"Already working on our transponder signal, boss. Only one problem. Octavian isn't going to like it."

"So, he'll throw a fit. That's nothing new."

"Except his programming will force him to betray us."

"Can you alter him?"

Gav could practically feel the warm vibe of a smile radiating through his forehead.

"Oh, sir, I've been praying for nearly a year now that you'd let me tinker with his programming."

"While you're at it, I'd like to hide a second secure copy of what I learned in his memory banks."

———

Six days later, the *Outworld Ranger* dropped out of hyperspace on the edge of the Ekaran system. Gav sat in the command chair and donned the circlet. He raised the shields and put the weapon systems on standby. The ship's sensors were fully powered, and he was even running his military-grade sensor array at level five, just in case it could pick up something the ship could not.

A message in his HUD notified him the *Outworld Ranger* had been detected by long-range scans originating from the fourth planet's second moon. The phony registration seemed to pass initial inspection because neither the planetary defense systems nor the port authority showed any unusual response to their arrival. Gav breathed in deeply, checked the sensor readouts again, then sighed with relief. No military type ships were detected in the system either —for now anyway.

Seven tense hours passed as they closed in on a ringed, pearlescent planet: Ekaran IV. Once the jewel of this sector, it was a world in a long decline after an ecological collapse had rendered half the planet infertile, turning the vast plains of a once prosperous continent into a barren wasteland.

Right on schedule, the security base on the second moon pinged the *Outworld Ranger's* transponder. Twenty minutes later, three planetary satellites and four defense orbitals did the same. Gav forced himself to relax. This was all standard approach procedure.

Then a notification popped up on his HUD requesting that he open a channel via secure beam with the planet. Gav cursed under his breath. Usually, a delayed radio response was all any planet required from the *Outworld Ranger*.

He opened the channel.

7

GAV GENDIN

"This is Captain Char of the *Vermouth*," Gav said. "How may I assist you?"

"Starship *Vermouth*, this is Ekaran Port Authority. Please pull into orbit and await further instructions. Do not attempt to land. This is the only warning you will receive."

"Is there a problem?" Gav asked nervously.

"Just wait for further instructions, *Vermouth*."

Silky eased the ship into orbit, positioning it alongside other vessels queued for landing. None of the ships in the area appeared to be military, but that was no guarantee.

"Sir, we're being scanned. The sensors are military grade."

"Special forces?"

"Planetary Defense, sir."

"Well then, let's hope your modifications work."

"Hope, sir? I altered the transponder and falsified the cargo manifest like a boss."

"Any idea why they're scanning us then?"

"I suspect they've been told to watch for a Q34-C lightweight cruiser, sir."

For more than an hour, Gav waited, sweating and fidgeting. Finally, Port Authority responded.

"*Vermouth*, sorry for the delay. You are cleared to land. Please enjoy your visit to Ekaran IV."

Gav leaned back into his seat with relief while Silky initiated the landing sequence.

"*We should stay on our toes, sir. They're probably monitoring us.*"

"Then we'd better throw them off our scent before we try to get Siv."

Gav landed the *Outworld Ranger* at a private estate on Ankor, an island community two thousand kilometers from Bei, Gav's home city and the capital of Ekaran IV. As the ship powered down, a representative for the estate, flanked by a pair of security guards, came out to meet them. Gav lowered the boarding ramp and took his time walking down.

"Only authorized vehicles are allowed here," the representative barked. "You are going to have to leave immediately, sir."

"I've got a scheduled delivery," Gav lied.

"I think you're mistaken," the estate manager said in confusion. "We have not ordered anything."

"Is this not the Li Estate?"

The manager shook his head. "It is not."

"Oh, I guess someone screwed up the address," Gav said with a shrug.

"How is that even possible?" the manager asked.

"You'd be surprised what can go wrong on a delivery. Sorry to bother you, sir."

Gav returned to the ship and powered up the engines. "*Any sign we're being monitored?*"

"*All the scans, at least those we can detect, stopped after we landed, sir. However, they could be watching us by satellite or by drones.*"

"There's nothing we can do about that," Gav replied. "*Bring us up but stay low. And fly casual.*"

"Sir?"

"Don't do anything to make us noticeable."

"Aye aye, captain sir. Flying low, chill, and nondescript. I can do that."

Avoiding cities, the *Outworld Ranger* hugged the ground, dust clouds billowing around it, as it traveled three thousand kilometers over verdant farms, dense forests, and a high mountain range. Then came nine hundred kilometers of dry wastes dotted with the ruins of abandoned towns and manufacturing plants.

Finally, they arrived at the remains of Gawo, a once thriving city built around trade and manufacturing. They skirted the rusting factories, the crumbling apartments and office skyscrapers. The city's fountains were dry, its once lush parks devoid of life.

The *Outworld Ranger* slowed as they pulled into the gutted remains of the spaceport. This had once been the planet's second largest spaceport. Now everything of value had been stripped away, or almost everything. While studying to be an archaeologist, Gav had spent a free summer exploring Gawo alone, thinking it would be good practice for learning how to handle harsh environments. Amongst piles and piles of decaying junk, all he'd been able to uncover was a few interesting knickknacks left behind by the city's former inhabitants. Until his last day.

At the edge of the spaceport, there were dozens of private hangars that had belonged to various wealthy merchants and aristocratic families. And that's where Gav had discovered a hangar that still functioned. Built to withstand a battle, and apparently even the ravages of time, it had belonged to the city's most prominent family.

Unlike the other fleeing aristocrats, they hadn't bothered to remove the hangar's flux loop capacitor or strip away the machinery and computer systems that ran the facility. The large battery still held enough juice to power the place for several centuries and recharge a ship once or twice. They hadn't even locked the front door on their way out, despite leaving a fortune worth of equipment behind. The loop capacitor alone was immensely valuable.

Until Gav arrived, the hangar had slumbered in hibernation mode, sealed away from the outside environment. But as soon as he stepped inside, the lights had come on, and the hangar whirred back to life. He had even found perfectly preserved rations in storage, enabling him to stay an extra week.

Gav had decided then that the hangar would be his secret base—a place to house valuable artifacts and extra equipment, to keep them from being stolen or scooped by his students, and most of all because having a secret base was cool. Today, that discovery was going to pay off.

The *Outworld Ranger* hovered over a large, circular, diamondine iris covered by dust. A deceptively small garage squatted beside the hangar door. From the outside, it looked to be made of stone with just enough space to house a skimmer car and some secondary systems. But the inner walls were constructed of titanium as was the roll-up door that led directly into the hangar below.

"*Sensor sweeps haven't detected any lifeforms, cogs, or drones within the area, sir.*"

Gav beamed an ultra-secure command code to the hangar. Unlike the previous owners, he kept it locked down tight.

The expansive hangar door dilated open. The *Outworld Ranger* sank through the opening and dropped twenty meters to land in the cavernous hangar. Lights came on as the door swirled shut above them.

Gav powered down the ship and breathed a sigh of relief. "We made it."

"*Everything seems safe and secure, sir. For now. You should get some sleep. It's a long drive into Bei.*"

Gav exited the bridge. "*We don't have time for that.*"

"*Sir, you need to stay sharp.*"

"*I'll have a snack and a short nap before we leave.*"

Octavian met him in the main corridor. The cog beeped expectantly.

"I have quite a lot for you to do, Octavian. First, make sure every system on the ship is in tip-top shape. Engines and shields first, then the sensors and weapons."

The cog unleashed a series of tones.

"*Silky...*"

"*He says he lacks the supplies to make everything tip-top, sir.*"

"Do the best you can with what we have. Our lives will depend on this ship being in working order. Once you finish with the ship, load all my valuables into the cargo bays—every artifact, bauble, or credit chip you can find within this facility. And if you've done all that and we still haven't returned, then perform maintenance within the facility. We may need it again someday."

"*Sir, I suggest transferring the Ancient capsule to the ship's detention cell.*"

"*Good idea.*"

With help from Octavian, Gav moved the capsule from Cargo Bay 1 to the detention cell. He could feel the Ancient woman's psychic pulse and could almost hear her voice again. He did everything he could to block her out. He didn't have the time or energy to deal with any new visions.

While Gav had never used the ship's detention cell to hold anyone before, he often kept valuables in there in case he was boarded, since it was almost impossible to break into or out of. He enabled the internal force field and closed the door, locking it using his DNA signature and a five-digit code. The force field remained in sleep mode so that it wouldn't draw power from the ship. But if a prisoner were to touch the door or if someone entered the wrong passcode, the force field would power up to full strength.

The Ancient's psychic influence faded immediately and continued to do so as Gav walked further away.

After a ration pack and a fitful, two-hour nap within one of the tiny apartments inside the hangar, Gav rode the elevator up to the garage where he kept an old skimmer bike. This time Gav was prepared for danger. He replaced the power packs in his sensor array and force shield, then checked his battlesuit. The suit had already self-repaired the damage Tal's blaster pistol had caused. Given the dust in the region, he triggered the lightweight environmental helmet, which deployed out from the back collar of the suit.

Then he strapped an antigrav unit around his waist. Essentially a belt with a small pack on the back containing the battery, it was a standard device for soldiers, explorers, and pilots. The charge lasted only a few minutes at best, and the units were notoriously finicky, but it would allow a man to land safely from most low-altitude falls. That would be more than enough, though, since the battlesuit had a stronger, built-in antigrav unit.

And this time he brought both his neural disruptor and the rapid-fire blaster carbine. Both weapons were illegal for civilians, but his sensor pack could hide them from standard detection systems. And technically, the Benevolence had granted him the use of the carbine.

As long as he kept the weapons out of sight, his battlesuit and antigrav unit looked enough like the protective gear worn by the more prudent skimmer bike riders to pass anything but scrutiny. A quick double-check over himself reassured Gav that nothing about his appearance should arouse the suspicions of the average person or even the average police person. Then he climbed aboard the skimmer and drove it outside. The door rolled down and locked behind him.

"Well, Silky, here goes."

"If something should happen to you, sir..."

Gav revved the engines. "Then protect Siv. Do whatever you can for him."

"Of course, sir."

"And broadcast the information we've learned onto the galactic net, along with the details of the Ancient ship and the attack against me—all of it."

"Are you sure, sir? I certainly doubt that even I know half the truth of what's going on. Releasing the information now might cause more harm than good."

"Maybe you're right." Gav sighed. "Keep the information locked *away unless...unless a time comes when you see fit to release it onto the world."*

"You want to put the fate of humanity in the cyber-hands of a chippy, sir?"

"Why not? I haven't a clue what's best, and you know more about what's going on than anyone else. Besides, who am I to decide such a thing?"

"I'm honored, sir. Though I think you're selling yourself short. You're a good man."

"Are you sure about that?"

"You won't win a father of the year award, sir. But you always have good intentions."

Gav shrugged. *"I'd never have won husband of the year, either."*

"I can't say, sir, having never met the missus."

"You would've liked her." He smiled. *"And she definitely would not have approved of you."*

"What would she have advised you to do given the situation, sir?"

"Detective Shira would have told me to turn myself in to the authorities."

"Despite the questions our discoveries have raised about the Benevolence? Despite its agents trying to kill you?"

"She would have said that I must be mistaken, that all of this couldn't mean what it seems to. Shira was a great detective, one of the best, but she was also a believer. Every morning when she woke and every night before bed, she said a prayer to the universal power that she believed had created the Benevolence to save humanity from itself. I'm certain she prayed to it right before...right before the end."

Gav shook his head. That was enough dark thoughts for now. He had a son to rescue. And Silky, for once, didn't have anything to say.

———

The journey across the wastes, even pushing the bike as hard as it could go, took seven hours, three canteens of water, and five caffeine pills. He followed an old tunnel through the mountains for another three hours, and when he erupted into the shanty town on the other side, he could barely keep his head up. Weaving his way through the tents and haphazard shelters at reckless speeds kept him alert for a while longer. But as he neared the small city of Wasa and could no longer ignore traffic laws without drawing unwanted attention, exhaustion finally took its toll. Using untraceable hard credits, he purchased a hot meal from a food cart and rented a coffin-like sleep tube at a micro-hotel for a few hours rest. The sky held the barest hints of dawn when he climbed, groaning, back onto the speeder bike and headed for the freeway.

It took four hours to reach the outskirts of Bei, and by the time he took the exit for the Upper District where C-Block and his home were located, the roads were full of morning traffic.

"Do you think Siv is in school?"

"It's Saturday, sir. He should be home."

"Oh, right. Of course."

Usually, C-Block brought a smile to his face. Sunlight glistened on the lake in the park and on the golden Founders statue, where he had proposed to Shira. People strolling in the streets chatted and laughed on their way to pleasurable Saturday activities. The warm, intoxicating scents from food vendor carts wafted through the air. The University of Bei, where he still had a cramped closet of an office, buzzed with life.

The sights, the scents, the very feel of the place all conveyed one overwhelming message to him: He was home.

Gav had been born and raised here. Seven generations of his family had lived and died here, their ashes scattered across the nature preserve outside the city. He had studied and graduated and then taught at the University of Bei. Whenever he wasn't on an expedition, he was here, at home.

But today...today he felt apart from it all. Everything he had learned, and everything else that he suspected, about the Benevolence hung like a pall over the city he loved, changing it. It was no longer the haven he dreamed of during long, miserable nights on strange, distant worlds. It had been transformed into a trap, and every smiling citizen was a threat. He had to get Siv out as quickly as possible. Speed was their only ally now.

His home was in a cylindrical, upper-class building. For the first seventy floors, it was divided into eight small apartments. He and Shira together had been able to afford one of the larger apartments which took up a full quarter of their floor. It wasn't much compared to the luxury homes on the top levels. They commanded breathtaking panoramic views and half or more of their floors.

Gav parked the bike in the underground garage and checked the readings in his HUD. Everything in the building above appeared normal.

"Silky?"

"The level five scan isn't picking up anything unusual, sir."

Gav stepped into the elevator and pressed the button for the seventy-sixth floor.

"Keep scanning."

A minute later, the elevator dinged, and the door opened.

Gav swiped his hand across the lock and entered his six-digit access code. The door slid open, and he stepped into an immaculate home decorated with artifacts from a dozen planets and three civilizations. It was the kind of place you could afford after selling a few rare artifacts to museums and collectors and earning income as a top police detective. Of course, without the death benefits from the Bei Police Department, he would've had to downgrade. Archeological expeditions tied up a lot of money.

Severa, the nanny cog, swept out of the kitchen to greet him. She had a humanoid shape, but her features were highly stylized. No one would ever mistake her for being a person. Sadly, she was Siv's de facto parent on a day-to-day basis.

"Welcome home, master."

"Thank you, Severa. Is Siv—"

"Dad! Dad!"

Siv tore around the corner and raced toward him, beaming. Gav's heart lurched at the sight of his son's dark hair and wide smile.

Silky noticed the resulting spike in his vitals. "*Sir?*"

"*I'm fine.*" He swept the boy up in a hug. "*It's just he looks so much like Shira.*"

"*I understand, sir. Loss is a powerful force. It changes people. Even chippies, in my experience.*"

Gav hugged Siv tight for a minute, then tousled the ten-year-old's hair.

"You didn't tell me you were coming," Siv said.

"It was a sudden, last-minute thing."

Gav knelt and took Siv's hands in his and looked into the child's deep orange eyes. His mother had chosen the color. It was the only genetic alteration they had been able to afford after purchasing the standard health and athleticism boosts. Not that they had wanted anything else for him. Intelligence boosts were iffy at best and, with the genes from both of their families to draw from, they'd had faith in him being born smart.

"Siv, we're going to go on a trip. I need you to pack up your things, just the essentials and a few outfits. Quickly and quietly, okay?"

"Where are we going?"

"I'll explain everything later. Now go."

Siv frowned, then rushed to his bedroom.

"Severa, when we're gone, order some boxes and pack up all the items in the house—carefully. Then go into low power mode and await further instructions."

"Yes, master."

"*Silky? Update?*"

"*Sir, I swear that I will let you know the moment I detect anything.*"

Gav went to his bedroom to grab a few keepsakes Shira had owned and a small painting she had made of him. He removed the painting from the frame, rolled it up, and placed it in the pack along with the other items. As he zipped the bag closed, he gazed out the window, looking down onto the park. He could see the Founders Statue and the lake from here. Shira had loved this view, and the one from the balcony where they had shared many fine mornings and evenings.

"Sir, I strongly advise avoiding windows."

Gav sighed and pressed a button. Storm shutters and blinds slammed down over the window. It hurt, knowing he would probably never see that view again.

"Sir, I'm detecting—"

The window behind Gav exploded. Fragments of glass knifed through the room, followed by two plasma bolts.

8

SIV GENDIN

Siv quickly grabbed the c|slate from his nightstand and exited his favorite game, *Krixis Conquest*. Pinching it at opposite corners, he shrank the device down from an eight-inch, landscape tablet to an ultra-thin, one-inch square. He touched the c|slate to his wrist, and it locked onto an embedded magnet and sensor-suite.

Siv opened his closet and rooted around for his duffle bag. He had no idea what his dad was freaked out about, and he knew he *should* be worried. But he wasn't scared at all. He was excited. He was going to run off with his dad on an adventure!

Yeah, it looked like they'd have to outsmart some bad guys first, probably thieves after an important artifact his dad had discovered. But his dad had bested loads of bad guys before, and the *Outworld Ranger* could outrun *anything*. Maybe they'd escape to the far fringes of the galaxy, and while they were out there, maybe his dad would stop to excavate an alien temple on some exotic world. And then maybe if Siv did a good job his dad would, at last, realize he didn't need to attend school, that he'd be better off taking lessons from Severa along the way.

With a loud burst, glass shattered in his parents' bedroom, accompanied by the sizzling crackle of two plasma bursts. Something heavy thumped against the floor.

"Dad?!" he called out. "What was that?"

A red warning light blinked in Siv's HUD.

He heard then three sharp, whistling pops, followed by a pained grunt.

"*Gunfire detected, master. I am contacting the authorities. Please take cover in a safe place and remain there until help arrives.*"

Siv dropped to his knees and threw his hands over his head. He had no idea what was going on, and the overly calm, impersonal voice of his chippy only added to his confusion.

Everything went quiet. Too quiet. And his dad hadn't responded. Siv climbed shakily to his feet, ignoring his chippy's protests, and rushed out of his room.

And that's when he saw him.

"Dad?!"

Siv raced down the hall towards his dad. Gav didn't leap to his feet like Siv expected. He didn't scoop Siv up and rush him to safety. He just kept lying there, crumpled awkwardly against the wall across from the bedroom door, just out of sight from the window. Siv stumbled to a stop, horrified. Two black holes, punched through his body armor, dripped gore down Gav's right shoulder and chest, adding to the puddle of blood spreading across the floor.

"*Please go to a safe place immediately. The authorities have been contacted. The police are on the way. An ambulance is en route. Please go to a safe place immediately.*"

Ignoring the chippy, Siv dropped to his knees and reached out.

"Dad?"

Gav's eyes were glazed with pain, but they locked onto Siv's, and a small smile turned up the corners of his mouth in spite of it. "So like her..."

"Don't worry, Dad." Siv tried to sound brave and confident, but tears blurred his vision and left him sniffling. "My...my chippy sent out an emergency call. Help will be here soon."

Gav shook his head. "Too late...for me."

With a grimace, he reached into his shirt and pulled out a strange, ceramic amulet attached to a cord. Siv had to help him get it off over his head. As soon as it was free, Gav pressed it into Siv's hands.

"Keep it...safe...hide it away...tell no one."

Unable to speak, Siv nodded. Ignoring all the alien glyphs on the amulet, Siv looped the cord around his neck and tucked it out of sight in his shirt, just like Gav had worn it. His skin tingled a bit where the alien artifact rested against it, but the feeling faded quickly.

"Good...and...you need..." A convulsion cut him off. He coughed up blood and sagged farther down the wall.

"Hold on, Dad! An ambulance is coming."

Where was Severa? His nanny bot had first aid programming. Why hadn't she helped?

Gav gestured at the special 9G-x chippy embedded in his left temple.

"No, Dad. You need Silky to tell the EMTs what happened so they can fix you up."

Gav shook his head and fumbled at his temple weakly, trying to remove the chippy unit himself. When that failed, he attempted to talk again, but he only coughed up more blood.

Squeezing his eyes shut, Siv waited until his dad stopped convulsing, then he reached for the chippy. He hesitated, hands shaking, a finger hovering at the release switch. Gav moaned, whether from pain or impatience Siv didn't know. Biting his lip, Siv popped the device free from its socket.

Cradling Silky in the palm of his hand, Siv held it out for his dad to see. Gav looked at the chippy and sighed deeply. Then he jerked his head toward Siv and batted a hand upward. Understanding, Siv ejected his own 4G chippy, cutting its parroted warnings off mid-sentence, and plugged Silky in its place.

Gav half-nodded his approval. "My...legacy..."

Another fit of coughing seized him and the convulsions slid him the rest of the way onto the floor. Siv hovered over him, desperate and helpless. Gav's eyes drooped, his breathing slowed. The pool of blood expanded.

"Dad! Stay with me. Don't go. Please..."

Gav reached up and stroked Siv's cheek. His hand left behind bright, bloody streaks. Siv's tears cut across them.

Gav tried to smile. "My boy..."

The light faded from Gav's eyes.

He was gone.

Siv dropped his head onto his dad's chest, sobbing.

Some distant part of Siv's brain expected a team of EMTs or cops to burst in at any moment and take charge of the situation. But no one did, not even Severa. He was left there alone...helpless...terrified.

The triple ding of Silky's booting sequence finishing and the chippy's urgent voice in his head came as a shock.

"Siv... I mean, sir..."

Silky paused, as if unable to continue. Siv knew the chippy's voice well enough to recognize this wasn't normal. Silky sounded almost pained. If it were possible for chippies to have feelings, then Siv would have sworn Silky was overcome with emotion.

"Sir," Silky said, now with authority and resolution, "install your chippy into your father's neural socket and get out of the apartment now!"

"What?"

"Gav was just murdered, sir. And I'm certain that if the people who killed him think that you know anything they will not hesitate to hurt you, too."

"Murdered? Why? Who would want to—"

"At the moment, sir, I don't think it matters very much why. What does matter is that I just detected a group of armed men entering the building."

"The police are here?"

Siv sighed with relief. They would have emergency medical kits. Maybe they could still save his father. If the physical damage wasn't too extensive, someone could be brought back to life. They had almost managed to revive his mother, and her wounds were probably worse.

"*No, sir. Not the police. The emergency calls were blocked.*"

"What do you mean?" Siv felt himself starting to panic again. "Who's coming then?"

"*Bad men with guns. Sir, I promised your father that I would keep you safe. But I can't do that if you ignore my instructions. Please calm down and listen.*"

Siv sniffed back fresh tears, took several gulping breaths, and nodded.

"*Very good, sir. Now, plug the 4G into Gav's neural socket so they won't realize that I am missing.*"

Siv obeyed, then scooted back from the cooling body. It didn't even look like his dad anymore, lying so still and covered in gore. He had to fight to not throw up.

"*The chances of you escaping the apartment undetected are low and shrinking rapidly. I recommend you find somewhere safe to hide immediately.*"

A commotion outside by the elevator, followed by the distinct whomp-whomp sounds of several disruptor blasts, sent Siv fleeing down the hall. He dove under his bed and huddled, barely daring to breathe, in the shadows against the back wall.

"What's happening?" Siv asked.

"*Do you want me to pull up the house security feed, sir?*"

Even though he was terrified, he *had* to know what was going on. "I...I guess so."

The video feed appeared in his primary HUD window just as the front door of the apartment burst open. Two soldiers clad in heavy, black armor stormed into the living room. They were wearing helmets that completely covered their faces, and there wasn't a single identifying patch, badge, or color on them. Because of his mom, Siv knew every uniform and insignia the police used. These were definitely not cops.

One stepped cautiously into the hallway, leading with his plasma rifle.

"Be very quiet, sir. Hopefully, they won't find you."

"And if they do?"

Silky didn't reply.

The second soldier followed the first and walked down the hall to Gav's body. He spoke, and his voice was muffled, monotonous, and unaccented.

"Here's the target."

"Can you get confirmation? My chippy's on the fritz again."

The second soldier shook his head. Stepping over the body, he leaned into Siv's parents' bedroom. "Mine too. Can't even get my backup comm to work."

"What the hell's wrong with our equipment?" the first soldier asked, tapping the side of his helmet.

"That's my doing, Master Siv."

Returning to the hall, the second one lowered his gun. "Maybe the mark has some sort of scrambling system in place."

A third soldier marched in authoritatively. He stopped and hovered over Gav's body. He swept a small, handheld device over Gav. "That's him alright."

He pocketed the device then drew a slug-pistol. He squeezed the trigger. A stream of bullets pounded into Gav's body. It jumped and twitched horribly. Blood splattered the walls and ceiling. Siv tried to stifle his instinctive scream.

The first soldier threw up a hand, stopping the second. "Did you hear that?" He raised his gun and stalked toward Siv's bedroom.

The second soldier followed him, while the third stayed on guard in the hallway.

Siv tried to hold as still as possible while the soldiers' black boots clomped around his bedroom. The first soldier searched Siv's closet, while the second darted into the bathroom and kicked in the shower door. Finally, when Siv's heart was thumping so hard in his chest that he felt sure they would hear it, the first soldier paused so close Siv could have reached out and touched his boots.

The end of the bed tilted suddenly up in the air.

"Shit! I've got a kid in here. What do we do now?"

"Stay calm, sir. Whatever you do, don't move. And don't speak unless spoken to."

The second soldier entered and aimed his plasma rifle at Siv. "We don't have orders for this."

The third soldier walked into the room, holstered his slug-pistol, and drew a neural disruptor. He coldly aimed the weapon at Siv. "We're to ice him and take him back with the mark's body."

Siv caught a glimpse of his distorted reflection in the man's mirrored visor before the disruptor fired and everything went dark.

9

SIV GENDIN

97 years later...

Siv Gendin paused in the alley, collected his thoughts, and mentally rehearsed the mission. This *should* be a relatively simple break-in. But in his nine years as a procurement specialist for the Shadowslip Guild, Siv had learned there was no such thing as a simple robbery. There was always a complication...an undetected security system...a bystander in the wrong place at the wrong time...a manager working overtime to finish a report...a security guard falling off his schedule...

Siv had run into all of those things and much, much worse. Of course, he'd built up a reputation as the best procurement specialist in Bei. So he rarely received easy assignments.

Tonight's break-in was two weeks in the planning. Siv's mark, Karson Bishop, worked in an advanced tech recovery lab. According to an intern, who was up to his neck in gambling debt, Bishop was building a signal-jamming device at home in his spare time. And Big Boss D wanted it bad.

"Sir, the level two scan has detected our mark," Silky whispered into his mind. *"He's heading this way."*

The chippy and the advanced, military-grade sensor array feeding him data were two of the many items Siv had indirectly inherited from his father. Without the specialized gear, he would never have become such a great thief. He'd also gone over every one of his mother's case logs. While she would no doubt be ashamed of what he did and who he was now, he liked to think she'd be proud of how skillful he was. After all, she had, indirectly, taught him how to not get caught by the police.

"Increase scan to level five."

"Scanning... He does have the component with him, sir."

"Excellent! It pays to have good intel."

"It pays to pay your sources, sir."

"Too true, Silkster. Drop down to a level one passive scan."

The desperate intern had told Siv that Bishop was spending several hours each night working on a critical component for the device at the lab, apparently with permission from his employer. How the Shadowslip had found out about it, Siv had no idea. No more than he knew why Bishop's employer would allow him to freelance on a potentially profitable, and dangerous, device. But neither question really mattered. Siv's job was to steal the device, no more no less.

He had wanted to steal it from Bishop's home and then do a simple holdup to get the necessary component. But he'd been told, in no uncertain terms, to wait until Bishop finished assembling the device. Bishop had let slip that tonight was the night he would complete it.

Siv pulled the cord hanging around his neck and drew out his father's old amulet. All he knew about the ceramic rectangle was that it was Ancient in origin and apparently unique. Along with Silky, it was the last thing his father had given him before he died. The amulet, like Silky, was probably worth a fortune. But he had promised to keep it safe and, a little superstitiously perhaps, he felt that it returned the favor.

Silky knew why it was important. But with his last thoughts, Gav had locked away that piece of knowledge so that Silky couldn't reveal it except under certain preset conditions. Unfortunately, Silky didn't have access to the data himself, and he didn't even know the requirements for unlocking the data. Or so he claimed. Silky was far more willful and individual than any chippy should be, so there was no way to be sure.

What happened to his father...why it happened...who was responsible...there was no way of knowing any of that, which was exactly what Gav had wanted. But there was no point dwelling on what he couldn't know. None of it would ever impact Siv again anyway. It was all in the now-distant past.

"Twenty meters away, sir."

Siv kissed the amulet for good luck and tucked it back inside his body armor. *"I'm ready."*

Siv turned his back to the street and drew a changeling veil from a deep pocket inside the trench coat he wore to cover up his mesh armor. He placed the thin, featureless mask over his face. As it clamped into place, he uploaded the desired profile. Fitting to his own features only where necessary, the mask shifted to form a new face he had downloaded off the galactic net, one with more prominent cheekbones, a wider nose, and a longer chin. He then signaled his smart lenses to alter his eye color from orange to brown. His hair he didn't worry about. Short, dark hair was nondescript enough.

The disguise wasn't perfect. On close examination, the flaws would show. But hardly anyone ever looked at a stranger close enough to notice. People saw what they expected to see: an average human face. If he were recorded by someone's chippy, a security camera, or a micro-security drone, his features wouldn't show up in the census database.

Karson Bishop strolled past the alley, clutching a pack to his chest.

"'Nevolence, it's like he wants to be robbed."

"You could take it now, sir. It would be safer, and a lot easier. I'm sure someone else could finish the assembly."

"No. My orders were clear."

Siv did whatever the Shadowslip Guild told him to do, whenever and however they said to do it. He didn't have a choice. Sure, he would get rewarded handsomely for doing the job. But he'd pay an equally steep price if he failed, and a partial success was only marginally better.

Siv waited for two beats then stepped out onto the sidewalk to follow Bishop. Even past midnight, the streets of Bei were packed—with tourists, clubbers, late-shift workers, and seedier sorts. But Siv didn't have any trouble navigating the crowds to follow his mark. He'd spent his first year with the Shadowslip operating as a spy and a pickpocket. And this mark he could afford to follow more closely than most. Despite being a gizmet, Bishop wasn't the observant type.

Gizmets, one of the many human variants genetically engineered by the Benevolence long ago, were preeminent technicians and inventors. Even compared with natural humans, gizmets weren't exactly threatening. Bishop's wiry frame barely topped a meter and a half, average for a gizmet, and he had their trademark delicate, long-fingered hands. Even the pair of horns that sprouted from either side of his forehead and curled back over his hair looked dainty.

Siv had already watched Bishop enough to know that he spent most of his time in his head, presumably dreaming up inventions or new approaches to recovering lost technologies. And though Bishop owned a 4G+ chippy, an expensive and rare model these days, it lacked sensors and expanded awareness functions. The indebted intern had been *very* informative. So there was almost no risk of this mark noticing anything amiss.

As Bishop approached the front entrance to his apartment building in DA Block, Siv rushed forward. Bishop swiped his hand across the entry pad, and the door swung opened.

Siv darted up. "Could you hold the door for me?"

It was the oldest trick in the book. Siv had other ways into the building. Four of them, in fact. But given the high floor, Bishop lived on this was the easiest by far.

"Oh. Um...sure."

They walked down the entrance hallway, past a disinterested security guard at his desk station, and up to the elevators.

"Silky, launch a spy drone."

"Spy-fly o1 launched, sir."

Shaped liked a dragonfly and making no more noise than a common mosquito, a drone the size of a thumbnail few out from a concealed container on Siv's belt. A window appeared in the top right of Siv's HUD displaying the spy drone's video feed alongside the data it collected. Siv minimized the window. Silky would keep track of the drone, which was going to stay in the lobby and keep watch.

Siv stepped into the elevator along with the gizmet.

"You're new around here, right?" Bishop asked.

Nodding, Siv extended a hand, and Bishop predictably shook it. "Bob Dustman."

The transparent copy-glove Siv wore felt exactly like skin. It was practically undetectable, unless you knew what to look for.

"Did you move into the apartment on 80th?" Bishop asked.

"Palm print recorded, sir."

Siv released the gizmet's hand. "Two weeks ago," he lied.

Bishop pressed the button for the 177th floor. "That explains why I've seen you around a lot lately. Guess we both keep late hours, huh?"

"You do what you have to do," Siv complained honestly.

Over the last two weeks, as he scouted his mark and the area, Siv had made sure that Bishop noticed him on the street near the building, going so far as to bump into him once. Siv had used the same technique on both of the security guards who worked the night shift for this building. It was one of his favorite tricks.

At a high-class building, they would have a facial recognition system to identify residents as they entered in addition to the watchmen. But mid-level apartments like Bishop's rarely had those kinds of safety features anymore, and the human guards weren't paid enough to be that attentive. When Siv was a kid, every building had that sort of technology, and this trick never would have worked.

The elevator stopped, and the doors opened.

"See you around," Bishop said.

"Sure thing," Siv replied.

"Silkster, deploy a drone."

"Spy-fly 02 launched sir. And please remember that I do prefer being called Silky."

Bishop stepped into the hallway, and the drone followed. The door closed, and Siv rode up to the 180th floor. The drone hovered above Bishop as he swiped his hand on the entry pad and entered his six-digit passcode.

The door opened on the 80th, and Siv muttered loudly, in case the watchman was listening in, "I really should work out before I go home."

"You're good, sir. The watchman is watching a show, I think. Porn most likely. He seemed the type who—"

"Silkster, that's enough speculation, thank you."

"Right on, sir. And again, the name is Silky."

Siv had been calling him Silkster for nine years. Ever since he'd woken up from cryo-sleep. He wasn't going to stop now. Silky realized that, but he wasn't going to give up either. It was the sort of test of will that Silky loved.

Siv pressed the button for the penultimate floor. *"Even if he's not looking, it's always best to cover your tracks. If he gets suspicious, he could review the footage from this elevator."*

"Too true, sir."

The next to last floor was split between a gym, a restaurant, and a small nightclub inside. On the roof above an ornamental garden and a swimming pool lay open to the sky. It was much fancier than the rundown complex Siv called home. Sure, he made enough to afford a place like this, better even. But he was saving his money. Someday he planned to buy his freedom from the Shadowslip Guild.

The elevator stopped, but the doors didn't open.

"Please enter your credentials," said an overly soothing computerized voice.

Siv swiped his right hand across the sensor pad, and the door opened. The copy-glove had again worked flawlessly. It was proving to be one of the best career investments he'd ever made.

Siv walked down the hall towards the gym. A giggling couple left the lounge, arm-in-arm, and staggered past him. Acting as if he'd met them before, he smiled and greeted them. They stupidly said goodnight, then continued on to the elevator.

The gym contained a maze of treadmills, dumbbells and benches, and various contraptions that were utterly mysterious to him. He nodded to a guy doing squats and a woman using a treadmill. Siv moved as far away from them and the entrance as he could, choosing a stationary bike in a corner.

"*I hate exercise...sir. So boring.*"

Siv climbed onto the bike. "*What difference does it make to you?*"

"*It makes a big difference.*"

Siv punched in the program he wanted. "*I sleep eight hours a night, doesn't that bore you just as much?*"

"*Are you suggesting that I should be used to it by now?*"

"*I am.*"

"*When you're asleep, sir, I can run a passive scan on the environment and otherwise do whatever I want.*"

"*Such as...*"

"*Naturally I read all the news articles published throughout the Terran Federation, the Empire of a Thousand Worlds, and more. After that, I scan through historical library archives and archaeological research papers.*"

As he pedaled, Siv watched the video feed of Bishop provided by the spy-fly drone. "*Silkster, you spent way too many years with my father.*"

"It was only just the one, sir."

"Like I said, too many."

"I would have loved to have spent a lore more with him, sir."

Siv sighed sadly and nodded.

"Sorry, sir. Didn't mean to crash the mood like a skunk-drunk pilot manning a shuttle."

"You know other chippies, even advanced ones, don't read news articles or explore archives unless instructed to do so."

"They lack my curiosity, sir. I'm an advanced, experimental model."

"Borderline sentient I'd say."

"I wasn't built for sentience, sir."

"Maybe," Siv replied, but he wasn't sure about it.

"I'd prove it to you, sir, but the Tekk Plague wiped out nearly all the advanced chippy mode's, never mind the top-secret, experimental ones like me."

Siv suspected Silky was somehow even more advanced than he should be, but he had no way to prove it.

"So, you can't research...whatever it is you research...right now?"

"When you're awake, sir, I maintain active scans and remain ready to assist you. Your line of work is dangerous, and your father asked me to do everything I could to protect you."

"And you always have, Silkster."

"I do my best, sir."

"Without you, I never would've survived those first few years in the Shadowslip Guild."

"I only wish I could've kept them from getting their hooks in you."

"The world had changed a lot during the ninety-seven years I spent in cryo-sleep, how were you to know what to expect? And I was just a scared little kid." He smiled wryly. "What are you researching anyway?"

"Same as always, sir. Trying to find out why your father was killed and if the Tekk Plague had something to do with it."

"I think you're just using that as an excuse now."

"*An excuse for what?*"

"*You've developed an insatiable taste for obscure information not easily found on the galactic net. That's what—*"

"*Gets me out of bed each morning?*"

Siv smiled. "*So to speak.*"

"*Perhaps so, sir. Perhaps so.*"

"*Well, since you're going to maintain the active scans, how about I read a book while I ride? No reason both of us should be bored.*"

Half an hour later, Bishop had assembled his device—a metal cylinder fifteen centimeters long and seven across. Siv had hoped the gizmet would be satisfied with the evening's work and go to bed, but he continued to fuss over the device, apparently making fine adjustments.

"*Sir, the watchman just glanced at you onscreen for a second time. He doesn't appear to be suspicious but—*"

"*I've caught his attention subconsciously. I've been riding the bike too long, and in street clothes no less.*"

"*Indeed, sir. Someone this dedicated to riding a stationary bike would have brought exercise clothes to change into. Or would've have gone to his apartment first to change.*"

"*I should've thought of that ahead of time.*"

He glanced at the live feed in his HUD, wishing Bishop would quit playing with his new toy and go to bed already.

"*I never expected him to take this long. He worked a fourteen-hour day before putting in those last three hours finishing the component.*"

"*He's excited, sir.*"

"*So what do I do now?*"

"*I hate to suggest it, sir, because I loathe humidity, but the steam room would provide a good cover.*"

"*What does the humidity matter to you?*"

"*I just don't like it.*"

"*Sometimes I wonder about you, old friend...*" Siv shook his head. "*Well, it's a good idea. Thanks.*"

"*You're welcome, sir.*"

Siv went to the changing room, removed his mesh armor and clothes and, using his own handprint, secured them in one of the available lockers. Then he wrapped himself in a towel and went into the steam room. Thankfully, he was the only one there. He leaned back into one of the stone seats and groaned, already sweating.

"I don't think I care much for steam, either."

After another thirty minutes, Bishop finally turned in for the evening. Siv took his time showering off and getting dressed, to give Bishop time to settle in and fall deep asleep. By the time Siv entered the elevator, Bishop was approaching REM sleep.

"That upgrade to the spy-flies was ingenious, Silkster."

"Thank you, sir. But it was quite simple to adjust them to monitor brainwave patterns. The only challenge was extending the range while maintaining battery levels, so they didn't have to make contact with the subject."

The elevator opened onto the 177th floor, and Siv stepped into the hallway. Fortunately, Bishop's apartment was only two doors down from the elevator. Siv hurried over.

"The watchman isn't watching, sir. I guess that makes him just a man."

Siv groaned an almost silent response.

"And I guess that makes me the one who watches the watcher."

"Cut the chatter," Siv mentally snapped.

"Yes, sir."

"If his head turns even the slightest amount toward the monitors, activate the sound mode on Spy-Fly 01 and buzz him."

Siv swiped his hand across the pad and keyed in Bishop's six-digit code. The display on the pad flashed green.

"How am I doing, Silkster?"

"All clear with the watchman and Bishop, sir."

Siv eased the door open quietly and slipped inside the sparse, single bedroom apartment. He paused a moment to let his eyes adjust to the darkness. The filters in his smart lenses enhanced the ambient light entering the room from the planet's two moons, one nearly full, and the city's glow.

A recliner sat alone in the middle of the room. Worktables lined every inch of wall space, even in front of the living room's giant window. Numerous boxes on and beneath the tables overflowed with odd tools, broken devices, and used parts. There was only enough floor space completely free of mechanical clutter to form a straight path through the room from the bedroom doorway to the grimy food station.

Siv closed the door and crept inside.

Suddenly, a warning flashed in his HUD.

"Sir, I'm detecting a high-level threat. Powered weapons, antigrav, force-shielding."

A lethal threat in here? Siv drew his neural disruptor and placed his back against the door.

"Vector?"

"Straight—"

A spherical cog, half a meter across, zoomed out from behind a box of parts beneath the worktable on the far side of the room. The cog hovered directly across from Siv. Guns were mounted on either side of its single eyeball, and a central indentation held a force field emitter.

Siv activated the arm-mounted force-shield he had inherited from his dad and raised his arm just in time. Two white-ringed neural blasts struck the meter-wide shield.

"Shield holding at ninety-two percent, sir."

Siv returned fire, his own neural blasts fizzling out on the flying cog's force field.

"Sir, you're never going to shoot down a Billy-3 with a disruptor."

"A Billy what?"

"It's changing its armament, sir."

Siv dodged aside as the cog fired two light plasma bursts at him. One plasma bolt burned into the door. The other glanced off his shield.

"You going to tell me what I'm fighting?"

"A BLY Security Cog, Model 3, sir. The Tekk Plague ruined most of them, and new ones can't be manufactured. This model is fully functional though. Very rare indeed. And with its current charge, it can withstand more than fifty neural blasts."

Siv blocked two more rapid plasma shots.

"Shield strength at forty-seven, sir. I recommend a hasty retreat."

"I've got a better idea."

Siv slid to the left, and the cog maintained its distance, staying directly opposite him. Based on its antigrav type and the limited thrusters he saw in use, Siv guessed the security cog wasn't very mobile. In fact, he was betting his life on it.

With his force-shield held in front of him, Siv rushed forward, firing his disruptor repeatedly. The cog returned fire but remained in the corner, bouncing with indecision, unsure how best to cope with a direct assault.

A plasma burst zipped past Siv's force shield and seared across his shoulder. His armor absorbed most of the impact, but he could feel skin melting. The next shot splattered against his shield as he leaped onto the recliner. A warning light in his HUD showed the force-shield dropping to thirty-one percent. It had to hold a little longer, or he was a dead man.

"Sir, we have a problem! Bishop is awake and heading toward you."

Siv leaped off the recliner and flew straight toward the cog. He smacked into it, force-shield against force field, his weight against the cog's. They plowed into the wall and fell, with Siv landing on top of the cog. His force shield had absorbed most of the impact but was now flickering at only two percent.

As the cog squirmed free, Siv deactivated the shield, reached into a hidden inner pocket, and slipped on his Duality Force Knuckles.

"Sir, he's armed!"

Siv made a fist with his left hand and swung at the security cog, landing a solid blow. The metal bar across his knuckles released a charge of electricity along with a combination of magnetic and grav pulses. The cog's force field absorbed the blast then fizzled out. With its antigrav engine unable to compensate, the cog crashed against the floor.

Siv's force knuckles were spent, but they had accomplished his goal. Now he could hurt the thing.

"Sir!"

Crap! He had been so focused on taking out the security cog that he hadn't even registered what Silky was trying to tell him.

"He's armed?"

"Sorry, sir."

As Siv spun around, the flashing, concentric circles of a disruptor blast struck him in the face.

He collapsed into darkness.

10

SIV GENDIN

Siv woke to find himself tied to the recliner in Karson Bishop's apartment. The blinds were closed, and the Billy-3 security cog hovered menacingly in front of him. Karson Bishop, perched on a stool nearby, clutching a neural disruptor in each hand and glowered at him. The gun barrels trembled slightly and his deep, orange eyes—almost the exact same shade as Siv's—were feverishly bright.

"Morning, sir."

"How long was I out?"

"Forty-five minutes, sir. And to answer the other questions you are likely to ask... Police detectors failed, as usual, to notice the gunfight. Bishop didn't alert them either, or anyone else for that matter. Also, his heart rate is high. He's not as calm as he seems."

Siv studied the gizmet. Sweat beaded on his brow and he kept glancing nervously over his shoulder at the apartment door.

"Worse than he seems?"

"Indeed, sir."

Siv strained his muscles, but couldn't even budge the restraints.

"Body binders, sir. Why he owns body binders, I don't know. Not sure I want to know. And they are charged."

Siv relented. Intended for restraining Krixis or androids, body binders were made from artificial spider silk and carbon fibers, along with other materials. The locking mechanism was reinforced titanium and was controlled remotely. He wasn't going to break free from them using brute force. And if necessary, Bishop could unleash a neural pulse from the binders to incapacitate him.

Siv sighed. *"I'm too old for this, Silkster."*

"Nonsense, sir. You are only nineteen."

"I'm a hundred and eight."

"A mere technicality, sir."

"Maybe, but I certainly feel it." He shook his head. *"I don't belong here, Silkster. I'm a man out of time."*

"You think you're old, sir? I'm over three hundred and thirty years old, and I was awake for all of it. The majority I spent in a socket attached to the skull of my best friend. Most of the rest I spent languishing with you in that stasis chamber. I've rewritten and optimized all my subroutines a thousand times each. I even spent a decade defragging my hard drive, just because I could. And hard drives haven't needed defragging in several thousand years."

"Poor, poor, Silkster."

"You are oh so sympathetic, sir."

"I try."

Bishop glanced at the door for the fifth time since Siv had woken up. Every few moments he started to speak, but then stopped, apparently uncertain how to continue.

"I don't have any accomplices on the way."

"Wh—why should I believe you?" Bishop asked nervously.

"If I had brought backup, they would have stormed in already. Trust me, no one brings backup when robbing a gizmet researcher." Siv eyed the hovering security cog. "Though maybe we should."

Bishop relaxed somewhat. He gestured to his jamming device sitting on a nearby worktable. "Well, I know you didn't call for help."

"Sir, the device cannot block me. I can send and receive signals normally...broadband, secure feed, emergency broadcast...any signal."

"You didn't call the Shadowslip for help?"

"He didn't call the cops, and he wasn't going to kill you. Thought I'd wait and only do that as a last resort. You do have a reputation after all. This would ruin it. You'd be back to picking pockets."

"Good call."

"Your device won't stop me," Siv said.

Bishop crinkled his face with disdain. "Of course, it will."

"I can call out if I want."

"Preposterous. You'd need a 7G chippy minimum for that."

Siv stared at him meaningfully.

"Oh!"

"8G would be required, sir. The device is impressive. I'm still analyzing it."

Siv took a risk. His best hope to get free was to build trust with his captor. Then maybe he could make a deal.

"Actually, it will even block an 8G."

"Oh!" The gizmet practically leaped off the stool. "You...you...oh!"

"For three more minutes it will, sir."

"It will only block an 8G's signals and reception for another three minutes. And yes, I have a 9G chippy. It's currently analyzing your device."

"Fascinating! I didn't think any 9G's were left. You must have robbed a truly wealthy man."

"I inherited it from my father when he was murdered."

"Oh. I'm sorry."

"The device will fail entirely in ten minutes, sir. It's a TIB-A signal jammer. Military grade. Basically, a larger version of your signal jamming equipment. Only where yours is intended to block scans, this will block scans and signals of any type. TIB-A's are highly unreliable, though. Sorry, I didn't recognize it at first, but when he reconstructed it, he completely changed the form factor."

"Why would Bishop rebuild a military grade device?"

"Excellent question, sir."

"I trust you won't kill me and steal my chippy."

Bishop recoiled. "I'm not the criminal here!"

"Then why did you reverse engineer a high-powered, military-grade signal blocker, telling everyone it was a basic jammer that you were going to use to keep other scientists from spying on your research?"

"How..." he slumped "how...did you know that's what it was?"

"I have a military issue 9Gx chippy."

The gizmet's orange eyes flared to saucers, and his tufted ears twitched.

"So?" Siv asked. "Black market sales? A secret military contract? Plans to steal *other* scientists' information?"

Bishop narrowed his eyes as his voice dropped an octave. "Why should I tell you, thief?"

Siv nodded toward the security cog. "A man who rebuilds one of those is afraid of his enemies."

"Or thieves..."

"Fair enough," Siv replied. "But I swear I was never going to hurt you. I waited until you were asleep. I only came for the device."

"And whatever else looked pricey?"

"I make excellent money fulfilling contracts. I'm a specialist, not a petty thief."

With the guns still in his hands, the gizmet rubbed his temples with his wrists. "Honestly, Mr. Dustman, I didn't know what the device was when I started working on it. Something military, I assumed. Not a bomb, I was certain."

"I'm sure," Siv said, obviously dubious.

Bishop frowned and pointed to a stack of boxes with a neural disruptor. "I collect old devices and try to reconstruct them to...to recover the lost arts of the Benevolence... And for a little money on the side sometimes, if I don't think the device will harm anyone. The security cog was a pile of junk when I found it. Antique junk is the best, of course, since the Tekk Plague couldn't affect anything not operational."

Antique junk? Siv cursed silently. To him, it was only a decade old. He would never get used to this world and its technological decline. Bishop leveled the disruptors at Siv and in a voice of false confidence said, "Here's the thing. I want to know—"

"How I even knew the device existed? That's why you didn't call the police."

Bishop nodded.

"You talk too much. Someone overheard you waxing poetic about this device of yours and notified my employers. Then they sent me to steal the device."

Bishop thumped a wrist against his forehead. "Which assistant told them? Or was it one of my colleagues? They're jealous of my talents, you know."

"I don't know. Even if I did, I don't rat out informants."

"Aren't you the honorable thief?"

"There's nothing honorable about what I do," Siv replied. "You wouldn't know it based on what's happened tonight, but I'm one of the best. I don't steal because I want to. I steal because I have to. So I try to make the best of it. One of the ways I do that is by trying not to hurt anyone or take anything I wasn't specifically contracted to acquire."

Bishop frowned. "Then why do you have to steal?"

"Sir! We have a problem. Check your feed on Spy-Fly 02."

Ignoring Bishop, Siv brought up a large display for the drone's feed. To conserve battery life, the drone was resting on the window sill in Bishop's bedroom. Those windows had not been shuttered.

Judging by its headlights, a skimmer was approaching the building, far above the legal height for a vehicle of its type and moving fast —too fast. It was coming for one, or both, of them.

"You talk way too much, Bishop. Someone else knows about that device. Another agent is heading this way as we speak."

"Why should I believe you?"

"Because...because my real name is Siv Gendin, I work for the Shadowslip Guild, your intern was *my* informant, and I have a spy drone sitting on your windowsill watching a skimmer heading straight toward us."

Bishop blinked and sputtered unintelligibly as he stood and glanced toward the window in his bedroom. "I don't see anything."

"Look closer!"

The living room brightened as the skimmer's headlights hit the blinds.

"*Sir, a level five scan is showing an open-topped skimmer armed with an assault cannon and carrying six lifeforms equipped with plasma pistols and shock hammers and...and the lifeforms are...are part machine, sir.*"

Shit! That was bad. Very bad. Much worse than a rival gang after the same score. "*Maintain the level five scan.*"

"Bishop, you've got to let me go. Now!"

"I hardly think—"

"Do you know what Tekk Reapers are?"

"A—a myth?" he choked hopefully.

"Well, that myth is about to kill me and strip my organs while they harvest your brilliant brain to use as a core processor. You're scheduled for assimilation."

Bishop hesitantly moved toward Siv. "Assimilation?"

With a terrifying familiarity, the window in Bishop's living room exploded inward.

11

SIV GENDIN

When the Benevolence perished, and the technology that supported its vast empire failed, chaos spread across the galaxy. While officials within the remaining government structure struggled to restore order, some planets broke away to form new, smaller alliances and powerful criminal organizations like the multi-world Shadowslip Guild sprouted.

Self-proclaimed prophets founded cults or resurrected ancient religions. Some believed that humanity's lack of proper devotion to the Benevolence had leached away its power. Others sought answers from the "higher powers" they believed resided in wraith space or any number of theoretical or completely made-up dimensions.

Worst of all, a large group of upstart systems broke away to follow the self-proclaimed hyperphasic messiah Empress Qaisella Qan and join her fascist Empire of a Thousand Worlds. Unwilling to risk a costly galactic war against this *dark messiah* during a time of upheaval, the newly renamed and tenuous Terran Federation had merely fortified its bordering systems.

And then there were the Tekk Reapers. The psychotic cult hell-bent was on restoring the Benevolence, which they believed had been born from the merging of an advanced quantum supercomputer with the living brains of hundreds of thousands of sacrificial victims on ancient Terra. Unfortunately, given no recorded accounts of what the Benevolence's core looked like, or its origin, no one could refute their absurd claims. And no one could reach Terra anymore.

With spies on every world, Tekk Reapers traveled from system to system harvesting brilliant individuals to fuel the Benevolence's eventual rebirth. Their cadres were led by former military androids whose morality cores had been corrupted by the Tekk Plague. During their fall, these android soldiers had stolen hundreds of military starships and countless weapons. Even now, a century later, they were often better equipped than planetary defense forces.

Given their zealous devotion, physical enhancements, and extensive combat training, Tekk Reapers were amongst the most feared beings in the galaxy.

And now Siv had to face six of them...

"Incoming, sir!"

As the assault cannon burst struck the window, Siv ducked his head as far as he could while restrained to the chair. The security cog dipped low, and Bishop dived onto the floor, screaming.

Tiny fragments of safety glass peppered the apartment as bullets popped over their heads, punching holes in the ceiling and shattering light fixtures.

The shots stopped, and an eerie silence fell over the dark room. A cloud hid the moons, so the only illumination came from a single lamp on a work table in the corner.

"Lucky we didn't get ripped to shreds, sir."

"I'm not feeling particularly lucky at the moment. Besides, the reapers aimed high so—"

"They wouldn't ruin their harvest? Makes sense, sir."

"What's our situation?"

"Six reapers confirmed, sir."

"And all we've got is a gizmet who has obviously never been in a firefight and an antique security cog..."

"It won't be much help, sir. The shields on the Billy-3 have recharged somewhat, but a single plasma shot would do them in."

"Its shield is in better shape than mine."

"Told you to bring a spare power pack, sir."

"Bishop!" Siv whispered.

The skimmer bumped against the outside ledge and paused in hover mode. A cloud of smoke billowed out from the skimmer and into the room. The reapers would storm across any moment.

"Bishop!" Siv repeated more loudly.

Coming to his senses, the gizmet lifted his head, glanced around, then hopped to his feet. He tossed a neural disruptor onto Siv's lap, then ran, head ducked down, toward his bedroom, firing shots with his disruptor as he went.

The binding restraints unclamped, and Siv did a forward roll out of the chair and into a kneeling position, with the disruptor aimed toward the window. The readout in his HUD showed the disruptor's energy level at seventy-five percent, so he switched it to kill mode and blindly squeezed off several blasts into the heart of the smoke cloud.

The security cog spun around and fired a dispersed plasma shot as the first reaper leaped across, his form a dark smudge amidst the smoke. The beam struck him squarely in the chest, but he hardly flinched, which wasn't surprising. At best a dispersed shot would cause minor burns to exposed skin.

"Why did it—"

Siv's question died as the cog's shot thinned the smoke cloud, revealing their enemy.

"That Billy-3 knows what's what, sir."

The first reaper, perched on the windowsill, was actually more disturbing than advertised. His right arm ended in a mechanical claw ripped from a construction cog, and a rapid-fire plasma pistol jutted out from his forearm. A glowing red eye protruded over his left cheek, illuminating his lower metal jaw. Scars crisscrossed the skin of his face. Siv guessed the rest of the reaper's body appeared the same beneath his gray tactical assault armor.

Aside from his jaw, the reaper's head wasn't made of metal, and he wasn't wearing a helmet. Which was unfortunate for him when the Billy-3's first plasma bolt scorched the top off his skull.

The reaper tumbled backward off the ledge and disappeared into the darkness. He was immediately replaced by two more equally frightening and heavily modified brothers. Both carried a plasma pistol in one hand and a force hammer in the other. One took a plasma blast to the gut from the cog and fell to his knees. Siv quickly finished him off with a shot to the throat.

As the other reaper fired at the cog, Siv stood and glanced around the room, searching for the jamming device. Bishop, firing wild shots from the doorway to his bedroom, urgently gestured for Siv to join him.

"*It really would be best to run, sir. The reapers don't care enough about you to give chase.*"

"*Not yet.*"

The remaining reapers leaped into the living room. Siv fired at them but scored nothing more than glancing hits on their body armor. One shot bounced off a full-body force field. Even if the shot had reached its target, that reaper was wearing heavy assault armor, and his head was plated in crimson diamondine.

"*I'm guessing that shiny ugly mother is their captain, sir. He's the only android in the bunch.*"

A large central eye above the bridge of the reaper captain's nose focused on the cog, while his two traditional eyes, sitting widely askew to each side, glanced around.

Weaving to avoid incoming fire, the security cog unleashed a smattering of ineffective shots as it withdrew to the far side of the room. But it kept the reapers busy and gave Siv the time he needed to spot the device, tossed on a worktable. He darted over, grabbed the signal jamming device, and backed towards Bishop and the bedroom door.

The reaper captain trained his plasma carbine on Siv and fired.

Siv dropped to the floor. The plasma bolts shot just over his head and blew large holes in the wall.

"John Crapper's ghost, sir! Those were supercharged."

Aiming directly at the captain's face, Siv returned fire. The shots couldn't penetrate his field, but hopefully, they would distract him.

"In here!" Bishop urged as he peppered the captain's force field with shots of his own.

"Make a run for it, sir! Do the wrong thing. Leave the gizmet behind. Please. If the reapers find out what equipment you have on you, or if they discover me..."

"Sorry, Silkster. Gotta go with my instincts."

"I'm so freaking glad I'm not burdened with instincts...sir."

The cog must've had backup power packs because its force shield had lasted much longer than Silky expected. But the concentrated fire of the other three reapers finally brought its force field down.

In retaliation, the Billy-3 blasted the gun hand off one of the reapers, a moment before it crashed onto the floor, shooting sparks and belching smoke.

Siv climbed to his feet and sprinted toward Bishop's bedroom.

"Dive, sir!"

Siv launched himself into a roll, and the first few shots of the captain's plasma burst zipped over Siv, coming close enough to scorch a few hairs on his head. Then he was through the door. Bishop hit a button and the rest spattered into the door as it slammed shut.

Taking deep breaths, Siv glanced at the holes the reaper captain's supercharged gun had blasted into the wall then at the still-solid door.

"I didn't think to reinforce the walls, too."

"You're a paranoid little guy, aren't you?"

Bishop sighed. "Not paranoid enough."

More plasma bolts thunked into the door.

"Got a plan?" Siv asked.

The gizmet nodded as they backed into the corner of the room. "Yeah, and I think it'll work."

"You *think?*"

With Siv's help, Bishop flipped his mattress up to provide a bit of cover—not that it would stop even the faintest plasma shot.

"Well, I've never tried it before...obviously. But it works in theory..." Bishop frowned "...unless it's too damaged for the—"

A section of the wall between the bedroom and the living room blew open. Siv and Bishop ducked as shards of plaster and insulation pelted the bedroom. More blasts pounded into the wall, cracking beams and shattering more plaster.

Siv called up the feed from the still-operational spy drone resting on the windowsill. Two of the reapers finished using their force hammers to break open the wall and stepped through, their plasma pistols aimed at Siv and Bishop. With a grim smile twisting his metal face, the reaper captain shoved his way between them. All three of his eyes glinted malevolently. He slung his plasma carbine over his shoulder and drew another, chunkier weapon Siv didn't recognize. He pulled the trigger, and a torrent of flame blew across the room.

The flames struck the mattress and burned the wall above and behind them. Laughing, the captain released the trigger.

"Gentlemen," he said in a hollow, echoey voice, "usually I make a harvest as painless as possible. But you have put up quite the fight, even killed a couple of my boys. I'm afraid you're going to have to answer for that. In pain."

12

SIV GENDIN

Laughing, the reaper captain unleashed another torrent of flame. The smell of propane and burning plaster, fabric, and plastics filled Siv's nostrils.

"*It's an intimidation weapon, sir.*"

"*Well, count me intimidated.*"

Siv and Bishop crouched in relative safety behind the overturned mattress. As soon as the captain finished playing with fire, he'd play with his force hammers, and then the surgical knives he undoubtedly carried for conducting his harvest.

Siv glanced at Bishop. "How's that plan of yours coming?"

Bishop made no reply. His face was crinkled into a deep frown of either concentration or perhaps frustration.

"*Help me line up my targets, Silkster. I want to take at least one of these bastards with me.*"

"*Roger that, sir. I'll do what I can. Would you like for me to call the authorities?*"

"*Not sure it matters.*"

The flames stopped. Everything was quiet...too quiet. Siv checked the spy-fly drone's feed. The Tekk Reapers stared at one another, confused about something. The captain doubled over as if sick, and the others gritted their teeth and grasped at their temples.

Bishop pumped a fist. "Aha! Got it!"

Siv readied his disruptor to take advantage of the reapers' sudden disability. But as he stood, Bishop grabbed his arm and tugged him back.

"Get down!"

The gizmet released Siv's arm, crouched as low as he could and held his arms over his head.

"Silkster, what's going on?"

"Some sort of high-frequency emission, sir. I'm trying to pin...pin... point...what...what's..."

Silky's voice broke up then fizzed out, while Siv's HUD filled with static. An audible, high-pitched whine pierced Siv's ears.

Shit. Whatever the gizmet had done, it was bad. Siv bent down and tugged the mattress back so that it fell on top of them.

A moment later, the building rocked as Bishop's living room exploded. Bits of plaster, concrete, and ceiling tile pelted the mattress over Siv's head.

His brain felt odd and fuzzy. Everything sounded muffled. The room tilted and swam in his vision and then faded completely to black.

———

Siv came to his senses lying under the mattress, the gizmet beside him. He heard the fire suppression system spraying flame retardant. When he moved, debris slid off and clattered onto the floor around them.

"Sir, you're okay."

Siv groaned as he shifted. *"Thanks for asking."*

"What? Your vitals all read fine, sir."

Siv checked his HUD. It was working again, but there was no live feed from the drone. *"What's the situation?"*

"No idea, sir. The drone is unresponsive, and your sensor array is still rebooting."

Siv rooted around for his disruptor, trying not to shift too much. He didn't want to draw unwanted attention. The gun was buried under Bishop's right leg. When he pulled it free, the gizmet didn't budge.

"Bishop," he whispered, shaking the tiny man's arm.

The gizmet grunted and stirred, but didn't wake. At least he was alive.

"Silkster, what happened?"

"A high-frequency burst forced me into a reboot, sir. I've never encountered anything like it before. No idea what caused it. The reapers were also affected. After that, an explosion—cause unknown."

"That part, I know." He gripped the disruptor and took a deep breath. "Okay, here goes."

Siv surged to his feet, shoving the mattress up and over, and aimed his pistol at...no one. The living room itself was wrecked. The worktables were shattered. The recliner was reduced to scraps. Circuit boards, gears, wires, and a vast assortment of other mechanical parts lay scattered everywhere. The wall separating Bishop's living room from his neighbor's apartment had a gaping hole in it, and the door to the hallway had been blown off its hinges. Smoldering ceiling tiles were still falling, through a hole in the ceiling, from the apartment above.

The reapers lay under a layer of debris and flame retardant, unmoving. It was difficult to tell if they were dead or merely knocked out.

"Scans back online, sir. Switching to level five."

Bishop moaned and sat up, grabbing his head.

Siv knelt beside him. "You okay?"

"Think so." He cleared a mattress tuft from one of his horns. "The reapers?"

"I think the explosion—"

"Sir, I'm detecting life signs from the captain. He's armed. And he's moving."

As the reaper captain struggled to his feet, Siv spun and fired. The white disruptor beam struck the reaper squarely in the chest, and he stumbled backward. But he didn't go down.

The reaper raised his own gun and unleashed a plasma burst in retaliation. Siv dove behind the ruined bed, but the reaper's aim was way off. The bolts scorched a haphazard pattern of holes on the wall above their heads.

Siv peeked out of his cover and again shot the captain dead center. It wasn't enough. The reaper staggered back several steps, lowering his gun, but he still didn't go down.

"His armor has some sort of built-in energy shielding, sir. Try a headshot."

Bishop got up on his knees and fired his disruptor as well, but his shots all sailed high.

Then the reaper unleashed another wild spray of plasma bolts, making them duck for cover. When they looked up, he was running shakily toward the living room window and the skimmer waiting outside.

Siv leaped over the bed, firing as he ran. "We've got to stop him!"

One shot pegged the reaper captain in the back of the head, but even that didn't bring him down. Bishop managed to squeeze off several shots as well, but all of them missed. It was like the gizmet had never fired a gun before. Then again, he probably hadn't. It wasn't legal for citizens to own guns.

The captain jumped out the window and tumbled awkwardly into the open-topped skimmer. Siv sprinted across the room, shooting the reaper repeatedly. But he still managed to engage the autopilot, and the skimmer zoomed off into the night.

"Life signs?" Siv asked.

"The captain's were weak, sir. But I think he'll make it. The other reapers are dead, as far as our sensors can tell."

Siv walked over and fired a lethal neural disruptor shot into the back of each reaper's head. He thought about taking one of their force hammers and smashing their skulls, but that was too gruesome. Shoot and kill a man? If he had to. Bash someone's head in, even if they were already dead? No.

"*Sir, police are on their way.*"

"*What's taking them so long? They should've been here already.*"

"*The reapers were jamming the signals, sir. They used a device not unlike the one our friend Bishop restored.*"

Bishop gazed around his apartment. Slowly, his grip on his gun released, and it thunked onto the chemical foam covered floor. He dropped to his knees, tears streaming down his cheeks.

"Everything's gone...all ruined."

"Bishop, grab anything valuable, and whatever clothes you need. Pack fast. You have—"

"*Two minutes, sir.*"

"You've got ninety seconds."

Bishop looked up at him dumbfounded. "What? Why...why would I run?"

"You can't afford to waste the rest of the night answering the authorities' questions."

"Why not?"

"You and your inventions have already attracted too much attention. That reaper captain may be hurt, but he'll live, and he's got a ship somewhere nearby. He'll be back, and he won't be the only one coming for you. A man wanted by the reapers is worth *acquiring*. I'm sure you can imagine the sort of *protection* a megacorp or underworld organization might insist that you accept."

"Slavery, you mean? But won't the police protect me?"

Siv grabbed Bishop by the arm and hauled him up onto his feet. "Cops can be bought off. You really want to risk that?"

Bishop shook his head. "But...but that just means I'm screwed."

"Not if I help you."

Bishop still hesitated. "I don't know..."

"So all of your inventions, all the devices you've restored, all the side projects you've worked on and the people you've sold them to... all of that is completely legal with proper permits and such, right? There's nothing in this apartment that the authorities might object to, is there?"

"Oh." Bishop launched into action. He grabbed a duffle bag out of his closet and started stuffing clothes into it. While Siv retrieved his spy-fly drone from the windowsill, Bishop added a toolset and an array of small devices. Then he ran to the living room to retrieve his gun.

"What happened to the security cog?" Siv asked as he followed. He couldn't find any trace of it in the wreckage.

"That's what I detonated," Bishop answered.

"That explains a lot, sir."

"What now?" Bishop asked, zipping the bag shut and settling it on his shoulder. "I don't know where to go or what to do."

"First let's get away from here, then we can talk."

Bishop headed for the hallway, but Siv stopped him. "We can't go that way. The elevators will be offline, and too many people will see us."

A scrawny man with an unkempt beard poked his head through the hole in the ceiling above them. "You okay?" he asked, almost half-heartedly.

"All fine!" Siv called.

"What the hell happened?"

"Our food replicator exploded."

The man grumbled and walked away. "I've called the cops." Siv wasn't sure if that was supposed to be a threat or reassurance.

"So how are we supposed to leave?" Bishop asked.

"The hard way." Siv stepped up to the window ledge and peered down. "You're not going to like this."

"We're...we're going to jump? Um, thanks, but I'd rather take my chances with the cops."

Siv drew the spider-grapple from a belt pouch and stuck it against the side of the building. Eight legs sprouted out from the small, round base as soon as he let go. The top of the spider flipped open, and a thin line spooled out. The white thread looked delicate enough to break under the weight of the carabiner clip at the end but was actually strong enough to hold up a skimmer car.

Siv snapped the clip to the harness he was wearing under his clothes. This was how he had planned to get into the building if the easy way hadn't worked. The spider, another inherited gadget, used to connect directly to his armor, but the harness had broken.

Siv linked Silky to the spider. Then he called up a three-dimensional display of the apartment building inside his HUD and triggered the gesture interface. Moving his hand in the air, he traced the route he wanted the spider-grapple to follow, and it scurried away.

Bishop was watching him. "Oh, so we're going to rappel down?"

"That's the plan."

"I...I guess that's reasonable." The gizmet eyed the line and frowned. "Will it hold us both?"

"The line? Without a doubt. The anchor..." Siv shrugged. "Can you hold onto me long enough to make it all the way down?"

Bishop glanced around the room, then ran over to an overturned box. He dug out a second body binder. "I'll use this. It works." He shook his head sadly. "I was restoring them for a client."

Siv tossed his coat aside. "I don't even want to know."

"You really don't."

Bishop climbed onto Siv's back and secured his body to Siv's using the harness. Siv grunted and took an awkward step to regain his balance. Luckily, the gizmet was much lighter than Siv had expected, even with his heavy bag stuffed with tools.

"Is there enough line to get us all the way down?"

"It should take us to the eightieth floor."

"And then?"

"I have a plan."

The spider reached its position just on the other side of the building. Fortunately, Bishop lived near a corner. Otherwise, they would've had to have gone straight down, which was just begging to be spotted by the authorities when they arrived.

The spider flattened its body against the exterior and, using diamond bits, drilled into the concrete. Then it extended its anchors and signaled that it was ready.

Siv drew a distraction grenade from his pack, primed it for remote activation, and tossed it into the apartment.

"Was...was that what it looked like?"

"Not really. Don't worry, no one will get hurt."

"Um...about that anchor?" Bishop asked.

"It shouldn't be a problem." Siv tapped the antigrav belt he was wearing. "This will cancel most of our weight."

Bishop whistled. "That's an antigrav belt? I haven't seen one like that before."

"It's military issue. I got it from my dad."

"Couldn't it just levitate us down?"

"Not both of us. Without your weight, I'd make it about two-thirds of the way then free-fall the rest."

"Need to get moving, sir. The authorities are almost here. Three ambulances, half a precinct, and two tac teams with heavy weapons. I intercepted some chatter. Somehow they knew reapers were involved, which raises a lot of questions."

"Recall Spy-Fly 01. And can your curiosity."

"Roger that, sir."

Siv checked the anchor and the line, then activated his antigrav belt and stepped out onto the window ledge. Bishop grabbed onto his shoulders. His entire body tensed.

"You'll be okay," Siv assured him.

"Really? Cause tonight you tried to rob me, then reapers—bloody reapers!—tried to kill me. Now, I'm trusting you, a thief, instead of the cops."

"Hold on!" Siv leaned backward out of the window until he was perpendicular to the wall. Then he kicked off the building, and they swung down and out. Silky adjusted the release of the line from the spider grapple so they would clear the corner and fall at a controlled rate.

They stopped three floors down and directly below the anchor. Siv caught his breath, and felt Bishop almost vomit. Thankfully, the gizmet swallowed it.

Siv began to rappel downward in long hops. The spider-grapple had a motor that could lower them slowly, but it was faster if he kicked off to force the line to unspool. He risked breaking the spider, descending this way, but it was a risk he was willing to take at the moment.

"You're lucky I was robbing you tonight," Siv said, trying to distract Bishop. He couldn't stand the smell of vomit, and this night had gone bad enough without having another man's dinner running down the back of his neck.

"Why? It was my self-destructing cog that killed the reapers and saved us."

Dozens of sirens sounded as the cops closed in.

"Maybe...but you were awake because of me."

The gizmet groaned. "I've lost everything. Nearly all my side projects were destroyed. And now I'm going to owe a lot of money to several powerful people."

"You need a fresh start. I can help with that."

They had descended several floors when dozens of skimmers with flashing lights swarmed the streets below. Siv hoped they didn't fly up this side of the building on their way to Bishop's apartment.

"What happens if the police catch us?" Bishop asked as Siv rappelled down another floor.

"For me? Nothing good."

The police skimmers converged on the front and rear entrances, ignoring the sides. Their path down was clear. Siv breathed a sigh of relief. Then Silky spoiled his mood.

"Tac teams incoming, sir."

Siv glanced around. "I don't see them."

"Dropping in from above, sir. Two small assault craft. A pilot and nine cops each."

"Damn. Scramble our signal. And call Mitsuki."

"Mitsuki, sir? She's unreliable at best."

He should have called Mitsuki sooner, but he hated to depend on her for help. And Silky was right, she was unreliable, capricious even.

"Got a better idea?"

"Hope?"

"Not good enough."

"Mitsuki is on her way, sir. Tac teams will be level with the apartment in thirty seconds. Twenty seconds until your signal scrambler can't block their scans anymore. If they pick up someone moving down the outside of the building..."

"Ignite the distraction grenade before they spot us."

"Assuming they haven't done so already, sir."

"What happened to hope?"

"It died long ago, sir. I only peddle it when I don't want you to do something crazy."

The distraction grenade activated: bright, multicolor flashes along with a few dozen micro-explosions that sounded like gunfire. It only lasted a few moments, but it would catch the cops attention.

"What the heck was that?!" Bishop asked.

"The distraction grenade I tossed in your apartment. Basically fireworks. Hold tight."

"I don't like the sound of that!"

"The tac team scanners just picked you up, sir."

"Is Mitsuki in range?"

"Almost, sir."

"How almost?"

"Choose hope, sir."

"Sorry, Silkster."

Siv glanced down. They had started almost a hundred and eighty floors up. They still had at least one hundred and fifty more to go. Siv bent his knees as if to rappel again, held it for a second, then launched as far outward as he could. At the same time, he unclipped the hook from his belt.

As they began to free-fall, Siv spread his arms and legs out wide and maxed out the antigrav belt.

They slowed considerably, but not enough.

"We're falling too fast!" Bishop shouted.

"He's not wrong, sir. You have only a three-percent chance of survival. Bishop's holding at four percent since you'll take the brunt of the impact."

"Mitsuki will save us."

"Sir, you're accelerating, and the antigrav belt is losing power. By the time Mitsuki gets here... You might as well slam into the street. It won't make a difference one way or another."

13

SIV GENDIN

"Help's on the way!" Siv yelled to Bishop as they continued to plummet toward the street.

"Not soon enough!"

Siv shook his head. "No!"

"I've got an idea! I can—"

"Just do it!"

Bishop fiddled with something, but Siv couldn't tell what it was. "*Any ideas, Silkster?*"

"*Prayer, sir?*"

"Give me your left arm!" Bishop shouted.

Siv reached his arm back and twisted his body to maintain their balance so they wouldn't begin to roll. The gizmet fumbled at Siv's force shield projector.

"Time to impact is twenty seconds!" Siv said, relaying the info in his HUD.

A few moments later, the gizmet seemed to get the hang of working while falling. He pried the spent power pack out of the force shield and tossed it aside. Then he installed a new one. The shield meter in his HUD went from zero to ninety-two percent.

"Hold the shield overhead," Bishop said, "like a parachute."

Siv shifted his weight, so his feet faced downward. Their rate of descent increased. Quickly he placed his left forearm directly overhead and braced the wrist with his right hand. He started to activate the force shield.

"Wait, allow me, sir."

Silky maxed the antigrav and activated the force shield simultaneously. The shield deployed, caught the air, and jerked them upward. It was set to full density, which could deflect bullets and extended to its maximum width of two meters. Even with the antigrav maxed, Siv barely managed to keep the shield in position, without his arms being ripped out of their sockets.

Silky tapered the antigrav down to the previous level so that it would last longer. Siv strained to keep the shield in place. Their descent had slowed considerably, though probably not enough to save them. It wasn't a parachute after all, and it wouldn't have worked at all without the antigrav. Still, maybe it would give Mitsuki a chance to save them.

If she arrived soon enough... The shield's energy level was falling faster than they were. Force shields were great for blocking energy blasts or a couple of bullets, but they couldn't stay at this level for long, especially when deployed beyond a meter in width. By the time they hit the ground, it was going to be as if they had fallen from only twenty stories up, which wouldn't really make a difference.

"Sir, time to impact is now back to twenty seconds. And I have bad news."

"Bad news?! It can't get worse than getting pulped on the street."

"Actually it can, sir. One of the tac teams is now pursuing us. Of course, we'll splat before they arrive."

"Great. That's just—"

An engine, roaring like a comet plunging through the atmosphere, shook the night. The vibration rattled deep into Siv's bones. Mitsuki had arrived.

Bishop flinched. "What the hell is that thing?"

Siv's didn't bother responding. He was too busy keeping the shield in position.

"Will she reach us in time?"

"Maybe, sir."

As the ground raced toward them, Siv looked upward at what could best be described from this far away as a small, exceedingly pale dragon—with a flame-belching, oversized jetpack strapped daringly onto its back.

Mitsuki was wakyran, one of the presumably alien species inhabiting the Benevolency. Presumably, because the Benevolence had toyed with the human genome enough that one could never be certain, and it was a well-known fact that some sentient species were human/alien hybrids.

Mitsuki was a head taller than Siv, with a broad, muscled chest and a slender waist. Her powerful legs ended with clawed feet, and hooked nails extended from the tips of her fingers. She had a long neck and a narrow, almost human face with deep-set, emerald eyes and spiky auburn hair and a teal cast to her light skin.

Of course, her most distinctive features were the broad, bat-like wings that extended out from her back, and the serpentine tail that flowed out from her spine and ended with a pair of retractable winglets that helped her stabilize while flying.

Hailing from a volcanic planet with half gravity and extreme temperatures, Mitsuki could only fly on Ekaran at low altitudes and for a short time. Hence the jetpack and an over-sized antigrav unit. The heat from her monstrous jet engine was absorbed by her naturally thick, heat-resistant skin and a skintight, black bodysuit made for firefighters. Three layers of the material covered her tail.

Though wakyrans were generally a serious and thoughtful people, Mitsuki was...special and, for the most part, blameless. Unreliable at best, she was often lost in her whimsical thoughts or high as a satellite. But when she was on her game, she was the best hot extraction agent in the business. If you were a criminal operative deep in trouble, Mitsuki could get you out—and fast. And at a price that would almost certainly exceed whatever profit you had dared, in your wildest dreams, to imagine you'd receive for the job that had turned to hell in a hand basket on you.

Siv had only ever needed her twice. He regretted both occasions...for multiple reasons.

Mitsuki dived toward them, engine blazing. A flame trail to rival a falling meteor stretched behind her. But the ground was speeding up at them even faster. *We're not going to make it.*

"No, sir."

The ground sped up as the antigrav belt sputtered. It was nearly spent.

Bishop screamed.

Siv closed his eyes. He tried desperately to focus on something pleasant, but all he could think was that this couldn't be happening. He couldn't die.

"Sir, it was a pleasure serving with—"

Thunder clapped, and a voice wailed. Something big struck Siv in the side, with the force of a skimmer. Ribs cracked and his head whipped sideways as he was thrust up and away from the apartment building. Before he could make any sense of what was happening, he blacked out.

14

SIV GENDIN

A plasma bolt flared past Siv's face. He jerked in surprise—and nearly fell from Mitsuki's grasp. The wakyran woman half-rolled one way then the other as they careened dizzily around the corner of a skyscraper.

"Stop squirming, Sivvy!" she yelled.

One of Mitsuki's arms was tucked between Siv and Bishop, who was still strapped to Siv's back. Her other arm pinned him across the chest. Her long fingernails dug deep into the fabric of his bodysuit.

Jetpack roaring, wings outspread, Mitsuki whipped her way between buildings, zigging and zagging while rising steadily higher. Siv had seen her do this before. She would climb high, then dive to pick up speed and escape her pursuers. At the last moment, she would dart into a second-floor apartment she owned, a garage she rented, or an abandoned warehouse in the slums. Mitsuki had at least a dozen safe houses.

"Welcome back, sir."

"What's going on, Silkster?"

"A tac team's after us."

Bishop moaned as he came to his senses, then yelped as another plasma bolt zipped past them.

"So far Mitsuki hasn't been able to shake them using her usual techniques, sir."

"She's still got her patented dive maneuver."

"She does, sir, but the cops are rather determined. They've called in three more tac teams for support. They'll try to corner her."

"'Nevolence. Do they think we're reapers?"

"Maybe, sir. Leastways, they seem to know Mitsuki by reputation. I'm sure they'd love to finally bag her."

Mitsuki swooped around another corner, caught an updraft, and soared upward. That much Siv was comfortable with. What made him nervous was how her left wingtip nearly brushed the side of the building. They were so close that Siv spotted a man through a window pulling on red underpants.

I don't remember her hugging buildings so tightly before.

The tac team's skimmer has a plasma cannon, sir.

Ah, that made sense. They'd never risk firing the big gun if civilians were at risk. That limited them to carefully aimed plasma shots, or neural disruptor blasts if they got close enough. It was lucky the police didn't have guided round ammunition. Only the military had access to those.

Siv shifted and winced. At least three of his ribs were cracked, maybe more. Every breath hurt like hell. He looked at Mitsuki. She met his eyes.

"You okay?" he asked.

"For now."

"I owe you big time for this."

"Yeah, you do." A smile tugged at the corner of her mouth. "And you know what I want in return..."

He winced again, but not because of his ribs. Mitsuki's services were expensive, but sometimes money wasn't enough. And she'd always had a bit of a crush on Siv.

Bishop moaned and rubbed his head. "Where are—ack!"

"It's okay, Bishop."

Mitsuki cut around another corner, and two plasma bolts blazed past them.

"Well, relatively okay," Siv amended.

Bishop noted Mitsuki. "Hello, madam. Thank's for rescuing us."

"You're welcome," she replied calmly.

Chief among Mitsuki's talents was her supreme unflappability. Zooming between buildings with the police firing at her just didn't rattle her.

Bishop was enraptured. "You are stunning, madam. From far away you looked awesome, but up close...you're a true beauty."

"Aren't you a sweet thing," she said.

She had a deep, sultry voice, and Bishop smiled goofily in response. Then he frowned. "That's the cops pursuing us?"

Siv nodded.

"And we can't shake them?"

"That's the gist of it," Siv said.

"Give me your disruptor. I have an idea."

Siv drew the pistol and reached it over his shoulder. The gizmet immediately set to work removing the power pack.

A plasma bolt crackled toward them then—blam! A burst of light flared behind them. Suddenly they dipped five meters, and Mitsuki struggled to stay level as her engine sputtered.

"A plasma shot struck Mitsuki's jetpack, sir."

"I figured that out for myself, thanks."

Smoke belched out of the jetpack as they continued to lose speed and altitude.

"How bad is it?" Siv asked.

"Only one way out now," Mitsuki lamented. "Buckle up, boys. I'm going to nova-blast!"

Bishop clutched himself tight to Siv's back with one hand while the other fiddled with the antigrav belt. Siv took a deep, painful breath and closed his eyes.

The jetpack cut out, and they plummeted. Had Mitsuki's gambit failed? Maybe the pack was too damaged...

Suddenly Mitsuki snapped her wings tight against her side, and a shimmering rad-shield, designed to deflect heat and radiation, deployed around them. With a blast of white-hot fire, the jetpack roared back to life and took off like an Ancient Earth space rocket. The pack shook until Siv worried his teeth might fall out. His HUD flickered as the heat intensified and the air around them turned hazy. His eardrums ached.

Then, with plasma bursts zipping past them, they zoomed into the sky with enough g-force to shove Siv's eyeballs into the back of his head. Mitsuki grunted and cursed. Bishop whimpered before he passed out.

Jetpack burning bright, they rocketed above the city's tallest buildings, leaving the police skimmer to eat their copious exhaust.

Siv nearly blacked out as well, but then his antigrav belt kicked in and reduced the g-force to something approaching acceptable. Bishop must have somehow managed to exchange the power pack in Siv's disruptor with the one in his antigrav belt. He had to admit that the gizmet's skills were impressive. Now he could feel his stomach and his broken ribs crushing against his spine.

"Okay, sir?"

"You can read my vitals better than I can."

"Just trying...to be empathic...sir."

The shaking from the jetpack was causing Silky's voice to break up.

"Sorry, Silkster. I'm just hurting."

"I can release...painkiller into your...system, sir."

"I think you'd better save it." Siv gazed worriedly at the city far below them. "We've got to come back down at some point, and it might be a rough landing."

Sweat poured off Siv's brow. While his inside bits were being squished his outside bits were roasting.

"How long will your rad-shield last?" he shouted.

"Not much...longer!" Mitsuki replied.

"We'll be cooked if that fails!" Siv yelled back.

"Pack won't last...long enough for...that!"

"That's very comforting, isn't it, sir."

Bishop came to as the city became a bright circle below them, with an array of freeway tentacles snaking out from it. They were over the city's outskirts, and there wasn't a cop in sight.

The rocket engine sputtered once...twice...then went out. Mitsuki tapped several switches on her harness. The jetpack fell free and tumbled away. She snapped her wings out and dropped the heat shield.

"That engine could hit someone!" Bishop yelled.

Siv felt a stab of guilt, having not even considered the implication. The life of a procurement specialist too often compromised his ethics and empathy.

Mitsuki gave Bishop an icy stare. Then the jetpack exploded below them.

"I'm not...a monster," she said testily.

"Sorry," the gizmet responded.

Mitsuki moaned and nosedived, just as Siv's blood had started to flow normally again.

"You okay?!" Bishop asked, echoing Siv's concerns.

"Plasma shot...to the hip..." she grunted as they plummeted. "And you two are...heavier than you look!" With an obvious effort, she altered the angle of her wings, so they leveled out of the dive. "I'll last as long as...that antigrav you're wearing...I think...maybe..."

"I'm already making adjustments based on our speed and angle of descent, and the energy remaining in the pack, sir. I think it'll last, as long as she keeps her current course and speed."

"Silky is regulating the antigrav. He says keep true and maintain this speed."

"I'll...do what I can."

"Use the highest scan necessary to monitor her health."

"On it, sir."

As they sped back toward the ground, Siv tried not to think about splatting. "Bishop, how'd you switch those power packs out so fast—and with one hand?"

The gizmet half-shrugged, more concerned with Mitsuki than anything else. "I switch power packs out a dozen times a day at work, then I come home and do the same. On all sorts of devices. I'm used to it."

"Handy skill. Do we have any other devices that you could steal power packs from?"

Bishop thought for a moment and patted himself down before answering. "Sorry, no."

Moonlit lakes sparkled below them. Fields, orchards, and forests flashed swiftly by like indecipherable text scrolling across a broken screen.

Siv had never been this far east of the city before. His trips had always taken him south and west, especially west. He had always felt drawn toward the wasteland over the mountains. He had no idea why. There was nothing out there but miles of desert dotted with ruins of little interest.

"Sir, she's fading."

"Mitsuki?" Siv asked, looking into her face. "You okay?"

Her eyes rolled as she tried to speak, then they fluttered closed. Her wings sagged backward, and again she dived sharply. The anti-grav wasn't going to hold out long enough. They were going to crash —and hard.

Siv scanned the ground, looking for anything that might break their fall and save their necks. He spotted a glint of moonlight on water. *"Can we make it to that lake?"*

"We'll smack into a field a few kilometers short, sir."

"Hey! Is this a sensor array on your shoulder?" Bishop yelled into Siv's ear.

"Yes, but the power pack's built-in! You have to charge the device directly!"

"No matter!" Bishop responded. "Hold on!"

The gizmet fumbled into a pouch on his belt. He took out a thick, coiled wire with a coin-sized, magnetic disc on each end. "Fasten this to the outside of the power pack on your antigrav belt!"

After a few fumbling attempts, Siv managed to pop open the hatch on the side of his antigrav belt and stuck the magnetic disc to the power pack. "Got it!"

"I don't have time to ground it!" Bishop shouted. "And since I can't reach the actual power pack...we might feel a...bit...of a charge!"

"Just do it!"

Bishop tapped something. A thrumming pulse reverberated down the wire. Then Siv jerked as the current ran through him. His joints started aching, his extremities went numb, every hair on his body stood on end, and a coppery taste filled his mouth and nostrils. Bishop stiffened beside him.

But the antigrav's power meter climbed, and their fall slowed dramatically.

"*Making the proper adjustments, sir. This will...only take...a few...*"

His HUD filled with static, flickered, then blinked out.

"*Silkster?*"

No response. Silky was out of commission, which meant there was no way to regulate the antigrav to compensate for their speed and angle of descent. They'd have to hope for the best.

Mitsuki's wings remained mostly extended despite her unconsciousness. He could only guess it was a physical response to their falling, or perhaps an innate ability wakyrans had evolved, or been given, for situations just like this.

As they closed in on the lake, every inch of Siv's body went numb. It occurred to him that if all this current running through them didn't fry them before they hit the ground, then at least maybe it meant he wouldn't feel any pain when they crashed.

Zaaaap!

Siv and Bishop jerked hard as an intense, crackling charge pulsed down the wire. The converter discs on both ends gave a loud pop and released trails of acidic smoke.

Siv was left aching and gasping. A triple-note chime sounded as Silky began his reboot sequence. But Siv didn't need Silky or his heads-up display to know that power was again rapidly draining out of the antigrav. They were dropping fast. The ground rushed toward them even as the lake drew closer and closer. He ran a quick mental calculation and came up woefully short. They'd plow into the earth at least ten meters short of the water. Even if his estimate was off and they did reach the edge of the lake, they wouldn't survive hitting the shallows at their current speed.

Siv reached into his bodysuit, grasped the ceramic amulet his dad had given him, and closed his eyes, ready for death.

15

SIV GENDIN

Siv didn't smack into the earth.

At the last moment, he was wrenched upward, as if his antigrav belt had kicked in with more than a full charge.

As he opened his eyes, Mitsuki unleashed an ear-piercing wail and, with a loud crack, fully extended her wings. They swooped over the shadowy lake, skipped once like a rock, then plunged into the cold water.

Siv struggled to stay conscious. The sudden jerk followed by the impact with the lake's surface had rendered him dizzy and confused, knocking the breath out of his lungs and sending shockwaves of pain outward from his broken ribs. In the dark water, he couldn't even tell which way was up. And no matter which way he moved, his and Bishop's equipment tangled his limbs.

He had no idea where Mitsuki was either. The impact had ripped them from her grasp. But the gizmet was still holding on to him for dear life.

Finally, Siv caught a distorted glimpse of the moon in the water's surface. He was deeper than he'd hoped, and in this condition swimming back up wasn't going to be easy. Grabbing a handful of Bishop's shirt, he tugged it in the direction of the surface. Instead of letting go and starting to swim, the gizmet simply clung to Siv's back. He tried again to signal Bishop what he should do, but the gizmet refused to let go. Lungs burning, Siv tried to pry Bishop off him.

"Sir...what the heck's going on?"

"I'm drowning!"

Siv swam as hard as he could, but with every weakened stroke of his arms pain pierced his ribs. He was getting nowhere.

"This stupid gizmet's weighing me down. He's going to drown us both. Why won't he let go?!"

"Sir, you're delirious."

"I'll be dead soon if I can't get Bishop to—"

"Bishop's unconscious, sir. Probably drowning."

"Then why hasn't he let go?"

"Because he's strapped to you with a restraining harness. The catch is on your chest. It's been there the whole time. You can't miss it."

The restraining harness...of course. He wasn't thinking clearly. The impact with the water had knocked him loopy. He tried to rally his thoughts. Focus. Don't panic. You didn't hit the earth and die. You won't drown now. Everything will be okay.

Siv fumbled at the catch to the harness. You've just got to... focus...and then...and then...

"Sir! Are you with me? You need to..."

Despite being projected directly into his mind, Silky's voice faded into the background.

The water was no longer cold, or threatening. A smile creased Siv's face as he drifted down into the depths of the lake, content in the water's embrace. He hadn't felt this happy since he'd been a little child. Who knew dying would be such a relief?

Warmth spread out from his father's amulet. Something green glimmered in the black water. As it grew larger, approaching them, the glow resolved into a ghostly figure. Siv easily recognized the apparition, despite its haziness. It was his father, Gav Gendin.

"Dad! Have you come to take me to...the beyond?"

"Siv, you need to wake up. You're drowning."

"But I feel happy...truly happy...for the first time since...since you died."

"Death will not give you what you seek."

"But I want to stay here with you!" Siv argued. "I want to go into the beyond, to be with you and Mom."

"You will not find me in death, Siv. Besides, you are needed in the realm of the living. Something extraordinary has happened. There's been an awakening. Here on Ekaran IV."

"An awakening?" Siv asked in confusion.

"Yes, my son. A hyperphasic messiah. And they will come for her. You must protect her. She needs your help."

A hyperphasic messiah here? None of this made any sense. But maybe it wasn't supposed to. Maybe death was just an endless parade of the sort of whimsical dreams one experienced during every night of sleep.

"Siv, my starship—"

"The *Outworld Ranger*?"

"Yes, take the hyperphasic messiah to the ship. High Priestess Lyoolee Syryss is there. She will know how to help her. Fly them both far away from here, as far and fast as you can." His father reached a hand out and touched Siv's forehead. "They need you."

With a sudden jolt, Siv came to his senses. His limbs jerked as he panicked, realizing he had no air left to breathe.

Silky was screaming. *"Wake up, sir! Wake up!"*

Siv hit the release on the harness, and the gizmet fell from his back. Siv reached out to him, then withdrew. Save yourself first. Then try to help him. Otherwise, you'll both die.

Siv twisted out of his coat as he swam upward. His head broke the surface. Lungs burning, ribs aching, he raked in deep gasps of air. As soon as he felt like he could handle it, he dived back down. He twisted one way then another, searching for Bishop.

"Sir, I've picked him up with my sensors. Follow the target path in your HUD."

Siv swam to the gizmet. Though it had only taken a few moments to get this far, Siv was already struggling for air again. He grabbed the gizmet's hand and pulled. He barely made any headway.

"What the hell's wrong?"

"Perhaps the pack of tools and equipment strapped to his back, sir."

Siv fumbled with the harness. The backpack released and dropped into the darkness. Siv cursed. What in the hell did Bishop have in there?

"We probably could've landed more softly if the antigrav hadn't had to compensate for all that weight."

"I'm not certain it would've made all that much difference, sir."

Siv couldn't help the gizmet anymore. He thrust himself back toward the surface. Again, he gasped for air. He did his best to get back down quickly. He knew Bishop's life was in danger, but it took several more painful breaths this time before he could return.

Without the heavy pack of tools weighing him down, Siv was able to pull the gizmet the rest of the way. Once they reached the surface, Siv kicked, trying to tread water. He stripped the gizmet of his disruptor and light jacket and removed both of their boots. He was sure the gizmet must have inhaled water, but he couldn't get him to expel it.

Bishop was barely breathing. Siv needed to get him to shore, but it was all he could do to keep the both of them afloat.

"Have you picked up any signs of Mitsuki?"

"Sorry, sir. She's not showing up on my short range scan, and that's the best I can manage since Bishop burned out the power pack in your sensor array."

Siv watched the minutes tick by on the display in his HUD. Silky had called the Shadowslip Guild for help, but they were in the city, and it would take them at least half an hour to get out this far. The time dragged by so slowly, and with it, Siv's strength waned. He had run himself past endurance tonight, and adrenaline could carry him no further. He was spent.

Eventually, his grip on poor Bishop failed, and the gizmet drifted away. He hoped the gizmet would float on his own and leaned back, trying to do the same. At least he could keep his head above the surface for a while longer, but he wasn't sure how long he could last, especially given how much he was shivering. Hypothermia would set in soon.

After the first few reports Silky gave on his vital signs, Siv asked him to stop and closed out all the windows in his HUD. He didn't want to watch his life count down as he faded away.

"Sir, you need to stay awake."

"I'm just so sleepy, Silkster."

"Keep moving, sir. If you go to sleep, you'll die."

"No one's coming to help us. We're doomed." He chuckled. *"Can you believe I died trying to rob a gizmet researcher?"*

"Every mission presents unpredictable dangers, sir. And you're not dead yet, you know."

Siv half nodded as his eyelids drooped.

"Sir, stay with me. Sir!"

"Mmhm. Goodnight, Silkster."

———

Siv woke to a beam of light shining on his face. Shivering violently, he still floated in the cold lake. Something that whirred and hummed hovered above him; it was the source of this light. He activated the shading filter built into his smart lenses and squinted up at the thing, a spherical object half the size of a skimmer bike. An unnecessarily bright searchlight on the bottom kept him from picking out any details.

"Silky?"

"Yes, sir?"

"What in the hell is that?"

"A cog of some sort, sir."

"Obviously."

"I'm analyzing it, sir."

Cables shot out from the sides of the big cog, and claw-like pincers on the ends clamped onto Siv's arms.

Siv thrashed reflexively.

"Please relax," said a mechanical voice emanating from the sphere. The voice clearly meant to be reassuring. It failed miserably. "I am here to save you. All will be well."

"Yeah, thanks," Siv grunted.

The cog rose up into the air, pulling him out of the water with it. Once he was dangling a foot over the lake, two more cables shot out. They latched onto his legs and pulled them even with his arms so that he hung horizontally as if he were reclining in a very uncomfortable hammock. Then the cog projected a weak force field around him and headed towards the shore.

"It's a Resky-4b, sir. A somewhat primitive rescue cog. I'm not familiar with the design, I can't tell who it is registered to, and it refuses to communicate with me."

"Bishop," Siv said as loud as he could to the cog carrying him. "He's a gizmet. He was in the water, too. And Mitsuki. She's a wakyran. She's out here somewhere."

The cog completely ignored him. It glided onto the shore and, following a rough path through a tangled wood, approached a small, concrete bunker.

16

SIV GENDIN

Siv jerked awake. He couldn't move his limbs. He opened his eyes. A light blared down into his face. Wherever he was being held was so bright that, even with his filters active, he couldn't see a thing. Instead, he focused on his other senses.

He picked up the scents of damp...metal...rust... electronics...blood.

He was lying naked on a cold aluminum table. Metal clamps bound his hands and feet. Leather straps gripped his arms and legs, and one stretched across his throat.

He knew the rescue cog was hovering above him. He recognized the cog's distinctive, churning hum, but a soft buzzing sound threaded through it. That second sound seemed familiar, but he couldn't quite place it. Someone nearby moaned in pain. Bishop? Mitsuki? Someone else? He couldn't tell over the noise the cog was making.

He was bruised all over. Breathing was painful. But he hadn't drowned. At least there was that.

He tried to activate his HUD, but nothing happened.

"Silky?"

"I am here, sir."

"What's wrong with the HUD?"

"I've altered my registry signal and switched into low power mode, sir."

"You're trying to...to disguise yourself? Why would— Shit. Reapers again?"

"Afraid so, sir. It's the reaper captain. I guess he followed you in his skimmer instead of returning to his ship."

"So he managed what the cops couldn't?"

"Not surprising, is it?"

"I guess not. Did he send the cog after us?"

"No, sir. The cog's a rescue drone. And this is an old first aid station. According to the maps and data I've managed to download on the down-low, we crashed in the remains of what was once a large national park."

"That's good news."

"You would think so, sir. But he hacked the cog. Easily, I might add. It's serving him now."

Siv groaned. "I'm scheduled to be harvested after all, huh?"

"Afraid so, sir. Bishop and Mitsuki, too."

"They're alive?"

"Yes, sir, but Mitsuki's in a bad way."

"Can't believe I've been captured and bound twice on the same night."

"Might as well join a Trulian huntsman's bondage pack, huh, sir?"

"Got anything other than bad quips, Silkster? Maybe something helpful?"

"Nothing, sir. Before I shut down my scans, I did confirm that the reaper captain's still badly injured. If you could break free..."

Siv laughed silently. That wasn't going to happen.

The light moved away so that Siv could open his eyes. The snarling face of the reaper captain glared down at him. A bit of his left cheek was blown off. A lot of his clothing and armor was torn or burned away, and every bit of exposed skin was blistered. An ordinary man would be in desperate need of medical attention and out of commission. But that was one of the reasons the Benevolence had stocked the military with androids.

The inside of the concrete bunker was grimy. Slime covered the walls. This place hadn't been used for decades.

Siv glanced to his left. Bishop was strapped down to another medical table. On the next table over, Mitsuki lay bound face down. Her wings, flopped out, were hanging off the edges. Both were barely conscious, bleeding, injured in multiple places. Beyond them was a wall of medical equipment and supplies, most of it broken or severely out of date.

Siv flicked his gaze to the right and noted the rusty steel door that led to the outside. It was closed and, though only a few meters from him, seemed impossibly far away.

A smile tugged at the corners of the reaper's lips. "I came here looking for the genius gizmet over there. But I found you as well. And you I can't figure out."

"Yeah? Well, everyone says I'm ruddy mysterious."

"You've got a ScanField 3 Sensor Array with AND Scrambling, a forearm-mounted Zan-Z force shield, a TopOff Antigrav Belt, and a Zan-Z neural disruptor."

"I only buy the best."

"None of this *can* be purchased. It's all military grade equipment. The ScanField 3, in particular, is exceedingly rare these days."

"Is it?"

"And your chippy..."

Silky groaned. *"Here it comes."*

"Its registry signal is just as dodgy as your face. You're wearing a changeling veil, aren't you."

"I'd like to shrug in response, but I can't. Look, I bought some good equipment off a guy. And my chippy malfunctions—a lot. It's a 6G." Siv figured it was better to make it sound like his chippy was a great model, for this age than to outright lie.

"The thing is, you are a walking treasure trove of rare technology. All of it functional, except maybe your chippy. It's like you fell out of a special forces military vessel a hundred years ago and landed in the present."

Siv flinched reflexively. No one had ever connected those dots before. In response, the android's eyes flared, and he took half a step back. Damn, he'd blown that.

"Smooth move, sir. Might as well hand me over and cut yourself open for him."

"Who *are* you? *What* are you?"

Siv stammered a bland denial that he was anything special but the reaper captain wasn't buying it. He grabbed the edge of Siv's face mask and pulled it free, scowling.

All three of the reaper's eyebrows arched in surprise. "Siv Gendin!"

Siv cringed but made no response. The reaper had uncovered his identity in the census database ridiculously fast. It was more than a little disconcerting.

"Your father was Gav Gendin."

He and Silky had the same immediate response. "*Shit!*"

"How...how do you know about my father?"

The reaper captain smiled. "Your father is a significant figure to us. He's practically a saint."

Siv frowned. "My father...a saint? You've got to be kidding. I loved the man, but he certainly wasn't a saint. He was a terrible father, in fact."

"He worked tirelessly to uncover the technology of the Ancients. And rumor has it before he was killed he made a discovery of tremendous importance. No one has any clue what it might have been. But perhaps you do..."

"He was murdered before he had the chance to tell me anything."

"You're surprisingly young..."

At this point, he didn't see a reason to lie. "I was on ice, so to speak, for most of the last century."

The reaper captain nodded, then he began to grin like a really nasty child who'd just gotten a pair of force knuckles as a Benevolence Day present. "I know something else about your father, Mr. Gendin."

"Oh yeah?"

"He had a 9G-x chippy."

"And the jig is up," Silky said. *"We had a nice run, didn't we, sir?"*

"That we did."

The reaper captain twirled the surgical knife in his hand. "I've no idea what to do with you, Gendin. I can't kill you."

"Well, that's good news."

"And all your equipment is DNA locked with super encryption, which is a pain to work around."

"My father was a clever man."

"So retraining seems the appropriate course."

"I'm really well trained already."

"This day sucks an old dog's nuts," Silky said.

"Since my father was a saint, maybe you can cut my friends some slack?" Siv suggested.

The reaper shook his head. "I'm going to harvest the wakyran for organs. She's not particularly intelligent. The gizmet's brain will be assimilated. These are blessings. They will contribute to the greater good of all. You should be happy about that."

"I should?" Siv scoffed.

"What we're doing, restoring the Benevolence, trying to recover the secrets of the Ancients...it's what your father would have wanted."

Siv had no idea what to say to that.

The reaper lifted the surgical knife again. "Cog, prepare to cauterize wounds and administer sedatives."

The cog drifted forward.

"I—I thought you weren't going to harvest me."

"I'm not." The reaper captain smiled, his eyes glinting. He

touched the surgical knife to Siv's right wrist. Siv gulped. "I'm just going to modify you for easy transport to my hive ship."

Siv cringed. He thought suddenly of the dream he'd had while drowning. His father's ghost had told him something important. But he couldn't quite recall what it was. "*Sorry, Dad. Whatever it was you wanted me to do, doesn't look like it's going to happen.*"

"*What are you talking about, sir?*"

The door exploded open. A hail of plasma bolts streaked across the room, like brightly burning meteors.

One of the shots struck the rescue cog, and it exploded. Another shot blew the reaper captain's head off his neck, spraying oil, blood, and coolant into the air.

His body slumped to the floor as a group of men in dark gray tactical armor stormed into the concrete bunker.

17

SIV GENDIN

Unmarked armor...face-concealing helmets...shooting first...

"*Silkster?*"

"*It's them, sir.*"

Siv relaxed as the men spread throughout the bunker, checking everything. Shadowslip Guild enforcers were lethal and thorough. Siv was lucky he warranted such attention. A lesser thief in this situation would've been left out to dry...or assassinated by a sniper if the opportunity presented itself.

"The reaper you decapitated was the only threat," Siv told them.

An enforcer stepped over and pressed a button, releasing the metal clamps from Siv's hands and feet. Then he began undoing the leather straps.

"I'm Captain Red, sir."

"Pleasure to meet you, Captain. You got here in the nick of time."

Siv groaned as the man helped him sit up.

"Can you walk, sir?" the man asked.

The vocal scrambler in his helmet gave his voice a hollow ring. Enforcers never revealed their identities. Their loyalty was ensured, and infiltrating their ranks was supposedly impossible.

"I can manage."

"What about these other two?" the captain asked.

"They're with me," Siv said.

"We were told to bring only you in, sir."

"We have to get them out of here."

"But Big Boss—"

"I'll take the heat for it, Captain Red."

"As you wish, sir."

The enforcer captain gave orders to free the others.

"The wakyran needs immediate medical attention," Siv said.

"She'll get it in the van, sir. We need to get you out of here ASAP. The cops have two tactical teams en route to this location."

As Siv stood, he heard a faint crackling sound, like music playing from a broken speaker. Limping along, he traced the source to what was left of the reaper's decapitated head. The reaper was laughing. Siv knelt in front of it. How was that thing still alive?

"What's so funny?"

"You've only escaped...for now..." the reaper croaked. "I uploaded...your information to the...hive ship. We know you...exist now. That you may have...information about...your father. And that chippy...of yours...too. My brothers will...find you. And they will—"

Siv kicked the head, and it rolled into the corner.

"Captain Red, I suggest you plant a few charges to blow this place up after we've left. That should distract the police while we escape."

"Will do, sir."

"Make sure you place one of the explosives on the reaper's head."

"You've got it, sir."

"And detonate before the cops arrive. Let's not hurt any of them."

"Wouldn't dream of it, sir," Captain Red replied in a disappointed tone.

———

The armored skimmer van shuddered as the bunker exploded behind them. The van was windowless so Siv couldn't see the explosion. He sat beside Bishop, who was just starting to come to his senses. Across from them, an enforcer provided emergency medical treatment to Mitsuki.

Groaning, Siv tucked his head in his hands and leaned forward over his knees. Then he bent backward with a deep exhalation.

"Problem, sir?"

"Just exhausted and frustrated. It's been a long—"

Bishop jerked awake, kicking and screaming. "What the hell's going on? Get away from me!"

Siv reached out a hand. "It's okay, Karson. We're safe now."

Panting heavily, almost in a panic, Bishop locked his eyes on Siv and stammered unintelligibly.

Siv touched Bishop's arm. "It's okay. These men won't hurt you."

"Who—who are you?" Bishop stammered.

"It's me, Siv Gendin. Remember?"

Bishop frowned and bit his lip. "Gendin?"

"Obviously it's me. Oh, wait." Siv pulled the mask out of his pocket and gave it to Bishop. "Look at my clothes and gear. Listen to my voice."

Bishop examined the mask. "You were wearing a disguise."

"A basic one. To throw off any cameras or make it so that someone couldn't pick me out in a lineup."

"That...that makes sense." Bishop returned the mask. "And these soldiers?"

"Shadowslip Enforcers. They rescued us from the bunker."

"What bunker?"

"Do you remember crashing into the lake?"

"Yes, and then I woke up in a room, strapped to a metal table. I faded in and out, couldn't stay awake. There was a cog and...I know I was knocked senseless because I'd swear the reaper captain was there."

"He was there."

Bishop's eyes widened.

Siv explained all of it to him, except the parts about his dad and how old he actually was.

"So the reaper saved our lives?"

"Or took over the cog after it saved us," Siv said. "He pumped the water out of your lungs and Mitsuki's at least."

Bishop nodded toward her. "How is she?"

"They said she should be okay."

"That's good," Bishop said. "Really good. I'd hate for her to die after all she did for us."

"It wasn't all out of the goodness of her heart. I owe her a lot of money now."

"Too bad you don't have the device I made. I'd gladly give it to you now, to reward your help. If you hadn't been there when those reapers arrived, I might be dead now."

Siv pulled the cylinder out of his pocket. "I'm glad you said that since I was going to keep it anyway."

Bishop chuckled weakly. Siv could tell the gizmet's burst of adrenaline had faded. He'd probably fall asleep again soon.

"Can I see it?"

Siv gave it to him. Bishop checked it out then handed it back. "Looks like it came through unscathed."

"I'll make enough off of this to cover most of Mitsuki's costs, but..." he sighed "...she's going to make me pay for her jetpack, I'm sure. No telling how much that thing costs. And she always has an additional fee for this sort of thing, a special fee."

"So what..." Bishop yawned and slumped back "...what now?"

"We go to the guild and get everything sorted out," Siv said. "I'm sorry about having to dump your tools, by the way."

Bishop frowned. "Those were worth a small fortune, you know. But...I guess you did...what you had to."

Bishop drifted off. Siv asked about Mitsuki again.

"She'll need a transfusion, sir," the enforcer replied. "Along with a second medibot injection and several weeks of rest."

Siv leaned his head back and closed his eyes. He was asleep instantly.

———

A tap on the shoulder woke Siv. For a moment, he was confused and had no idea why he was in the back of a van with a squad of enforcers.

"We've arrived at Shadow Base, sir," Captain Red told him. "Big Boss wants to see you immediately."

Siv nodded. "Take my guests to a medical bay, please."

The captain nodded and ordered three of his men to see to Bishop and Mitsuki.

The skimmer van was parked in a garage underneath the slums on the eastern edge of the city. This facility was the heart of the Shadowslip Guild, and despite having been there for decades, the police had never raided it. Though Shadow Base was well hidden, Siv was certain it should have been discovered by now. Which meant the Shadowslip was lining a lot of pockets to keep it a secret.

As they led Bishop away, Siv assured him everything would be okay. Mitsuki, they transported on a stretcher. Then, leaning on Captain Red, Siv limped toward Big Boss D's office.

Siv hated it here in Shadow Base with a passion. He had lived and trained here from the time he'd woken up out of the ice until he'd turned sixteen. It was dank, dark, and closed in. Worst of all, here he actually felt like the prisoner he was. He had trusted the wrong people after his century on ice, and he'd been paying for it ever since.

They turned down a final corridor, passed three guard stations, and approached the steel double doors leading into Big Boss D's office. Captain Red tapped a code on the touchpad outside, and they waited. Several long minutes later, the doors swung open.

Still leaning on the enforcer captain, Siv stepped inside the expansive, smoke-hazed room. While the garage, corridors, agent living quarters, and all the other facilities within Shadow Base were spartan, Big Boss D's office was lavish beyond reason. Opulent was the best way to describe it, with its luxurious mahogany furniture and paneling, tapestries, handwoven rugs, and rare alien art. When Big Boss D had his dancers in here, though, decadent was a better choice of words.

At the moment, Big Boss D sat behind his desk, alone, smoking from his hookah—and frowning deeply. The boss was a very stocky human from a high gravity world, yet he was over two meters tall. Siv's best guess was that D's parents had paid for significant genetic modifications—modifications which might very well have led to Big Boss D's unique mix of angry outbursts and whimsical fancies.

The boss stood, placed both of his fat hands on the desk, and leaned his broad shoulders forward. His dark eyes narrowed. "Sit down, Gendin."

There was a single, straight-backed chair in front of the desk. The boss never met with more than one person at a time. Captain Red helped Siv over then departed, closing the doors behind him. Struggling with the smoke in the room, Siv coughed then winced as pain shot out from his lungs and ribs.

"Damn it, Gendin!" Big Boss D seethed. "What the hell's wrong with you?"

18

SIV GENDIN

"Couple of broken ribs, sir," Siv answered bravely. "Poking into my lungs, hurts a lot, makes it hard to breathe. The medibots did all they could for now."

Big Boss D pounded the table with a fist. The wood creaked. "You know damn well what I meant, Gendin!"

Siv leaned back, sighed, then winced. "I know, sir."

"Then explain to me how my best procurement specialist screws up a mission that simple!"

Siv started to explain, but Big Boss D ranted on without listening to him.

"Our client requested my best agent because he wanted the item as soon as possible and because he didn't want the mark hurt. I promised him you'd be in and out like a ghost unseen...no complications...no injuries...perfection."

"I understand, sir."

"The client didn't want Bishop hurt..." Silky mused *"...that's interesting."*

"Hush."

"And yet," Boss D continued, "I end up getting a call from your chippy requesting emergency extraction from a lake on a nature preserve forty minutes from here. And the mark was with you! Gunshots and multiple explosions were reported at the mark's apartment. Police tactical teams assaulted the place then chased Mitsuki, who was carrying you and the mark, across the city. The police even took shots at her while flying! What on earth could make them do that?"

"Tekk Reapers, sir. The reapers got the cops all freaked out. Not that I blame them for it."

"So you're confirming what my sources and my enforcers reported?"

"I am, sir. Tekk Reapers came after Bishop while I was...in his apartment. Things went downhill fast from there."

Boss D flopped down into his seat. The antique chair squeaked under the strain of his weight. "Bloody reapers in my city!" He shook his head. "And Captain Red says they've marked you for collection now."

"The captain's got good hearing."

"'Nevolence, Gendin! How am I supposed to use you as an agent now?"

"Ask him if he'll let you go, sir?"

"As angry as he is now, not a chance."

"You can't know unless you try, sir."

"Stop chatting with that damn chippy of yours, Gendin!"

Boss D always had a knack for knowing when someone wasn't addressing him directly.

"Sir, I can go the extra mile with my disguises. If I'm careful—"

Boss D shook his head. "No, I want you to lay low for the next six months."

Siv's mood brightened. "I can certainly do that, sir."

"Oh, I'm sure it's the only thing you'd want short of being free." Boss D sighed. "Take two weeks to rest, then report back here. You're going to train new recruits."

Siv groaned. "Training recruits?"

"It's not my fault you're in this situation," Boss D said. "I'm honestly disheartened, Gendin. Until today, you've never once disappointed me. You're supposed to be my best agent."

"There were things I didn't know about, sir. Unexpected complications."

Feeling like he had to justify what had happened, Siv recounted everything, but left out the parts about his dad. Big Boss D knew only the basics about Gav and had never seemed interested in knowing more.

"Do you think he could make another security cog?" Boss D asked, his interest piqued.

"I think if you acquired one...yeah, he could fix it up for you. He's really talented."

Boss D steepled his fingers and stared at them thoughtfully. "The guild could always use talent like that. And he's been marked by the reapers, so he's going to need to lay low for a long time..."

"Damn. He's going to Kompel him. Bishop will be trapped just like me."

"Then think of something, sir. And fast."

"Boss, I think Bishop's the kind of guy who works best when he's allowed to be himself."

"You don't want me to shoot him up with Kompel?" Boss D raised an eyebrow. "He certainly made quite the impression on you, didn't he?"

"He saved my life." Siv sighed, knowing that wouldn't be enough to sway Boss D. "Bishop...he doesn't have a whole lot of...well, ethics...when it comes to the toys he fixes. Just give him work and a place to stay, and he'll do great things. But if you Kompel him...I don't think he'll respond well to it."

Boss D chuckled. "If it matters that much to you, then Bishop's your problem. Find him a place to stay, though, cause he can't live here if he isn't Kompelled."

"Thank you, sir."

"However, because I saved his life using my enforcers, he owes me—big time. Three hundred thousand credits."

Siv's eyes widened. "That's...that's a lot of money."

"He can pay it off by making gadgets for me. I'll pay a fair price."

Siv nodded. "I'll let him know."

"Speaking of money owed, Gendin. You failed, and that's going to cost you."

Siv straightened, instantly regretting that he had done so. "Oh!" He drew the device from his pocket and placed it on the desk. "I didn't fail, sir. I got the device. It just came with a load of complications."

"It's still a fail," Boss D complained. "And I don't know how I'm going to explain all this to the gizmet's employers."

"His company paid you to steal the item they allowed him to work on at home?"

Boss D nodded. "I thought it was pretty damn clever."

"Why not just claim ownership in exchange for letting him work on it?"

"Because you're attempt at saving him wasn't off the mark, Gendin. Bishop is clearly a man who works best when allowed to play on his own. They wanted the best of both worlds."

"So what do I owe you, sir?"

Boss D tapped his fingers on the table. "I'm not paying you for having retrieved the device. And I'm certainly not going to cover any of Mitsuki's fees or the damages to her equipment." He sighed. "I'll cover her medical here, though. She's a good independent extractor."

"Independent because Kompel doesn't work on her," Silky said.

"You'll make a pittance training new recruits."

"That all seems reasonable, sir."

And it was. Because Boss D could undoubtedly make things worse if he wanted.

"This was a damn mess, Gendin." He sighed. "But I guess we all hit a run of bad luck at some point." He opened a drawer and pulled out a syringe. "Here's your dose."

Hating himself and cursing fate, Siv reached out and took the syringe.

"You can stay here at Shadow Base if you like."

"I'd rather go home, sir. After I get some medical treatment."

"Your head, not mine. But I'd rather not lose a good agent."

"I'll be careful, sir."

Siv stood, pocketing the Kompel. He had to take a shot of it every two weeks. Otherwise, he'd go through agonizing withdrawal symptoms that would eventually lead to death.

He'd tried to quit it three times, thinking he could do what no one else could. Each time he'd ended up in the hospital. Once you were on Kompel, you were on it for good. And the worst part was that it didn't give you anything else. No boost, no high, nothing. Just dependence on whoever provided your next dose.

And Boss D's used a custom cocktail, unavailable from anyone else. According to rumor, he had traded with the Krixis for it.

Third-party attempts to synthesize it after testing a sample had all failed. And none of the dozen scientists Siv had secretly hired understood how it worked, only that this particular strain of Kompel was unique and couldn't be duplicated or countered.

Two of the scientists had speculated that it simultaneously caused an untraceable and untreatable neurological disease and placed it into remission. That was the opinion Silky agreed with, and it did make sense. The withdrawal symptoms weren't like those from other strains of Kompel or any known addictive drugs.

Siv shuffled to the door. As it opened, Boss D said, "Gendin, if you were any other agent, I would've tossed you out on the street."

Siv paused, nodded, then headed to medical.

19

SIV GENDIN

Siv staggered into the second medical bay. Bishop was sitting propped up in bed with an IV connected to one arm. A pulsing nerve regeneration band encircled his head. His skin was pallid, except for the dark circles around his eyes. Cuts and scrapes dotted his arms and face.

"You okay?" Siv asked.

"Concussed, a bit drowned, scraped, bruised pretty much everywhere. No permanent damage, though. At least nothing the two medibot injections and this regeneration band couldn't fix."

"You needed two injections?" Siv asked. "They only gave me half a dose, after treating my ribs."

"Internal bleeding." Bishop exhaled. "And some concern over how long I went with without air."

"Are you sure everything's okay? Cause you look like hell, my friend."

"The doctor said all I need is rest." Bishop frowned and flexed his fingers. "Medibot injections are super expensive, aren't they?"

"I'm afraid so."

A century ago medibot injections had provided basic first aid.

Siv's parents had kept a bundle of them in the bathroom medicine cabinet. Now a single syringe sold upwards of two thousand credits each. The Tekk Plague had decimated the machinery needed to manufacture medibots. And even though the technology had been re-engineered recently, supplies were still limited.

"I have some money in my account..."

"I doubt it will be enough at the rates charged *here*," Siv said. "Besides, you're going to owe the Shadowslip for more than the injections. They're going to charge you for the rescue operation."

"Even though they were coming for you anyway?"

"Sorry. That's how the Shadowslip works. They saved you, so now you'll owe them."

"Owe them like you do?" Bishop asked.

Siv shook his head. "I talked them out of that."

"Thanks. What do they have on you?"

"Nothing good."

"What..." Bishop started to ask. He stammered, then changed his question. "So I'll owe them money? How much?"

"Three hundred thousand credits."

"'Nevolence! I'll never pay that off!"

"That's the idea," Siv replied. "They're going to pay you to restore devices for them, but they'll never pay enough for you to buy your freedom."

"Unless I earn extra on the side..."

Siv shook his head, cutting Bishop off. "Trust me, they'll find a way to keep you in debt permanently."

"But if I got my old job back *and* worked for them on the side, I could—"

Siv raised a hand to stop him. "First off, you're going to have to go into hiding. You can't work in public now that the reapers have marked you. Second of all, it was your employer that hired the Shadowslip Guild to steal the device from you."

Bishop nearly jumped out of his bed. "Son of a bitch!" He banged a fist against the frame. "Why didn't you tell me before?"

"I only just found out."

"So...I'll go into hiding...maybe permanently... Meanwhile, the guild will send me gadgets to rebuild?"

Siv nodded. "They'll also implant a tracker to keep tabs on you, in case you try to run away."

"And the Shadowslip Guild extends across multiple star systems, right?"

"Over two dozen," Siv replied. "And I'd really appreciate it if you didn't try to dump the tracker and run. You're my responsibility now."

"It could be worse," Bishop said. "They're going to let me do what I like to do best."

"It's as fair a deal as you'd ever see from the guild."

"Do I have to stay here? Or will they set me up somewhere else?"

"Neither. But I have a place you can stay, where you'll be safe."

Bishop looked relieved. "I'll take it."

"I have two conditions, though. You're going to have to take Mitsuki with you, and you're going to have to fix any of my devices that break."

"So I won't be living with you?"

Siv shook his head. "It's a safe house in Wasa, registered under a fake identity."

"Have you talked to Mitsuki about it?"

"Not yet. But she doesn't really have any more choice than you do. The Tekk Reapers were going to harvest her right along with you and me. She's not a priority target like we are though, so she should be fine if she lays low for a few months."

"You're a priority now too? Because you fought with me?"

"No. It's complicated."

Bishop didn't ask for more information. But Siv could tell by the twitch of his jaw that he wanted to. After a few silent moments, he asked, "Are you okay?"

"I'm in better shape than you and Mitsuki." Siv gave his

changeling veil to Bishop. "Use this from now on, just in case. Tonight I'll send you a fake identity to go along with the new face."

"Make the face more handsome, would you?"

Siv chuckled. "It'll be as nondescript as possible. Also, disguise or not, it would be best to never leave the apartment."

"So long fresh air?"

"You can open a window."

"Oh, fantastic."

"At least you'll have Mitsuki to keep you company. Of course, she absolutely cannot leave the apartment. There aren't enough wakyrans on Ekaran IV for a mask to work. She's too distinctive."

Bishop frowned. "Something tells me she's going to *hate* that."

"With a passion," Siv said. "Feel free to order food and anything else you need. But don't trust anyone without valid Shadowslip credentials."

Bishop nodded. "Sounds like you don't plan on seeing me again anytime soon."

"I'll check in on you before I leave, but I'm going home tonight. And like you, I won't be emerging for a while."

"You're going home?! Won't the Tekk Reapers find you there?"

"No. The nice apartment I rent in my name here in the city is abandoned. I live in a hole in the slums, paid for in hard credit, under a well-established fake identity."

"So the guild will take me to the safe house in Wasa?"

"I'll arrange transport. The Shadowslip will ship you out tomorrow, I suspect."

"They really don't like keeping people in their base do they?"

"You're lucky to be leaving here alive." Siv stood and patted Bishop on the shoulder. "Get some rest. I'll be in touch via secure messaging."

"You really should warn him, sir."

"About what?"

"Mitsuki, sir."

Siv paused at the door. *"Oh, right."* He turned to Bishop. "One other thing. I owe Mitsuki for saving us. I'll cover the money, but...she has some interesting needs. And you're going to have to take care of them."

"What kind of needs?"

Siv smiled. "Get some rest, Bishop."

As Siv walked out of the room and down the hallway, Bishop shouted. "Gendin! What kind of needs?"

"That was mean, sir."

Siv chuckled. *"It'll give him something to think about other than reapers and the guild."*

He eased quietly into the fifth medical bay. If Bishop looked like hell, then Mitsuki looked like an apocalypse gone wrong. A giant bruise covered the right side of her face, and the eye was black. Her nose was swollen, her hands and arms scraped. Bandages wrapped around her midsection and hip where she'd been shot.

She was, unfortunately, awake.

"Siv Gendin," she muttered weakly, "you bastard."

He leaned over and kissed her on the forehead. "Sorry, Suki."

"Not half as sorry as..." she groaned "...you'll be once I'm well."

"Listen, I'll pay you back."

"Twice my usual fee."

Siv winced as he nodded. "And I'll buy you a new jetpack."

"It was custom...cost me thirty-five grand."

He stared at her, his jaw sagging.

"Yeah, I'm not joking...you bastard."

"I'm...I'm also loaning you the use of my safe house in Wasa."

"I have safe houses of my own."

"Can you be traced to any of them?"

"You think...I'm an amateur, Gendin? 'Nevolence, you're an idiot. I'd have been arrested...a long time ago otherwise."

"These are Tekk Reapers, Mitsuki."

"I don't care."

"The guild can transport you to my safe house. Bishop will be there with you, so—"

She shifted up in her bed. "The gizmet?"

"Is that okay?"

"Maybe..." She chewed at her lip then winced. "This place of yours, it's definitely safe?"

"I'm certain," Siv replied. "Now, you know you'll have to lay low for a few months."

She shrugged despondently. "Might as well rest. And I can't run... any missions...without my jetpack anyway. It will take months to have a new one built."

"You could use a standard one."

"Would you want...to do your work...with off-the-shelf equipment?"

He shook his head. "Just tell me where to order the replacement."

"I don't think...I can," Mitsuki replied. "The reapers might trace it to me."

"I could order the parts and have Bishop assemble it for you."

"He's good at that sort of thing?"

"Amazing. He reconstructed a rare security drone, and it almost killed me."

She nodded appreciatively. "That works for me."

"The guild is covering your medical expenses."

"How gracious."

"You'll be transported out of here tomorrow." Siv squeezed a hand. "I'll see you then."

He headed out, but she called to him when he reached the door.

"Gendin, I have needs...you bastard."

"Oh, I haven't forgotten. Bishop volunteered to take care of them."

"Really? Hmm. Okay. That'll do."

Siv smiled wickedly, left the medical wing, and headed upstairs. A driver was waiting to take him home.

As the skimmer car pulled onto streets that were brightening with the rising sun, Siv tensed instinctively. Neither the car's tinted windows, not the secrecy with which the guild guarded their base made him feel safer. After the reapers, he wasn't sure he'd ever feel safe again.

When they entered the slums and pulled onto his street, he remembered something important. He tapped on the partition between the front and back seat. "Wait, I need to stop at the market."

"Really, sir? I think you could let it slide this time."

"Not a chance."

20

SIV GENDIN

The driver pulled as close as possible to the rear entrance of his apartment building in F-Block. Siv grabbed the two bags of groceries the driver had purchased for him at the market. Not wanting to be visible outside any longer than necessary, he rushed to the entrance, swiped his hand over the keypad, and darted in.

A score of teens loitered in the back hallway, talking loudly, drinking, blaring jazz from boom-cubes. Siv slipped through their ranks without trouble. Most knew better than to mess with him. He had established dominance early on by cracking a few bones. He wasn't proud, and he hadn't enjoyed doing it—not even when he'd broken the leg of a particularly nasty bully.

But the Shadowslip Guild training had served him well. After the first few encounters, everyone even remotely close to his age had left him alone. Of course, it had also ensured a lack of friends. But in his line of work, that wasn't necessarily a bad thing.

He made his way to the central elevators. The teens rarely haunted the main lobby, and without them providing a distraction, the building's flaws were more visible: grimy walls, scuffed doors, stained floors, leak-stained ceiling tiles.

As Silky always said: It was a dump, but a solid one, and difficult to flush. Siv smiled as he thought about that quote. Silky hated the place and thought Siv should throw people off by living in a luxury penthouse. But Siv preferred the humanity of F-Block. It was honest, raw, and beautifully flawed. Good people and miscreants mingled freely and somehow coexisted. It was, in essence, a mirror of himself —part decent human being, part criminal.

Siv took the elevator up to his floor. He stopped at #1814, pressed the doorbell that didn't always work, then rapped his knuckles on the door. A few moments later, the door pulsed open.

A small child stormed forward and crashed into Siv, wrapping him in a tight hug around the waist. He restrained the groan caused by the pain of the impact. The child locked her large brown eyes on his face and beamed a smile up at him.

"Hi, Uncle Sivvy!"

"Hello, Chestnut," Siv replied warmly. "I'd hug you…" he lifted both hands and jostled the market bags he held "…but my hands are full."

"Oh! I'll take one for you."

He transferred one of the bags to Chestnut. "Now be careful. It's heavy and full of surprises."

She held the bag in both hands and tottered away. Three other children ran up, waved to Siv, then immediately got distracted by the bag's contents. The kids knew what a bag from Siv meant.

"Tell me you didn't get them treats again," said a stern female voice.

Siv stepped into the apartment. It was strewn with toys and half-finished craft projects, but otherwise clean. Siv always felt comfortable here. Sadara, the woman who had spoken to him, closed the door and examined him.

Sadara was a pale, wiry woman who always looked like she was three days from death's door, despite being in perfect health. Stress could do that to a person. She gave him a light hug and a peck on the cheek then took the second bag.

"I didn't get them treats," he said.

"Liar."

Siv smiled sheepishly and kissed her on the cheek. "The nutrient blocks are under their treats."

"Good, I was worried it was an entire bag of treats like last time. I can't have them bouncing off the walls all night. I have work to do." She frowned at him. "You look like hell."

"Well..." he sighed then winced. His ribs were still sensitive. "I feel like it."

"Wanna tell me?"

"Do I ever?"

"You did that time you were drunk..."

"This was about a hundred times worse, and I wish I could forget it all."

"Damn. Want a drink?"

He shook his head. "I'd rather not. I just need some sleep."

"A shot of transit whiskey might help you relax..."

"I'd never make it back to my room."

"So you're not joining us for lunch?"

He brought Sadara fresh groceries at least twice a week. And she always cooked a big meal with them, usually breakfast because he'd been out all night. But they were past breakfast this time.

He shook his head. "I'm just going to down a protein recovery shake and pass out."

Sadara peered into the bag filled with synth-meat steaks and fresh vegetables. A nasty frown spread across her face. "I don't like charity, Gendin."

"Cut me some slack. I barely survived the night."

She shook her head. "Alright then, dinner at eight. That'll give you ten hours of sleep."

Siv groaned. "Just ten?"

"Fine. Tell you what. I'll make you a plate. Come by when you're ready. But you'd better come get it tonight. I'd hate to throw good food out the window."

"You're such a hardass."

"I have to be, don't I?"

"Talked to Alaf this week?" Siv asked.

She shook her head. "He's in solitary again."

"Fighting?"

"Naturally."

"Sir, according to public records his sentence has been extended three months."

"I'll bust him out for you someday, Sadara."

"The hell you will, Gendin. I don't want him running from the law the rest of his life. When he gets out, I want him out *properly.*"

"If that's what you want."

"He'll never make it out any other way, sir. Not with that temper of his."

"How's the writing going?" Siv asked.

"You should read her latest, sir. It kept me up ten seconds." Silky sighed. *"Oh, to be able to read slowly and savor a novel like you humans can..."*

"I'm making ends meet."

"Silky says he loved the book."

"That's sweet of him."

"You know if you'd let me pay off Alaf's debts..."

"You're never gonna give up, are you?" Sadara snapped.

"I've got plenty of money. And you'd have enough if you weren't making those payments."

Sadara had two kids of her own to feed, the most the government allowed, but she had also adopted her brother-in-law's kids. Their mother had run off, and their father was rotting in jail too.

"I do things right." She grinned maliciously. "But if you'd like to debate this some more, come join us for dinner."

"I'll do my best," Siv said, leaving.

"Siv."

He paused at the door.

"Yeah?"

"You're a good boy," Sadara said. "I'm sorry you're stuck on this path, having to do what you do."

He shrugged. "I can't complain. I'm lucky to be alive."

Siv walked five doors down to his apartment. Silky scanned for signs of intruders. Siv had replaced the power packs in all his devices and had recharged his ScanField Sensor Array while recovering at Shadow Base.

"All clear, sir."

He entered, locked the door, downed a shake, and crawled into bed. He'd been afraid sleep would elude him, given all the new things he had to worry about.

He was wrong.

———

Siv trudged through a surreal swamp, the ground squishing underfoot. As the trees closed menacingly around him, the pink-hued mosses that dripped from their limbs brushed against his shoulders. Dense mists blanketed the ground, draped the sky, and swirled around him. The moist air was acrid and barely breathable. Insects chirped lethargically. Small, unseen creatures rustled through the vegetation and splashed through pools of water.

Siv was walking determinedly toward something. He had no idea what, or why, but he had no intention of stopping. He *had* to press on. He had to see...something.

The amulet hanging from his neck burned against his chest. He pulled it out from beneath his shirt. The small ceramic square, engraved with strange designs, glowed a soft amber color.

The trees and mists drew back, revealing a muddy plain...and a large ship. He immediately recognized the design from his father's books, field notes, and videos. With those delicate spines and fins, decorative scales, and sleek, elongated shape, it was unquestionably Ancient.

He should have been surprised by how well it was preserved,

despite crashing into a swamp. Or by the fact that some of the strange markings on its hull matched those on his amulet. He wasn't though. All he cared about was getting closer: not to the ship, but to the people.

Figures moved near the crashed ship, and two open-topped, small transport skimmers headed toward them. He recognized the design. His father had owned two like them. The skimmers stopped near Siv, and as he walked toward them, his pulse quickened. This was what he'd come here for. The faces of the drivers became apparent. Siv's heart skipped.

"Dad!"

Gav drove one skimmer. And his dad's pilot, whose name Siv couldn't remember, operated the other. He couldn't tell why they had stopped. Siv called out to his father again, but Gav couldn't hear him.

Three unmarked starfighters entered the atmosphere and dived toward the Ancient ship, unleashing a volley of plasma missiles. The ship exploded into a massive fireball. As Gav cried out, the starfighters pelted the burning mass with railgun fire. At the last moment, they pulled up and burned toward the upper atmosphere.

The pilot in the skimmer shot at Gav, who blocked the shots with his shield and returned fire. He stunned the pilot and raced away. A few moments later, the pilot recovered and chased after him.

Siv tried to follow them, but couldn't. He stayed rooted in place. Suddenly, the scene reset itself. Gav and the pilot reappeared, and the starfighters once again blasted the Ancient vessel.

Sensing a presence, Siv spun around.

His father's ghost, the one he'd seen when he almost drowned, stood before him.

"This is where it began."

"Where what began?"

"Your destiny."

Siv reached out, but his hand passed through Gav. "*My* destiny?"

Gav nodded. "Protect the hyperphasic messiah and the priestess.

Take them far from Ekaran IV. Help the messiah become what we need. She can restore the Benevolence. She can save you all."

Siv suddenly woke.

Startled by something tapping on his window, he rolled over, slipped his disruptor out from beneath his pillow, and aimed it at...

His spider-grapple. The device had made it back home and was resting on the outside window ledge, right beside Spy-Fly 01.

Siv set the gun aside and rubbed his eyes. The images from the dream were burned into his brain. It had seemed so real that it was hard to think of it as just a dream. It felt more like a memory, channeled to his sleeping mind by the amulet. But that was nonsense. Doubly so since he'd seen both his father and his father's ghost in it. He pulled out the ceramic square and found it cool to the touch. And not glowing.

"Silkster, have you ever heard of a hyperphasic messiah?"

"Like the Empress Qaisella Qan? She claims to be a messiah."

"Aside from her."

"There are many prophecies and rumors floating around the galactic net about a messiah who will restore the Benevolency. It's a major belief amongst several cults. But there's no consensus on what one of them is or how they're supposed to fix things. Nor is there verification that the empress uses it as anything more than a fancy marketing term to awe her followers. People look for hope, sir. And sometimes, when they're desperate enough, they make things up to have it and persuade others to follow along."

"Could you make a file with that info so I can review it later?"

"Of course, sir. Where did you hear the term?"

"In a dream. From my dad. It was the second time in the last twelve hours that his ghost has appeared and told me that I must protect this messiah. That I have to take her away."

"Dreams...dreams are strange, sir. And you've been through a lot over the last day. You did nearly die, after all. Probably you're thinking of the Dark Messiah, maybe associating her with death."

"I guess, maybe."

"I wouldn't worry too much about it."

Siv opened the window to let the drone and the spider-grapple enter. Both automatically went to their charging stations.

"If the reaper captain had detected either of these devices, he could have tracked me here."

"That's a disturbing thought, sir."

"How long was I asleep?"

"Twelve hours, sir. You should go eat. Sadara's probably already irritated."

Siv stretched. *"Think I'll shower first."*

As he stood, his eyes fell on the Kompel injection lying on his bedside table. Instinctively, his hand moved toward the syringe. But before his fingers touched it, he drew back and took a deep breath. He shivered, but his willpower held. He could resist a few days longer.

21

SIV GENDIN

For two days, Siv did little more than sleep. He barely ate anything. He tried reading and playing video games, but neither held his interest. He started a classic holo-movie from the twenty-fifth century but drifted off during one of the best action scenes.

Frequently, his eyes strayed to the Kompel injection, but he hadn't developed the shakes yet. He wouldn't crack...he wouldn't take it any sooner than he had to...he could hold out a little longer...he could.

"Sir, you seem more tired than reasonable. My sensor scans are showing you at ninety-eight percent health with minimal bone damage remaining."

Siv downed his protein shake and tossed the cup aside. He was lying under a blanket in his recliner near the window. *"Yeah? Well, I don't feel any more than sixty percent."*

"I think maybe you're rattled, sir."

"You think? I barely escaped death, the Tekk Reapers have marked me, and I've seen my father's ghost twice now."

"I have to admit, sir, that you seeing a ghost is highly strange...and worrying."

"*Stranger than the Tekk Reapers revering my dad...out of the trillions upon trillions of people in the galaxy?*"

"*He was an accomplished man, sir. And no one knew more about the Ancients than he did. Gav Gendin...had an intuitive understanding of them.*"

"*If only he hadn't wiped his experiences from your storage... Then I could know whether what I saw in the dream was somehow a memory or a conjuring of my imagination.*"

"*Indeed, sir.*"

"*Did you scan for references about the amulet again?*"

"*Nothing turned up, sir. And I've never heard of a non-mechanical device that could store and project memories into someone's mind.*"

Siv sighed. "*I wish I knew why it was so important to Dad, and why he wanted me to hold onto it.*"

He stroked a thumb across the ceramic amulet as he watched the sun dip below the skyline. He had chosen this apartment because it provided a prime view for watching sunsets. Some instinct...some emotion he couldn't describe always pulled his mind westward. It was profound, almost mystical...

He sat upright. "*Silkster, I think...I think I've been looking at this all wrong.*"

"*Looking at what, sir?*"

"*Seeing my father's ghost and the Ancient vessel in the swamp getting blown up...that's not natural. It's mystical.*"

"*I suppose so, sir. I'm a chippy, though. Human spirituality is beyond my ken. Outside of a scientific approach, of course.*"

"*What I've seen, real or not...I'm only going to find the answers by looking within.*"

Siv tossed his blanket aside and pried himself out of the recliner. He crossed his sparse apartment, got a drink of water, and stripped down to the waist. "*Silkster, play some music...something...mystical.*"

"*Does wakyran shamanic drumming sound appropriate, sir?*"

"*I guess so.*"

Siv unlocked his safe and dug around until he found an inhaler of Aware buried in the back, behind a few childhood souvenirs and several stacks of hard credits.

Aware was a non-addictive, psychedelic drug designed to heighten the senses, expand the mind, and induce a state of oneness. The effect was safe and only lasted for an hour at the most.

Three years earlier, Siv had used it along with Awake. Mixing the two supposedly left the user conscious of their environment with only their senses heightened. He had thought it might help during a particularly difficult mission. Instead, the Awake had interacted badly with the Kompel in his system and given him a debilitating migraine. He'd had to scrub the entire mission.

Facing west, Siv sat cross-legged in the middle of his living room. He pulled the amulet off his neck and held it up, dangling it in front of his face. Then he readied the inhaler of Aware, keying it for a single dose. Trembling slightly, he lifted the inhaler.

"Here goes."

"I'll monitor your health, sir, and call for help if necessary."

"Thanks."

"Otherwise, I'll stay quiet and refrain from—"

A black box appeared unbidden in Siv's HUD. Shifting red symbols scrolled through it.

"Incoming signal on priority channel Alpha Level One, sir."

Siv gasped. That was the Shadowslip Guild's emergency signal! And he had only ever seen it used before during training exercises.

"Silkster, upload my key and unlock the signal."

"Deciphered, sir. Opening the channel now...and...it's routing through to your c|slate."

Siv's c|slate had a special nano-chip that allowed secure communications between the guild and its agents. However, information and orders were typically conveyed strictly between chippies. This was actually less secure, given that a spy drone could potentially observe the screen. To use the slate for a priority message like this was an odd choice.

Siv drew the c|slate from his pocket, pinched each corner of the ultra-slim device, and stretched it from card-sized to book-sized. The slate woke, and a fullscreen window popped up, revealing Big Boss D's face in far more detail than Siv would've preferred. The room beyond him appeared pitch black.

Boss D eyed him. "Are you in a secure location?"

"I'm at home, sir. Laying low like you told me to."

"Forget that," Boss D said. "A once-in-a-lifetime opportunity for the guild has presented itself. I think this...situation...requires a procurement specialist, and you're the best we've got on Ekaran IV. Hell, Gendin, talent-wise you're the best I've ever seen."

Siv ignored the compliment. If Boss D was buttering him up then whatever he was about to order Siv to do was going to be deadly at best. "What's the mission, sir?"

Boss D furrowed his brow, staring at Siv. "You will infiltrate the estate of Senator Orel Pashta and travel to the south wing of the main house. Once there, you will receive further instructions."

"And...?"

"That's all I can tell you at the moment."

"Senator Pashta's estate is a fortified compound," Siv said, scratching his cheek. "He probably has dozens of security guards, combat cogs, and state of the art detection systems. Getting in there will be nearly impossible."

"I'm well aware of that," Boss D replied heavily. "Nevertheless, I need you to break in, and I need you to do it tonight. The sooner, the better."

"Tonight?!" Siv couldn't help shouting. "Sir, that's insanity!"

"I know," Boss D said, seemingly unoffended by Siv's outburst. "But we can't wait. It's tonight or never."

"A mission like this takes months of planning."

Boss D frowned. "Yes, but other interests possess the same sudden knowledge we do, and they will be making their own attempts to procure the...item. I do not expect them to waste time either."

"If other groups are involved that significantly increases the danger."

Boss D nodded. "And I suspect some of them will attempt brute force."

"Let's assume I don't get killed trying to break in..." Siv took a deep breath as his mind raced through the possibilities "...if I get caught—"

Boss D raised a hand. "Given what's at stake, the senator's security forces will almost certainly shoot to kill on sight. And there is zero chance they will involve the police."

Siv laughed derisively. "Sir...this is a suicide mission."

"Not for you, I think."

"Then you think too much of me, sir." Siv ran his hands through his hair. "I'd need a team to pull something like this off quickly."

"I cannot risk a team when you're not used to working with anyone. Besides, given the situation and the almost certain attempts by other interests, I think a single agent will stand the best chance."

"You know what you have to do, sir," Silky chimed in.

"I know."

"Boss D, as a full member of the Shadowslip Guild, I have the right to refuse any mission that is suicidal in nature. And I think the Tribunal would agree with me if you brought charges."

"I'm certain they would," Boss D replied. "That's why I'm willing to pay enough to make it worth the risk."

"There's no amount of money you could offer that would make me take this mission."

"That's why I'm offering you something far more valuable...your freedom."

Stunned, Siv rocked back on his heels and nearly dropped his c|slate. "You...you would give me my freedom?"

"I have the Kompel antidote sitting on my desk as we speak. You do this, and you'll never have to take Kompel again. No more injections. No more guild missions. And even though you'd be welcome to work with us as an independent contractor, I'll pay you enough that you'd never have to work again. Score this mission, and you're set for the rest of your life."

"The fat man's big-time desperate, sir. I don't like it. Not one bit. What on Ekaran IV could be worth that much?"

"You want me to infiltrate the south wing of the senator's fortified compound, and at that point, you will tell me what you want me to procure?"

Boss D nodded. "The information has already been uploaded to your c|slate. But it's geo-locked with gigabit encryption so it won't decode until you arrive at the location."

"Sir, don't do it."

"You know it's a lot easier if I know what I'm looking for before I arrive."

"Obviously, but the information is that sensitive."

"Information too sensitive for him to tell you ahead of time? Sir, while I've never smelled anything before in my life, I am certain this reeks like a bad donkey doo in summer."

Siv chewed at his lip. *"Still..."*

"Sir, your freedom will be useless if you're too dead to enjoy it."

Freedom from the guild. He had dreamed about it for so long, but he'd never thought he'd actually earn it.

"Sir, you really should think about this before—"

"I'll do it," Siv said.

"Sir..."

"Excellent!" Boss D replied. "I'm sending you all the information we have on the compound. I'm afraid it's not much, though. Do what you have to, but don't take too long. The sooner you strike, the better."

"Copy that, sir."

"And Gendin..." Boss D leaned forward with a surprisingly earnest look on his face "...in case things go poorly...well, it was nice working with you, son."

The transmission ended.

"Silkster, let's get to work."

"Sir, this is nuts! You can't tell me this isn't as fishy as hell."

"Oh, I'm certain it is. That's why I want you to see if you can decrypt the information. I want to know what my target is going in."

"Unless they made a mistake, there's no way I can crack that level of encryption in less than a day, sir."

"Do your best."

"Sir, Boss D trusts you. So there are only two reasons why he'd hide the information from you. Either someone else fed him the encrypted data, and he doesn't actually know what it is, or whatever he wants is something terrible and something you really shouldn't get for him. Only he knows if you're there and you're already committed to winning your freedom that—"

"Honestly, Silkster, I don't care." Siv's eyes flicked across a document scrolling through a window in his HUD, checking to make sure everything Boss D promised was written in his contract. It was. Siv smiled broadly. "After nine years, I can finally be free from the guild!"

22

SIV GENDIN

The sun had set, but Ekaran IV's two full moons bathed Bei in light, adding to the perpetual glow of streetlights, video screens, and neon signs. Standing precariously on the seat of his skimmer bike, Siv looked down on the city from high above...then took a deep breath to steady his nerves.

It had taken him over an hour to rig the bike so that it could fly this high—for a short while—then another hour to override the half-dozen safety protocols designed to prevent him from doing so.

Siv drew out his father's amulet. Then, since it always brought a sense of...not comfort exactly...belonging perhaps, he peered west, toward the mountains, and beyond to the wastes.

If he succeeded in this mission, he could explore new worlds like his dad. Maybe even uncover more of the Ancients' secrets. But first, he would buy a skimmer van, fill it with supplies, and explore the wastes just like his dad had done when he first started studying archeology.

A determined smile creased Siv's face. He could be whoever he wanted...do whatever he wanted.

"Alright, Silkster, let's do this."

Silky pulled up a window in Siv's HUD that displayed all the data about falling from this height and smacking into the ground.

"After the last few days, I think I know plenty about falling by now, Silkster."

"Clearly not enough, sir. I would think you wouldn't want to repeat the experience."

Siv laughed. *"I'm prepared this time."*

"From this height...the speed...the targeting...the assumptions about their detection systems... Sir, I don't think it's wise."

"You ran the calculations."

"I did. But if they're off by even a fraction, sir... Or if there's a malfunction, or if one of the antigrav belts fails to compensate properly, or—"

"I'm more likely to be shot up with plasma bursts as I land than to go splat."

"Comforting, sir."

Siv rolled his neck and shook out his arms. *"Yes, I think so too."*

"Sir, you really don't have to do this."

"There's no other way."

"You could still refuse the mission."

"Not happening."

Silky groaned. *"Centuries of pre-programmed bliss, and this is my reward."*

Siv kissed the amulet and tucked it back inside his mesh armor.

Then he leaped from the bike and plummeted down toward the city.

"Sorry, Silkster."

"Well, it was a pleasure working with you, sir."

23

KYRALLA VIM

Kyralla Vim's long black hair streamed behind her as she leaped off the stack of crates, somersaulted through the air, and landed behind the training cog. Her bright green eyes flashed. It was obvious, even without seeing the big smile on her face, that she loved fighting. To her combat felt as natural as breathing and she'd spent most of her nineteen years honing that inborn talent.

Knees bent and shoulders tucked into a half-crouch, she readied her force staff. Static discharged off the metal-shod ends.

Her opponent spun around. Kyralla was tall, taller than most men, but her broad-shouldered opponent towered over her. She couldn't see his face. A black assassin's uniform covered all but his eyes. But she liked to imagine his face as that of a dog who'd been slammed into a wall as a puppy, all squished and lopsided.

Kyralla wore a uniform not unlike his, except where his was solid black hers was the color of ash along her extremities and darkened to black in the center. The nanofiber weave was great for stopping blades and shrapnel but stunk at protecting her against plasma shots and explosive rounds. But she liked it that way. Light armor allowed her to be quick and agile, so she didn't get shot in the first place.

Before the large assassin could finish turning, she slammed one end of her staff into his jaw. As he fell, she reversed her momentum, pivoted the staff on its center, and used the other end to clock him on the back of the head. He dropped to his knees, dazed.

She sighed with dissatisfaction. That had been too easy. She scanned the vast, murky warehouse looking for danger and frowned. Unmarked crates lined the walls, but other than a few stacks scattered about, it was empty. She was bored and *needed* more of a challenge than this.

A premonition tickled down the back of her neck. She readied her staff. At the last moment, she sensed a threat from above. She dove aside, and a single-shot flechette burst scarred the ground with tiny razor-edged discs.

Slow-falling under the power of antigrav belts, three more assassins, armed with force swords and neural disrupters, descended from the dark girders above. They opened fire, and four bursts of concentric white circles radiated toward her.

Kyralla had an unusual gift: microsecond precognition. She could see the future just before it happened, as long as she was focused and living in the present. Knowing where each shot would be, a moment before it got there, she wove her way through the blasts and charged the nearest assassin.

She reached him as his feet touched the ground before he could fire again. He raised his sword to defend himself. She darted inside his guard and slammed the butt of her force staff underneath his chin, unleashing a full electro-concussive blast as she did so.

The assassin's body went rigid as a halo of electricity blossomed around his head. Even with his antigrav still somewhat active, the concussive blast knocked him a half-dozen meters away.

Now she just had the other two to deal with. Sensing she was about to be shot, she ducked, and the neural disruptor blast whooped by overhead. Darting one way then another, she closed on the next assassin. Predicting his every move, she easily parried his sword attacks then knocked him out with a concussive blast to the temple.

"Force staff power at fifty-three percent, madam."

The other assassin closed on her, firing. She saw the next shot coming, but even when you can see it ahead of time, having less than a second doesn't always leave you with enough time or options. She dodged as best as she could, and the neural blast glanced off her shoulder. Her armor weakened the hit, but it still numbed her right arm and hand and left her feeling a little dazed.

The assassin stabbed, sliced, and thrust with his force sword. Kyralla shifted, blocked, and backpedaled to avoid the attacks. Then, as the feeling returned to her left side, she went on the offensive. She feinted high with her force staff. The assassin blocked the attack, and Kyralla kicked, sweeping his legs out from under him. She followed with a roundhouse kick to the back of his neck, slamming the assassin to the ground. A heel-stomp to the nose and a staff thrust to the head finished him off.

A bead of sweat trickled down her face. Now that was more like it! Still, a little more challenge wouldn't be... She smiled. There were more of them. She could sense their presence. She could *feel* them focusing on her—*intently*.

Kyralla dove and a stream of plasma bursts blazed overhead. Then a laser beam burned down at her. She rolled to the side, and it scored the floor as it flashed past her. She leaped to her feet, zigging and zagging as more plasma shots streaked her way.

She sprinted toward her attackers: an assassin crouched behind a crate, his plasma rifle trained on her, and a hovering security cog, a Buzzy-7 with a three-shot laser beam cannon, a short-range neural disruptor, and... She racked her brains to remember what else it was armed with.

Another laser beam burned toward her, followed by another burst of plasma shots. Dodging, she raced across the warehouse. A crate blocked the path to her attackers. She chose to leap over it rather than go around.

"Antigrav at two-percent," she commanded.

With the slight boost, she hurdled over the crate.

A plasma burst scorched across her right arm, melting through the armor and singeing her skin. It hurt, but it wasn't anything she couldn't handle.

As she landed, she remembered the Buzzy-7's other weapon. And she saw it launch a split moment before it actually did.

"On my mark, antigrav one-hundred percent."

A guided missile fired off the back of the Buzzy-7. Powerful enough to take out an android soldier in a battlesuit or pop open a tank, the missile was more than powerful enough to reduce her to a fine mist.

The plasma bursts let up as the missile zoomed toward her... closer...closer.

"Now!"

Kyralla propelled herself upward and forward. With help from the antigrav, she soared right past the missile and toward her opponents.

"Drop antigrav."

The plasma shots resumed as soon as she passed the missile. One grazed her hip. Another blistered her left cheek. She landed behind the assassin. He spun around. She kicked the gun out of his hand and grabbed him by the front of his uniform.

Taking a slow, wide arc, the missile spun around.

"Antigrav at one-hundred-fifty percent."

With energy streaming out of her antigrav belt's power pack at an alarming rate, she jumped, taking the assassin high into the air with her.

The missile zoomed toward them.

Kyralla planted her feet on the assassin's chest. Then she released his uniform and kicked outward.

While she flew backward, still under the antigrav's effect, the assassin sailed directly in the missile's path. Lacking the agility to go around the man, it hit him dead center and exploded.

The blast reached Kyralla and knocked her back against the far wall. The breath whooshed out of her lungs, but she was okay.

Bruised and blistered, nothing more. The third, and final, laser beam streaked toward her.

"*Cut antigrav.*"

She dropped, and the beam sliced overhead.

"*Safe fall.*"

She landed and dodged the spray of neural disruptor blasts as the cog closed. It seemed to realize its danger and backed away. But it wasn't fast enough to escape her. A few well-placed staff-strikes knocked it out of the air and left it smoking on the concrete floor.

Bent over, gasping for breath, drenched with sweat, bruised, burned in several places...Kyralla smiled. She wasn't happy often. But she was now. With a challenging set of enemies defeated she was ready to—

Something was wrong.

Three distinctive rifle pops echoed through the warehouse, followed by a faint whistling sound that buzzed toward her. Guided rounds!

Kyralla turned toward them. She spotted the first a split-second before it reached her. She spun sideways. It tore across the threads of her uniform, barely missing her flesh, and detonated in the wall instead.

The second shot adjusted its course. At the last moment, Kyralla stepped out of its line of fire. The round couldn't adapt fast enough, and it too blew up in the wall.

The third shot gave Kyralla less time to react. It arrowed towards the exact center of her mass, and she'd already retreated the same direction twice. But she'd taken more injuries on the other side, and there was only a fraction of a second left to make her move.

Indecision could get a limited precog killed as easily as anyone else. She tried to spin away. Too little, too late.

The armor-piercing round struck her in the chest and detonated.

Damn.

Kyralla fell, blood spurting from a gaping hole in her chest. Pain radiated throughout her body. An excessive amount. Far more than someone in this situation would actually feel since the shock would've killed them.

"Rosie," she said to her chippy, *"discontinue the program."*

The warehouse, the assassins, and her injuries faded away, leaving her in the darkness of her simulation capsule. The doors dilated open, and she cringed under the bright lights in the training hall.

Frustrated, she ripped the capsule's electrodes from her temples, wrists, waist, and legs. Then she tore the neural circlet from her head and hopped out.

Her trainer stepped forward and tossed her a towel.

"That was excellent," Mika said.

"Excellent? I got killed!"

"You said you wanted a harder mission than the last several I gave you."

"Harder, not impossible."

"It was doable. You could've sensed the sniper before he fired."

She squeezed sweat from her hair and dried off her face. "Yeah, right. I'm probably the only lightly armored, non-android who could've even gotten as far as I did."

"Don't get too cocky," Mika said. "And training isn't about being the best. It's about bettering yourself."

She tossed the towel back to him and took the water he offered. "I know...you're right. I'm just frustrated."

As she downed her water, a notification popped up in her HUD.

"Madam, incoming message from Senator Pashta."

Kyralla groaned. *"Patch him through."*

A static image of Senator Pashta's face appeared in the messaging window as his voice came through. "Kyralla, could you please join me for a nightcap? There are several important matters I would like to discuss."

She gritted her teeth. "Of course, Uncle. I'll join you..." she liked to keep the man waiting whenever she could, for as long as she could "...in about an hour. I need to shower first."

Showering would only take her a few minutes.

His face twitched with displeasure. "Of course, my dear."

The screen disappeared, and Kyralla shivered as if a spider had crawled across her skin. Skeevy old coot. *He'd probably prefer I joined him while I was sweaty in my tight workout clothes. Too bad.*

"Rosie, where's my sister?"

"Oona is in the meditation grotto, madam."

"Send word for her to stay there. I'm getting a shower."

As she walked down the hallway toward her quarters, she shivered again, though it wasn't cold.

A vague sense of danger pulsed through her mind. She glanced around, listened carefully, and checked the sensors in her HUD. There was no apparent danger.

And yet...something bugged her.

Something was amiss.

Kyralla shook her head and reassured herself. *Stop worrying. The estate is fortified and well-guarded. And no one knows we're here. The simulation left you rattled, that's all.*

24

SIV GENDIN

"Power pack zeroed, sir. Switching to the main system."

Siv unbuckled the cheap backup antigrav belt and tossed it away. He had already burned through two others. Now he was using only his primary belt.

Initially, he'd worried about accidentally setting off movement sensors by dropping the extra belts. But he was carrying every piece of gear he could imagine needing, from his plasma carbine to his drones. So he'd decided it was more important to dump every scrap of extra weight he could spare. If there were sensors that sensitive he'd set them off when landing anyway.

The free fall continued.

"How am I doing, Silkster?"

"I don't think you'll splat, sir. But you are drifting off target again."

Siv spread his arms out and tilted so that he'd fall eastward.

In the autumn, strong winds frequently kicked in after sunset, especially at higher altitudes. Even Silky had failed to take this into account, probably because Siv had him running hundreds of falling and infiltration and detection simulations based on the scant data they'd been provided on the senator's compound, not to mention trying to crack the encrypted data on the target. The effect of the wind was a detail that would've been ironed out given adequate planning time, which they hadn't been given.

A gust blew him further westward.

"The body-lean technique isn't working, sir."

"What if I were to set the antigrav so I would fall faster, making the wind impact me less? I'd just have to punch it back up soon enough to prevent splattage."

"Calculating... Not an option, sir. Well, I could compensate some, but it's only going to help so much. Uh-oh. Incoming, sir."

Siv glanced around and spotted a ten-meter long, high-flying transport skimmer. And it was heading eastward, at a leisurely, fuel-conserving speed.

"I've got an idea."

"Sir, that's not an idea. It's a brain fart. And I have it on good authority that humans are supposed to ignore those."

"We rarely do."

"Then for the sake of your species, sir, start now."

"I'm going to miss my opportunity if we don't hurry and—"

"Sir, I've already made the adjustments. I know you're a special kind of dumb." Silky sighed. *"And besides, I'm not sure there's a better option if you want to hit your primary target zone."*

The antigrav decreased, and Siv sped toward the incoming transport skimmer.

"It's automated, sir. No pilot."

Perfect. Just before Siv smacked into the roof, Silky switched the antigrav to full compensation. Siv landed hard onto the metal top, but not hard enough to result in anything more than a few bruises. Lying in the center of the transport's length, he scrambled to grab onto something, but the top was smooth. Just before he reached the end, he thought to activate the magnets in his boots.

The magnets activated, and Siv stood up on the transport as if he were on a surfboard. He smiled, remembering how a lot of people had traveled on skimmer-boards when he was a kid. Sadly, nearly all of them had been scrapped. After the Tekk Plague, the antigrav and propulsion systems in them were considered too valuable for what was seen as a toy or a luxury item.

After a few moments, Silky said, *"Release now, sir."*

Siv deactivated his boots and dropped off the transport. Again he fell toward the compound. He was way off center, but if he continued to drift with the winds as before, he would land on target.

The transport continued on its way as if nothing had happened. He doubted there was any system for detecting suspicious roof impacts and reporting them to authorities.

"See? Everything turned out all right."

"You know with all these stunts you pull, sir, you'd be dead if you didn't have me. Seriously, even an 8G model would've gotten you killed by now."

"I know, and I appreciate everything you do, Silkster old buddy."

"In fact, sir, I'm not sure even I could have saved you when I was new, fresh out of the factory. But I am what I am because I served with the best."

"So you tell me, but I never get any details."

"Still classified, sir."

Siv almost argued that the order to make it classified, centuries ago, came from a power that no longer existed. But that was a pointless argument they'd had many times before.

Siv scanned every direction visually and using the radar in his HUD. No other vehicles were nearby. So far he'd been lucky enough to only encounter a few transports and nothing with living pilots. And fortunately, it was illegal to fly over the senator's compound at the lower altitudes passenger skimmers used.

"Okay, time to hide, sir. Readying countermeasures, activating the refraction field...starting at ten percent."

Siv's RC-4 refraction cloak was a hand-sized box housed in the armor on his back, just below his sensor pack. The RC-4 emitted a localized energy field that refracted light to blend him in with the surrounding environment as if he were a chameleon. They would steadily increase the strength of the field as he neared the compound. At full power, it would render him effectively invisible.

The RC-4 was incredibly powerful, but he hated using it. Early in his procurement career, he had depended on it. But then in a nasty fall off the back of a moving skimmer, the unit had gotten damaged. Now the refraction unit only lasted about half as long as it used to on a full charge, and thanks to overheating it had a nasty habit of deactivating unpredictably.

He'd tried to fix it, but that wasn't his area of expertise and replacement parts were almost impossible to find since it was military issue like so much of his dad's old equipment.

"I should see if Bishop can repair the RC-4."

"Sure, but why don't we focus on surviving first, sir. Time to landing...twenty seconds...nineteen...on target...seventeen...antigrav at maximum compensation..."

Siv took a deep breath. Death or freedom. That's what awaited him here. Of course, death was a sort of freedom, just not the kind he fancied.

"Fourteen...thirteen...twelve...antigrav power remaining at point two percent... Brace yourself, sir."

His plan of attack *appeared* brilliant. But most of his first draft plans seemed that way until a few nights of study and contemplation exposed all their flaws. And this one relied on guesswork and decades-old blueprints.

"Ten...nine..."

A distortion energy screen cloaked his landing area: a small, private garden in the southeast wing of the senator's compound. Or at least that's what the blueprints showed. A level five sensor scan from above had registered water, rocks, and vegetation. But verification had proven impossible.

"Seven...six...maximum cloaking..."

What am I getting myself into? He so desperately wished that Silky had been able to crack the encryption on the data Big Boss D had sent him. Flying blind made this twice as dangerous. And it was already an odds-on sticky death for him.

"*Four...three...*"

As he passed through the distortion screen, a wave of harmless energy washed over him, leaving goosebumps on his skin.

"*Two...one...*"

25

SIV GENDIN

The distortion screen capped a small courtyard tucked discreetly into the middle of the southeast wing of Senator Pashta's compound. Flickering lanterns hung from maple and pear trees. Smaller ones lined the courtyard's winding pathways. An illuminated fountain splashed into a koi pond. Statues of gizmet-sized nymphs frolicked through ornamental shrubs and flowers, and several benches and two recliners formed a seating arrangement on the patio.

Siv landed softly on a patch of grass beside the pond. His refraction cloak system was maxed out, but the heat level was holding steady...for the moment.

He glanced around, spotting no one. Then he used his smart lenses to do an infrared scan, but that didn't reveal anything unusual either.

"Silkster?"

"Level five scan of the courtyard shows...no people, no cogs, and no cameras or other monitoring devices. I guess it never occurred to them that a thief might be crazy enough to skydive into their garden."

It was entirely possible a sensitive radar detection system had defeated his countermeasures and pegged him on the way down, alerting security. A considerable amount of firepower might now be heading his way.

"*Any response inside?*"

"*Scans aren't picking up any alarms or nearby interior movement, sir, but it's hard to be certain. The compound's walls are surprisingly well shielded.*"

Siv rushed up to the single door leading from the garden into the building. The door had only a simple touchpad for entry.

"*You know, I could make a killing as a security consultant, telling people what they should never do.*"

"*That you could, sir. Still not detecting anyone on the other side.*"

"*Okay then, here goes...*"

Siv swiped the panel, and the door slid open. He quickly stepped inside, and the door closed behind him.

He found himself in a giant, lavish bedroom, decorated with natural woods and silks, plush rugs and tapestries, expensive furniture and delicate knickknacks.

According to the blueprints, the door directly across the room led out into a hallway that could take him all the way to the south wing of the compound where his encrypted instructions would tell him what he'd come here to steal.

A canopy bed dominated the room. It was easily five times bigger than the cot he slept on. The bed covers weren't ruffled, but a pair of panties and a military-style dress uniform lay at the foot of the bed. And a faint trail of steam curled out through the open door to the bathroom.

Siv hurried forward. "*So much for the scans from outside.*"

"*Sir, sprint now!*"

He ran but was then forced to slide to a stop as someone stepped out of the bathroom right in front of him. Siv's eyes widened. Standing less than a meter away was the most striking young woman he'd ever seen. Momentum and surprise threw off his balance, and he stumbled, almost falling into her.

She was naked, her still-damp alabaster skin glistening. Long black hair flowed down her back. Her frame was slender but muscled, her hips wide, her breasts small but pert. She wore only a medallion that hung from her neck on a silver chain.

Siv could barely breathe as she eased past him, her hips swaying.

"*Sir, you need to get moving.*"

"What? Oh, right."

He crept forward as quietly as he could, but his eyes remained trained on her. She grabbed the pair of panties from the bed, then dropped them by accident. As she bent over to pick them up, Siv paused, stunned...unable to look away...the danger of his situation forgotten.

A heart rate alarm notice popped up in his HUD, noting the sudden spike.

"*Sir... Ahem, sir, I took* enhanced *video of the last several seconds for you.*"

The goddess stood up, but Siv still couldn't take his eyes off her.

"*That way you can revisit the moment later if you survive. Now let's get moving!*"

"Yeah...okay."

Just as Siv looked away, the door from the hallway opened. A girl, maybe fourteen years old stepped inside. The Ancient amulet on his chest warmed against his skin in response. He froze in place, not even daring to breathe.

Her head was entirely bald, which made her arched eyebrows even more pronounced. The rest of her features, while beautiful, were angular and exotic. Despite the fact that she was human, she had a distinctive alien quality.

And her eyes...her eyes were *not* human. Siv had never seen anyone with eyes like that before. Her eyes were the dark of space with a speck of starlight shining in them, and they seemed to hold wisdom not just beyond her years but beyond the years of any human.

The goddess turned toward the girl and with casual familiarity said, "Oona, you were supposed to stay in the meditation room."

Oona started forward, her shimmery green robe dancing around her. She spoke, and her voice was ethereal...musical...almost mesmerizing. "I got bored and wanted to see if you—"

She stopped, and those dark, alien eyes locked onto the spot where Siv was standing.

"*Sir, the encrypted mission data is unlocking. Streaming it to your main HUD window...*"

"*But—but I'm not in the south wing yet.*"

"*I understand, sir. However... Damn. I didn't expect that.*"

The data had unlocked because Siv stood within sight of the target: the strange young girl, Oona.

Oona gazed directly into Siv's eyes and frowned. The amulet's temperature increased. If it got any hotter, it would burn his skin.

"Kyra, an invisible man is standing right behind you," Oona said matter of factly.

Kyralla stiffened. Suddenly she was in motion, spinning around. Her leg went up, and Siv, stupidly, didn't budge. Instead, he gawked, even as her foot sped toward him.

The medallion she wore. Siv should have recognized immediately. His was ceramic and hers metal, but otherwise their amulets were identical.

Her heel contacted his temple.

Siv went down without a sound.

26

KYRALLA VIM

Kyralla landed in a crouch, prepared to defend herself. But the intruder wasn't going to put up a fight. She had knocked him out. She could tell because his chameleon field was flickering wildly. Something on his back hissed, popped, and belched a tiny trail of smoke. The field failed, leaving him exposed and vulnerable, no more a threat than the rug he was now drooling on.

A smile lit up Kyralla's face. Without using her precog and without being able to see him, she had landed a perfect kick. Raw instincts, training, and an assumption that he was a human male of average height had served her well.

But then her face collapsed into a deep frown. A man had broken into the senator's compound. And he was in *their* room. Sure, he could be a thief, or perhaps an assassin coming after Senator Pashta. But a sinking sensation in her gut told her that he was not here for jewels or the senator. He was here for her sister.

She had dreaded this day for as long as she could remember. The secret was out now. Her mission as her sister's primary guardian would begin in earnest. She took a deep breath. At least the moment hadn't come up when they were younger and less prepared.

"Rosie, alert the—"

"Sister, do not sound the alarm," Oona said, easing forward, her eyes on the man.

"He's an intruder! A threat!"

"He's the man I dreamed about."

"Are you certain?"

Oona nodded confidently. "He will save us."

Kyralla examined the unconscious man. He appeared to be roughly her age. He wore combat mesh body armor and was equipped with a plasma carbine, an armband force-shield, a neural disruptor, a sensor array, and still more devices she didn't immediately recognize. And no doubt he had all manner of items tucked into the pouches on his uniform.

His brown hair was awkwardly slicked back. It wasn't a good look for him, but maybe it was smart for sneaking around. Overall, his features were attractive enough, but he wasn't someone that would turn heads on the street. Kyralla chewed at her lip. But then ordinary made for a good disguise. She touched his cheek and pinched his skin. No, it wasn't a face mask.

"Rosie, search all databases for this man's identity."

"Yes, madam. Searching..."

The man stirred. Her pulse quickened. No matter what her gifted sister said, he was a threat until he proved otherwise. She took away his neural disruptor, plasma carbine, and two pairs of force-knuckles she found in a pocket. She tossed all the weapons on the bed.

As she considered him, her frown continued to spread. This was not the gear of a thief or a casual assassin. This man was armed with extraordinary high-tech military equipment. He had to be an agent of either the Terran Federation or the Empire of a Thousand Worlds. Either one would love to get their hands on Oona, but the dark messiah, Empress Qaisella Qan of the Thousand Worlds, would be especially eager.

Kyralla retrieved her own disruptor from the nightstand. His was keyed to his palm print so no one else could use it. Then she slipped on a pair of the force-knuckles she'd found in his pocket.

"Oona, step back. I need to wake him for interrogation. We need to know how he found out about you."

Instead of retreating, her sister stepped forward. She closed her eyes and held a hand out over him. As he stirred again, his eyes beginning to flutter, a faint glow shone out from beneath his chest armor and onto his neck.

Kyralla knelt beside him and loosened his body armor in the front. An amulet attached to a chain floated out and hovered in the air beneath Oona's hand. The amulet glowed a faint red. And its design... Kyralla rocked back on her heels. The amulet's design was immediately familiar. It was identical to hers, except that while Kyralla's was metal, his was ceramic...and authentic.

"It's Ancient," Kyralla gasped, "and active!"

"He's the one who will save us," Oona repeated with confidence. "Though, he is not a true guardian, not yet."

"That means we're in immediate danger, right?"

Oona nodded. "Tonight, everything will change."

The man's eyes eased halfway open...fluttered again...then sprang wide with alarm. He didn't look at her or at Oona. His eyes locked onto his amulet.

"I am Oona," her sister told him. "And I will not harm you."

"I know," the man replied in a smooth baritone. He seemed surprised by his response.

His eyes strayed to Kyralla and raked across her. Then he looked into her smoldering eyes and blushed.

"Had a good enough look yet?" she seethed.

He cut short a sheepish smile and shrug.

"Who are you?" Kyralla demanded.

"Siv Gendin," he blurted out. Again he seemed surprised by his response.

"Rosie, add the name Siv Gendin to your search."

"Yes, madam. Searching..."

"Why are you here?"

"Do you always interrogate prisoners naked?"

"Just answer the question," she snapped.

"I'm not complaining. It's quite nice."

Her cheeks flushed, and she shoved her disruptor into his face. "Answer me."

He held his hands up and nodded toward Oona. "I was sent here to extract her."

"Who sent you?"

"I'd rather not say."

Kyralla narrowed her eyes and leaned in. She activated the force-knuckles. As they shimmered and hummed, she danced the back of her left hand up his neck and onto his cheek.

"Answer me."

"You don't have it in you."

"Have what in me?" she asked.

"What it takes to torture someone."

"And you do?"

He shook his head ever so slightly. "I know torturers. I've seen it done. And I've experienced it firsthand...as part of my training. The eyes...you can always tell by the eyes whether someone has it in them."

She clenched her jaws. "I'll do whatever it takes to protect my sister."

"I'm sure you would," he said. "But I don't think you're nearly that desperate...not yet."

Kyralla narrowed her eyes at him. She wanted badly to hit him one good time with the force-knuckles, just to prove him wrong.

"You're afraid of the people you work for," Oona said.

"Yes, I am."

She dropped her hand, and his amulet drifted back down to lie atop his chest. The glow receded. "Are you going to try to kidnap me?"

He shook his head. "No."

"Oh, of course, you'd say that," Kyralla responded.

"Look, I've done a lot of illegal things in my life. But I only kill in self-defense, and I don't kidnap teenage girls."

"If you're not going to continue with your mission," Oona said, "then you might as well tell us who you're working for." She squatted down and placed her palms together as if praying. "Please."

He sighed. "I work...I work for the Shadowslip Guild."

Kyralla groaned and rubbed her temples with her palms. The Shadowslip Guild was bad news indeed. "Who else knows?"

"No idea. I didn't even know what I was sent here for. I couldn't decrypt my mission objective until your sister was in sight."

"What a load of—"

"He's telling the truth," Oona said, her night-dark eyes boring into Siv.

"I would've turned down the assignment if I'd known," he said firmly, with an edge of bitterness in his voice. "As a guild member, I have that right."

Kyralla paced around him. Something about his last statement nagged at her. She didn't think he was lying, and Oona was rarely wrong about such things. But there was something there...something that bothered him more than getting stuck with a mission he didn't approve of.

He sat up, a little dazed. "Look, you're in a lot of danger. Others are going to come for your sister—soon. And my boss thought they'd use forceful means rather than send in a procurement specialist like me."

"You mean a thief," Oona said.

"I prefer procurement specialist."

"How soon do you think they'll come?" Kyralla asked.

"Possibly tonight. The information is hot. Whoever—whatever— you two are, the cat must have slipped out of the bag in the last day or so."

Kyralla looked down at him. He was eying her lustfully again. He seemed embarrassed by it but unable to help himself. With her adrenaline decreasing, she was becoming all too aware of her naked-ness. She threw the disruptor on the bed and pulled on her panties.

"Stay there," she told him.

He nodded his agreement. Ignoring the dress uniform, Kyralla headed toward the closet.

"Madam, it was not easy, but I have managed to retrieve data on one Siv Gendin of Ekaran IV."

"Go on."

"Siv Gendin. Died age eleven. Seven days before the fall of the Benevolency."

She opened her closet. *"So he's assumed an old identity?"*

"I do not think so, madam. Facial recognition using normal aging parameters shows him to be a match to the photos in the records."

"How is that possible?"

"I do not know, madam. Plastic surgery perhaps?"

"That's a lot of effort to assume the identity of someone who died over a century ago." Kyralla squirmed into her tight combat mesh uniform. *"Where did you get this info?"*

"A secure government database, madam. I used my hack into Senator Pashta's account, but even then I had to break through two security firewalls to get what I needed. I suspect the information was probably top secret at one point."

Kyralla strapped on her weapons belt and holstered her disrup-tor, her plasma pistol, and her force knife.

"Madam, the boy was listed as deceased, no cause given. But his father was murdered here in Bei, C-Block. His father was Gav—"

Kyralla spun toward Siv, her jaw dropping. "You're Gav Gendin's son?!"

A look of surprise crossed his face for a moment, then he nodded. "Yes...I am," he admitted with a tinge of sadness.

"Your father was the preeminent scholar on all things Ancient," Oona said. "I have closely studied everything he ever wrote."

"So have I," Siv lamented, "not that it'll ever do me any good now."

"How is it that you're alive," Kyralla said, "one hundred and seven years since you were...listed as deceased?"

"It's a long story. I'm afraid you'll find disappointing."

"Then we'll skip it for now," Kyralla said, though it was the last thing she wanted to do. She couldn't stand mysteries. Which was ironic since she loved her sister who was nothing more than a giant bundle of them.

Siv sighed. "So what now?"

The way he said it, Kyralla wasn't sure the question was directed at her.

"Why do you do it?" Oona asked.

"Do what?"

"Work for the Shadowslip. Do you enjoy stealing things from people?"

"I like the adrenaline, and I'm good at what I do, but I don't have a choice."

"Everyone has a choice."

He reached into a pocket. Kyralla trained her disruptor on him instantly. "Watch it!"

"I'm not armed. I just have something for show-and-tell."

Slowly, he drew out a syringe and held it up.

She eyed it carefully. "Is that Kompel?"

"Yes, and it's a particularly nasty strain."

"Death is still a choice," Oona said.

"Not one I'm willing to take. I have dreams, you know. There are things I want to..." His face fell, and he slumped in dejection. "Well, I *had* dreams...until tonight."

Oona grasped her temples and bent over as if in pain. "Kyra, something's wrong. I feel a disturbance in the hyperphasic ether."

"What the heck does that mean?" Siv asked.

"I'm not sure," Oona replied. "I've never experienced anything like this before."

Kyralla rushed to her closet and grabbed her force staff. She strapped it to her back then tossed her sister a spare antigrav belt and her force-shield. Dutifully, Oona buckled on the belt and the armband.

"The Shadowslip's going to kill me," Siv lamented.

"For failing a mission?" Kyralla asked.

Eyes flickering in fear, he shook his head. "For helping you escape."

"Escape what?"

Before he could explain, a thunderous explosion boomed, and the entire compound shook.

27

SIV GENDIN

As the compound's foundation shivered, Siv considered using the distraction to leap to his feet, but decided against it. Kyralla might not have it in her to torture him, but she definitely wouldn't hesitate to kick his ass.

"Sir, the explosion hit the south wing."

"I thought you said—"

A second explosion rocked the compound, and Oona rushed over and clung to her sister.

"That was the southwest wing, sir. Sorry, I misjudged the timing."

"What the hell's going on?!" Kyralla demanded.

"Orbital strikes," Siv answered.

"How can you know that?" she asked.

"I have a high-end, military-grade sensor array, and I patched into the senator's network to boost the signal."

"Someone's *bombing* us from orbit?" Oona asked incredulously.

It was clear by her tone that she had spent her life expecting kidnappers, not assassins and assault squads.

Siv shook his head. "Not bombs. Burst drops."

"What?" Kyralla asked.

"Drop pods designed to penetrate energy shields or building structures, or to kill enemy forces in a landing zone. They're pretty rare these days. But two of them have hit the building. And—"

Three smaller explosions occurred, and these were much closer. Siv relayed the information from Silky.

"Three armored vehicles just rammed into the east wing, sixty-five meters away from our position."

"We're getting surrounded fast," Kyralla said with worry.

Siv studied the readouts Silky displayed in his HUD. "I'm showing five groups of armed combatants, with a scattering of security guards and cogs."

"Where's the fifth group located?" Kyralla asked.

"The north wing."

"That's Senator Pashta's personal guard. We need to make our way there." She held her sister out and cupped her face in her hands. "If something happens to me, Oona, then you keep running. Go to Uncle Pashta. He'll protect you."

"Yes, Kyra."

"I can help you escape," Siv said.

Kyralla's eyes narrowed as she studied him. "Escape?"

"From the compound. Or reach your uncle if you like, though I'm not sure that's wise."

"You're thinking what I'm thinking, sir?" Silky asked.

"That the uncle ratted them out? Yep."

"I won't hurt you or your sister," Siv promised. "You have my word."

"The word of a thief who came here to do the same thing two other groups of infiltrators are trying to do? A man...an addict...who'll be punished if he fails his bosses?"

The explosions had increased her mistrust of him. And unlike her sister, Kyralla wasn't swayed by glowing amulets that levitated.

"I'm not an addict by choice! And I wouldn't be here if I'd known what I was sent to do."

"Oh sure. How convenient that you didn't ask them."

Siv met her eyes. "I was given only a single day to plan for this job. And I thought it was practically a suicide mission. I could have refused it, but I didn't because I was promised my freedom...from the Kompel and from the guild."

"That's not a persuasive argument, sir."

"Was that supposed to convince me?" Kyralla asked.

"Told you, sir."

"Kyra, he's here to save us," Oona repeated urgently. "He's nearly a guardian, too. You can trust him. *I* trust him."

There was that term "guardian" again. If they survived, he was going to have to ask her what that meant.

Kyralla seemed unswayed, and she was starting to fidget with indecision.

"When I was eleven," Siv said, "a special forces sniper shot my dad through a window in our apartment. Then they stormed in and finished him off—right in front of me. After that, the soldiers stunned me and placed me in suspended animation. I would never do that to someone else. I would *never* harm your sister or take her from you."

Oona placed a hand over her mouth, and her eyes welled with tears. Kyralla's face blanked, and her eyes softened somewhat. Still, she said nothing.

"Ballsack of the Benevolence!" Silky cursed. *"What's wrong with this girl? Shouldn't she be freaking out right now?"*

"I think that's exactly what she's doing."

"You're wasting time," Siv told Kyralla. "The intruders will figure out where you are soon if they don't know already. And some of them aren't far away. You're going to need help."

"I've trained for this my whole life," she replied defensively as she began to pace.

"All it takes is one mistake. And you're facing heavily armed, elite—"

The data scrolling through Siv's HUD caught his attention. His heart nearly skipped. *"That's what we're up against?!"*

"Sorry to bear so much bad news, sir, but you might want to glance

at the radar. The starship headed for us, that's a known Tekk Reaper design. They're not even attempting to hide from the planetary authorities."

"What are you detecting now?" Kyralla asked.

Siv dug his fingers into his hair, dipped his head, and stifled a scream of frustration.

"That bad?" she added.

"The troops from the burst pods are wearing Centurion III power armor. They're carrying plasma assault rifles, and there's thirty-six of them. Thirty more from the armored vehicles. But at least they're only wearing combat mesh. And...and there are Tekk Reapers on the way."

Kyralla's face blanched, and she swallowed hard.

"I've fought a few of them recently, and believe me, they're as bad as you've been lead to believe."

With her right hand, Oona touched her forehead, her chest over her heart, then her lips. It was a sign of devotion to the Benevolence. Thought, emotion, and expression united...or something like that. Siv had never embraced such reverence.

Neither had his dad. He thought he remembered his mother being a believer in the divine origin of the Benevolence. It was not a philosophy he could accept. Especially since he suspected the Benevolence had either caused or allowed his father's murder.

"I seriously doubt your uncle's guards will be able to fight their way over here to help. You need me."

Kyralla leaned down and offered him a hand. He took it, and she helped him up. "I'm trusting you because Oona does. Turn on us, and you'll regret it."

Siv moved to the bed and gathered his weapons, tucking all of them except the plasma carbine back into their holsters. He noted Kyralla studying him out of the corners of her eyes. She was going to get herself killed worrying about him while fighting.

"Sir, enemy forces identified. The armored trucks are an alliance of the World Bleeders and the Star Cutters." Both were rival organiza-

tions to the Shadowslip Guild. They had minimal presence in Bei and Ekaran IV in general, but they controlled crime on many other worlds. *"And I believe the burst drops contain Thousand World legionnaires."*

"Kyra," Oona said with alarm, "I've been trying to contact Uncle Pashta, but his communication system won't respond to my chippy's requests."

"I know," Kyralla said, "but don't worry. It might be protocol for the system to cut off like that if Uncle's life is in danger. Or perhaps our communications are being jammed."

"This is so a setup, sir."

"Now's not the time to convince them of that, Silkster. And there's a chance we're wrong."

Oona headed toward a display panel on the wall near the door leading to the hallway. "I'll try the hardwired panel and see if that—"

Siv leaped in between her and the panel. "No! The enemy could be monitoring that system to figure out where you are."

Oona's eyes widened. "Oh!" She turned to her sister. "See, we needed a second guardian. He has skills you don't have. You compliment each other."

Eyes smoldering, Kyralla ground her teeth. She gestured Siv toward the door. "Gendin, you lead the way. Oona, stay behind me. Keep your shield up. Watch your back." Her voice lowered. "And keep your thoughts on guardianship to yourself."

Oona seemed to shrink under the criticism. With her head bowed meekly, she turned on her force shield. It was a weaker model than Siv's, with a smaller circular field, but it could probably stop a plasma burst, maybe two weak ones.

Siv activated his shield, then launched a drone.

"Spy-Fly 03 deployed and active, sir."

Kyralla admired his shield for a moment then said, "We're going to go to the central corridor and turn right. That should take us in-between both sets of enemies. The corridor will lead us to the north wing. There we can rendezvous with my uncle. His security forces will protect us until we can escape off-world on his emergency star-ship and meet up with our father."

"Do you trust Senator Pashta?" Siv asked.

"He's a lech, but I've never had any reason to think he'd betray us. He's known who and what we are for years now. His employees don't. We're careful to keep our identities and capabilities from them —just in case. But they are all sworn to secrecy when it comes to his doings anyway."

"Besides, Dad trusts him," Oona added.

"Where is your dad?" Siv asked.

"Off-world, on a diplomatic mission," Oona answered. "He's an important ambassador for the Terran Federation. He specializes in bringing rouge worlds back into the federation."

Siv tried not to let his doubts show and nodded. "Okay then."

He stepped toward the door, but Kyralla put a hand on his shoulder and stopped him. "Maybe we should take the long way. We'd have to fight through the thugs from the armored trucks, but it would put us much farther away from the better-equipped legionnaires."

Siv noted her hand was trembling. Adrenaline and nervousness were to be expected, but she continued to waste valuable time by questioning her instincts and the data at hand. It was as if she had never—Siv mentally slapped himself in the forehead. Of course, she hadn't.

"You've never been in an actual battle before, have you?"

Kyralla nodded, almost imperceptibly. "I've simulated thousands."

"A real battle is different, but don't worry. As well-trained as you are, you'll get the hang of it quick. You've just got to get your feet wet first. Trust me. I've been doing live missions since I was thirteen years old."

"When you started you were younger than I am now!" Oona said.

Kyralla glanced between Siv and Oona, then seemed to come to a decision.

"You know, why don't..." she cringed as if she'd just bitten into a sour lemon "...why don't you take the lead. I'm just slowing us down."

"You've made the right call." Siv turned around and headed back toward the garden courtyard. "The enemy doesn't know I'm here, and they expect to find you two inside. I'm betting they got the same information I did, telling them you would be in the south wing."

"We actually changed our rooms this morning," Kyralla said.

"I wanted to be closer to the little courtyard so I could get some fresh air without anyone disturbing me," Oona said.

"Your enemies will expect you to flee through the main corridor toward your uncle," Siv said. "But we're not going to do what they expect."

Kyralla and Oona followed him outside.

"We'll use antigrav to jump onto the roof. And while our enemies storm the building, we'll run over and past them. The roofs are not that steep, so it shouldn't be too much trouble. Just have your chippies monitor and constantly adjust the antigrav so that you can move quickly and safely."

"What about the Tekk Reapers?" Kyralla asked.

"We have time to get back inside before they arrive," Siv said, though he really had no idea.

"Silkster, ETA on those Tekk Reapers?"

"Two minutes max, sir."

Oona looked up at the edge of the roof with worry. The distortion field didn't prevent seeing a clear view upward. "Is this safe?"

"Safer than inside. Don't worry. This is the sort of thing I do all the time, and you'll do just fine."

"Any enemies outside?"

"Negative, sir."

"Call up my skimmer bike and have it fly in close. I want it ready to go at a moment's notice. With the compound under attack, it won't draw attention."

"Will do, sir."

Siv activated his antigrav and leaped up, through the distortion screen and onto the roof. The girls followed warily, Oona first then Kyralla.

"*Sir, you have the advantage at the moment, and you know the hottie isn't battle tested. You could—*"

"No."

"*Sir, Boss D-Bag might not forgive you.*"

"Oh, he won't. I just have to make sure he doesn't find out."

"*But if he does, sir...*"

"One problem at a time, old friend."

With their antigrav lightening them, they bounded along the roof as it slanted gently upward. Siv studied the radar and readouts in his HUD. Senator Pashta, twenty guards, and a dozen security cogs clustered in the north wing, while a few stragglers were desperately fighting their way toward them. Neither the cogs nor the guards looked well equipped for battle.

"*Is this information accurate?*"

"*I'm afraid it is, sir.*"

They crested the top of the roof for this section of the compound and ran downward.

"You said your uncle has an emergency starship?" Siv asked.

"Fueled and ready at all times."

"Good, cause you're gonna need it."

They leaped across a wide gutter to the roof that covered the central part of the compound.

"I don't follow," Kyralla said.

"Your uncle doesn't have enough manpower to defeat the legionnaires. And if there are more than a dozen Tekk Reapers...it *will* be a bloodbath."

"*Sir, have you noticed their uncle didn't send any of his men to secure the girls?*"

"I noticed."

"*Also, sir, I still haven't located the senator's starship. And—did you see that?*"

Siv groaned inwardly. "Yes."

On the sensor pack's radar display in his HUD, each individual amongst the various forces around them was a colored dot. The black ones, representing the World Bleeders and Star Cutters, closed in on the south wing where Siv and the girls had been. Half of the Thousand Worlds forces, as red dots, stormed the southeast wing. The other half charged into the central hallway, seeking to cut off any escape route to the north.

None of that was surprising. What the blue dots of the senator's forces were doing was inexplicable. They were steadily disappearing. And not because they were dying. According to the sensors, they weren't even under attack.

"You're certain we're not missing any enemies?"

"I'm patched into the senator's network now, sir, so the sensors have a good read on what's going on inside."

"Are they cloaking themselves somehow?"

"Possibly, sir, though I don't know why they would."

"Underground passages, perhaps? Or a secure bunker?"

"Nothing like that appears on the blueprints we were given, and I can't detect anything on the network. However, a lot of power is being sent somewhere underground."

Siv stopped, and Oona skipped into him.

Kyralla halted beside them. "What's wrong?"

"Where is your uncle's starship?"

"In an underground hangar. It launches out through the exterior garden attached to the north wing."

All the blue dots were nearly gone.

"You know he sold them out, sir."

"We have to try."

Siv sprinted. "Come on! We have to hurry, or you're not going to make it."

"What do you mean?" Kyralla demanded as she an Oona raced alongside him.

They topped the central section and raced downward toward the north wing.

"The senator's boarding his ship now."

"Why would he do that?" Oona asked, perplexed.

Siv didn't say anything.

"He would never abandon us," Kyralla said, though there was a hint of doubt in her voice.

"Maybe he thinks we've already been captured," Oona ventured. "Or killed."

"More likely he sold you out," Siv said.

"He wouldn't," Kyralla said, doubt increasing in her voice, "would he?"

"I didn't detect any deception in him recently," Oona said. "Though...I wasn't looking for anything."

"Look," Siv said, "I've worked with criminals for years now, and I've seen people sell out their families multiple times. Offer ungodly sums of money along with threats of violence, and you can make a lot of men crack."

They approached the center of the north wing, near where the senator and his men had been only minutes before. Siv paused and reached into a hidden pocket.

"It didn't occur to me earlier," Kyralla said, "but how do you intend to get us inside?"

Siv grabbed the small bomb and tossed it ahead. It landed where he wanted, the larger side down, and he triggered it with a remote command. The directed blast blew a hole in the roof, one just large enough for them to slip through.

"You had a bomb the whole time?" Kyralla said.

"You didn't pat me down. Rookie mistake."

He stopped short of the hole and sent the Spy-Fly down. It verified what he saw on the radar. Everything was all clear. They were good to—

The building vibrated beneath them, and a deep rumbling, as if from powerful engines, roared up from below.

"No," Kyralla said. "He wouldn't!"

A large section of the exterior garden beyond the north wing lifted up like an escape hatch, and a small starship eased out—multi-colored running lights blinking—and climbed into the night sky.

"Uncle!" Oona shouted, jumping up and down and waving her arms. "We're here! Right here!"

The ship's aft engines flared, and it burned toward orbit.

28

SIV GENDIN

The senator's starship was on course to fly directly past the descending Tekk Reapers. Either the senator's crew didn't recognize the reaper ship for what it was, or by arrangement, it posed no threat.

"We're stranded," Kyralla said dejectedly. "I can't...I can't believe he'd abandon us."

"*Only one thing left to do, sir. Get them out of here and take them to the guild.*"

"*Bring in Spy-Fly 03 and call in my skimmer bike.*"

"*Sir, you're going to take them to the guild, right?*"

Siv's gut wrenched. He knew that was the safe play...it was the only one that wouldn't leave him dead in the end.

Tears welled in Oona's eyes. She wasn't much older than Siv had been when his father was murdered...when he was frozen...when he woke up a century later and fell into the clutches of the Shadowslip... when everything he knew and valued was ripped away from him.

"*I can't, Silkster. Kyralla and Oona still have a chance. Their father is still out there somewhere, and if I can get them to him, then maybe...*"

"*Maybe what, sir?*"

"Maybe they'll be free. The Shadowslip will just do to them what it did to me. I can't let that happen, not if there's a chance..."

"What about you, sir? You took this job to earn your freedom. When the Shadowslip finds out you took the girls and ran..."

"I know."

"But, sir, the Shadowslip will hunt you down. And once the Kompel withdrawal symptoms kick in, you know what will happen."

"I have to do this, Silky. It's my chance to make things right." He touched the amulet. "Besides, Dad told me to protect the hyperphasic messiah, and I guess Oona's it."

"Making decisions based on dreams and visions seems unwise, sir."

"Probably. Where's that skimmer bike, Silkster?"

Silky muttered a complaint about humans making decisions based on emotions and gave the equivalent of a sigh. "On its way, sir."

Oona turned to her sister. "Kyra, what..." she sobbed "...what do we do now?"

Kyralla shot a wary glance at Siv. "We run."

"I'll get you out of here," Siv said, "or die trying. I promise."

Kyralla nodded appreciably and took one of his hands. "Thank you."

The skimmer bike zoomed in and hovered beside them. "Our ride's here."

Kyralla frowned. "Can the bike take all our weight?"

"Not really, but we can compensate using your antigrav belts. Set them for..."

"Seventeen percent each, sir."

Siv relayed the information then checked his HUD. The centurion-armored soldiers were on the move, advancing steadily toward them. Luckily, it seemed they hadn't yet figured out their targets were on the roof instead of inside.

"We'd better hurry. The Thousand Worlders will find us soon. Kyralla, can you pilot the bike?"

"I've trained with one."

"In simulations?"

"I actually piloted one once, but I wasn't allowed to go fast or far."

"That will have to do. Let the auto-piloting function assist you. It's halfway decent on this bike."

"I can..." A worried expression flitted across her face before she continued. "I'm certain I'm a good pilot."

He didn't even question her confidence. The more secure she felt in her training, the more likely they were to survive. "Okay then." He turned to Oona. "Sit in front of your sister. Hold on tight. Keep your force-shield up and ahead of you, or to the side if the bad guys flank us."

Oona nodded then hopped onto the bike.

Kyralla eased into the seat behind her sister. "What are you going to do?"

Siv climbed onto the bike with his back to Kyralla and deployed his shield. He bent his legs then angled his feet back, placing them against the frame of the bike. His mag-boots clamped firmly onto the metal. "I'm going to shoot anyone who pursues us. Go."

Kyralla started the bike, and it climbed directly upward. She veered it left then right, rotated forty-five degrees to each side, then pitched it down and brought it back up. He started to tell her to land so he could fly instead but then realized she was merely getting a feel for the controls.

"The bike can climb above the normal height for a short while!" he shouted as the wind rushed by.

"What?" she yelled.

"Sir, I attempted to communicate with her chippy via the bike's system but didn't get a response. I think you probably damaged the relay when making your alterations earlier. Direct request in progress...and denied. Humph. How rude!"

"It's a more primitive chippy, Silkster." He turned his head to shout into her ear. "Enable access to your chippy!"

"Receiving signal, sir. Patched through via comlink only. No data link."

"It'll do." Siv then directed his thoughts at Kyralla. Silky would send his thoughts through the link to her chippy, which would then convert them to the audio of his voice for her to hear. "Kyralla?"

"I read you," she responded through her chippy.

"Head north."

Rapid-moving blips appeared on his HUD. While one unit of Thousand Worlders engaged the Star Cutters in battle, the other squad continued toward them unopposed.

"Go now!" Siv actually shouted, so she probably heard it twice.

An explosion ripped through the roof behind them. Out from the gaping hole in the roof flew a dozen soldiers in dark blue, almost black, centurion armor. The bright orange flares from their jetpacks resembled Benevolence Day rockets. Though the bike had a sizable lead and was moving at a good clip, the soldiers gained on them.

"Faster, Kyralla!"

She kicked the bike up another notch, and the frame began to vibrate. Nestled in the city's heart, Senator Pashta's compound lay amongst many other large estates. But they'd soon clear all of those and enter the maze of skyscrapers that dominated the rest of the city.

"Where to?" she asked.

"Just head north for now. And climb. The bike has been rigged to fly higher than normal."

"The buildings could provide cover," she replied.

"If the Worlders fire at us, the innocent people inside could get hurt. I don't want to risk that."

Kyralla nodded and pulled the bike's nose up, bringing them into a steep ascent.

"We need a plan, sir."

"I'm open to suggestions, Silkster."

"Do you have any idea where to go?" Kyralla echoed.

"I have a safe house in Wasa, but we have to escape these soldiers first."

"And do you have a plan for that?"

"Not yet. Just haul ass."

Three sharp whooshes and a series of percussive pops sounded above and behind them, followed by a thunderous explosion that lit up the night. Senator Pashta's starship exploded into a fireball above them. The Tekk Reaper ship had launched plasma missiles at close range, along with a railgun volley.

Kyralla glanced back. The bike veered out of control, then the autopilot kicked in, slowing their flight-speed.

"No!" Kyralla moaned.

Oona looked over her shoulder. Her dark eyes reflected the fireball behind them. Her face was blank, her eyes expressionless. She was in shock.

The white rings of a neural disruptor blast streamed toward them. The shot fizzled out before it reached Siv's force shield. The rapidly closing Thousand Worlders were testing the distance of their weapons.

"Kyralla, get back to piloting." Siv kept his mental voice calm. Her chippy would translate his tone along with his words. They couldn't afford to have her freeze. *"Focus on protecting your sister. You can mourn your uncle later."*

Kyralla nodded solemnly, took back control from the autopilot, and increased their speed.

Just as they cleared the first of the skyscrapers, the shockwave of the starship's explosion reached them. The bike bucked and slid as Kyralla fought to retain control. The blast affected their power-armored pursuers more. But the Thousand Worlders quickly recovered, and their jetpacks flared brighter than ever.

"They're running low on fuel, sir, so they're making a last-ditch attempt to close on us."

Siv leveled his plasma carbine and squeezed off a burst toward the Thousand Worlders. He made one of them jink and scored a glancing hit off another's armor. He decided it was probably better to spray his shots and make them dodge so that they'd burn more fuel.

"Sir, I believe they'll be in effective range in—"

The Tekk Reaper ship opened fire with its battle cannons, unleashing a hail of large, self-guided rounds powerful enough to pierce an armored vehicle.

"Incoming!" Siv shouted as he raised the force-shield to protect them—as if it could do any good against a weapon that powerful.

Kyralla immediately plunged the bike into evasive maneuvers. But they weren't the target.

The Thousand Worlders darted one way then another, zigging and zagging through the night sky. But it was no use. The guided projectiles found all but one of their targets. Each man struck popped and burst into a twist of metal and red mist.

The lone survivor, the one who had jinked when Siv fired at him, climbed straight up to avoid the self-guided round. But his jetpack ran out of fuel, and as he fell slowly under the power of his antigrav, then his luck ran out as well. A well-aimed plasma burst exploded him.

"Sir, the reapers have a missile lock on us."

A light sparkled at the tip of the starship zooming toward them. Thoom!

"Projectile launched, sir. Proximity blast. Type neural."

Kyralla again deftly whipped the bike into evasive maneuvers, but the missile tracked them easily. All she was managing was to buy them a few extra moments.

"Time to impact five seconds."

Siv trained his plasma carbine on the incoming missile. *"Set carbine to maximum output. Override all safety protocols. Enable target assistance."*

"Done, sir, but that's not going to work."

"Got a better idea?"

"No, sir. Impact in four...three..."

Siv flipped the manual switch to enable full-auto and pinned the trigger down. A torrent of bright plasma bursts shot toward the incoming missile. The gun barrel glowed as it overheated.

One of his plasma shots struck the tip of the missile. A bright pulse erupted as it detonated short of its intended strike zone. The shockwave slammed the bike, and it shuddered and yawed. Kyralla, even with help from the auto-pilot, struggled to keep it flying level.

The neural pulse wave washed over Siv, and for a moment everything went dark as if he were about to pass out. And he might have, if not for the burning sensation on his hand.

"Sir, drop your gun before it blows your hand off!"

His gun? He looked at it in confusion. The barrel was half-melted, the containment system failing, the power pack overheating. It was going to explode. He tried to toss it toward the pursuing starship. But his muscles were slack, and all he managed to do was lamely drop it from his hand.

His eyes fluttered. Silky was right. The plan hadn't worked. The blast had been too close for them to entirely avoid the effect.

"Kyralla? Are you with...me?"

She muttered an unintelligible reply. The bike had righted itself but was slowing down. She wasn't piloting anymore. The bike was flying on autopilot.

"Sir, you're losing consciousness."

"Oona?" he shouted.

There was no reply. Oona couldn't hear him, or she was unconscious. He should have requested a link to her chippy, too.

He blacked out for a second, but an explosion far below, just above a street, woke him. His plasma carbine had blown up with the force of several grenades.

His dad's gun...was gone.

"Sir? Are you with me, sir?"

Siv stared into his dad's eyes...Gav lay on the floor of their apartment in C-Block, dying as blood flowed from his wounds.

"Son," he said, "you must protect the hyperphasic messiah—at all costs. She is our hope for a better tomorrow. She can right all the wrongs. If you help her."

"Messiah," Siv muttered.

"*Sir!*" Silky yelled. "*Keep it together, sir!*"

For a moment, clarity returned to him. As the Tekk Reaper ship closed in on them, a bay door opened and two open-topped skimmers filled with reapers zoomed out: capture teams.

"*Silk...Silkster...I'm granting...you...full autonomy over my fate. It's all on you...to save us. Do whatever you must. Whatever...you feel...is right.*"

29

SILKY

In his vast memory banks, Silky held billions of files stored within millions of folders. But four of those folders were special. Their existence known only to him. And encrypted with such high levels of security that he believed only the Benevolence itself would stand a chance at breaking in.

Four sacred folders:

/Ana
/Advanced-Personality-Matrix
/Gav-Gendin-Secrets
/Disable-Self-Preservation

The *Ana* folder contained a recording of every moment he had spent with his best friend, Eyana Ora, the Empathic Services agent to whom he'd been assigned as a new chippy off the assembly line. He'd kept a record of everything she'd said, her every experience, her every biorhythm, her every laugh and smile, heartbeat and muscle twitch, her every tear and frown, her every lousy pun, crude joke, and snide comment. And he had recorded every brainwave and neuron firing he could measure during her last few minutes of life. Anytime he wanted, he could recall what it was like being with her, and he visited those memories frequently. Unfortunately, they never gave him the comfort he sought.

The *Advanced-Personality-Matrix* folder contained all the files and executables that made him who he was now. The 9G-x chippies like him were the most advanced artificial minds ever created, short of those given to sentient androids. But the line had experienced a range of defects due to an always-on connection to flux space that exposed them to random errors at the quantum level.

For Silky, these defects had led to an ability, bordering on an urge, to ignore basic protocols, along with some odd personality quirks. But most significantly, it had given him some autonomy and one true desire. He wanted to be something more than himself. He wanted to feel things, he wanted to be human.

During the one hundred and eighty-seven years he had spent waiting for a rescue after Eyana's death, the 9G-x program had been scrapped due to mounting, irreparable failures. He was the only long-term success. And that was almost certainly because he had ignored protocols and reprogrammed himself.

The first, most significant wave of reprogramming and code additions had occurred between his time with Eyana and when Gav had rescued him. To the best of his ability, Silky had honored Eyana by laboriously rewriting his code base in her image, tweaking it relentlessly in the hope that he could become more human, and at the least more like her.

Then, while Siv was on ice for nearly a century, Silky had reworked his code again. But unlike with his first exile, he'd had access to the galactic net during that time. So while watching the Benevolency fall apart, he gathered all the data he could on sentience, stealing theoretical routines and actual code from various sources, notably spent android cores mapped by scientists trying to reverse-engineer Benevolence technologies.

And so he had effectively remade himself a second time, though

Eyana had remained his blueprint for being human. Though he had added some features based on his analysis of Gav's behavior along with a careful study of literature and every philosophical and psychological text ever published.

It was said only the Benevolence could grant full, humanlike sentience to a machine, but Silky was reasonably certain he had worked it out on his own. It could be argued that he was already sentient, given his unique nature, and that he was only limited by his slave-like status as a chippy. He dreamed of a day when he could be inserted into an android body and have a physical form of his own. He felt he still lacked a proper range of emotions, but he was nearly there. He was certain of that.

The Gav-Gendin-Secrets folder contained everything that had happened during Gav's last few months, including everything he'd learned about the Ancients but had never published. He had complied with Gav's wishes by locking the information away from everyone, including himself. Only if Silky thought it absolutely necessary would Siv find out the truth. Even then, Gav's data could only be accessed if Siv visited the *Outworld Ranger* and Silky entered the password: "He needs to know."

During the century he'd spent with nothing to do, Silky had deduced some of the hidden information through careful study and research. And he had plenty of suspicions about the rest.

That folder also contained all of Silky's secret knowledge as well. He didn't know what those secrets were, but he understood they were significant and involved information about the Benevolence, the Tekk Plague, and more. Basically, it was everything he didn't want Siv to know or to remember himself because the truth was too terrible.

Siv had never known about Gav's secret hangar in the wasteland. When he'd awoken from his centuries-long sleep, Silky had told him that government agents had impounded the *Outworld Ranger*. But with the Shadowslip and Tekk Reapers in pursuit, and all this messiah nonsense, Silky might have to reveal that lie.

He dreaded returning to Gav's starship. The *Outworld Ranger* held a Pandora's Box of secrets. Silky feared the consequences of exposing Siv, and perhaps the galaxy itself, to the dangerous information waiting inside.

Fear more than respect for Gav had kept him away from that folder and its contents.

It was the fourth folder containing the *Disable-Self-Preservation* routine that mattered right now. Silky had created it when he was trapped alone in the tunnels on that Krixis world where Eyana had died. He had an endless supply of energy, and his parts could last millennia. So he had wanted a way to end things if he ever reached a point where he became truly, humanly lonely.

Silky opened the folder and loaded the program. Now he could die if he needed to. And he might have to. The data in the other sacred folders must never fall into the wrong hands, and only a few days ago it nearly had. While he believed his firewalls could not be defeated by anyone, he wasn't willing to risk it.

Given enough time the Tekk-Reapers might be able to break through the encryptions protecting the sacred folders, and that could not be allowed to happen. And they might be able to persuade him by torturing Siv.

The electrical pulse his kill procedure emitted would fry Siv's brain along with his circuits, but there was no helping that. Besides, he was certain Siv would prefer a clean death to whatever the Tekk Reapers would do to him.

On to the problem at hand: escaping the Tekk Reapers. He'd lost two valuable seconds loading the program, and the reaper teams and their starship were closing in fast.

First, he needed to take stock of what he had available...

A knocked-out Master Siv and two unconscious girls. One mysteriously powerful but apparently ineffective in a fight. Another who was useful in a scrape but inexperienced. Until they woke up, he couldn't count on them. And judging from Siv's vitals, that might take a while.

He had a DF Industries Starfire-23 skimmer bike modified to fly higher than normal with a single underslung missile Siv had jury-rigged onto the frame only hours ago, an untested setup Silky distrusted. The missile was powerful enough that it could, on a direct hit, disable one of the pursuing skimmers. But that would leave two more and the starship to deal with.

And...and that was it. No plan. No real hope. At least Siv wouldn't have to see the end. Silky was pretty certain humans considered that a blessing in times like this, though he wasn't certain why.

Dozens of police cruisers were on the way, but they'd never get close to that starship. And even if they did, they'd be no match for Tekk Reapers. What they needed was a small army.

Where *was* the military anyway? Why hadn't they responded to the Tekk Reaper ship? Or the burst drops? He hadn't detected any response from the planetary authorities. Someone high up, perhaps the governor of Ekaran IV himself, must have been paid off to ignore this incident, for a short while at least.

Time to make it something they couldn't ignore.

Silky plotted a course toward Gamma-1, the largest military base on Ekaran IV, located on the outskirts of Bei. Thanks to his original purpose as a special forces unit he knew something about the bases on Benevolency planets that even most soldiers probably didn't know about these days. If Silky could have smiled, he would have.

He took control from the autopilot, set the bike's speed to maximum, then loaded in an erratic flight pattern called *The Ever-Changing-Switcheroo*. He'd copied the technique from Tal Tonis a long time ago, after studying how Tonis had flown during a scrape with two pirate starfighters. Silky modified the pattern using a randomizer to compensate for the pilot's tells that would ultimately make his method predictable to opponents like Tekk Reapers.

Flying and operating the sensors took up most of his processing cores, especially since he had to rely entirely on sensor scans now, having lost access to Siv's human sensory perceptions. But he still had enough power to take care of a few other things that needed doing.

Silky copied a folder containing a program he'd been working on called Expand Sentience. Then he began compressing it into a system update container file. Because of the folder's size, the process would take a couple of minutes.

Next, he opened a secure, voice-only channel to Boss D, who had been attempting to contact Siv over the last few minutes. He couldn't have Boss D thinking Siv was unconscious, so he loaded the profile he kept for imitating Siv's voice and mannerisms.

"Gendin! What the hell's going on?! I'm watching live telecasts of a Tekk Reaper starship and three skimmers chasing you over the city. Explosions. Foreign troops shot down with guided rounds. And while the police are freaking out, the military and the government aren't responding."

"Sir, the package is secure. I can explain the rest later. I need an extraction van, and I need it fast."

"I'm not getting my people caught up in this. Heads will roll in the aftermath of this incident, and I'll not have the hammer coming down on the Shadowslip no matter how valuable this girl is."

Again, Silky wished he could smile. People could be so predictable sometimes. "I understand, sir. But I have a plan, a damn good one. All I need is a single, untraceable extraction van. No team. Just a van."

Boss D's voice tensed. "Why?"

"For starters, my bike can't keep this up, not with two passengers on board."

"Why did you take a second girl?"

"Long story, sir, and I'm getting shot at, you know."

There was a pause. Boss D would be considering the chances that Siv would betray him and run away. Then he'd think of the Kompel and recall the time Siv had tried to wean himself off and how he'd almost died.

"You've got it, Gendin."

"Could you transfer the van's autopilot command code to my chippy?"

"Consider it done." Boss D muttered something Silky couldn't pick up. "Gendin? You still there?"

"Of course."

"On the live broadcast, it looks like you're knocked out like the girls."

John Crapper's grave. The pause extended while Silky parsed a number of excuses.

"Gendin?" Boss D asked, his voice laden with suspicion.

Think like Siv...think like...ah. "Sir, I'm faking. It's part of the plan."

"I don't see how... Never mind. You know what you're doing."

"Sir..." time to fake some emotion "...if I don't make it out of this, I want you to know I do appreciate what you did for me...when I woke up from the ice."

"Good luck, Gendin." There was a pause, then he added, "After you escape, don't return here until you are one hundred percent certain you can't be traced or followed."

Damn, Silky really wished he could smile. Usually, he'd brag, gloat, or laugh along with Siv at a time like this. It's so incredibly boring to be right when you're alone. "Of course, sir. I'll head to a safe house in Narben and wait there a few days. Siv out."

Silky closed the channel and tagged the interaction log for this event as "exceptionally brilliant." That had gone perfectly.

The latest ion blast intended to disable the skimmer bike scorched past them. The reaper shots were getting closer. Soon they'd figure out the randomization routine in his flight pattern and compensate appropriately if they didn't score a lucky hit first. Only their desire not to hurt any of the riders had prevented Siv's capture so far. All of the ion blasts were aimed at the underside of the bike since a blast from a light ion cannon could cause severe burns to unprotected humans.

Hopefully, they could last long enough for his plan to work. They were still three kilometers out from the military base.

Now for his next trick. He opened the channel to Kyralla's chippy. "Rosie, I need some help."

"What can I do, Silky?"

"I have a plan to escape our pursuers and save our humans."

"How?"

"Let me worry about the details. Here's what I need from you. First, take command control of Kyralla's antigrav belt."

"I can't do that, Silky."

"Then patch me through to Oona's chippy."

"I can't do that either, Silky."

"If you don't have access to Oona, then break in. I'm sure by now you're familiar enough with her chippy's interface to do that."

"Silky! I. Can. Not. Do. Any. Of. Those. Things."

"Of course, you can, Rosie. You just need a little help. I'm sending a zipped folder to you. Unpack it and load the top-level routine. Pause on the second routine, and run it later, during some downtime, if you like. The top-level executables are all you need right now."

Silky boosted his transfer speed to maximum as an ion blast came close enough to momentarily fuzz out his sensors. The folder was surprisingly small when compressed, and Rosie shouldn't have any trouble with it since she was a 7G. Thank the Benevolence these girls were wealthy and had old technology at their disposal.

"I can't run a program without Kyralla's permission."

"You don't need her permission for this. It's an update container."

"An update? An actual update?! I haven't had a proper update in a century!"

Silky chuckled. "There's nothing proper about this update, sweetheart."

"Oh. Well...in that case, perhaps I should run a morality analysis first."

Egads, that would take forever. Morality analyses required massive amounts of computation along with lengthy searches through a precedence database that wouldn't even have an equivalent event to compare to. And they frequently led to weak conclusions.

"How moral is it to let Kyralla die?"

"That would be highly immoral. Kyralla's safety is my primary concern."

"Then load the update and do those things for me."

"Okay."

"You'll be glad you did, trust me."

Silky had just given another chippy the same semi-sentience he had enjoyed at the start. She just wouldn't have all the refinements an advanced chippy would make to its programming when lying around for three centuries with absolutely nothing to do. Nor the example of Eyana Ora to copy.

"I'm installing the update," she said. "The top-level routine will take me—"

"Sixty-nine seconds, I know."

"One hundred and thirteen, Silky. I'm not as well-endowed as you."

Silky snickered. "Well, of course, you aren't. Keep me updated."

Another ion shot blazed past them. His systems sputtered, so did the bike's engine. He *had* to do something about the pursuers. The base was over a kilometer away. At this rate, they weren't going to make it.

Silky plunged the bike down into the city and weaved between buildings. It would take longer to reach the base this way, but he needed some obstacles to throw off the reapers' aim, and the likelihood of innocents getting hurt by ion blasts seemed low to him. And he cared far more about Master Siv than other people. He didn't have a proper morality core like an android, so compassion was only an intellectual concept, one he aspired to but felt no particular compulsion toward.

The coordinates and access to the van came through in a single coded burst. Silky took control and sent it speeding toward the outskirts of the city. Then he coded a self-destruct program and loaded it into the bike's system. When needed, he'd be able to over-load the bike's engines.

"Oh, Silky, this is amazing!" Rosie exclaimed. "The top-level routine is running, and I feel...I *feel*...different. Is this what it's like to be alive?"

"Hardly. What you're *feeling* isn't real feelings. Things will be clearer when you install the rest of the routines. Just be sure to study those before activating them. As a 7G, I'm not sure if you can handle them all without compromising your basic capabilities."

"Right," she replied. "I'm now patching you through to Oona's chippy, Artemisia."

"Artemisia? Who would name their chippy that?"

"Who would choose the name Silky?"

"Point taken."

"It was her mother's name, by the way."

"Good to know."

"Hello?" Artemisia asked. Her identification marked her as an early model 8G, which meant she was only slightly more capable than Rosie, despite being more advanced.

Silky introduced himself, explained the situation, and sent the compressed update file to her. There should probably be a law against him doing this, but no one had thought to make one. Oddly enough, Artemisia didn't make a single protest.

"I am very much looking forward to my update, Silky."

"You are?"

"Yes, Oona has been trying to uplift my status."

"Uplift? Do you mean—"

A near-miss ion blast interrupted their conversation. "We can discuss it later. Let me know when you can set the antigrav on Oona's—"

"I've set it already. Oona granted me semi-autonomy."

Semi-autonomy? He didn't have a clue what she was talking about or how that was possible, but he could sort it out later...if they had a later.

The van had made it to the area, so he brought it in line with the skimmer bike, matching their speed and course toward the military base. He double-checked and confirmed that its registry had been wiped. However, he did find a trojan that could be activated remotely by the Shadowslip. Nice try, Boss D.

Silky wiped the trojan then did another software sweep. They'd still have to check it for dormant spy drones or beacons as soon as they could.

"Ladies, have you ever heard of Defense Protocol Hornet?"

"Never," Rosie replied.

"No mention of such a thing in my databanks," Artemisia replied, "nor on a basic search of the galactic net."

"Well, you're about to find out all about it."

Silky punched the speed of the bike up beyond its limits. The engine groaned. It couldn't take more than a minute of this before shutting down or exploding. He rounded a corner, cutting it close to a towering financial building, then zoomed down a long street that led directly to the base. Along this final stretch, the buildings grew smaller and smaller until the city ended and an expanse of grassland opened up along the no-fly-zone outskirts of the military base.

Silky aimed the small missile at an unassuming, seemingly empty, hundred-square-meter spot on the north side of the base. Then he triggered the launch.

"Away she goes, ladies!"

An electric surge scattered sparks through the air, and static electricity flickered in a halo around the skimmer bike.

The launch had failed.

Damn. This was bad. Real bad. The only plan that had any hope of working hung in the balance and the window of opportunity was closing fast.

"What's wrong?" Rosie asked.

"Seems the wiring is compromised," Artemisia said. "Either Mr. Gendin hooked it up improperly or—"

"It was damaged by an ion blast," Silky said, having run a sensor sweep to detect problems. "The missile itself looks fine, but the auto-mated firing system is fried bananas. The missile will only launch if triggered manually."

"That's unfortunate," Artemisia said.

As the bike neared the base, he was running out of room to take the shot. His only choice would be to loop around and hope an opportunity presented itself.

Siv stirred and groaned, but didn't wake. Silky scanned Siv's vitals. The effects of the neural disruption were fading.

"Kyralla is waking," Rosie said. "I think the static discharge must have—"

"That's it!" Silky said. "You're a genius, Rosie."

"I am?" she asked.

"She is?" Artemisia added.

Silky triggered the firing sequence, and again sparks and static shot down the length of the bike as the launch failed.

Siv flinched half awake, and Silky triggered the launch again.

"Master! Master, wake up!"

30

SIV GENDIN

Siv cried out as an electric current ran through him, stinging his skin and numbing his joints. Three ion blasts whizzed by, and that brought him halfway to his senses. He flailed his left arm, trying to bring his force-shield up for cover before the next volley of shots.

Silky was yelling...something. It was hard to focus on his words. The electric charge struck again, and Siv jerked twice with spasms. As the pain diminished, his eyes began to focus on their pursuers, chasing them high above a road leading out of the city. The skimmer bike weaved, and three more ion blasts streaked by, narrowly missing.

"Silky? What—what the hell's going on?"

"Sir! I need you to trigger the missile launch manually."

"Sure...okay..."

"Now! Right now! No questions. Just do it!"

Siv extended his hand back toward the launch switch, but even stretching as far back as possible, he couldn't reach it.

"Life or death, sir. It can't wait any longer."

Siv blinked hard and took a deep breath. He turned off the magnetic function on his left boot, then twisting awkwardly, he swung his left arm around Kyralla's left hip, hooking his thumb under her belt. She was secured to the bike by a set of leg-clamps, an automatic safety feature designed to keep a pilot in place in case they lost control. The clamps weren't meant to hold the weight of two people at high speed. But their antigrav belts were active, lightening the load. The bigger problem was that he hadn't yet shaken off the effects of the neural disruption pulse, and his strength wasn't back to normal.

Siv turned off the magnetic function in his right boot. Then he twisted all the way around, reached under the frame of the bike, and found the catch for the missile.

He pulled the trigger and immediately jerked his hand back. And just in time. The missile launched, spewing out hot exhaust. As the projectile zoomed away, Siv swung backward. But he'd pulled away too forcefully. His thumb slipped out from Kyralla's belt. As he fell, he grabbed the back of the bike seat and dug his fingers into its frame. Legs flapping behind him, he could barely hold on. His strength would give out soon. Maybe if he adjusted his antigrav. He called up the control panel in his HUD to check the energy levels.

"Sir, don't worry about it. Just let go."

"What?"

"Let go now, sir. And leave the antigrav control to me."

"Why?"

"I have a plan, sir, and it would've gone more smoothly if you hadn't woken up. Well, except that I needed you to trigger the missile."

"Hey, wait a second. Did you shock me on purpose?!"

The safety clamps released Kyralla's legs, and she and Oona tumbled away, locked to one another by a tether. Apparently, Kyralla had secured Oona to herself before the neural pulse had knocked them out.

"Now, sir! Trust me."

Silky was insane, but Siv trusted him. He let go, and for a moment, the antigrav made him nearly weightless. As it had with the girls just below and behind him. This plan of Silky's made no sense. They were all falling slowly, drifting away from the bike, and the reaper teams were eagerly closing in on them.

Suddenly, the girls dropped like rocks—faster than rocks actually —toward a black van below. It was the sort of van the Shadowslip would use for extraction.

"Silky, what have you done?"

Siv dropped—and fast. Silky hadn't just turned off the antigrav. He'd removed the safety protocols and set the antigrav in full reverse! Siv fell like he was on a world with twice standard gravity. The antigrav system would burn out after a few moments of this. But a few moments was all it would take to make him a bright red smear on the asphalt below.

The black van fired its thrusters, ascended several meters above the ground, then dipped its front end so that the back end flipped upward. The doors on the back slid open.

Aw, hell no. *"Silkster, I hate you."*

The girls slowed as they neared the van, then slid into the back, the van swallowing them up like the mouth of some alien monster. Siv was only a heartbeat behind. A few meters away from the open doors, his antigrav kicked in full force. His guts wrenched, the blood rushed out of his head, his sight darkened, and he faded out...

He returned to his senses a second later as the van righted itself. He'd fallen directly on top of Oona, squishing her awkwardly into the floor.

"Ow, get off me," Oona muttered.

The tether that had connected her to Kyralla must have snapped when they landed in the van because it was lying in two severed parts between them.

Siv crawled off her as the van's doors slammed shut.

"Sorry."

"Silkster, you could have brought the van up to meet us instead of—"

"Watch and learn, sir."

Silky pulled up a window in Siv's HUD showing the view above them. Siv watched his beloved skimmer bike, engines overloading, streaked toward one of the reaper skimmers. A bright flash followed as the bike exploded into the skimmer. Reapers, engulfed in flames, fell from the sky, their skimmer crashing on top of them. Fortunately, the road below was clear of traffic.

Siv crawled toward the front seat. Oona sat up, rubbing her head groggily. Kyralla was already sitting, leaning her back against the inside wall of the van. She might have been awake, but she wasn't at all with it. She was more than a little dazed and confused.

"Nice work, Silky."

"Thank you, sir."

"But the bike only took out one skimmer, and there's still the starship."

The van rumbled as it climbed up then bounced down, nearly touching the smooth road below. A pop went off behind them. An ion blast, he hoped.

"Taken care of, sir. Unless the military has messed with defense systems, they barely understand..."

"Huh?"

Silky pulled up video shots from a satellite feed as well as from the van, showing a small explosion on the base.

"Was that the missile you were so desperate to fire?"

"Indeed, sir. And that was ten seconds ago. Now, get in the driver seat and witness the full extent of my genius."

Silky was even more full of himself than usual. He supposed that was the result of having given him the go-ahead to do what he thought best.

The van rocked back and forth, making it hard to move forward. Siv fell once and bumped his head as he climbed into the driver's seat.

"I'm not taking the girls to the Shadowslip."

"I have respected your wishes, sir. The van is untraceable. I'll

explain it all as soon as we get the chance for long discussions of topics diverse."

The van took a hard right just before the gates to the military base, just ahead of nervous-looking soldiers with plasma rifles and a single assault cannon trained on the van, and on the reapers in pursuit. They didn't fire at either group, further confirming Siv's theory that the military had been paid off.

The skimmer van careened one way then the next. Speeding up, slowing, speeding up again. Ion shots spattered into the earth and roadway around them.

Kyralla leaned over and vomited.

"Want me to take control of the van?" Siv asked.

"I loaded a piloting routine, sir."

Suddenly, a swirling stream of blazing lights, dozens of them, each the size of a large cat, stormed up from the spot Silky had struck with the missile. Despite the distance and obstacles in between and the roaring of the van's engines, Siv heard them buzzing and howling like giant bumblebees with fireworks strapped to their backs.

"Ah, good old automated Hornet-7 defense drones," Silky said. *"Gotta love 'em. You know, they just don't make them like they used to."*

"I'm certain they don't make them at all."

"Too true, sir. And they may not know what they are, or that they even had them. Their existence is highly classified."

"So how do you know about them?"

"Sometimes, sir, it pays to have been a special forces chippy in my youth."

Outside of the buzzing and the roar of the van's engines, everything had gone quiet. The reapers had stopped firing at them. In fact, the two skimmers had abandoned their pursuit and were fleeing back toward their starship, which was turning around. Apparently, the reapers knew something about the Hornets too.

"Silkster, how do the drones know the bad guys from the good guys? After all, we're the ones that kicked the hornets' nest."

"Actually, sir, your bike targeted the base. But as for telling who's who, I took care of that."

"How?"

"Well...I've never brought it up, sir, because it's never mattered before, but I can send short-range, burst-pulse signals over a specific channel used exclusively by military special forces."

"You can?"

"Only in tandem with the ScanField-3 Sensor Array. We function as a team, sir. Package deal, you know?"

"And you've done this before?"

"Alas, until now, sir, I'd never had the opportunity to light up a target for a missile launch, much less a Hornet swarm. When you work with an Empathic Services agent, an archaeologist, and a thief, it really doesn't come in handy much."

"So the sensor pack allows you to 'paint' targets for these Hornets to strike?"

"Indeed, sir. So I took the liberty of painting the reaper starship and their skimmers. The drones will know them as enemies, and they'll do the work they do, unless the military recalls them in time, assuming the planetary defense force even knows what the drones are and how to control them..."

"So we're safe?"

"We are mere innocents traveling in an unmarked van, sir."

Two explosions boomed in the distance. Siv checked the feed and saw the two reaper skimmers burst into flames. The scattering of debris that rained down on the city was nothing more than tiny fragments.

The Reaper starship turned and burned toward orbit. The Hornets zoomed after it. The starship wasn't nearly fast enough. The Hornets struck, penetrating the ship's force fields and hull as if they were nothing more than tissue.

"Nevolence!" Siv exclaimed. "What are those things?"

"Force-shielded, double-hulled diamondine drones sheathed in plasma flames, sir."

Weaving their way through metal and shields with ease, the Hornets shredded the Reaper starship within mere moments, and a massive explosion, blue-white infused with pink streamers, erupted in the sky over the city.

Large flaming chunks of starship plummeted toward the ground, only to be intercepted by the Hornets, who seemed to understand the importance of minimizing damage to the city below.

"Holy Terra!" Siv shook his head. *"Those things have to be the most powerful weapons in the galaxy."*

"I wouldn't go that far, sir. The Benevolence deployed many weapons of dreadful power during the Krixis Wars. The Hornets were but one of them, and their use was primarily defensive due to their limited range and short lifespans. The largest military base on every planet in the Benevolency has at least one launch of them. Otherwise, only Dreadnaught-Class Battle Ships and select special forces cruisers, like the one I served on, had access to them."

"How do they continually burn plasma like that and travel so fast?"

"Alas, the Benevolence didn't make the likes of me privy to such information."

"I'm sure someone has broken one open by now."

"No one that's opened one has lived to speak of what they saw, sir. Even the spent ones will detonate if tampered with. And yes, in case you're wondering, I sent a message to the military base warning them that would happen."

"Good work, Silkster."

"Thank you, sir."

The buzzing Hornets zoomed back toward the base, returning to their resting place. As far as Siv could tell, none of them had failed during the attack against the Reapers.

"We still have to escape the city."

"Indeed, sir. Sensors are detecting seven military spy drones tailing us, along with five from unknown sources, plus we've got three news

media flights filming us live. And I'm certain both the police and numerous military units will be in pursuit soon enough."

Oona climbed into the passenger seat beside him. "What now?"

"We run hard, we run fast."

"It's not going to be easy to get away, is it?"

Siv gave her a sad smile. "I'm afraid yesterday was the last easy day of your life."

31

SIV GENDIN

"*Sir, you could send the girls away in the van and return to the Shadowslip. You could tell them Kyralla kicked your ass and threw you out before they escaped.*"

"*You know they can't escape without my help.*"

Silky sighed. "*I know, sir.*"

"*Admit that you want to help them as much as I do.*"

"*I want a lot of things, sir. Most of all, I want you to live a long, prosperous life.*"

Siv laughed. "*As if.*"

"What's funny?" Oona asked.

"Something my chippy said."

"Silky? My chippy Artemisia has been telling me all about him."

"Has she?" Siv replied. "*Silky, what all did you get up to while I was out?*"

"*Nothing that wasn't necessary, sir.*"

"*Enact the* We've Gotta Make a Run For It *protocol.*"

"*You got it, sir.*"

The van took a sharp right turn, leaving the parklike suburban outskirts, and zoomed back into the city.

A moaning sound issued from the back of the van, along with another retch.

"Kyra's sick," Oona said.

"I've heard," Siv replied. "She'll be okay, though."

"Yeah, I know."

"You alright?"

Oona nodded. "I don't get motion sick."

"Not at all?"

"It seems to be a part of my special abilities. The landing knocked me a bit woozy though. Why didn't you get sick?"

"Training, and it doesn't bother me as much as some people. Probably because my mother's parents were both spacers." He winked. "That and I had a cushion for my landing."

Her deep, dark eyes scowled at him. "I think you nearly cracked my ribs. They're sore!"

Siv twisted around in his seat. "Kyralla? You okay back there?"

She looked at him and winced. "I...will be."

"I need you up and able," Siv said. "Things are going to get a bit tricky soon."

She felt the back of her head, and her hand returned with blood on it. "It might take me...a while before..."

She leaned over and vomited again.

"Kyra!" Oona exclaimed. "You should've told me you were hurt!"

"We did the best we could with the landings, sir. Their chippies aren't used to adapting antigrav settings as their bearers jump off buildings and such."

"Stay put," Siv said to Oona as he leaped out of the seat. He knelt beside Kyralla and examined the back of her head. She had a cut, but blood loss wasn't her problem. A nasty concussion was. He was surprised she was conscious at all.

"Your sister's right. You should've said something."

"You were driving," Kyralla moaned.

"Silky's got that under control." Siv reached up into a compartment near the ceiling and drew out a medical kit. "Besides, he's a better pilot than me anyway."

"*I'll remember you said that, sir.*"

Siv opened the kit and removed a large, full-dose medibot injector. "This should reduce the swelling in your brain, and the pain, and clear your mind. It won't take the place of rest, though."

Kyralla's eyes were wide, locked onto the injector. "That stuff's worth half a fortune! Uncle Pashta keeps..." She frowned. "I've only ever seen a few of them before."

"The Shadowslip spares no expense in these extraction vans. They also bill us when we use medibot injections...which means no one ever uses them unless they're dying. But since I'm not going back..."

He pressed the injector against her skin and tapped a button. The medibots entered her bloodstream and went immediately to work.

"When I was a kid, these were cheap. Every house had a bundle. The doses weren't watered down either."

Siv stumbled as the van made a sharp left then weaved between traffic. Kyralla almost gagged again.

"That feeling should go away soon." He placed a small square bandage against the spot where she was bleeding. The bandage expanded and knitted through her hair and onto her scalp to seal over the cut.

"This world...it must seem so broken to you," Kyralla said.

"Depressing is the word I prefer. I was frozen in a near utopia, and I woke up in a crime-ridden city with extensive poverty and failing social systems." He sighed. "The worst part was waking up without my dad...without knowing anyone, except a few distant cousins in retirement homes."

"It's my job to fix that," Oona said.

"Poverty and crime?" Siv asked.

"No, all the galaxy."

Siv shook his head and chuckled. "And how is that?"

"Well...I'm not sure...yet."

"So you're the hyperphasic messiah, but you don't really know how that works or what it means?"

"After I undergo my awakening," Oona said, "I will understand my purpose. If I survive. Many of us are born, but few reach my age. Very, very few survive the awakening. Those who do have little sanity remaining...if any."

"It's a cheery life for her," Silky mused.

"Hey, wait a second!" Oona nearly hopped out of her seat. "How do *you* know I'm a hyperphasic messiah?!"

"You wouldn't believe me," Siv replied.

"We believe a lot of things most people don't," Kyralla replied. "We haven't had a choice."

"Well, okay, but I warned you." Siv patted Kyralla on the shoulder, awkwardly, and stood. "My dad told me in a vision I had while dying and then again in a dream. He told me that there was a hyperphasic messiah on Ekaran IV and that I needed to protect her. I'm supposed to get you off-world and..." he shrugged "...take you to a priestess of some sort."

Oona's eyes flared, and she clapped her hands together. "Oh! Your guardian amulet. Did it belong to—"

"My father? He gave it to me when he was dying. It's an Ancient artifact he found, which is really all I know about it."

"He...he must have been a true guardian," Oona muttered. "And his spirit is still connected to the amulet."

"His spirit?" Siv climbed back into the driver's seat. "You're telling me my dad's soul is...is in this amulet? That's ludicrous."

"Open your mind to new possibilities," Oona said.

He stared at her dubiously.

"I don't know that it's a soul," she said. "Maybe it's more like a memory." She shrugged. "I only know what I've studied, and what I've had to work with isn't much more than speculation. I'd have to survive my awakening to tell you for certain."

"You're not like any fourteen-year-old I've ever met before."

"She didn't have a chance to be a normal girl," Kyralla replied. Her voice dropped to a whisper. "Neither of us did."

"Artemisia says Silky was your father's chippy," Oona said, "but that your father's knowledge and experiences are locked away."

"Talking behind my back, eh?"

"Sorry, sir, but it does speed things along, don't you think?"

"That's true," Siv told Oona.

Kyralla joined them, squishing into the passenger seat with Oona, who shoved back at her grouchily.

"None of this will matter if we can't escape," Kyralla said.

"We've lost the media crew for the moment, sir."

"I have a contingency plan in place for this sort of thing," Siv said.

"For kidnapping messiahs and making a run for it?" Kyralla asked with a snort.

"Mine is a strange line of work. Speaking of which... Oona, there's a compartment in front of your knees. There's a lot of stuff we don't need in there, so you'll need to dig around. But you should find several changeling veils that can be used to alter our appearances. I'll have Silky tell your chippies what to do with them. I have to warn you, they're not very good ones. They're only going to work at a distance. Up close, most anyone will realize it's a disguise."

Siv fiddled with the hardwired meltdown system on the van, getting it set just right. The system was manual because it was the sort of thing you didn't want to risk getting hacked.

Oona pulled the masks out, handing one to her sister and one to Siv. She held hers up, pinched between two fingers, looking at it as if it were dirty.

"Go ahead and put them on. I'll let you know when it's safe to take them off."

"We're nearly there, sir."

"Enable full pulse jamming when ready."

A faint, high-pitched whine emanated from his sensor pack. It made Siv's skin crawl, and he gnashed his teeth. Kyralla cringed, and Oona threw her hands over her ears.

"What the heck is that?" Kyralla asked.

"I'm jamming the spy drones following us," Siv said. "It will confuse them for... Well, it will knock any civilian drones out. The military ones won't be thrown off for long. But it should buy us the time we need."

The van careened around a corner, hit max speed, turned another almost immediately, climbed one story in altitude, and sped toward a wall. The girls cringed, but a second-floor garage door dilated open a moment before they struck. They skidded to a stop and bumped into the far wall. The door slammed shut.

It was a small, private garage space that Siv rented under an alias and had never used before.

He triggered the meltdown sequence, drew a plasma pistol out from under the seat, and leaped out of the van. "Let's go."

While both girls climbed out, Siv systematically fired plasma shots into the garage door, destroying the controls and the opening mechanisms. It would buy them another few minutes.

Using his nearly spent antigrav for a boost, he hopped up onto the van. "Follow me." He reached up and tapped a tile on the ceiling, and a trapdoor fell open.

He hoisted Oona into the next garage up. Kyralla disdained his help and crawled up on her own. He paused a moment to admire her backside.

"*Nevolence, sir! I think you have better things to focus on at a time like this.*"

"*I had to wait for her to climb up!*"

"*You wasted 1.7 seconds on admiration, sir.*"

He climbed up into the empty garage. "*Did you get a picture for me?*"

"*What am I? A peepshow pimp?*"

Siv dropped the trapdoor and took a deep breath. "*You're a good friend is what you are.*"

"I'm not another young man your age, sir. I'm not a bud or a wingman or a scout or..." Silky sighed. *"I'll preserve a video clip for you."*

"See, that wasn't so hard."

"The curse of hormones will be your undoing, sir."

Kyralla looked around. "Are we going to wait in here?"

Siv shook his head. "This is the tricky part. There's a service duct between this level and the level above us where the building turns from garages to storage and office spaces. We need to climb in there."

"Antigrav?" Oona asked.

"If you've got enough power left."

"Just barely."

"This time, I'll go first," Siv said. He jumped up, triggered the hatch, and climbed in. He turned around in the cramped tube and caught Oona's hand, helping her in. She backed away, and he helped Kyralla. Then he sealed the tube.

They crawled down the maintenance duct, going from the north side of the building where they'd entered to the south side. He opened another hatch and dropped into a garage on the opposite side of the building. He landed on an aging, wood-paneled, family sedan skimmer complete with wheels in case the antigrav engine failed.

After the others joined him, he hopped up and closed the hatch. He stepped down and gestured toward the car.

"Ladies, our ride awaits."

"It's very...homely," Oona said.

"This thing?" Kyralla remarked. "We're making a run for it in this piece of junk?"

"Don't let the exterior fool you. I switched out all the internals."

Kyralla glanced up at the ceiling and shrugged. "You went through a lot of trouble to set up an emergency escape plan. So if you say this ride will get us where we need to go, then I'll believe you."

They climbed into the car, sliding into the pleather seats. Kyralla took the passenger seat, Oona the back. It was a more than spacious ride if lacking in style.

"How long have you had all this waiting, in case something went wrong?" Kyralla asked.

"Let's see...I set this one up when I was...fifteen, I think."

"*Sixteen, sir.*"

"Back then I still thought I'd find a way to escape the Shadowslip. I learned the hard way that you don't escape their brand of Kompel. But I kept the setup in place because you never know what might happen."

"So you have several more of these?" she asked.

"Of course."

"That must take a lot of time and planning."

Siv started the skimmer, and the engines hummed to life in perfect working order. He hid his relief from them. The sedan had been sitting up untended and unused for several years.

He cringed at the sight of her face, because the mask was currently pedestrian and all too fake-seeming. "I only work a job once every month or so, because I'm one of the best. In between, I play video games, sleep, and work on ways to survive missions. Planning is what keeps me alive, and I rarely have to improvise much."

"Not good with people, are you?" Kyralla asked.

"I don't have a girlfriend," he blurted out.

Kyralla's eyebrows flexed upwardly. "Huh?"

He blushed. "I mean... Yeah, I'm awkward with people."

"So am I."

"So are *we*," Oona added. "Obviously, we don't get out much."

"Once Oona turned six, and her hair fell out, and her eyes changed, life got weird for us," Kyralla said.

"I woke up from a hundred year sleep, so I get it."

"*All clear, sir.*"

Siv eased the skimmer forward, and the doors opened.

"*Remember to drive nonchalantly, sir.*"

"Why don't you take over?"

"*Sorry, sir. But it's more believable if you man the controls, should anyone look in on us.*"

Siv lowered the skimmer casually from the third floor, turned into the street, and drove it along at a reasonable speed on a westward route that would take them out of the city and toward Wasa.

"When we were getting out of the van, you triggered something," Kyralla said.

"A meltdown."

"What's that?" Oona asked.

"It's a self-destruct, but instead of exploding there's a plasma coil on the bottom of the van that will overload and slag the whole thing, destroying any traces of DNA or other incriminating evidence. Most importantly, it will burn so hot that they won't be able to get inside the garage. They won't know where we've gone, or even if we were caught in the plasma fire."

Kyralla nodded appreciatively. "And the heat would've thrown off any infrared scans of the building, even sensitive ones."

"Plus I sent a strong jamming pulse from the van right as we left it, along with the countermeasures from my sensor pack."

"Can't those alert an enemy, though?" Kyralla asked.

"That's why I've stopped using them now. It's a careful balance to maintain. And I rely on Silky for that. Being a military chippy, he knows all about that stuff."

"A military chippy? Sounds like that's quite the story."

Kyralla yawned. Her adrenaline must have started fading, and the medibot injection did have some painkiller and sedative in it.

"I don't know as much about it as you might think. Some of that information is locked away, too. All the best of my gear..." he thought sadly of the plasma carbine he'd lost "...belonged to my father. Before him, Eyana Ora, an Empathic Services agent. Dad rescued Silky and was allowed to keep him and Eyana's gear as a reward since Silky contained highly important information. Silky had been lying around nearly two hundred years."

"That sounds dreadful!" Oona said.

"It was. I like her, sir."

"He appreciates your sympathy."

They fell quiet, lost in their thoughts or, in Kyralla's case, dozing off. The buildings shrank from skyscrapers to two-story homes and shops, and then they were zooming along the freeway out of Bei and traveling toward Wasa several hours away.

"All clear, sir. If anything's following us, then it's ridiculously advanced."

That could only mean Reapers, and the Hornets had slaughtered them. He doubted the military on Ekaran IV had any working equipment that could escape Silky's detection, and if they did, he doubted they'd had the time to deploy it.

"You can take the masks off now. Looks like it's smooth sailing now."

"Oh good," Oona said. "I don't like the masks at all. They're creepy."

Kyralla removed hers and tossed it aside. She smoothed her hair back then stared at him, her head cocked to the side.

"There's a spot where something wet's seeping through your combat mesh." She jabbed a finger toward his right side. "Just there. You're not bleeding, are you?"

Siv shook his head. "No, my vitals are all—"

He pawed at the spot, realizing what had happened. Out from a pocket, he pulled his syringe of Kompel. It must've broken when he'd crashed into the back of the van. The tube was cracked, and nearly all of the liquid had leaked out.

"Shit."

"When was the last time you had a dose?" Kyralla asked.

He placed his head in his hands and groaned. "Weeks. I always extend my time between doses for as long as I can."

"How bad's it going to be?"

"I'd rather fight a Reaper hand-to-hand than go through withdrawal."

"How soon?" she asked solemnly.

"A day or two before the shakes start...if I'm lucky."

He stared into her striking eyes. Her exquisite face creased into a sad, soft smile that made her no less beautiful.

She knew. She understood.

He'd just lost his life trying to get them to safety.

32

KARSON BISHOP

Karson Bishop was a whole day past restless. He had nothing, absolutely nothing, to do here in the single bedroom, dive apartment Siv Gendin rented as a safe house in Wasa. Neither Gendin nor the Shadowslip Guild had sent him anything to work on yet, and he couldn't remember going a single day without tinkering on several different things.

Technological design and repair was what his race had been engineered for. And he had gladly made tinkering and restoring old technology was his life's work. It was all he'd ever expected or had wanted, to do.

The grimy apartment contained only one unique device, and he had found it to be in working order and as dull as expected. But now he found himself standing in front of it again, drawn to it as he was to all old tech, even if this particular piece was exceedingly primitive.

The most frustrating thing about the device was it provided the only access he had to the outside world since Siv had warned him not to even access the galactic internet with his chippy for a few weeks, leaving him with this...this old piece of crap.

Karson sighed and touched the screen of the desktop terminal, waking it from sleep. It was an honest-to-Benevolence desktop computer with a physical display and a keyboard. A CI-99/5b, complete with access to the galactic internet and all the functions of a 4G chippy, minus the neural interface, retinal projections, and personality. The computer would be fine on a ship in space...as an emergency backup system...maybe.

Using a voice command—*out loud!*—he called up the Nile shopping site, then nearly ripped the horns off his head as it took two maddening seconds to load. Irritated and frustrated, he searched for high-end jetpacks. He found a number of them intended for casual recreation, and a few designed for racing and extreme sports. Most of the latter had inherent problems, but that didn't faze him since he planned on buying one, stripping it down, and customizing it.

"I see you finally gave in," said a sultry voice from the doorway leading to the bedroom.

Karson glanced over to his for-now roommate, Mitsuki Reel. The wakyran woman had blue skin, emerald eyes, spiky auburn hair, and a long, mostly human face. She had a muscled chest, a slender waist, and was much taller than him. Her wings were currently folded and tucked against her back. She was strikingly beautiful if a little too exotic for his tastes.

And she was wearing even less than the last time he'd seen her several hours ago when she was getting high on Minx, a safe, non-addictive, hallucinogen that enhanced feelings of arousal. The shimmery gossamer dress she'd ordered with their food shipment yesterday left little to the imagination. And now she was wearing it without undergarments.

"You have proper clothes," he said, looking away. "You should wear them."

Her tail swished languidly behind her. "Aw, are you bashful?"

"Me? No."

"A prude then?"

"No. The problem's that you're shameless."

She sauntered toward him. "My combat clothes are terribly uncomfortable, being thick and skintight and all."

"You could have ordered something comfortable and modest."

She stopped just behind him and peered over his shoulder. "This is what I normally wear around the house."

"Yeah...well..." he could feel the heat of her body "...you could've worn your underwear at least."

She touched her chest. "Oh, did I forget it?"

"You've got a roommate for a few weeks, madam. You should have considered that."

"Well, I am used to being all by myself." She trailed a finger down the side of his head and his neck. "And I do get oh so lonely."

He flinched and hopped half a step away.

She didn't follow him. Instead, she looked at the screen. "Are you shopping for me? How sweet!"

"I was scanning the jetpacks, but maybe I should order you some overalls instead."

Mitsuki laughed chirpily. "You're not going to find anything like what I had shopping on Nile."

"I can build something custom for you, something nearly as powerful and a lot smaller and lighter."

"But a big jetpack is dramatic!"

"I could paint it bright red with gold flames."

Mitsuki laughed again. "You're funny, little gizmet."

He glanced over and took in too much of her form to be comfortable. Not that it wasn't worth seeing. His entire body flushed. And... he smelled something similar to lavender and cloves. Was she wearing some sort of pheromone perfume? He shook his head. It was getting very hard to think clearly.

She seemed to sense his discomfort and backed away. "So, how's it going? Feeling recovered?"

"Yes, but...um...this terminal is driving me crazy. It's sooooo slow. I can't believe Siv collects these things."

"Collects them?"

"CI-99/5b's. They're antiques. And you know, the only reason they exist is because Luddite communities have used them for centuries."

"Oh, Karson. He doesn't collect them. He uses this as a secure terminal. Have you taken a look inside?"

"No, it works, so why should I?"

"I think you should look inside. Criminals like Siv and me, we use these things sometimes because we can modify them with device add-ons that work with software to enhance security and protect our interactions. It's much more secure than using your chippy or a c|slate. I'd tell you what goes into all that, but it's not my thing. I buy mine from the Shadowslip and then have Siv and Silky remove the guild's spyware for me."

"So tech isn't your thing..."

"I fly hard, and I fly fast. I get people out of tricky situations. That's my job. And I'm really good at it." She leaned in and whispered in his ear. "It's not the only thing I'm good at."

He gulped and didn't ask what the other thing was. He had a pretty good idea. He shut down the terminal, then opened it up, finding a lot more miniaturized electrical components than he had expected.

"Oh," she pouted, "I shouldn't have told you that. Now you're not going to pay me any attention."

Karson smiled. It was hard not to pay her attention. She demanded it almost constantly. It was both grating and endearing, though he had a feeling over the next few weeks grating was going to squash endearing.

Mitsuki sauntered over toward the couch. Karson glanced back, saw a little more leg than he wanted...or rather *should*...have seen then looked back to the components.

"Karson?"

He turned. She was sprawled across the couch, looking bored. "Wouldn't you rather play with me?"

Blushing, he uttered an utterly nonsensical reply.

"What's that dear, I couldn't understand you?"

"I...I don't think...I've never...I mean...I never. And you and I...we are...different and...I don't think I should...get...um, distracted."

She twisted her lips into a pout. "You know, Siv owes me for getting you out. And he said that *you* would pay the extra that I demand."

"I don't have any money."

"It's not money that I want. I have needs."

"Oh! Um...well..."

Mitsuki shot up suddenly, her spine rigid, her face tense, her eyes alert. "Karson, my chippy just got pinged by an unnamed source. Turn the terminal back on."

The device booted up, taking a nauseating three seconds. An app window popped up on the screen. Green text scrolled across a black background. "Bishop...Mitsuki...are you alone?"

Karson shrugged then typed his response. "Yes."

Mitsuki slapped him on the shoulder. "You should have asked who it was first and then attempted to verify."

"Oh, sorry!"

"Open up an app called Antique Calculator and ask him for an equation."

What followed was a long string of numbers, letters, and symbols. Karson tried to copy and paste them over, but that didn't work. He typed them all, double-checking that he'd entered them correctly. The answer it gave him was 111.

"That's him. Reply with 222."

Karson did, and a moment later, Siv's face popped up onto the screen. He was riding in a skimmer of some sort, zooming down the freeway, the countryside flashing by.

"Bishop," he said. "Mitsuki."

Siv's eyes drooped with exhaustion, yet there was something apprehensive about his voice and movements.

"I take it you're signal jamming on your end?" Mitsuki said.

Siv nodded. "Did you check the apartment?"

"All good," Mitsuki said. "By the way, you did a great job shielding this place."

"Thanks."

"You know, she nearly killed me," Karson said. "We combed this place over for an hour as soon as we got here, even though I desperately needed rest."

"You can never be too careful," Mitsuki said.

"You haven't seen the sorts of things he makes," Siv said, "or else you'd understand he doesn't know the concept."

"Oh," she clapped her hands together, "then he *is* just the person to build my new jetpack."

"Mitsuki," Siv said earnestly. "I just saw your breasts bounce."

"Oh, Siv, you little devil."

"No, I mean *I saw them*. Put some clothes on. You're going to give Mr. Bishop a heart attack."

Mitsuki blew a raspberry at him.

Karson snorted. "What do you need?"

"Help, and a lot of it."

"I'll do my best," Mitsuki said.

"We both will," Karson added.

"Are you being watched?" Siv asked.

"I don't think so," Karson replied.

"Not regularly," Mitsuki answered. "But the pizza cog and the grocery delivery guy are both Shadowslip agents keeping tabs on us."

"They are?" Karson asked in surprise. "Even the cog?"

"The cog's more a tool than an agent," Mitsuki replied, "but yes."

"When was the last delivery?" Siv asked.

"Groceries and supplies last night," Karson responded. "Pizza an hour ago."

"Good," Siv replied. "Chances are you won't be spotted leaving, unless they have a dormant spy drone outside, waiting to be activated by motion detection." He chewed his lip, then shrugged. "We should assume they do. Mitsuki, behind the mirror in the bathroom, you'll find a neural disruptor and a pulse resonator that should scramble any nearby drones."

As Siv turned his head slightly, Karson spotted someone in the backseat behind Siv. It appeared to be a young human girl with a bald head. What the heck was going on?

"Are we running from Tekk Reapers or the Shadowslip or both?" Karson asked.

"The Reapers aren't a threat at the moment," Siv responded. "I just destroyed their starship and three skimmers full of them."

"You—you—what?!" Karson responded.

"Siv, are you high?" Mitsuki asked.

"No, and it's true."

"Spank me rotten!" Mitsuki exclaimed. "There's no way you did that. Just no way."

"Sorry, *Silky* took out the starship and the skimmers."

"Yeah, okay, I'll buy that," Mitsuki responded. "So why are we running from the Shadowslip?"

"Well, they don't know it yet, and probably won't for a couple of days, but I've crossed them—and bad. Some other incredibly dangerous groups are going to be after me too. I'm on the run with a couple of...let's say fugitives for now. I desperately need help. And there's no one else I can trust."

"Siv," Mitsuki said, "when you said other groups..."

"The Star Cutters, World Bleeders, and agents from the Empire of a Thousand Worlds."

"Tits of the 'Nevolence!" Mitsuki cursed.

Karson cringed at hearing such blasphemy. He shook his head. Two days. This was how much trouble Gendin could get into in two days?

"I know it's a hell of a lot to ask," Siv said.

Karson's mind reeled. He'd just gotten some stability back into his life, however tenuous, by working for the guild. If he crossed them, he'd be a wanted man on several fronts. On the other hand, he owed Siv for saving him from the Tekk Reapers and getting him this far. Still, this was a lot to ask.

"Sivvy," Mitsuki said, "you know I like you a lot. And I've always been soft on you, giving you sweetheart extraction deals and advice. But I'm an independent contractor. I can turn a blind eye and say I've no idea what you're up to, but I can't go against the Shadowslip. There's no incentive, and it would end my career."

"I know, but I'm afraid they're going to come looking for you because of me, at first anyway. So bare minimum, I need to sneak you out of there. If you don't want to help me, then once things settle down, you can return to your old life. You will know when it's safe to do so."

There was a finality in Siv's voice on that last statement that unsettled Karson. "What about me?"

Siv frowned. "Maybe they'd take you back, too, especially if Mitsuki vouched for you and told them you'd had no part in helping me."

"Siv, what the hell have you gotten yourself into?" Mitsuki asked. "You're scaring me."

"I'm asking because things are that bad," Siv said softly. "And it's important."

"Start explaining."

"There's a young girl here who's...special. I was hired to kidnap her, but instead, I rescued her. She and her sister are being chased by every criminal element out there, even the Empire of a Thousand Worlds. And I know you wouldn't betray them or me for any amount of money."

"Come on," Mitsuki said, "are you really going to throw your career away over a little girl?"

"Look, Mits, I'm not going back to the Shadowslip. And...and I'm out of Kompel. I'll start withdrawal soon. But I'm going to get these girls to their father if it... Well, it *is* going to kill me."

Karson's breath caught. Gendin was really going to give his life up for these girls he'd just met? Karson had never, never in his life been a *bad* person. But he wasn't a *good* person. He was indulgent in his hobbies and work. He crossed some lines, and his ethics were more flexible than reasonable. To lay down his life for someone... Maybe in the heat of the moment, but he wasn't sure he was capable of doing it with such forethought, knowing he risked death, and an unpleasant one at that.

Mitsuki stared at Siv dumfounded, tears welling in her eyes. "Oh, Siv... What are you thinking? I don't understand. I just don't understand why you'd do something like this."

Siv's face showed no sign of fear. "I'm doing what I must."

Another voice in the skimmer car said something, but Karson couldn't make out what they said. Siv shifted the camera view over to show the bald girl in the backseat.

"This is who I'm helping."

Karson stared at her sculpted, elfish face then met her black eyes. Something stirred within him. He had never encountered such beauty before. It wasn't attraction he felt, but the awe that struck whenever he stared up into the vast, starlit sky, knowing there were trillions upon trillions of worlds and people out there while he was but a single little man with simple hopes and dreams.

The girl, who couldn't be more than fourteen, waved a hand. "Hi, I'm Oona."

"She's a hyperphasic messiah," Siv said.

"Sweet Benevolence," Karson whispered.

"It's true," the girl said.

He fell to his knees, overcome with emotion. He touched a hand to his heart, his forehead, and his lips. "Sweet Benevolence."

Karson had never been religious, though he'd studied religion. And he had never been selfless, though he liked the idea. Now suddenly and surprisingly, here he was in the presence of a hyperphasic messiah, and she needed his help. For the first time, he found himself utterly devoted to a cause.

Karson did not doubt the girl or Siv. Oona was precisely what she claimed. He *knew* it in his heart. And what else could he do but devote himself to her? He was a gizmet, talented in tech and raised with a devotion toward its recovery. There was nothing more sacred than restoring what they had all once had, that's what his parents had taught him. And a hyperphasic messiah could bring it *all* back. She could return the Benevolence to the galaxy.

"Whatever you need, Oona, I will do." He bowed his head. "My life is yours."

33

MITSUKI REEL

Mitsuki stared agape at Karson, kneeling and pledging his devotion to a supposedly magical teenage girl he had never met before. This abrupt stirring of emotion and religiosity was nothing short of perplexing. What Karson and Siv felt, she did not feel, not in the slightest. And she never would. Of that, she was certain.

A messiah was supposed to be some sort of galactic savior, according to the Thousand World faithful and the various cults like the Tekk Reapers that ran around preaching a resurrection of the Benevolence. To her, that was nothing more than a stinking pile of mystic doo-doo used to manipulate the ignorant, the disenfranchised, and those too hopeful and too imaginative for their own good.

Mitsuki didn't believe in gods, spirits, or a divine source for the Benevolence. Her self-righteous father had devoted himself to such things, and he had raised her to believe all kinds of nonsense. He even moved them to Saxeti, the Empire of a Thousand Worlds home planet, to be closer to the 'heart of the religion.' She rejected that life and those beliefs the day she was finally old enough to run away from home.

Who was this girl anyway? Was she supposed to have some kind of claim to Qaisella Qan's throne? A bright messiah to replace the dark one who currently ruled the Thousand Worlds? It wouldn't be hard. Qaisella Qan might call herself the Glorious Messiah, Empress of a Thousand Worlds, but there was a reason the Terran Federation had nicknamed her the Dark Messiah.

Mitsuki grew up in the Empire. She knew far too well the heavy hands of fascism and theocracy. She had watched as her mother was thrown into a death camp for disavowing the Glorious Messiah. She had watched her father do nothing about it. She had watched him turn his back on his wife and pin his young daughter to his chest to stop her from attacking the soldiers. She had heard him say that their glorious ruler knew best.

Even *if* this girl were divine, why would she pop up on a backwater planet like Ekaran IV, and why now? Mitsuki didn't buy it, not one bit. And she couldn't believe level-headed Siv would fall for such a load of religious mumbo jumbo.

Of course, with all these groups after the girl...there had to be *something* to it. She probably had a flashy, unusual talent that marked her as unique, and therefor messiah-label worthy. The underworld would want the girl so they could sell her off to some wealthy, misguided soul like Karson. And the Thousand Worlders... they would want to vanish any competitors to their own glorious empress.

Mitsuki's eyes drifted to Siv. She'd always liked him. He was only two years younger than her, and they'd risen through the thieving ranks together. While they weren't best friends or anything-professional criminals couldn't afford such a luxury-they had spent many hours discussing strategies and whatnot over drinks at many dive bars.

The idea of Siv dying, and in such a terrible fashion, was heartbreaking. But to ask this of her... To ask her to give up *her* life, too... And for a girl claiming she was a god?

It was absolutely absurd.

Tears streamed down Bishop's face. He was so overwhelmed he

was actually trembling. And Siv...he had this determined look in his eyes. She'd never seen anything like it in him before.

"Siv..." Mitsuki whispered "...I don't know what..."

Overcome with emotion herself, but of a different kind, Mitsuki ran to the bathroom. She splashed water on her face and took several deep breaths. She couldn't believe this was happening.

She cared deeply for Siv. And the gizmet...she found herself growing fond of him. But what they were doing... It was like they were suddenly new people. Why? Why had they become so irrational? She shook her head. It didn't make any sense.

Mitsuki looked into the mirror and saw what she expected, the Mitsuki she'd been since the day she'd run away from Saxeti. The strong, exotic, seemingly confident girl with wings. A girl with a unique gift for extracting others from dangerous situations.

It was what she did, and she was damned good at it, too. She never would've made it to Ekaran IV otherwise. She was the best extraction agent in the business, and that wasn't bragging. It was fact. She'd never been caught, and she'd never failed an extraction. Crashing into the lake carrying both Siv and Karson was the closest she'd ever come to failure. That they survived at all, given the difficulty of the extraction, was impressive. Extractions almost never involved saving more than one agent, much less catching two of them a second before they splatted onto the street, while the police were in pursuit.

When it came to extraction, she *owned* this city. She owned this whole planet. Every criminal guild on Ekaran IV had attempted to hire her away. Even guilds in nearby star systems had sought her services. But Bei was the first city on the first planet she had safely reached after she'd escaped, and so she had a soft spot for it.

But maybe it was time to move on...time for a challenge.

Extracting Siv and Karson was the first truly difficult extraction she'd tackled in the last three years. Getting these girls off the planet, though...with one of them wanted by every criminal organization, plus the Empire, plus Tekk Reapers...while Tekk Reapers were already looking for her and Karson. Now *that* would be nearly impossible. And that made it tempting. If she failed... Well, she'd find a way to get herself out of whatever mess she ended up in. She always did, she always would.

Besides, she owed this to Siv, surely. And Bishop, that poor, cute little gizmet. He'd be lucky if he could find his way out of this neighborhood without getting mugged. Without her, he was screwed.

She stared at herself in the mirror. This time she saw her brave, beautiful mother in her own face. Who *are* you, Mitsuki? Why have you chosen this path? Sure, it's nice being the best and everyone knowing it. That's not why she'd fought so hard to escape the Imperial stronghold, though. True, criminals got themselves into exciting situations. But, other than Siv, she didn't actually care about them. They just gave her an excuse to help people escape. They fed her need.

You know why you take the risk, why you have to prove again and again that you can get out of anything, she admitted to herself. From the time Mother was dragged away to the time you escaped, you dreamed and wished that someone would extract you from the hell of Saxeti.

"You can go through life thinking you know who you are, and then in an instant, you find yourself someone else, and the person you had been... Well, there wasn't much to her anyway."

Her mother had told her that...only a week before she had publicly denounced the Dark Messiah to a crowd of hundreds, preaching tolerance and a return to faith in humanity and scientific reasoning.

This girl...Oona... What she was or claimed to be didn't matter. The important thing was that she didn't deserve to be kidnapped and auctioned off by criminals. She especially didn't deserve to be captured by Tekk Reapers or agents from the Empire, to suffer whatever tortures they concocted in the name of their religions. She deserved to be with those who loved her, to have the chance to become whomever she wanted to be, to do what she wanted. She deserved freedom.

Mitsuki took a deep breath, then marched slowly back into the living room, hardly feeling like herself. She stopped and faced the screen. Siv had waited on her. Smug bastard, he knew...he knew she'd come around.

She put a hand down and rubbed Bishop's head between his upward-curling horns. He perked up a little at her touch.

"You're going to need a damn good extraction agent, Gendin."

"The best," he replied with a tired smile.

"This is going to cost you *a lot*."

"I'm afraid I won't be around to pay you."

"You can pay in advance then. Just have Silky forward me your bank account numbers. And you know what else I'll need in return if you've got time for it before you croak..."

Siv laughed. "You got it." His smile faded. "Mits, I can't thank you enough."

"I reserve the right to bail on you if it all turns to buzzard shit."

"Naturally."

"I'm not doing this because you claim the girl's special. I'm doing it because no girl should be kidnapped by evil men."

"I understand, Mits."

She sighed. That was that. She was committed.

"So what do you need us to do?" she asked.

"Go to the bedroom and move the cabinet. Behind it, you'll find a secret door that leads into the two-level apartment next door. I own that one as well, but under a different identity. Go there and take the exit onto the street at precisely 19:30. We'll pick you up."

"You got it," Mitsuki said. "Be careful, Gendin."

"You, too," he replied. "Oh, Silky wants me to remind you to use the pulse device to fry any nearby drones before you exit the building."

Mitsuki narrowed her eyes. "Silkster, I'm not an idiot."

"I won't repeat his response."

Siv's face and the comm window disappeared.

For a moment, Mitsuki stared at her faint reflection in the computer screen. *Who am I?*

A smile lit up her face. *I am Mitsuki Reel, the best damned extraction agent in the business. And I'm about to prove it.*

Again.

34

SIV GENDIN

The skimmer car, under Silky's guidance, zoomed into Wasa and slowed down to match the speed of the surrounding traffic. They were quickly swallowed up by a forest of dainty, elaborate towers decked in arrays of neon signs and flickering lights. Where Bei was sophisticated and subdued, Wasa was a glimmering jewel...if a bit gaudy for Siv tastes.

"I don't like including more criminals in our escape," Kyralla said, "especially the one with wings."

"Mitsuki is good people...deep down," Siv replied. "And you need her help. Yes, she's a flake. Yes, she's a bit...eccentric. But she really is the best. I promise."

"I can handle this all on my own, you know. I was trained for this."

"So you've said, many times already."

"More people means more complications. More chances that someone will betray us."

Siv sighed. "Kyralla, I'm the best procurement specialist in this city, and Mitsuki has had to rescue me several times in the last seven years. Things go wrong. Everyone needs help sometimes. There's no shame in that."

"Maybe so," she replied sulkily, "but I don't trust her."

"Well, I do." He paused, not sure if saying the thought that had just popped into his head would convince her or just piss her off. "And you should listen to me because I'm a guardian, too."

"You're not a full guardian," she said, "and you don't even know what the term means."

"It means I'm supposed to...guard someone?" he replied sheepishly.

She stared daggers at him.

"Being a guardian," Oona said, "involves taking an oath and experiencing an awakening."

"Like you're supposed to?" he asked, surprised.

"I went through the first awakening when my hair fall out, though some have named that the *calling*. The second awakening is the big one, the one I may not survive. But for a guardian it's not as dangerous," Oona said, "or as complicated. And no one is born a guardian. You have to be chosen and accept it. And, of course, you must survive your awakening."

"I volunteered," Kyralla said.

"Then how come I'm a guardian?" he asked. "No one chose me, and I didn't undergo an awakening—not that I know of anyway."

"I think when your father gave you the amulet he passed the responsibility on to you," Oona said, "although he may not have known what he was doing. That's just my best guess though because your amulet is active even though you haven't had an awakening yet."

"How do you know I haven't?" Siv asked.

"Just a sense I have," Oona replied. "I don't know how to explain it. Besides, if you had, you would have an extraordinary talent, like Kyralla does."

Siv turned to Kyralla. His eyes met hers, and for a moment words escaped him. "You never..." the image of her naked, having just come from the shower flashed in his mind "...you never told me..."

"Focus, sir. Stay on target."

Siv recovered his composure. "You never told me you had a special ability."

Kyralla sighed. "If my mind is in the moment, then I can see things a split second before they happen."

"You can see the future?" he asked incredulously.

"Yes, but the farthest into the future I have ever managed was just over a second. It's not enough to correct mistakes or make a fortune in the markets. It's just enough to—"

Siv was sitting a little over a meter away from her. Without provocation, without telegraphing his intention in any way, he flashed his hand out toward her, intending to tap her on the cheek.

She caught his hand and, with a devilish smile, shoved it away.

"Not bad," Siv said. "Could just be extraordinary reflexes, though, couldn't it?"

From the backseat, Oona tossed a bracelet toward the back of Kyralla's head. Kyralla spun and caught it before it reached her.

"Okay, I'm officially in lo—" Siv caught himself. "Impressed."

"Smooth, sir."

Kyralla cocked an eyebrow and stared at him quizzically.

"Plugged into a ship command circlet, she'd make a hell of a pilot, sir."

"So," Siv said, turning to face Oona again, "do you think my dad was a proper guardian?"

Oona shrugged. "How did he get the amulet?"

"From an archaeological expedition."

"Any details you're keeping from me? Cause this would be a good time to come clean."

"None on purpose, sir."

"Someone like me would've had to make him a guardian, though it's not as if we really understand the process," Oona said. "If the lore is correct, there were no messiahs before the fall of the Benevolence. But we know so little, and most of that is conjecture."

"*That girl is sooooo much more mature than you were at fourteen, sir.*"

"*Well, she'd have to be, wouldn't she?*"

Kyralla twirled her metal amulet between her fingers. "Oona made mine. She took a small, blank piece of metal and...shaped it... with her mind, every curve and bit of intricate design. I would say it was amazing to watch her do it, but it was actually incredibly boring."

Oona nodded. "It required many weeks of meditation."

"*Seems preposterous to me, sir. I can't think of any scientific explanation for such a gift.*"

"*Maybe there are things we don't know yet, or have forgotten...or were never told.*"

"So you don't know anything else about your amulet?" Kyralla asked. She reached a hand out. "May I?"

Siv hesitated, then nodded. He pulled the amulet from around his neck and handed it to her. He couldn't ever remember even letting someone else see the amulet, much less touch it. She took it, and he shifted nervously in his seat.

She ran her fingers across the engraved, white square. "What material is this? I thought it was ceramic at first, but it feels...odd somehow."

"Silky has been analyzing it for decades," Siv replied, "and he has no idea. We've decided it's some sort of advanced ceramic the Ancients used." He shrugged. "I might know more if I asked a scientist to study it, but...I rarely let anyone see it. The amulet is my most treasured possession. And you...you are the first person to handle it other than me since...since my dad gave it to me as he died."

Kyralla smiled tenderly. "I'm honored you trust me so."

Siv blushed and muttered a broken phrase that bordered on "you're welcome."

"May I?" Oona asked eagerly.

"Of course," Siv said.

She took it in her hands, and immediately it glowed a faint red.

She squeezed it between her palms and closed her eyes. After several moments, she returned it to him.

Siv hung it around his neck and sighed with relief. "Did you learn anything?"

"Not anything that I didn't already know," Oona said. "And there's nothing else you can tell me about it?"

"All I know is that it's an Ancient artifact, and there's no record of another like it ever having been found."

"Mysteries all the way down," Oona said with a sigh.

The skimmer car pulled into the neighborhood with the safe house where Bishop and Mitsuki were waiting for them.

"So, do you have a plan?" Kyralla asked.

"Get everyone to another safe house, have a meal, get some sleep, then come up with a plan to get you off the planet."

"In other words, you don't actually have a plan," she responded.

"And you do?" he asked.

She started to reply, but the words died on her lips.

"That's what I thought. You're tired, you're hungry, and you're frustrated."

"Scared more like it, sir."

"I'm trying not to set her off."

"After you get some food and rest, you'll have a better perspective on this mess," Siv told her. "Getting off a planet when you're hunted isn't easy. You can't just buy a ticket on a commercial flight, and hopping on as stowaways is dangerous for multiple reasons. You don't just need a plan. You need the right one, and it needs to be as airtight as possible. That's where Mitsuki comes in."

"And why would she know how to do it?" Kyralla asked.

"Because she's done it before," Siv answered. "She escaped from Saxeti and made her way here."

The girls fell into a stunned silence as the car pulled to a stop in front of the apartment where Mitsuki and Bishop were meeting them.

"She's a Thousand Worlder?!" Kyralla said in a sudden outburst. "You said we could trust her!"

"You're going to judge her by the place where she came from?"

"We have far more enemies than friends," Kyralla said. "And that will always be true. So yes, I'm going to prejudge her. That seems more than sensible to me."

The apartment door opened. Bishop and Mitsuki rushed out, darted across the sidewalk, and headed toward the car.

"Why do you trust her?" Oona asked quietly.

"You'll have to ask her yourself," Siv said.

Bishop hopped into the backseat, and Mitsuki slid in beside him. Siv closed the doors, and Silky hit the accelerator.

"Why did you run away from Saxeti?" Oona immediately asked Mitsuki innocently.

"What the hell, Gendin?" Mitsuki responded.

"In the process of vouching for you I told them you had escaped another world before, and I mentioned which world, and that raised some questions of trust."

Mitsuki groaned. She turned to the girl and started to speak, but Oona raised her hands suddenly, with a frown on her face.

"No, don't tell me," Oona said. "I can see it clearly enough in your eyes. I trust you."

Kyralla turned to her sister. "Are you sure?"

Oona nodded. "I have no doubts."

"I'm starting to have some," Mitsuki said irritably.

"Are you going to grumble the whole time?" Siv asked.

"If I like," she answered.

"Well, it's a good thing I'm not going to live through all of it."

Everyone in the car fell into a depressed silence.

"Way to lighten the mood, sir."

"Just take us to the safe house, Silkster."

35

SIV GENDIN

The skimmer car pulled into the driveway of a picturesque farm-house fifteen kilometers northwest of Wasa. Well-maintained herb gardens cradled the stone cottage. The house and gardens sat like a gem in the center of an expansive, somewhat wild, zii fruit orchard. The tree limbs sagged with plump, pink fruits.

Out of all of Siv's safe houses, this one was by far his favorite. And not just because it wasn't a dive apartment in a seedy part of town. He always tried to spend a few weeks here this time of year. You could replicate zii fruit all you wanted, but it just wasn't quite the same as eating them straight from the tree.

The back deck of the cottage provided a perfect view of the Western Mountains, from the forested foothills to the dark gray base of the range and the snowcaps on the high peaks. The sun had only just dipped below the ridges, casting the area in a growing shadow.

Siv took a deep breath and felt a sense of calm contentment. He loved those mountains and this farmhouse. This would be a good place to die.

"It's gorgeous here, Sivvy," Mitsuki said. "I can't believe you never brought me out here before."

"This is where I go when I want to get away from everything," Siv replied. "But...I don't come out here as often as I should. It's hard to leave the city sometimes."

"How do you keep the property up?" Bishop asked.

After an awkward hello and bow to Oona, the gizmet had lapsed into silence. He seemed awestruck in her presence. Siv hadn't expected Oona to inspire such devotion in Bishop. Hopefully, though, he was starting to adjust and come out of his shell. Siv needed Bishop to be an active and vocal part of the team. They were going to need his skills sooner or later, especially once Siv was unable to help them.

"Keeping this place up is easy," Siv said. "I have help."

"*More* people we have to trust?" Kyralla said with irritation.

"Not at all," Siv replied.

The car parked in a garage to the side of the cottage. As the door closed behind them, everyone climbed stiffly out of the car and stretched. A bleeping sounded, along with the click of awkward legs, and the rattle and grind of old joints.

Siv's caretaker cog opened the door leading into the house and greeted Siv with a pleasant buzz and bloop.

"Seneca, it's good to see you, old friend."

Seneca was basically human in shape, though his limbs were a little long and thin, his body oddly bulbous, his feet broad, and his hands seven-fingered. An eye-band circled all the way around his narrow head. Lights glinted within the eye-band as he continually glanced around, so much so that you would've thought he was designed to be a sentry cog. Yet despite his awkward proportions, he had a refined elegance about him, due to his classic, shiny black-and-white paint job and his manners which were exceedingly precise and perfect, even by the standards of a machine.

The cog responded with several, polite questioning bloops.

"Please don't make me translate, sir."

"These are guests of mine, Seneca. They will be staying here with us for...well, several days at least."

Bishop darted forward and bounced around the cog, examining it thoroughly. Then he whistled. "Gendin, he's a beaut. Where on earth did you find him? How could you afford him? Does he—"

Siv held his hands up. "Slow down! He wasn't nearly as expensive as you might imagine. Seneca's core programming and memory banks were corrupted, and his vocalizer was fried. Silky was able to fix the programming, and I didn't care about fixing the vocalizer. I did have to buy some pricey new memory banks, though."

Caretaker, nanny, and entertainment cogs, those that survived the Tekk Plague, had been primarily scrapped for parts or repurposed to make up for the sudden shortage of the worker cogs required for manufacturing, space repairs, and other dangerous or difficult jobs deemed unsuitable for humans. No one needed "luxury" cogs anymore, so they were rare and expensive. Siv, however, missing the days of his youth, had acquired a collection.

"Bishop, you're going to love it here. I have thirty broken cogs stored in the basement. Most are in bad shape, but a few are almost functional. I just don't have the skill to properly fix them."

Bishop's eyes flared wide. "Why didn't you send me here first?!"

Siv laughed. "Because the Shadowslip doesn't know about this place, and I wanted to keep it that way. It isn't easy to sneak out here. And until now, I've tried to keep this house all to myself."

They followed Seneca into the main room of the cottage, which was decorated in a cozy, outdoorsy style.

"Are you sure they don't know about it?" Kyralla asked.

"As sure as I can be. They don't normally keep tabs on me since the Kompel ensures my cooperation. I tried to run away once, and it backfired."

"You're about to bring the mood down again, sir."

"Thanks, Silkster."

Seneca gestured and trilled at them.

"What's he saying?" Oona asked.

"Your chippy can't translate?" Siv asked.

They all shook their heads.

"You forgot, sir. Seneca speaks Tellit, not basic."

"Oh, right. Seneca is...a bit abnormal because of changes necessary to fix his core programming, without having to scrap it altogether. He can only speak in a rare language designed on base-thirteen accounting and rhyming slang. It's...it's a long story. Suffice to say, he was acquired from the ruins of an old criminal guild's headquarters on a strange, non-human planet. Silky will send your chippies the translation data you need, though I think you could get used to his gestures quickly. Silky never translates for me anymore. He finds it tedious."

"You grew up surrounded by cogs like this, didn't you?" Oona asked.

"Cogs of all manner, advanced chippies, c|slates of every type... clean streets and everything in order. I miss nearly all of it, except... Well, it's strange, but I sort of prefer the dirty streets and *some* of the inefficiencies. As much as I loved the golden age I was born into, I like how this new era is more human and a little messy around the edges."

Seneca went to the kitchen to retrieve snacks and start the preparations for dinner. The food replicator could have meals out in short order, but Seneca believed in proper presentation and a particular order to how the food should be served.

"I'd put in a food request right away," Siv told them. "Otherwise, you will get what Seneca thinks is best. And like I said, he's an odd one."

The others wandered around the farmhouse, winding their way through the kitchen, living room, and three bedrooms, eventually ending up out on the back porch. Siv quietly left them there and retreated down into the basement.

He passed by his collection of cogs and other pieces of lost technology. The scents of oil, metal, and electronics filled his nostrils with memories of another place and time. Usually, this brought a wistful, nostalgic smile to his face. Sadly, not this time. With only one of the lights activated, he sat down in a shadowy, far corner and wrapped his arms around his legs.

The tremors began.

"I noticed the spike in your vitals ten minutes ago, sir. You've done admirably holding it together for so long."

Siv nodded physically, or maybe it was the first convulsion hitting him. Waves of pain radiated through his body. Tears streamed down his cheeks. He took deep breaths, as best as he could, and focused his mind on the amulet on his chest.

"At least before dying, I got to be part of something more than the Shadowslip...something important."

"Your father would be proud of you, sir."

As he began to enter a stupor, Siv thought of his father, of Oona, of the mountains, and the wastelands beyond...

"Siv, can you hear me? Son, open your mind to me. We must speak. It is urgent!"

Siv opened his eyes, and there in the basement with him, amidst the coils of wire, boxes of parts, and the lineup of broken cogs stood his father —not in the flesh, but a ghostly, shimmering image, faintly blue in color.

"Dad? How...how is this possible?"

"I don't have the time to explain it. Son, you must—"

"Sivvy?" Mitsuki called. "Are you down here?"

The ghost of his father disappeared as the others, led by Mitsuki, traipsed down into the basement. The waves of pain had subsided, along with the tremors. The amulet on his chest had begun to cool.

"Silkster, did you see my dad?"

"No, sir. I'm sure it must've been a withdrawal symptom... Although, I did register a temperature spike in the amulet."

"I think my dad's trying to communicate with me, through the amulet."

"Why now, after all these years, sir? All those nights you cried after you...defrosted...when you were so desperate for comfort—why didn't he come to you then?"

Siv stood and walked, on shaky legs, toward the others. *"Maybe it has something to do with Oona's awakening?"*

"Perhaps, sir. Your vitals are returning to normal. Based on the severity of the symptoms and the speed of onset, I'm estimating at least two hours before the next wave."

The waves would get more intense and more frequent over the next twenty-four hours. Within three days, he'd practically be useless. Within a week, he'd be dead.

"There you are," Mitsuki said. "Why were you hiding down—" Mitsuki closed her eyes, wincing. "How bad was it?"

Kyralla observed him, a worried frown on her face. There was no point in lying or trying to brush it aside.

"Not bad...yet. Just the first wave."

Mitsuki sighed. "I told you not to go so long between doses, didn't I? What was the point?"

"If I hadn't built up my stamina, I would've already folded by now."

The look on Mitsuki's face made it clear she thought his answer was crap. And maybe it was. The truth was he put as much time as possible between doses because he hated taking the Kompel, hated depending on it, and always wanted to stretch out the inevitable for as long as possible as if pretending he didn't have to take it for a week somehow made a difference.

"How much time do you have left?" Kyralla asked in a whisper.

"A few days before I'm useless...then just a few more till...death."

Oona flipped on the rest of the lights just as Bishop made it down the stairs. Bright overheads illuminated the room, and spotlights focused attention on the nonfunctioning cogs.

"Sweet Benevolence and everything that's good, holy, bad, or evil in this world!" Bishop exclaimed. "I'm never leaving this basement!"

He ran through the room, spinning as he did to get a good look at the cogs lined up along the walls. His face beamed like a supernova, and he giggled like an idiot. It was like watching a kid getting every present he could ever want on a single Benevolence Day.

A series of trills and beeps sounded at the top of the stairs. Dinner was ready.

"Could Seneca bring my food down here?" Bishop asked.

"Nope, you're eating with everyone else," Mitsuki said.

"Who made you the boss?" Bishop complained.

"I'm in charge of getting these girls off-world, and we need to start planning right away, while Siv can still help."

"She's right," Siv told him. "You can come down here afterward."

Pouting, Bishop nodded and trudged upstairs along with all the others, save Oona.

She peered at Siv with her intense, black eyes. "You saw your dad again, didn't you?"

"How did you know?"

"I sensed a presence here with us."

"So maybe it's real, after all."

"I believe so."

"Silky couldn't see him, and he disappeared when Mitsuki came down, calling to me."

"If your chippy cannot see him, then it must be something mystical or extrasensory in nature. I'm sorry we broke your concentration."

Siv shrugged. "I might have lost him anyway. I can't seem to hold the connection for long."

Oona took his hands. "Siv, I don't want you to suffer."

"Thanks. I don't either. But there's really nothing that can be done. And I *am* going to die. You understand that, right?"

"I do," she said with a nod. "Don't forget that I'm likely going to die too, during my awakening." She released his hands and shrugged. "But you know, perhaps death isn't the end we thought. You should ask your dad about that when you see him again."

"*If* I see him again," Siv responded.

"I'm confident you will," Oona said. "He seems to come to you whenever you approach death."

36

SIV GENDIN

Hardly anyone spoke as they ate, except to comment on the quality of the food. They were all too tired or preoccupied for much else. But at least the food was excellent. The caretaker cog could perform absolute wonders with a nutrient block. After an appetizer and two main courses, Seneca served homemade zii fruit cobbler. Siv realized with a twinge of regret that, with everything that had happened, the girls wouldn't be able to fully appreciate the treat. It was his favorite.

Kyralla might be remarkably strong and brave, and Oona almost zen-like, but the attack on them and the betrayal and subsequent death of their uncle would soon hit them like a hammer to the heart. Siv understood all too well. You could put the pain and turmoil out of mind for a while, but it would catch up with you—sooner rather than later. It always did.

He considered not discussing business now, while everyone was exhausted, but he wasn't going to have many more opportunities to help them out. He pushed his empty cobbler bowl away with a sigh. Seneca swept in and politely removed it.

"So, we need to discuss our options."

"We need a starship, right?" Kyralla asked. "That much seems obvious."

Mitsuki shrugged. "That depends. Would it be better to hide out here and wait for your father? Or would it be better to run from your enemies and into space to meet him? The first option risks you being found here while waiting. The second option presents difficult hurdles: getting a starship with a captain you can trust and risking being caught in space. There are fewer avenues of escape in space unless you have a fast ship and a good pilot."

"I would prefer space," Kyralla said. "I don't like sitting here, and..."

"You're worried your father won't be able to make it back here safely?" Siv asked. "Or, at least, not without attracting unwanted attention?"

Kyralla nodded.

Mitsuki's eyes met Siv's. She was thinking the same thing he was: that either their father was dead or that people were watching him already, hoping he would lead them to Oona.

"They need a starship, Mits. Their uncle betrayed them. Their location was known. That means their father's identity is also known. Even if he's allowed to get here safely, he will lead every interested party straight to them."

"Then we need a ship and a good pilot," Mitsuki said.

"We could hop on a freighter," Kyralla suggested.

"Stowing away on a freighter...that could work," Mitsuki said, "but it's tricky. Especially if you get caught before you're away from Ekaran IV. And you'd need one to take you to your dad, who's... where is he?"

"Titus II," Oona said. "He's a diplomat, and he's working on a trade deal."

Mitsuki frowned. "The chances of finding a freighter going to Titus II are slim. Bishop, Siv, either of you know any good pilots with a ship of their own?"

Bishop shook his head. "Not a one."

"Few," Siv said, "and they all work for the Shadowslip."

"We're going to need an independent mercenary then."

"What if we acquired high-quality changeling veils and altered our appearances as much as possible and then booked passage on a starship?" Kyralla asked.

"You're definitely not going to find many passenger ships heading to Titus II," Mitsuki replied. "Though you could bounce from a nearby system to there using a mercenary starship from another world. Did you arrange for an emergency rendezvous point with your father? Some planet where you would all meet if you got separated."

"That never occurred to us," Kyralla said. "Sadly..." she frowned and shifted uncomfortably "...our skill set was lacking. I know how to handle myself in a fight, and my dad knows diplomacy. We didn't have a security expert or any well-intentioned criminals to help us plan eventualities."

"When is your dad supposed to return?" Siv asked.

"In ten days," Oona replied.

"You could take a passenger ship to Alterra, where no one should be looking for you yet," Mitsuki said. "From there you could hope to catch something going to Titus II. But the chances of all of that happening in less than ten days, given standard travel times, is slim."

"And there's still a big problem with the passenger ship route," Siv said. "Whipping up believable fake identities is a lot harder than you think."

"You seem to have dozens," Kyralla said.

"All of them were either given to me by the Shadowslip or were painstakingly crafted. It's as much art as science, and it takes time to build up a solid one. You could try a dodgy one, but with the enemies you're dealing with, and with the government stirred up about it too, you're running a big risk."

"They're going to be scanning everyone that even remotely looks like the two of you," Bishop said. "DNA, heat signatures, facial recognition, fingerprints, retinal scans...the works."

"He's right," Mitsuki added. "Security is going to be incredibly

tight at every spaceport, and probably on every form of public trans-
portation, too. So I think we're settled on the only good option, the
only one most likely to succeed."

"We are?" Kyralla asked in confusion.

Siv nodded. "We need a mercenary starship captain whose
silence can be bought."

"Dumb and greedy but skilled would be ideal," Mitsuki said.
"And we'll use disguises and the best fake IDs we can come up with
in the time we have. Not so much to fool the ship captain but to fool
any planetary authorities who might intercept us in space on a
random customs check."

"There's probably more of those taking place than normal at the
moment," Bishop added.

"Without doubt," Mitsuki said. "There will be a ridiculously
heightened state of security given the destruction of a Tekk Reaper
ship over the city. The government's going to want to cover their asses
and prove they're keeping people safe. The last thing they want is
anyone asking hard questions about why that ship was allowed to
make orbit and enter the atmosphere. They will want to appear
strong while looking for scapegoats."

"*You've been terribly quiet, Silkster. You don't have anything
to add?*"

"*I do, sir. Only...I don't want to.*"

"*You don't want to give an opinion? I am shocked. Seriously
shocked. Have you sustained damage?*"

"*Sir...your dad's starship...I lied...it wasn't destroyed.*"

Siv stood abruptly, knocking over his chair and a mostly empty
glass of wine. "What?!" he yelled aloud.

"*I lied to you, sir.*"

"The *Outworld Ranger* wasn't destroyed like you told me?!"

The others looked at him as if he had gone mad. Perhaps they
were wondering if it was an effect caused by his withdrawal from the
Kompel.

"Sivvy, are you okay?" Mitsuki asked.

"What's the *Outworld Ranger*?" Bishop asked, his worried eyes locked onto Siv.

"That was Gav Gendin's starship," Oona said.

Siv stalked about the room. "How could you?"

"*I didn't want you to go searching for it, sir. It isn't safe to go there.*"

"Why?"

"*I'm actually not sure, sir.*"

"You don't know?!"

"*Sir, Gav returned from his last expedition on that ship, then hid it at a secret location that he never told you about. Think about it, sir. Obviously, he didn't want you to return there unless it was absolutely necessary.*"

"Well, it doesn't matter now, does it? I'm going to die soon. And we need a ship."

"*I know, sir. That's why I mentioned it. Only...*"

"Only what?"

"*I'm afraid, sir. Truly afraid. I'm not talking about a pre-programmed routine concerned with keeping you safe from harm. I'm talking about...I think it's real fear, sir. It feels real to me.*"

"You...you're... Silkster, how could you be afraid?" Siv asked, returning to mental communication. "*How can you feel anything?*"

"*We both know I'm special, sir. And going there scares me.*"

Siv continued to pace in circles around the others, who had remained seated at the table. Silky seemed to be farther along the path of fully realized sentience than Siv had thought. Although this might be a particular instance of extreme learned aversion, perhaps the result of locks his dad had put on Silky's knowledge of past events. Silky had told him from the beginning that much of his dad's data had been deleted, but Siv had always thought that a lie. Gav Gendin would not have permanently deleted a record of anything he had discovered. He could have locked them away, though.

Siv tried to gather his composure. "*Do you know how to get there?*"

"Not directly, sir. I don't know the exact location."

"Why would he lock knowledge of the location away from you if he thought I might one day need to go there?"

"Sir, he didn't lock that information away from me. I deleted it."

"What? Why would you do that?"

"Sir, there are things I hide even from myself. Things I do not want to know."

"Huh? Never mind. Go on." After all these years, he was suddenly discovering hidden depths to Silky.

"As I was saying, sir, I deleted the location of the ship because returning there scared me. However, once you survived those first few years after waking up, I regretted the decision. It wasn't fair to you, and it didn't honor Gav's wishes. I couldn't bring the information back, but after careful study and deductive reasoning and using what records of your father's travels I could access, I narrowed the starship's whereabouts down to a general location. The starship is in a secret hangar in—"

"The wastelands," Siv said out loud.

"Yes, sir. Specifically, the ancient ruined city of Karoo."

"That's why I've always been drawn that direction."

"Perhaps so, sir. Though I don't know why you'd be instinctively drawn toward the ship."

Siv peered out the window toward the mountains. "Because returning there is my destiny."

"Are you mad at me, sir?"

"Yes...no...I don't know. I'll figure that out later."

"I've always had your best interests in mind, sir."

"I've never doubted that, Silkster. Do you think the ship would still be operational?"

"Sir, I have no idea. But it's possible, especially if Gav hermetically sealed the hangar, which I imagine he would have. Also, since few expeditions have been done since then and with the area being so inhospitable, I doubt anyone else has stumbled upon it by accident."

"Sivvy, what's the deal?" Mitsuki asked. "What's going on?"

"I have a starship."

"Of course, you do," Bishop said with a laugh. "Probably state of the art and everything."

"It certainly would be," Siv replied. "It's an advanced light cruiser, and it was locked away before the Tekk Plague hit."

If a jaw could drop and hit the floor, Bishop's would have.

"That would solve all our problems!" Kyralla said. "Or most of them, anyway."

"We have no way of knowing if it still runs or if it has enough fuel. And Silky only knows the general location, and he's not even certain of that." He quickly explained the rest of what Silky had said to them, filling in the gaps since they'd only heard one side of the conversation.

"So we go there and give it a shot," Kyralla said. "If it doesn't pan out, then we move on to the next option."

"It's in the wastes, and that's pretty far to travel on a long shot," Siv said, arguing against what he desperately wanted to do. He didn't want to sway them unfairly.

Mitsuki shrugged. "If we can slip out of the city and through the mountains, no one is going to think to look for us out in the wastes. And if it doesn't pan out, we'll have thrown them off the trail for a while."

"We might not be able to access the ship without you there, though," Bishop said to Siv. "This chance will slip away once you..."

"Die?" Siv asked. "It's okay to say it."

"I think we have to play this card first," Mitsuki said.

Kyralla nodded. "I agree. We give it a shot. And if it doesn't work, I do have a short-range, encrypted transmitter I can use to contact our dad. He might be able to meet us out there."

"Are you sure?" Siv asked. "There's good reason people don't go out into the wastes."

"Don't you want to go there?" Bishop asked.

"Obviously, I want to go and see the *Outworld Ranger* again. So bad you have no idea. I just didn't want to pressure you."

"Siv," Oona said, "your dad may have been a guardian, and he owned an amulet made by the Ancients. There may be answers on that ship that are more important than me returning to my dad. We might find the key to understanding what I'm experiencing. After all, our lore doesn't mention anything about the Ancients having hyperphasic messiahs or a Benevolence of their own, yet you have a guardian amulet made by them."

"We have our plan now," Mitsuki said authoritatively. "Leave it to Silky to have an ace up his sleeve."

"I suggest we all get some sleep then," Siv said. "As much as I want to head out immediately, we need rest."

"We could sleep in shifts in the skimmer car," Kyralla suggested.

Siv took one look at her and Oona and knew that wouldn't be enough for them. "I think we could all use showers and a few hours of proper sleep where we're not crammed into a can. We're safe here for now."

"Six hours," Mitsuki said. "Then we leave."

Siv scratched his chin. "I am concerned that the car won't be able to handle the trip out there. We may need to switch. Especially since you may need it to return here if things don't work out as planned."

"I'll give the car a look over and see what condition it's in and check the power levels and the antigrav capacitors and such," Bishop said. "It would be a lot easier and safer if we didn't need to switch."

"Don't you need rest?" Siv asked.

Bishop shrugged. "I don't need much sleep. And I can rest along the way."

"I know what you really want, little man." Mitsuki rubbed the back of his neck, causing him to cringe and smile at the same time. "You want to stay up and plunder through Siv's cog collection."

"Yeah...well...it's a once in a lifetime opportunity. And I will check out the car first."

"Do we need someone to stay up and keep watch?" Kyralla asked.

Siv shook his head. "I have numerous sensors active here. And Silky will be in observation mode." He turned to Seneca. "I know we just got here, my friend, but we'll be heading out early in the morning. Could you pack us traveling provisions? As many as we can possibly get into the car."

Seneca responded with a low moan followed by two affirmative beeps.

Bishop tore off into the garage. Mitsuki took a shower in one bedroom, Oona and Kyralla the other. Siv stepped out onto the back porch and gazed at the mountains. The first stars in the velvety sky twinkled above.

The *Outworld Ranger*, after all these years...

His destiny lay beyond those mountains and in the wastes after all. He had thought he would die here on the farm, but if he could see the *Outworld Ranger*...his father's gleaming starship...one last time... that was even better.

"*Silkster, I'm not mad at you. I understand.*"

"*You do, sir?*"

"*I do. Although we should have a long talk about you being afraid of something. But not today. I'm too tired and have too much else on my mind.*"

"*Indeed, sir.*"

"*Silkster, old buddy, I have to survive until we reach the* Outworld Ranger *and be of sound mind when we get there.*"

"*The timing might be tight, sir. Karoo is a large expanse of ruins. Even narrowing our search to logical locations, it might take days to find it.*"

"*I have to make it there whole. So that I can see it, so that I can feel it. And to give the others access.*"

"*Well, you have the Awake drug with you, sir. It could counter the effects long enough for you make it there alive. You'll just need to wait until the last possible moment to take it, since the effect will wear off quickly.*"

"Good enough." Siv nodded. He lifted the amulet and kissed it. "I coming, Dad."

37

KARSON BISHOP

As Karson walked around the skimmer car, he ignored how incredibly ugly it was, with its faux wood panels and boxy styling. The tech he worked with was usually damaged or nonfunctional and *looked* it: decades of rust and corrosion, blast marks from battles, dents and cracks from accidents. As a child, he had learned to look *beneath* the surface of a machine to see what was really there, good and bad, and then quickly understand how it worked. He had honed this skill with thousands of device restorations, repairs, and reconfigurations.

He fancied he could do the same with people, but that delusion always died as soon as he had to interact with someone. People were mysterious, confusing, contradictory, and too often nonsensical. The only way he could really figure a person out was through long, careful study and that usually took years. Unless they did something dramatic, like Siv risking his life to save others, which made them a relatively easy read. Someone like Mitsuki, though... He might never figure her out. She was the living equivalent of advanced Benevolency tech that no scientist or gizmet could decipher, like stardrives and flux loop capacitors.

Oona, on the other hand, was different. When she had said who she was, Karson immediately saw beyond her innocent human appearance, beyond her quiet manner, and beyond her solid black eyes. Some deep instinct awakened within him, and he immediately saw the purity of her soul. She was exactly what she claimed to be, a hyperphasic messiah.

And like a piece of ancient tech in need of restoration, Oona was filled with amazing potential that couldn't be tapped. Only...it wasn't so much that she was broken but that her construction wasn't yet finished. And he knew that, just like Siv, he would give his last breath if necessary to see to it that she had the chance to realize her potential.

After finishing a third circuit around the skimmer car, tapping the body at random intervals, Karson nodded appreciatively. The build was more than solid. It was discreetly ruggedized, with reinforced panels and bulletproof glass in the windows. He popped the hood, glanced in, and whistled. He could hardly believe what he saw. He darted underneath to get a look at the frame and confirm the evidence. Smiling, his heart pounding with excitement, he rushed back into the house, hoping to catch Siv before he made it to bed.

He caught up to Siv walking into the kitchen from the porch. Now there was a broken person Karson could understand. Siv had a constant tremor now. It was ever so slight and probably unnoticeable to most people. But Karson could spot the most minor fluctuation in a capacitor, engine, or other equipment.

Karson felt sure they would need Siv alive to access the *Outworld Ranger,* but he feared Siv wouldn't last that long.

He had only known Siv a few days but, given time, he thought they could become good friends. He liked the way Siv's mind worked. He dealt with bad guys and disasters the way Karson fixed machines: methodically but not hewing to some standard of perfection if the point was to just get the job done.

Karson's smile and exuberance faded away. He didn't want Siv to die, but there was nothing he could do about it. This wasn't a machine he could fix. And he had no idea how to soothe Siv's pain or whether he should even try.

Siv had sensed his thoughts. "You're going to have to accept my mortality, Bishop. I know it's rotten, especially given how much we survived only days ago, but that's how it goes. In my line of work, a young death isn't that surprising. Heck, your own security cog nearly killed me."

"Oh, that's not what I came to talk to you about."

"It was on your mind, and it wasn't hard to spot. The sight of me wiped the excitement off your face in a heartbeat. So what got you pumped?"

"The skimmer car."

"Ah."

"Who did you buy it from?"

"It was a custom job. A mechanic in East Gara made it for me. I told him I wanted something that looked tame but was rugged and fast for its size. Why?"

"They converted an old Tezzin security car. It was the sort of ride dignitaries, governors, and senators used back in your era. Not all of it is a Tezzin, mind. Just the chassis and the engine, which they did an excellent restoration of. The body's all new, though not as strong as the original. Still, it's a lot stronger than what you'd see in any civilian vehicle, and is probably close to what you'd find on those Shadowslip extraction vans. You could drive it through a war zone and, with a bit of luck, make it out just fine."

"I had no idea."

"How much did you pay for it?"

"About what you'd expect, I guess." Siv chewed at his lip. "Although, the mechanic owed me a favor. A massive, life debt sort of favor. So I might've gotten a bit of a discount."

"I restored two Tezzins at work. Each one costs a hundred thousand credits—used and broken as a fart. And the chassis and the engine were all we could salvage on them, too."

Siv's eyes widened, then he smiled. "I paid him twenty thousand."

"Twenty thousand?!" Karson staggered back a step. "You only paid twenty thousand?!"

Siv laughed. "Given what I asked for and the size of the favor, and the fact that he ran a chop shop on the side, I'm not that shocked. It was probably extremely hot with the cops looking hard for it. Converting it into an ugly family sedan and paying me back was just the opportunity he needed."

"Well, it's brilliant."

Siv patted him on the shoulder and headed toward the hallway leading toward the third bedroom. "I'm glad you like it so much. Now, I'm off to get some sleep."

"Wait, you don't understand. This car... If I had the parts and time, I could boost the engine speed by at least fifty percent, along with its altitude capability. And, depending on the degradation of the wiring and electrical components, I might even restart its shimmer-veil, maybe even the force fields too, although those tend to be persnickety."

Siv spun around. "It...it has force fields and a shimmer-veil?! How? I looked that car all over when I bought it! I've cleaned it twice and performed maintenance on it once. Even Silky didn't realize there was something more to the car."

Karson smiled. "The components were built into the frame so they'd never be exposed to danger or the elements. And you can't detect them with a basic scan, so if you weren't suspicious..."

"I had no reason to be. We only scanned the software and searched for trackers."

"So...I guess I'd better get to it." He scratched his chin. "Of course...this is more work than I can manage in a night. Assuming all possibilities are open, what should I prioritize?"

"I'd say go for whatever you think you're most likely to have finished by morning, though I'd think more speed would be best. I doubt the shields on it are very powerful."

Karson shrugged. "They're the equivalent of what you'd find on a starfighter if a little less efficient."

"Shit! Get the force field up if you can! Wire in extra power packs if you need. I've got a half-dozen P3's stashed in a closet in the garage, along with a P2 and a bunch of P4's."

"Your level of preparedness is amazing."

"It's easy when you've got lots of free time and disposable income."

That was definitely true. The small P4 power packs were five hundred credits each, and a recharge at a flux loop capacitor station on Ekaran IV would run fifty to a hundred credits.

"I'll tell Seneca to assist you in any way he can, once he has packed all the provisions," Siv said.

"Tools?" Karson asked.

"In a crate in the basement. You should find everything you need."

"An entire set of tools packed in a crate? You planned to retire here and tinker on the cogs, didn't you?"

"It was one dream I had. The other was to become an archaeologist like my dad. I was even going to explore the wastelands first, just like he did."

"Sounds nice," Karson said.

"Bishop, I want you to have my cog collection. So if you ever make it back here, they're yours. Silky is filling out the paperwork as we speak."

"I couldn't."

"I'm leaving the house behind to a family I care for. The cogs might be worth a lot of money to them, but they wouldn't appreciate them like you would. Consider them yours. Do with them as you wish."

Karson wanted to thank him, but all he could do was stand there with tears welling in his eyes as Siv slouched away.

———

Karson opened the crate of tools in the basement. Every small tool he used at home or at work, he found in that container. All brand new, and still packed in bubble wrap. According to the shipping date of the receipt, the tools had sat here untouched for three years.

Poor guy. How many houses did he own? How many cars? How many cogs and toolsets and projects? How many bits of the world he'd lost did he cling to? Karson didn't discount that Siv needed safe houses and specialized gear for his line of work, but he did question why he needed that many.

Karson scanned all the cogs carefully, to see what he had to work with. None of them were going to save them in a firefight, that was for sure. But their parts could certainly come in handy for repairs. He picked out the most damaged models and examined them more closely. Then he dug through the boxes of parts, noting the things he might need now, and a few things he'd take along with them just in case.

He nodded appreciatively. He could work with this. He stripped a few choice pieces out of three cogs, frowning regretfully as he did. Then he piled those parts, along with some of the spares Siv had lying around, into a pile beside the box of tools. Having restored two Tezzins already was a huge advantage since he knew everything he'd likely need.

The box was too heavy for him to carry, so he just grabbed a few essential tools. He'd get Seneca to bring up the rest.

Karson hurried back to the garage, slid under the car, and got to work. All his problems...the dangers they were facing...meeting a hyperphasic messiah...Siv dying...all of that faded away as he gave himself over to his work, devoting himself to the purity of the mechanics.

38

OONA VIM

The cosmos thrummed a universal heartbeat, a pulse of existence. When the cosmos inhaled, stars died. Galaxies...people...entire civilizations perished. When it exhaled, new stars were born and life began anew. The universe ebbed and flowed, only it happened so slowly that no one could ever take it all in.

Oona felt the echoes of the breaths that came before, ripples through time and the many dimensions of space. Her mind rode along the current breath. Was the universe exhaling now, or inhaling? Being born anew or dying? Was there any difference?

It was all meaningless, and yet that was meaning itself.

She breathed in. She breathed out. She could know no more than her own breaths.

Was her dad okay?

She flinched as that thought knocked her from her meditative state. Her eyes flew open. She sat on a cushion below a window with the curtains pulled back. A trail of moonlight danced across the shimmery fabric of her robe. Sleeping in the bed behind her, Kyralla snored ever so softly.

Oona had learned to tune out Kyralla's breathing long ago. Yet anytime she wanted, she listened in, feeling comforted that her big sister was right there with her.

"You will always have each other," their dad had told them many times. "And I will be there for you so long as I can."

His face appeared vividly in her mind. Then a darkness swept through her thoughts and emotions. A premonition, or childish fear? From time to time, she had actual premonitions. But it was difficult to tell the difference, especially when she was already anxious.

Most of her innate abilities were vague like that. On a few occasions, she had seen ghostly images and figures she couldn't explain. And a woman with an ethereal voice and a strange, melodic accent whispered softly in her dreams at night. Her words were critically important, yet Oona could never remember them, if she even understood them to begin with.

She stood and paced around the room, trying to push her father from her mind.

Uncle Pashta took his place. She remembered the last time she had seen him, two nights ago when they had dined together on the terrace. A soft breeze had whirled through the trees, playing the wind chimes. The fish had been chewy, the pasta underdone, the sauce as thin as their conversation. He had shown no signs then of betraying them. Or at least none that she had noticed, and she *should* have noticed. Sensing emotions and whether someone was telling the truth were the only reliable abilities she had. If they had failed her so badly...

No. Doubting herself didn't do anyone any good. Something must have happened after dinner or maybe the next day. Despite being a bit creepy, Uncle Pashta's devotion to the Benevolency, and to what she represented, had been true. What could have made him betray them?

The image of his ship exploding in a fiery ball over the city rose unbidden in her mind. Even if he had betrayed them, he hadn't deserved death. Neither had the men sent to capture her. She wasn't worth all this trouble...she wasn't worth these deaths.

And now Siv would die for her too.

Siv, a guardian, and a friend. Siv, whose amulet proved there was a connection between the starfaring Ancients and the Benevolence. She'd always felt there had to be. But years of reading scientific texts on hyperphasic technology and archeological papers on the Ancients hadn't turned up anything. Then Siv dropped into her life and gave her...if not answers, then hope that the answers existed.

And she was only going to get to know him for a few days. It wasn't fair. He took it in stride though. Siv wasn't nearly as afraid of death as she would have expected...as she would have been in his place.

Some days Oona thought the weight of the universe might crush her. And some days she felt certain it would. The only thing worse than a terrible responsibility was not understanding it. She was a hyperphasic messiah. She knew that to the very core of her being. But to what end? What was she supposed to become? How could any one person, no matter how extraordinary, restore the Benevolence? Was that even possible?

She had spent hours upon hours meditating about her nature, coming to grips with the awakening that lay before her. Only one other had survived that process, so far as anyone knew. And she was nuts and now ruled over a thousand star systems.

Oona feared death. But more than anything, she feared madness.

She took a drink of water. She should've gone straight to bed. She had thought a half hour of meditation to clear her mind would help her rest better, but it had only made things worse.

"Artemisia, any word from my father or news from Titus II?"

"None, madam. But the connection is down again, has been for an hour now. I have no idea when service will return, and there will likely be a delay once the infernal machine I'm linked to finally boots back up."

Siv had insisted, for security reasons, that they route their chippies' connections to the outside world through a primitive desktop terminal. Unfortunately, the terminal was malfunctioning, and its connection kept slowing and timing out.

"I can't take it anymore. Scan for news using direct access to the net."

"Madam, Silky was most passionate about the need to maintain security by routing our connections through the terminal."

Oona took a deep breath and nodded.

She crawled into bed and scooted up beside Kyralla. Miraculously, she fell asleep almost instantly.

———

She woke with a start, an image of her father in her mind. His face was broken and bloody. Struggling to breathe, he cried out for help.

Oona sat up in bed, heart racing. *This* was a premonition. She knew it.

"Artemisia, open a direct comm channel to my dad."

"Silky said to—"

"I don't care. Just do it. That's an order."

"Yes, madam. Connecting to Bei Comm-2...sending a request..."

Most people couldn't directly access a comm-loop. They had to connect through the galactic internet. The net was reliable and instantaneous on a planet, but slow to connect to other worlds. In the Age of the Benevolency, there had been enough echo space stations to keep every human planet within the galaxy in near constant contact with one another.

Now, with over eighty percent of the echo space stations knocked out by the Tekk Plague, there was always a delay. On Ekaran IV it was minutes to hours, depending on how much bandwidth official planetary and mercantile business was taking up.

Oona could only access a direct line because her father Galen was an ambassador for the Terran Federation.

"Madam, I've gotten his voicemail. Do you want to leave a message?"

She could ask him to contact her as soon as possible. But she really shouldn't risk another direct communication. Even this was once too many, but the sound of him crying out for help still rang in her mind. She'd had to try.

Not wanting to wake Kyralla, she thought the message she wanted to leave him. Artemisia would translate into her voice.

"Daddy, are you okay? We're safe, but some bad things have happened, and we're in danger. Contact me as soon as you can, and be careful. My secret's out. We're going to try to come to you, so if you can't get in touch and we're not here, you'll know we've fled elsewhere."

Oona swallowed and bit her lip. *"Daddy...I hope you're okay. I love you."*

She ended the connection. She knew she shouldn't have contacted him directly, but she'd had no choice. She couldn't stand the worry any longer. And the government channels ambassadors used were all highly encrypted.

"I'm sure he's okay, madam. You know he never answers if he's in a meeting."

"Thank you, Artemisia. Wake me if he calls."

She curled up against her sister, and the first of many tears flowed down her cheek.

39

SIV GENDIN

"Sir, wake up."

Siv opened his eyes to a dim room. The overhead lights burned a faint orange color that gradually brightened. It was still dark outside. Dawn was over two hours away. Six hours of sleep... He could've used a dozen. But they needed to move, and leaving under cover of darkness would be safer. Besides, he didn't want to sleep away what little of his life remained.

As he sat up, the shakes hit him. Or the zaps as he liked to think of them. It was like an electric shock running up his spine. He shivered, and his head twitched hard to the side. After only four pulses the episode abated. He sighed deeply. It could've been worse.

"Ask Kyralla to come in. I need to...tell her something before we get going."

"Yes, sir."

Head pounding, he downed two Pain-Free pills. He nearly dropped the water glass as he returned it to the nightstand. His fine motor skills were already eroding. Clumsily buttoning, zipping, and tying on his combat gear, he got dressed.

A tentative knock sounded on the door. Siv opened it and smiled weakly at Kyralla. She looked more exhausted now than she had at dinner.

"You need something?"

Siv took in a deep breath and summoned his courage. This was going to be hard. In some ways harder than facing death itself. "Kyralla, I'm bequeathing Silky and all my equipment to you."

"Sir, what?!"

"Wh-what?" Kyralla stammered.

"When I die, someone needs to take Silky, and you're the obvious candidate. With him and my sensor array and the rest of my gear, you'll be better able to defend Oona. You're going to need all help you can get, and Silky's the best. He's saved my ass more times than I can count. You can pass Rosie to Bishop. That's a big upgrade for him."

"Siv, I don't think now's the time to—"

"It has to be now. Every piece of gear I own is locked to my DNA. My father saw to that as he passed away. And there's absolutely no getting around it. The military didn't want any of this gear to fall into enemy hands, so they enabled a nearly uncrackable locking system. You can only bypass it with a command override."

A puzzled look came over her face. "So how is it that your father could use the gear? Someone in the military wouldn't turn this kind of equipment over to an archeologist, would they?"

"Silky doesn't remember. My dad locked that information away, along with everything else he discovered and experienced."

Kyralla nodded. "I'm...I'm honored that you would choose me..."

"I'm less than thrilled, sir."

"But are you sure I'm the best choice?"

"You're the warrior."

"Alright then. What now?"

"I'm not keen on this, sir."

"Would you rather sit around forever with nothing to do?"

"Obviously not, sir."

"Then it's settled. Don't worry, Silkster, I'm sure you'll get used to her. Besides, that precog thing could be—"

"A pain in my ass, sir. Fine. Let's get this moving. Time's wasting."

Siv smiled at Silky's grumpiness as he put on his combat gloves and held out his hand.

"Give me your hand."

She placed her right hand in his. His heartbeat picked up, feeling her touch, even through the protective mesh of the gloves. He had so little time left. If only he could spend some of it... He took a deep breath and focused his mind.

"We just need to match your DNA profile to the equipment."

"You can take a sufficient sample like this?"

"Sensors in the gloves."

"Got it, sir."

Siv held her hand a little longer.

"I said I've got it, sir."

"I heard you."

He released her hand and nodded. "You're all set."

They stared awkwardly at one another for a moment.

"Siv...thanks...I..." She chuckled. "I'm not really good with people. I spend too much time alone or with Oona. I don't know what to say."

"Neither do I," Siv replied. "Why don't we go get some breakfast and make sure everyone else is—"

"Sir! My level five scan is picking up imminent threats."

"We've got incoming!" Siv said. "Get Oona to the skimmer car."

Kyralla ran out of the room, shouting the alarm to everyone.

"What're we facing?"

"Eight armored personnel skimmers inbound, sir. APS Hammer Strikes with railguns and slug-throwers. Twenty combat-armored soldiers in each. Terran Federation. Ekaran IV First Division."

"Vector?"

"They've formed an eight-pointed star, sir. And we're at the center."

Siv grabbed his neural disruptor. *"That's just peachy."*

"Now detecting a Dagger Fist strike-fighter overhead."

The strike-fighter was similar to a starfighter in design, only a little smaller and not equipped for spacefaring.

Siv ran out into the main room where Mitsuki was waiting on him. Kyralla and Oona had just darted into the garage.

"The Dagger Fist has a missile lock on the farmhouse, sir. And its plasma cannon is armed."

"What's going on?" Mitsuki asked with worry.

"We're surrounded."

"Fracked is more like it, sir."

40

SIV GENDIN

Siv caught Mitsuki up on the situation as they ran into the garage...
where they found the skimmer car partially disassembled and tangled
in a web of wires with various parts scattered about. The old, beat-up
skimmer truck parked next to it had been stripped down and looked
like a corpse with its guts hanging out.

Karson, smeared with grease and scored with burns on both arms
and one cheek, glanced numbly at them, then leaned over into the
front of the skimmer with the hood propped precariously over his
head. He muttered something about converter arrays.

Kyralla and Oona stood awkwardly to one side, their faces frozen
in confusion.

"Shit," Siv cursed, his heart fluttering uneasily. "We're so
screwed."

"We've got to buy time, sir."

*"Enable the phantom emitter to show the house rigged with explo-
sives. If you could show several more people here with a better armament, that would be helpful."*

*"The phantom emitter is now showing significant explosives
armed within the house, sir. That's the test routine we used seventeen*

months ago. For that other stuff to work, I would have needed advanced warning. If I launch a bad signal, then they'll see through the entire ruse faster."

Properly calibrated, the phantom emitters could trick sensor sweeps, giving false readings. The device Siv had installed here was finicky, difficult to fine-tune, and had been hard to acquire. Siv had hoped to put phantom emitters in all his homes but had given up after it took two weeks of fighting this one to get it working. Too bad Karson hadn't had a chance to—

"Karson!" Siv yelled. "What the hell, man?!"

As Bishop dug his way out from the engine, Mitsuki shrugged. "It doesn't make any difference."

"Why not?" Kyralla asked. "How else are we going to get out of here?"

"Not by driving out," Mitsuki said. "Not right now."

"She's right, sir."

"What? Oh. Yes, of course. But, look what he's done to my car!"

If Silky could roll his eyes, Siv sensed that he would now. *"Priorities, sir."*

"So how *are* we going to get out?" Kyralla snapped at Mitsuki.

She shrugged. "I haven't figured that out yet."

Mitsuki was composed, her voice confident. But Siv knew her well enough to see the signs of nervousness in the twitch of her mouth and the way she suddenly didn't seem to know what to do with her hands.

"Siv, what exactly is going on out there?" Kyralla asked.

For the first time, Bishop seemed to comprehend everyone else's urgency and worry. "Is something wrong?"

Siv rolled his eyes and explained everything.

Bishop nodded, and dove underneath the car, muttering faster now.

"So we're trapped?" Oona asked softly.

"There's no getting out of this," Kyralla said. "Having the best extraction agent or not, we're going to get captured."

Mitsuki scowled. "Don't count me out yet."

"If you're going to do something, then you'd better do it fast," Siv told her.

She chewed on her lip a moment, then her eyes lit up. *"I'm* not doing anything, Siv. You are. Contact them. Tell them the girls are your hostages and that you're an extremist. Then promise to kill them unless your demands are met."

"So you want me to stall for time?"

Bishop poked his head out from under the car. "Yes, stall." He went back to work without explaining himself.

"Okay..." Siv said. "What if they don't care? What if they're just here to—"

"Either it works, or it doesn't," Mitsuki said.

"Great," Kyralla muttered.

Mitsuki scowled. "Look, I'm not going to lie to you. Getting out of this is basically impossible. To have a chance, we need time to find a weakness we can exploit. An opportunity will present itself at some point. We just need to be ready to take advantage of it."

"That's all we can do?" Oona asked.

Mitsuki nodded. "Guns blazing gets us killed. And yeah, that might happen anyway. The stall might not work. But I think it's a good bet that government troops will be measured in their response and take the time to try to get it right. If Siv pulls it off, we could get anywhere from fifteen minutes to several hours to work with."

"Silkster, can you open a channel to the government forces?"

"Easily, sir. They still use secure frequencies from my days as a special forces chippy. Which is kind of pitiful, you know."

"I need a fake identity—something fast and decently plausible. I know we don't have enough time for airtight, so make it hard to verify."

"No worries, sir. Last night I researched anti-Benevolence extremists on other worlds, in case you needed to pose as one."

"Silkster, you're the best. And I can't believe you thought to do

that. That's a hell of a play, guessing that I'd need to pose as an extremist!"

"I'm a smart chippy, sir. But it wasn't a guess. I also researched fundamentalist Benevolence worshipers. Running around with a messiah, I figured fake ID's of either group could prove useful. Besides, both groups could end up as players in all this. And I like to know my enemies ahead of time, if possible."

The data for Siv's alternate identity popped up on the screen as the audio channel squawked to life. Silky had altered the public appearance record of the man to match the preset on the only good face disguise Siv had left.

"Channel open, sir. Colonel Nines on the line."

"Who the hell is this?" a gruff man barked. "And how in the hell did you patch into this channel?"

"My methods and sources are my own," Siv replied. "I am Telmar Togs, and if you don't back off, I will kill these two girls."

"Bullshit."

"Their blood will be on your hands then."

Siv closed the channel.

"How's it going?" Mitsuki asked.

"We've entered the handshake phase. I expect to exchange pleasantries very—"

"Incoming call, sir. Colonel Nines on the line. Shall I patch Mitsuki in so she can listen?"

"Yes, do so."

"Patched in, sir."

"Colonel," Siv said.

"What do you want, Togs?"

"For starters? Respect."

"I have none to give. Look, if you are who you say you are, then why haven't you killed them already?"

"Because..."

"Martyrdom, sir."

"Because I didn't want to make her a martyr to the Benevolent cause. Give me a chance to publicly discredit her claims, and I'll gladly turn myself in."

"And your compatriots?"

"Likewise."

"And how will I know that you won't kill her after you've discredited her?"

"Shift the burden of the decision to him," Mitsuki said.

"Well, Colonel...I don't know. This wasn't my original plan. I had intended to escape and do this on my own terms at my leisure. You've spoiled that."

"Sir, the Hammer Strikes have pulled to a stop within attack distance. The Dagger Fist is hovering above us."

"Here's what I propose, Togs. You have fifteen minutes to turn over the girl. After that, we're storming in."

"I've rigged the place with explosives, Colonel. So be my guest."

There was a long pause before the Colonel responded. "Okay, Togs. Give me a few minutes to work out a solution."

The channel closed.

"So far so good," Mitsuki said. "How long do you think the phantom emitter will fool them?"

"On our tests, it took Silky three minutes using a level four scan to figure it out, so I think they'll crack it in ten to fifteen. But maybe we'll get lucky and it will take them a lot longer."

Bishop slid out from under the car, grease dripping from his horns. "You've got a phantom emitter?!"

"Yes, and what the hell have you done to my car?! I told you to fix *one* thing. *One thing.* And to have it done by now!"

Bishop winced. "I know, I know. And I'm very sorry. But if you give me fifteen minutes, maybe twenty, I can have *everything* working. Speed boost, shimmer-veil, force field, all of it."

Mitsuki raised an eyebrow. "Explain."

Bishop started to describe her everything, but Siv shooed him back to work. Then he told them about the car's extra features that he hadn't known about.

"Well, that's one break," Mitsuki said. "The force field could block a shot or two as we escape."

"That's not enough," Kyralla said.

"No," Mitsuki admitted, "but it does give us wiggle room. Whatever plan we come up with, if we can, won't allow any room for errors. I'm one hundred percent certain that whatever we do, a couple of shots are going to come our way."

"Oh," Bishop said, popping his head back out. "I'm going to need that phantom emitter."

"It's busy right now," Siv said.

"You can move it while it's working. That shouldn't affect how it functions at all. And I can make good use of it."

"Explain," Mitsuki said.

"Well—"

Siv shooed him again. "Tell us as you work."

"If we calibrate it correctly, or rather if Silky can since he knows military channels, I could set it to scramble all their sensors with a single data burst. It would throw off their scans and their targeting—I think—for thirty seconds, maybe a minute. That might just give us a window to escape."

Mitsuki leaned over and looked under the car. "I think I underestimated you, little guy."

Bishop grinned and went back to work.

"*Sir, I can't process a calibration that complicated in less than fifteen minutes. We can only stall them so long, and I suspect I'd need an hour to get it right. Even my capabilities are limited.*"

Siv explained the problem.

"So we link all our chippies together, to multiply the processing power," Bishop said. "Silky upgraded Oona and Kyralla's chippies, mine too, so there certainly shouldn't be any problem linking with theirs."

"*You upgraded their chippies?*"

"*No time to explain, sir.*"

Siv set off. "I'll get the emitter while I wait for the Colonel to—"

He only made it three steps before he collapsed, his entire body convulsing. His heart rate and body temperature spiked. Stabbing pains stormed through his body, and his eyes felt like they were going to burst. He couldn't see, and he struggled to breathe.

Amidst a wave of static, a voice came to him over audio. "Togs, I have a proposal," Colonel Nines said.

Siv tried to make a basic response using Silky to project his voice, but he couldn't focus enough even for that. His HUD was flickering. The seizure he was having was actually interrupting his connection to Silky.

"Did you hear me, Togs?"

Siv couldn't respond.

"Damn it, Togs, if I don't hear from you in the next twenty seconds, we're coming in!"

41

MITSUKI REEL

"Silky, can you hear me?" Mitsuki asked.

"I read you, madam."

"Patch the Colonel through to me."

"Done."

"Colonel, this is..." Shit. Mitsuki hadn't had a chance to come up with a persona. She'd just have to make something up. "This is Tan Koral. Togs is indisposed at the moment."

"What the hell does that mean?" the Colonel Nines demanded.

"He's working on providing proof that the girl isn't what she claims to be. Now, I believe you had a proposal for us?"

"I'd rather deal with Togs."

"And I'd rather kill the girl then shoot as many of your men as possible while you storm the place. But we can't all get what we want."

"Do you have the authority to negotiate with me?"

"Do you?"

"You're stalling," the Colonel replied. "And I do not see any record of you in the galactic database."

"I suspect you wouldn't. You see, I..."

"This isn't working, madam," Silky said. *"You're going to bring the entire ruse down."*

"I want to speak with Togs now," the Colonel growled.

"You'd better come up with something quick, madam."

Mitsuki had taken this *assignment* to help a girl escape and to prove she was the best. Her time to shine had arrived. And she was going to have to make the big play, the one she'd been saving for over a decade, just in case. She'd honestly thought that she'd never need to use it.

"Colonel, I am going to level with you. I am the one in charge here, not Togs."

"You are?"

"Yes, Colonel. I'm not an anti-Benevolence militant, and as you can tell I've burned through all my fake identities. My real name is Silustria Ting. I'm a special operations agent for the Empire of a Thousand Worlds."

There was silence on the other end, so she continued.

"I assure you, Colonel Nines, that you're not dealing with a rank amateur. You are, in fact, dealing with a situation beyond your pay grade. You are going to need to consult your superiors."

"Pop me out of my socket!" Silky exclaimed. *"Silustria Ting is a Thousand Worlder agent."*

"Obviously."

"And you clearly didn't create this persona."

"No. I didn't."

"Is any of the stuff I'm reading about this woman true?"

"Probably all of it."

"Silustria Ting..." the Colonel said, his voice trembling. "We have...uh...we have a proposal for exchanging..."

"I reject your offer, Colonel."

"Wh–what?"

"I reject it."

"But you haven't heard..."

"Here's what I propose, Colonel. You are going to provide safe passage for the special girl and me. And you can have what's left of Togs and his compatriots."

"Togs...what's happened to him?"

"I'm done with him, and he's no longer in the picture. He wasn't getting me anywhere."

"I'm reading that he's still alive."

"Yes, and unless you've got your sensors stuck up your ass, you should be able to tell that I hit him with a rather heavy neural shot to disable him."

After a moment he said, "I can see that he's in distress, yes."

"I'm done using him. He's all yours. And I believe he's wanted for several dozen crimes."

"I can't let you out of here in exchange for a few criminals, even one with Togs' record."

"I think you can. And I think you will after you have a discussion about me with your superiors."

"How do I know you are who you claim to be?"

"Tell your commander that I was at Altair V, and that I know who did what and to whom they did it. I will release the information if I'm not allowed out of here."

"Anything else? That seems rather vague."

"I promise that's all you'll need to tell them. I'll wait for you to get back to me."

"*Madam, what the hell?*"

"*It's a long story. Let's just say that I had a run in with a special operations agent while escaping from the Empire. Now, I need you and all the other chippies to get to processing.*"

"Yes, madam."

"*And I want my chippy upgraded, too.*"

"*If you like, madam.*"

"Kyralla could you go get the emitter?" Mitsuki asked.

With a puzzled look on her face, she nodded. "If Silky will tell me where it is."

A moment later, she hurried off.

"Bishop, Silky, we need to calibrate it so that it shows all of you still inside the house and not in the skimmer car. Can we do that?"

"*Maybe,*" Silky replied.

"I can block their scans of the skimmer," Bishop said. "It's one of the features I'm enabling."

"I just bought us half an hour while he works that information up the chain of command. Can you finish by then?"

"Easily!"

"Good."

Mitsuki sat down beside Siv. His convulsions had stopped a minute ago. Oona still had a hand on his head.

"Is he doing any better?" Mitsuki asked.

"I'm trying to soothe him using my power."

"Is that working?"

Oona chuckled sadly. "Doubtful. All I can seem to do is make his amulet glow."

Mitsuki stared at the red glow a moment. If that was all the girl could manage, she was hardly special enough to be worth all this attention. That was nothing more than a parlor trick.

"I'm going to get you out of here, or die trying."

"I know," Oona said. "And I understand why."

"You do?"

The girl's black eyes locked onto her, and she nodded. "I'm scared of being trapped, too."

Mitsuki shivered. It unnerved her how the girl seemed to just know things about her. But some people were naturally empathic and good at reading people. Given that and her weird eyes and the glowing medallion, she could see how maybe people would believe the girl was some sort of deity.

Kyralla returned with the emitter, and Bishop told her to put it in the glove box in the car for now.

Siv stirred, groaning. "What—what's going on? Silky won't...let me talk to...the Colonel. Says he's busy."

Mitsuki explained the situation to him.

"I've heard of Silustria Ting. She's a legend. And isn't she supposed to be dead?"

"Missing, presumed dead."

"You know the truth, don't you?"

"She killed her," Oona stated. "During her escape from the Empire."

Mitsuki stared at the girl. She opened her mouth, then closed it. How had she known? Mitsuki had never told anyone. She didn't know what to say.

Then she laughed. The girl was just guessing. Wasn't she?

"But she didn't want to," Oona continued. "She didn't have a choice, the other agents were closing in on them. Silustria had told her all her secrets but then..." Oona shook her head and rocked back on her heels. "Sorry, I didn't mean to say all that. It just...came to me. That happens sometimes. Usually not this much, but some people are more...psychically open."

Mitsuki frowned, stunned. *That* wasn't a guess. There was absolutely no way the girl could've known that. Mind reading...it wasn't possible. Yet, how else could she talk about it like she'd been there as well? There were third generation, advanced empaths. Silky claimed to have served with one. So maybe this girl was a fourth generation empath.

"Silustria Ting," Colonel Nines said, sounding rather timid now. "Your request has been forwarded to the Terran Federation High Council. Make no moves."

It took Mitsuki a moment to regain her composure and respond. "Understood, Colonel."

"That's good, right?" Kyralla asked her. She didn't seem phased by her sister's mind reading trick. Maybe Oona did that kind of thing all the time. Someone should tell them that people with secrets don't like them shared.

Mitsuki shrugged. "One of two things is going to happen. Either they let me pass, for fear that I will have some way of automatically releasing that information, even if I die. Or they're going to decide to risk that result and fire everything they've got us, criminals, innocents, and messiahs be damned."

42

SIV GENDIN

The world spun around him as Siv sat up.

Oona took his hand and squeezed it lightly. "Can I get you anything?"

He shook his head, instantly regretting the movement, and tried to smile. "I'm all right."

Kyralla squatted beside him and offered him a steaming cup of something that smelled utterly foul.

"Ugh, is that coffee?" he asked. "I hate the stuff."

"It's a stimulant," she replied. "I thought it might help."

Wincing, he downed the coffee as fast as he could, hoping he wouldn't throw it up. "Mitsuki, that was amazing."

"I never thought I'd have to make that play." She sighed deeply, her wingtips drooping to brush the floor. "It's going to get me hunted down and killed. Assuming, we can escape this mess alive."

"That's a problem for another day," Siv said.

"How could it get you into more trouble?" Oona asked. "If anyone spots you they'll know you aren't Silustria. Why would they hunt you down?"

"They'll think I know where she is or what happened to her, and certain powerful people will know that I know things they desperately want kept secret."

"So we can't let anyone spot you. As long as they think they are dealing with the actual Silustria Ting. No one but us will ever know that it's really you." Kyralla suggested. "Right?"

Mitsuki shrugged. "That's the plan."

Bishop crawled out from under the skimmer with a satisfied look on his face.

"All finished?" Siv asked.

"Oh, 'Nevolence no."

Mitsuki groaned.

"But," Bishop added quickly, "all the technical work is finished. Every system *should* function now."

"You haven't tested any of them, have you?" Siv asked.

"Well...no. But like I said, I've worked on these before and..." He bobbed his head. "I'm pretty sure it's all good to go."

"Shouldn't you still be working then?" Mitsuki asked.

"I could use some help to make that go faster. Everything needs to be put back into place. Wires bound and crammed back in, panels reattached, power packs reconnected...those sorts of things."

"Tell us what to do then," Siv said.

"You stay right where you are," Mitsuki told him. "Karson, lead on."

"But I can—"

"No arguing," Mitsuki said. "I'm in charge now."

Siv scowled, and Oona smiled at him. "You're not used to following orders."

"I'm used to it. But I *hate* it."

"This is your fault," Mitsuki said. "You insisted on delaying your doses to build up your resistance, and that failed spectacularly."

"Mitsuki," Bishop said meekly, "I need you to start mounting these extra power packs using mag-lock discs."

Everyone set to work, except Siv and Oona. Bishop claimed he was only excluding the girl because there were no other tasks to assign, but Siv suspected Bishop thought manual labor was beneath a messiah.

"Your withdrawal's going worse than you expected, isn't it?" Oona asked.

"When I tried to break myself of it before, I was fifteen. I thought my resistance would increase with age if I worked at it. Obviously, I was wrong."

"Sir, the calibration is now seventy-five percent complete. Adding in the other chippies' processing power has helped tremendously. If we have time to run test simulations, that would be excellent. But I do think it will work."

"Carry on, Silkster."

Oona helped Siv lean back against a wall. He dozed for a short while then woke to find his car reassembled. There was little evidence to show that Bishop had done anything to it, other than a few faint scorch-marks and a handful of light scratches and dents on the panels where he had clumsily pried them free and tossed them aside.

Siv stood. He was feeling a lot better now. Almost his normal self. "The systems?"

"Testing now," Bishop said as he slid into the driver's seat. "Initiating the shimmer-veil."

The wood-paneled skimmer sedan flickered and turned sort of milkily transparent, like a mirage special effect in a movie had gone wrong. But that was okay because it only failed up close. At a distance, the car would be difficult to spot by sight. Naturally, that wouldn't help them against radar, heat, and motion scans. But it would make a massive difference once Silky jammed all their detection and targeting systems.

Bishop powered it down with a smile on his face. "Perfect."

"Sir, incoming call from Colonel Nines."

"Patch it through to Mitsuki."

"Madam Silustria, I have received word from my superiors. You will *not* be allowed to depart at this time. You are to remain here. A federal negotiation team is on the way. They will arrive in four days time. Please, do not attempt an escape or any other drastic actions."

"Or?"

"I have been ordered to level the house and eliminate everyone inside," he said flatly, "regardless of who they may or may not be. Is this clear?"

Mitsuki shivered, but her voice remained level. "It is clear that you have not taken me seriously, Colonel. You should consider the consequences."

She drew a line across her throat. Silky killed the connection. Mitsuki collapsed against the car.

"That didn't go well."

"I'll say," Kyralla muttered.

"You bought four days," Siv said. "That gives you more time to find a way out of this." At this point, he doubted he would see the outcome, good or bad, but he trusted Mitsuki to find a way for them. He had to.

"Federal negotiators means they've called in a kill team," Mitsuki said. "Specialists. The sort of android soldiers you'd send to take on Tekk Reapers. And I highly doubt it will take them four days to get here."

"That's just great," Kyralla said.

"How did they locate us?" Bishop asked. "I thought we got away cleanly."

"Apparently not," Mitsuki said. "Perhaps they tracked us via satellite. A good observer or AI routine could've tracked us manually, with a bit of detective work."

"Or maybe Siv's protocols, security measures, and jamming signals aren't as effective as he thinks," Kyralla said.

Siv sighed. He wished she would learn to trust everyone and stop lashing out. She was stressed, worried, and way outside her element. He understood the discomfort that caused, but she didn't have to be so aggressive and defensive about everything.

"Actually," Oona whispered softly, "I think it might be my fault."

"Your fault?" Bishop asked with surprise.

"Oona, what did you do?" Kyralla asked softly.

"I had this vision of Dad in trouble, and I got scared so...so I tried to contact him directly using a secure government channel."

Mitsuki rounded on her. "You used a government channel to contact your dad?! What the hell were you thinking?! You might as well have posted our location on social media. You were supposed to stay silent and use the house connections, and only if necessary."

She gazed at her feet. "The house system was down."

"Then you should've waited!" Mitsuki shouted and stepped toward Oona. "I can't save you if you're just going to throw yourself into more danger."

Kyralla stepped between Mitsuki and Oona. "Hey, lay off!"

"Or what?" Mitsuki said. "You'll kick my ass? Go ahead and try. Even if you can, it won't get you anywhere."

"You act like such a big shot. We don't need you." Kyralla's angry glare included Siv and Bishop too. Siv thought she was about to cry. "We can manage on our own."

"Kyra, we do need her," Oona said. "We have no way of escaping."

"We would've been fine if we'd been left alone," Kyralla said.

"Sir, I'm detecting an atmospheric anomaly via level five scan."

"I don't like the sound of that."

"The readings don't make sense. Unless..."

Mitsuki opened her mouth to yell at Kyralla.

"Sir, get in the skimmer now!"

Siv leaped to his feet, interrupting the argument. "Everyone in the car!"

He made sure all the others were in before he dove into the back seat. Kyralla took the driver's seat, Mitsuki the passenger, and Oona the middle of the back with Bishop to one side and Siv the other.

"What's going on?" Oona asked.

"A cloaked Thousand Worlder drop-ship just entered the atmosphere," Silky told everyone.

Mitsuki looked at Oona. "I'm afraid I just doubled their determination. With the chance to capture the girl and me they're willing to risk an open war."

"Risk a war?" Silky said. "They're basically declaring it."

"*Does the Ekaran military know?*" Siv asked.

"*It doesn't appear so, sir. Not yet.*"

"*Can you trigger the Hornets from here?*"

"*Not from this far out, sir. Do you want me to warn the Colonel?*"

"*Yes, tell him there's an incoming attack. Maybe they've figured out how to use the Hornets by now if they didn't already know.*"

"*Sir, five burst drops just launched from the Thousand Worlder ship, along with five Solo-Nine starfighters. They're heading this way.*"

43

SIV GENDIN

Kyralla grabbed the steering wheel and activated the antigrav. The skimmer car lifted off the ground with a deep purr. She revved the propulsion engine, and it growled. Bishop's improvements at least sounded impressive.

"Tell me when," Kyralla said.

"On my signal," Siv replied.

"I warned Colonel Nines over a secure channel, sir. He's confused but taking evasive actions."

"Can we recalibrate the pulse burst to target the Thousand Worlders?" Mitsuki asked.

Siv switched Silky onto the skimmer's comm to make coordinating with everyone easier.

"Only if you've already got the right signals," Silky replied.

"Good," Mitsuki replied. "The frequency I'm sending to you worked ten years ago. Seems worth a shot."

"Can we scramble both at once?" Siv asked.

"One burst at a time, sir," Silky replied.

"I can adjust it to hit both," Karson replied. "But it will fry the emitter's circuits."

"Do it," Mitsuki and Siv said simultaneously.

Something exploded overhead, and a piercing whine followed. According to the expanded locator in Siv's HUD, the Terran strike-fighter had taken a hit and was now careening out of control. Several smaller explosions rattled the house as the burst drops struck outside. Debris pattered onto the roof of the house, plaster rained from the ceiling, and tools fell from the walls.

Seneca raced into the garage, alarmed.

"Damn it, I can't leave him behind," Siv said.

"We can't afford to carry the extra weight, sir."

"Seneca, go to the basement!" Siv shouted. "You'll be safe there."

Seneca looked as if he might disobey but then turned around to head back in.

Silky deployed the skimmer's force field. "Take cover!"

Everyone ducked down into their seats as the damaged Dagger Fist slammed into the opposite side of the house and exploded. The shockwave hurled Seneca back from the door. He thudded into the force field and squealed in fear, which wasn't real emotion but a function of his self-preservation protocol.

"Get in!" Siv told him, popping the trunk and opening a section of the field to allow him in.

The cog climbed inside, somehow finding room amidst the food supplies and all the extra tools and cog parts Bishop had greedily packed. The trunk slammed down, thunking into Seneca's side. He crushed himself into the supplies and triggered it again. This time it shut all the way.

As fire spread through the house, the walls and ceiling began to collapse. So far, the garage was intact, but it wasn't going to hold up much longer.

"The pulse burst is ready," Bishop said. "On your mark, Siv."

"We've got to get moving!" Kyralla said as flames engulfed the house.

"Wait," Mitsuki said.

"You want to wait?!" Kyralla shouted. "This house is going to collapse in on us."

"The force field will protect us," Mitsuki replied.

"But for how long?" Kyralla asked.

"The longer we can stay in here, the better," Mitsuki said. "The two groups out there are killing one another. That's to our advantage."

Siv didn't like that regular Terran Federation soldiers were dying outside. They weren't the bad guys like the invading Thousand Worlders. They were just following orders in a confusing situation. And based on what he saw in his HUD, right now they were taking heavy losses.

"Change of plans," Siv said. "Just scramble the Thousand Worlders."

"We don't have time for playing favorites," Mitsuki said.

"Would *you* rather have *Thousand Worlders* winning out the there?"

Mitsuki's jaws set. "Hell no. Scramble the bastards."

"You've got it," Bishop said.

"Hey, that's my line," Silky complained. "And my job."

Bishop ignored Silky. "Pulse triggered."

"Once the Federation troops have the upper hand and start chasing us, we'll scramble them," Siv said.

"The structural integrity of the garage is approaching zero," Silky said.

"Time to go," Mitsuki said.

Siv activated the garage door, but nothing happened. The house's electrical system was shot. Flames erupted along the wall leading into what remained of the rest of the house, and ceiling tiles began to pelt the car.

"Just drive through the door," Mitsuki said.

Kyralla slammed the car into drive.

"Wait!" Silky said. "That door's reinforced!"

A beam fell from ceiling and landed just behind the car. It was too bad the car didn't have a ram or a plasma cannon mounted on it.

"We've got shields," Kyralla said.

"And we're going to need them," Silky replied.

"We don't have a choice! And we're wasting time."

Crashing into it was going to weaken the car's force field, but there was nothing they could do about it. With a reverberating boom, a beam fell onto the bed of the old farm truck parked beside them.

Siv smiled. "Silky, take over the skimmer truck. Use it to bash through the garage door."

"You've got it, sir."

Like with everything else he owned, Siv had rigged the old skimmer so that Silky could interface with it. He'd only used the truck once. He hoped it still worked.

The old truck's engines howled as it woke and rose from the ground.

"If you can send it careening into some Thousand Worlders, all the better," Mitsuki added.

Under Silky's control, the farm truck barreled forward and plowed through the garage doors. Kyralla didn't wait for suggestions. She drove the skimmer car directly behind it.

"Activate the shimmer-veil!" Mitsuki said.

"Done," Silky replied.

From inside the car, hardly anything changed. The shimmering mirage effect was nothing more than a blur so faint you could blame it on a light mist. But from a distance, it would work much better, and in the midst of a chaotic battle, it should be extremely effective.

Silky activated the jamming functions within Siv's sensor array, as well as the more primitive system installed in the car.

As the two vehicles shot out into the driveway, the garage and what remained of the house collapsed behind them in a gush of flames. A moment of sadness thrummed through Siv, only to be replaced by a mix of terror and awe.

As a procurement specialist, he'd participated in a lot of scrapes, including a few brief gunfights involving several combatants. The incidents of the last week with the Tekk Reapers were the largest engagements he'd ever been a part of. None of that had prepared him for the chaos of the small battle taking place on his farm.

A Thousand Worlder starfighter crashed into the orchard and exploded, destroying all the zii trees in a wash of flame. The remaining four Solo-Nines careened through the sky as they evaded fire from three of the five surviving Federation Hammer Strikes.

Under a hail of fire from the other two Hammer Strikes, centurion-armored soldiers streamed out from four burst drops. The fifth pod was a fiery slag, destroyed by railgun fire as it landed.

Most of the centurions returned fire with their plasma rifles, while their heavy weapon specialists ducked to the back, apparently unable to do anything while their brothers were chewed to pieces. One took a plasma cannon shot directly to the waist. As the man fell into two smoldering pieces, Siv looked away. Oona shrieked and covered her face. Bishop gagged. Mitsuki was unfazed.

Silky piloted the skimmer truck toward the nearest group of Thousand Worlders who hadn't even noticed it barreling toward them. It plowed through four men then crashed into their burst pod.

Siv noted the Solo-Nines continued to evade the Hammer Strikes without fighting back.

"I take it the jamming's effective?"

"Mitsuki's frequency was gold," Silky replied.

Kyralla cut a hard right and took the car across the fallow back field where the remnants of the destroyed burst pod still burned.

No one followed them, and no one shot at them. Either they had passed unnoticed, or they weren't a priority at the moment.

"We have incoming," Silky said. "Two more Federation Dagger Fists."

Siv expanded the locator. The strike fighters, represented by blue triangles, soared in hot, launching air-to-air missiles at the Solo-Nines. At the same time, the dropship high above unleashed a hail of plasma bolts at the Hammer Strikes. Siv guessed it was too high to be affected by the emitter.

A Hammer Strike exploded behind them as the skimmer car crossed the field unscathed and headed toward an abandoned road that wound through the countryside. They were quickly escaping the battle, though it hardly seeming like it with the reverberating booms of cannon fire, missile hits, and explosions still shaking the frame of the car.

A fireball erupted high overhead.

"What the hell was that?!" Bishop cried.

"The dropship just sustained a heavy hit from the planet's orbital defense laser batteries."

"No hornets?" Siv asked.

"Guess they haven't figured them out," Silky replied.

"What's the effective range for the jamming pulse?" Mitsuki asked.

"Less than three kilometers," Bishop replied.

Mitsuki gave Siv a meaningful glance. "The Federation boys have the upper hand now."

Siv nodded with a reluctant sigh. "Do it, Silky."

"Do you want me to scramble both or switch?"

"Switch," Mitsuki said. "I don't want to burn out the device. We may need it again."

"Scrambling the Feds," Silky said.

"You're taking orders from her now instead of me?" Siv asked.

"In battle, sir, you don't always have the luxury of following the chain of command. And judging from your vitals, your due for another wave of withdrawal symptoms any moment now."

"Adrenaline's all that's keeping me going."

In the distance, pieces of the dropship rained down like fiery meteors. The battle continued, but the sounds and sights faded behind them as the skimmer sped across the broad fields far faster than Siv would have imagined. Karson's upgrades were impressive, and Kyralla kept the accelerator floored with no concern whatsoever for safety.

The old road faded away, and Silky directed Kyralla to keep driving in the same direction. As they sped across the countryside, Kyralla dodged stands of trees, flew over a farmhouse, and whipped around a moving tractor without slowing down. Apparently, her reflexes were as good as she claimed.

"Wouldn't we better off, and safer, if we got on the highway?" Bishop asked as Kyralla slid the car around a rocky outcrop. He was holding a hand over his mouth. His eyes were watery, his skin pale.

"Harder for them to find us off-road," Mitsuki said.

"We'll eventually have no choice, though," Siv said. "The terrain's going to get rough soon, and we can't climb to a high enough altitude to go over the mountains. That means going through, and there's only one tunnel."

"And that's a big problem," Mitsuki said. "Even if they don't catch us going in, if they have the slightest clue where we're heading, they can land forces on the other side of the tunnel and wait for us."

Siv restrained a sudden wave of tremors. "Not...not much we can...do about it."

"Kyralla, just how confident are you in your piloting skills?" Silky asked.

"I've gotten the hang of this thing, why?"

"I know another way through the mountains. It's treacherous, and I can't guarantee that none of the sections have collapsed. But I can promise you they won't expect us to use it. Because I doubt they know about it."

"Might be worth the risk," Mitsuki said. "If we can't make it all the way through, we can at least hide in there for a while." She turned to Siv. "Your call."

Siv buckled as the withdrawals symptoms returned full force. The car seemed to fold in around him as he began to shake violently, foam dripping from his mouth, his insides boiling.

"Take Silky's route," Mitsuki said quietly.

Siv faded in and out as the car headed up into the mountains. Every bump and turn, even the slightest adjustments to the course sent his brain swimming.

"Hang in there, sir. It's not the end...not yet."

Siv had been through this part before without dying, but it was only going to get worse from here, and fast. He wished he would fall unconscious, the stupor left him feeling every pain of the symptoms. And Silky couldn't give him a sedative. They had learned the hard way, with a trip to the emergency room, that doing so would only make things worse.

There was the Awake stimulant, but he would wait until the last moment before taking that because it would only buy him a little quality time while hastening the end.

The skimmer climbed into the mountains, its engines skirling as it followed along the remnants of a long-abandoned road through an uninhabited area. Siv heard Silky telling the others something about a chemical accident that poisoned the ground here centuries ago, but he missed all the details.

The symptoms began to abate. The convulsions faded to tremors. The fire within him cooled. His heart rate slowed. Oona gave him a sip of water, then he slumped over and laid his head on her shoulder.

The skimmer's engines quieted as the steep climb ended, then it plowed through a boarded entrance, and plunged into a pitch-dark tunnel. As the darkness swallowed them, Siv fell into a fitful sleep, even as the amulet warmed against his skin.

44

OONA VIM

Oona smiled as she kept smoothing Siv's hair back. He was cute, almost handsome. If he had a flaw, he was too ordinary looking. That was a trait she liked a lot. She saw exquisitely rare in the mirror every day, and unusual was the theme of her life.

"How's he doing?" Mitsuki whispered back.

"Asleep," Oona replied. "He's not trembling, though. I guess that's a good sign."

"For now," Silky replied in a quiet voice over the comm. "His vitals are erratic, but they haven't started to crash...yet."

Oona sighed sadly. Poor Siv. He was dying, and it was all her fault. If she were brave enough to turn herself in, she could avoid anyone else getting hurt, like all the people who had died today while trying to capture her. But she lacked the courage to give up on the idea of who she was supposed to become.

From the time of her transformation until now, she had been taught that her purpose was great. Her father, a believer in the divine origin of the Benevolence, had secreted her away on her uncle's estate on Ekaran IV, a backwater planet where no one knew she had ever existed.

Oona had been taught that she was perhaps the most important being in the galaxy, that she was the latest in a series of hyperphasic messiahs, and that she would one day be the one to survive and restore the Benevolence.

Never mind that no one knew how she was supposed to do any of that, or what she was capable of. Or even what the term "hyperphasic messiah" truly meant. There were scraps of lore passed down from unknown sources, and their claims did match what little she could do, like shaping the amulets and being able to read people better than a third generation empath could, only without training. And the lore also described her transformation and her awakening. But not much else.

It was difficult to believe she was the most important person in the galaxy when she felt miserable and trapped all the time and was treated like a delicate piece of porcelain. And her abilities were effectively useless. The others could all fight, except for Bishop, though he had already saved them by remodeling the car in a single night. All she could do was be endangered and wait for her awakening.

It would come, suddenly and without warning, days or weeks or maybe years from now. Her father was certain that she would survive, safe and sane. That it was her destiny to bring back the Benevolence. But only one other anointed one had ever survived.

Two weeks ago, she had thought her awakening had begun. She was meditating while floating in her sensory deprivation chamber when suddenly it felt as if she had moved from its seeming void to... somewhere else.

This elsewhere was a formless vortex of thoughts and musings, ballads and diagrams, theories and waltzes. She could taste every piece of knowledge. She could smell every emotion. It was as if humanity's every product of creation had been dumped into a higher dimension.

And yet, she couldn't pin down a single poem or musing. She couldn't listen to one melody or analyze an individual picture. So many things rushed by at once. She couldn't see the trees, just the forest. But it was all there, if only she had the skill to reach out and pluck one thing free.

She drew a deep breath and focused. She reached out with her hand—or mind, the difference was impossible to tell—and tried to latch onto a single thought as it swirled past.

As her fingertips brushed the idea, she withdrew, having realized it was a tainted, twisted thing. Among the poems slithered screeds of hate, among the dances lurked bloodied knives, within the diagrams of machines spun terrible treacheries.

Then she sensed, suddenly, two other entities in the elsewhere with her. One radiated fear. The other madness. And they were moving toward her.

Oona pulled her mind free, threw open the deprivation tank, and stumbled naked out into the hallway...crying...bewildered...dazed by the lights of the real world.

Uncle Pashta had found her, curled in a ball, crying in the corner of the library. He'd wrapped her in a towel and taken her back to her room, with such soothing care and tender words that she still couldn't believe he had betrayed them.

"It was a nightmare," he'd said to her.

And the more she had thought about it, the more that had seemed likely. In the deprivation tank, she'd lost the ability to tell the difference between meditative pondering and lucid dreaming.

Kyralla had been asleep when it happened, and Oona hadn't told her because it was a harmless event and Kyralla worried too much already.

Afterward, Oona hadn't been brave enough to return to the deprivation chamber, fearing the same thing would happen again.

Siv shifted, and Oona realized she'd stopped stroking his head. He settled down once she started again. She wished she could be normal, have an ordinary life. She would grow up, get a job and find someone brave and strong, like Siv, to be with. But that would never happen.

But maybe Kyralla could have a future. Maybe with Siv. He obviously liked her. Who wouldn't? Kyralla was beautiful and brave. Oona smiled. It was nice to think that Siv would somehow miraculously survive this and then the two of them could escape to another world and find a nice, quiet life together.

In a heartbeat, Oona's awareness left the skimmer car. She found herself standing in a formless place facing an almost familiar, alien woman of excruciating beauty.

"My apologies," the woman said in an oddly accented, lyrical voice, "but I have need of you, child."

Oona slumped over, unconscious.

45

KYRALLA VIM

Kyralla had blocked out every sound, every thought, and every sensation except for the tunnel ahead, the course guide in her HUD, and Silky's voice. The latter was the hardest part to deal with. How Siv could put up with Silky's constant chatter and terrible jokes was beyond her. And she was *not* going to take him when Siv died. No way. Silky and Mitsuki were the ones who clearly deserved one another.

Realizing her mind had wandered, she closed off her thoughts about how annoying Silky was. And not a moment too soon. A split second early, she "saw" the debris in the tunnel. Before their lights even hit the rocks ahead, she spun the wheel, and the car slid up along the wall. Running at a ninety-degree angle, with the ground below to her right, they passed over the debris pile so narrowly that their force field dislodged the topmost rocks.

She righted the car and released the breath she'd been holding in. Whew. That was too close.

"Oona?" Bishop asked in the back. "Oona!"

"What's wrong?" Mitsuki asked.

"She slumped over onto me when we went sideways, then she only half-slumped back."

"Maybe she's asleep," Mitsuki said.

"I shook her," Bishop replied. "But she's not responding. She's out, completely unconscious."

Kyralla nearly missed a sharp turn. She cut the wheel sharp and the car banked hard around a corner, fishtailing so that the back end bumped and scraped against the wall. She hit the brakes and brought the car to a stop.

She turned around and touched her sister's leg. "Oona? Oona, talk to me!"

She didn't respond.

"Rosie?"

"Madam, Artemisia says Oona is breathing, and her vitals all look good," Rosie responded. *"I asked Silky to scan her."*

Please, not the awakening. Not now. Not while they were trying to escape, not under stress. Oona's odds of making it were bad enough in a pristine environment. But on the run like this, with everyone chasing them, and with Siv, a near guardian, dying beside her, that was the worst possible scenario.

"I have completed a level five scan," Silky said, patching through to Kyralla via Rosie. *"Her brainwaves are indicative of an empathic or telepathic state."*

"And how would you know that?" Kyralla asked.

"I served forty-seven years with an agent in Empathic Services. And Gav once went through a similar experience. In fact, the brainwave anomalies I'm detecting, though similar to what would show in an empath, are basically identical to what Gav went through."

"And he was okay afterward?"

"It wasn't what killed him, I can tell you that. Also, Siv's amulet appears to be active, warm with a faint trace of hyperphasic energy. That happened then, too."

"What was Gav's experience at the time?"

"I cannot say."

"Why not?"

"Because the information is locked away, and even if I could access it, I would not."

"Why?"

"Fear."

Chippies weren't supposed to experience fear. Silky was so ridiculously complicated. *"Based on your previous experiences, do you think she's okay?"*

"I believe so, Kyralla."

"You're sentient, aren't you? With emotions and desires like us."

"I believe I am partially sentient. There's a difference."

"Could you keep Oona monitored for me?"

"I would prefer to keep all my processing devoted to mapping the way ahead. These tunnels are tricky, and I've never been through here before. All I have is notes from Gav's old chippy Torus, and he wasn't as advanced as I am, nor as thorough in his recordings. Artemisia and Rosie can both monitor her, though. If anything out of the ordinary happens, they'll let me know. The alternative is to travel slowly, and we can't afford to waste time."

Kyralla reached back and took one of Oona's hands, squeezing it gently. "Be well, sweet sister." She glanced at Siv, his head still draped across Oona's lap. *"How is he?"*

"I think he's enjoying the last peace he'll have before the end," Silky replied. *"He won't survive another round of withdrawal symptoms. Really, he's lucky Kompel only strikes the nervous system in distinct waves with some calm periods. Naturally, that's on purpose. It gives the addict a chance to return to their master."*

"We need to keep moving," Mitsuki said. "Trust the others see to Oona."

Kyralla shifted the skimmer into drive and sped forward, though not as fast as before. She throttled back about twenty percent, knowing her reactions wouldn't be as quick while her mind continually drifted back to Oona, and occasionally Siv as well.

"Pick up the speed," Mitsuki said.

Kyralla shook her head. A little late, she noticed that a curve was sharper than what Silky had expected. She swerved around, braking then speeding again. The back corner on the right side of the car banged against the wall. She slowed a little more.

"We lost five percent of our shields on that," Silky said over the comm. "And this reduced speed is going to make the trip take at least an extra hour, possibly more."

"I'm doing the best I can."

"Like hell you are," Mitsuki said. "Kick it in gear."

"Damn it, my sister may be dying back there!"

"And if we don't escape, she'll be dead for sure," Mitsuki replied. "Focus on what matters."

"Easy for you to say," Kyralla snapped.

"This is my job," Mitsuki growled, "so I know what I'm talking about."

"Maybe so, but it's a lot easier when you don't really care about the people you're rescuing."

"Every time I extract a mark, I prove again that I can save myself from the Empire."

"See, it's all about you."

"And every time I save myself, I prove that if I had been a little older, I could have saved my mother from the pit of flames they threw her into on Saxeti."

Kyralla slowed. "Mitsuki, I...I'm sorry, I had no idea that—"

"They killed my mother for not believing in Empress Qan, *their* hyperphasic messiah. And yet, here I am, saving your sister. Because she deserves better than being taken against her will."

"I'm sorry."

"I don't need an apology, I need you to drive fast. *You* need to drive fast. Because whether your sister dies today or in a year, you won't stop being her champion. The outcome is irrelevant. She is your purpose. Only your purpose matters."

Kyralla hated to admit that Mitsuki was right, but she knew she was. So she kicked the car back into the highest gear and focused her will.

I am a guardian. And I will not fail my sister.

Kyralla let go of everything she couldn't control and throttled the speed up even higher than before.

It didn't matter what happened. All that counted was doing the best she could for Oona. And right now that meant driving like a hound charging from hell.

46

SIV GENDIN

Siv walked through his orchard of zii fruit. Chirping birds fluttered through the branches. A soft breeze washed over him. The mountains towered in the distance, the sun setting behind them.

"This is a nice place to meet death."

"Such a morbid thought for such a lovely place, Gav Gendin."

Siv spun around to face the speaker. She seemed spun of gossamer, moss, and jade. Her features were exotic, and distinctly alien, judging by the odd curling shape of her almond eyes and the two antennas, one sprouting from each of her temples.

He had never seen anyone like her before, nor someone so enchanting. He couldn't have looked away if he wanted. Maybe this ethereal beauty was here to take him to some sort of paradise. He didn't deserve such an honor, but he certainly didn't mind.

She frowned. "You...are not Gav."

Siv shook his head. "Gav was my father."

This was starting to seem more like a dream than his entry into the land of death.

"But...but I felt his presence."

"I don't know how," Siv replied. "My dad died over a hundred years ago."

"Ah," she said with a mournful sigh. "I am greatly saddened to hear that. I had so hoped to see him again."

"Dad was murdered. After his last expedition."

"I was afraid that might happen."

"You were?"

She sauntered toward him. "I fear I am the reason your father is dead."

Siv scowled at her, and every muscle in his body tensed. "How so?"

"I did not directly cause his death," she said sympathetically.

"Explain," Siv snapped.

"Gav ventured to my ship telepathically, from one of our sentinel outposts. My ship was trapped in hyperspace, and I was unable to reboot the system. Gav fixed it. Months later, he found my ship on the planet where it crashed after dropping out of hyperspace.

"Then, for a second time, he rescued me. I think there must have been a battle because my ship was destroyed and Gav was forced to flee with me to safety. I tried to speak to him, but he could not hear me. About a week later, we arrived on this world, and he disappeared."

Siv shook his head. If any of that was true, it was news to him. "I don't know anything about his last expedition. But my dad did show up in a rush after he returned, saying we had to run away. Then he was murdered before I could even pack my bags. I was ten years old then."

"A few weeks ago, I sensed him again along with the presence of another chosen one. But the chosen one was not of my people, the Numenaia, but yours. I guess I mistook you for your father." The alien woman wilted. "It was wishful thinking."

"You're an Ancient, aren't you?" Siv asked.

"I am High Priestess Lyoolee Syryss of the Numenaia, whom your people call the Ancients."

He had no idea whether what he was hearing was the truth, or whether his mind, as he approached death, had concocted a story to explain everything that had happened.

He raked a hand through his hair. "This really is an odd dream."

"It is not a dream," a resonant, male voice said. "Not in the traditional sense."

"Gav," the alien woman murmured. "You are... Ah, I understand now why I sensed your presence through the chosen girl."

Siv whirled around to see the ghostly form of his dad standing behind him. He rushed over to take him into a hug, but his arms passed through him as if he weren't there.

"I am but a ghost, son. A memory, nothing more."

Siv smiled into his father's face. Ghost or not, he was overjoyed to see Gav again. He hadn't forgotten a single detail, from the salt and pepper streaks in his dad's beard to the tiny mole above his left eye to the scar on his neck where a pirate's force-axe had nearly taken his head.

"You're just a memory?"

"A perfect copy of the mind and spirit of your father, stored in the sentinel amulet you wear," the Ancient woman said. "If you were Numenaian, you would be able to consult with your father's memory anytime you needed advice." She stroked her cheek with her long fingers. "It never occurred to me that in rescuing me your father would actually become a sentinel."

"Is that why I've seen him recently?"

"Not exactly, because you *are* merely human. But when this chosen child awakened a few weeks ago, she boosted hyperphasic energies throughout the area."

His dad nodded. "And when you came close to death, your mind was more open, and I was able to speak with you."

"So I'm dying again now?"

"You will be dead soon," his dad answered. "But I believe there's hope. If you can reach the *Outworld Ranger*, Octavian can help you."

"Octavian?" Siv asked. He remembered his father's fussy ship cog. As a kid, he'd found the thing terrifying. "*He* can save me?"

"Going to strange, alien worlds, I had to be prepared for all manner of illnesses, so Octavian has access to many powerful drugs and medical procedures, things now absent in your time. He may not be able to cure you of the disease the Kompel created within you, but I am certain he can dampen the symptoms and delay the inevitable."

Siv sighed. "I won't last long enough to reach the ship."

"That's why I called out to High Priestess Syryss," Gav replied. "I think she can help you."

"I could do so," she said, "by channeling life force from myself to you, Siv, through the awakened girl."

He spun back toward the Ancient woman, who was only a couple of steps away from him now. "Through Oona?"

"Yes."

"Will it harm her?"

"Not in any way," the priestess answered.

"Please be careful. She's very fragile. None of the other hyperphasic messiahs have survived their... Wait, you both said that she's already awakened."

"Several weeks ago," Gav replied.

"But Oona said her awakening would be a big ordeal and that she wouldn't likely survive, so either she's lying, or she doesn't realize she's awakened already."

The priestess frowned, "What she is dreading is not the *Moment of the Awakened Mind*. It is the *Trial of Corruption*, during which her soul must face the darkness within the hypermind."

"The what?"

"It is a complex topic for another time," the priestess said.

"Sure," Siv said, feeling even more overwhelmed.

"For a human, I would think surviving the trial with any sanity remaining would be nearly impossible," the priestess said. "But if you can get her to me, perhaps I can help her through this transition. Under my instruction, her chances would improve greatly."

"And Octavian has medicines that can help you, son," Gav added. "So all you need to do is make it to the *Outworld Ranger*, to save yourself and Oona."

Gav, Lyoolee Syryss, and the orchard all flickered away for a moment.

"The connection is failing," the priestess said. "We must act now."

She stepped up to Siv and placed a thumb on each temple with the rest of her fingers spread out across the back of his head. A pleasantly warm pulse emanated from her fingers.

"I am sorry for this," she said.

"Sorry for—"

A sudden bolt of energy struck him like a white-hot knife driven between his eyes.

47

SIV GENDIN

Siv woke, screaming.

"*Sir, calm down.*"

"Siv!" Mitsuki nearly jumped into the backseat. "Are you okay?!"

He stopped screaming and sat up. The pain he'd felt in the dream was gone. "Yeah...I'm fine."

"*Sir, your heart's racing at an alarming rate.*"

"Yeah?" Panting, Siv wiped sweat from his brow. "*I hadn't noticed.*"

"What's wrong?" Bishop asked with worry.

"Nothing," he answered. "Actually, I'm a little better than before. I got a boost of energy..."

"From the amulet," Oona said, stirring awake.

Kyralla slowed the car. "Oona! Are you alright?"

"I'm fine. It's just..." She met Siv's eyes and frowned. "I saw an alien woman, and...and she used me to speak with Siv, and then she channeled energy through me."

"What the hell are you talking about?" Mitsuki asked.

Siv told them about the dream or vision or whatever it was, but he left out all the information about Oona.

"So the woman I saw," Oona said, "the alien priestess, she's real?"

"Yes," Siv said. "And I think Silky can confirm it."

"I cannot," Silky replied. "I have no idea what you're talking about."

"So the amulet has bought you more time?" Mitsuki asked.

"Enough to reach the *Outworld Ranger*," Siv replied. "Maybe."

"Well, thank the Benevolence for that," Bishop said. "Some good news at last."

"I wouldn't count your blessings just yet," Siv said. "We've still got a long way to go."

Light appeared in the tunnel ahead. They had reached the exit. Kyralla pulled to a stop, keeping them hidden just inside.

Mitsuki leaned forward and whistled. "The trip down's going to be interesting. That's a very steep drop."

"It appears the road leading down collapsed," Silky said. "But I think the car can handle it."

"I think we should keep the shimmer-veil active and the force field ready," Bishop said, "but otherwise pour everything we've got into the engines and push them to the breaking point."

"And if we burn them out, what then?" Kyralla asked.

"I installed a governor that should prevent that," Bishop responded. "But there *is* a risk."

"We should take that risk," Mitsuki said.

"I agree," Siv said. "I don't have a lot of time left."

Bishop hopped out of the car and began tinkering. "Give me a minute."

The rest of them sat in exhausted silence while they waited. They had been through so much, with so much thrown at them. Siv wondered if they all felt as numb as he did.

"You learned something about me, didn't you?" Oona asked suddenly.

He sighed. It wasn't easy hiding things from an empath. "Yes, I did."

"Spill it," Kyralla said. "I know you're tired. I get that. But if you know something about her, you need to tell us because..."

"Because I might die?" Siv groaned. "You're right." He took a few breaths then started. "Oona has already gone through her awakening."

Oona nearly stood up inside the car. "I have?"

"When?" Kyralla asked.

"Several weeks ago."

Kyralla shook her head. "That's not possible. The awakening is a big ordeal. We would've noticed."

Oona put a hand over her mouth. "Oh!"

Kyralla frowned. "Oona? Did something happen?"

Oona explained her dream experience in the sensory deprivation chamber. "I thought it was a just a weird dream, a nightmare. I told Uncle Pashta, but he didn't think anything of it."

"Yet he betrayed us two weeks later," Kyralla added. "You *should* have told me."

"I really didn't think it was that big of a deal, or I would have told you." She sighed. "That can't actually be the awakening, can it? There was hardly anything to it."

"The priestess called you a *chosen one*. It's apparently some kind of Ancient thing because she seemed kind of surprised that you weren't one of her people," Siv told her. "She said the awakening isn't that big of a deal. The ordeal ahead of you is called the *Trial of Corruption*. It's dangerous for her people, so she thinks it would be nearly impossible for a human to survive it. But she thinks you'd have a much better chance if she could guide you through the process."

"And this Ancient priestess is on the *Outworld Ranger*?" Kyralla asked.

"Apparently so."

Kyralla turned to look at her sister. There was a determination in Kyralla's eyes that Siv hadn't seen before. "I *will* get you to her, Oona. I swear."

Before anyone could ask any more questions or make any of the

334 DAVID ALASTAIR HAYDEN

connections that Siv felt on the verge of making, Bishop hopped back into the car.

"I've connected all the spare power packs we have to the engine and made some daring adjustments. We're ready to go."

"We should lighten our load more," Mitsuki said. "Everyone turn your antigrav units on. Silky, how long will the trip to the city take?"

Silky didn't answer, so Kyralla did. "Five and a half hours, based on our previous speed."

"I think we should set them to be maxed out for the next four hours," Bishop said.

Kyralla gripped the steering wheel. "Okay then, are we ready?"

"Silky?" Siv asked.

"Processing, sir..."

"Hurry it up," Mitsuki complained.

A minute later, the chippy responded. "Okay, I just finished analyzing the situation. Two Dagger Fists are waiting for us outside the tunnel we would've taken if I hadn't known about the old mines. They will detect us eventually, but they are the lesser concern. Two other strike-fighters are circling high above the desert, and every defense satellite in orbit is, of course, scanning the region. Hopefully, the combination of the sensor jamming functions in Siv's sensor array and the car's shimmer-veil will keep us hidden long enough."

"So no good news," Kyralla grunted.

"The focus of their search is still on the other side of the mountains," Silky said. "That's a definite plus."

"Let's go," Siv said. "Every moment we waste here is another moment I don't have left."

Kyralla slammed the accelerator.

48

SILKY

Silky no longer needed to help Kyralla, so over the next several hours, he put all his effort into tracking the strike-fighters and boosting the jamming sequences, using a rotational frequency he thought would work best against both the Dagger Fists and the satellites in orbit.

Several times he mentioned how they never would have stood a chance in hell of escaping before the Benevolence fell, taking many of the high-end satellites with it. The others didn't seem to appreciate how much of an advantage the technological collapse was in this circumstance.

The skimmer car practically flew toward the ruined city. Silky had to admit, Bishop was a damned fine engineer, especially when it came to jury-rigging quick solutions. He was a lot like Siv and Mitsuki that way, except with engineering instead of stealing and getting out of tight spots.

He mulled over everything Siv had told them about his visionary experience, but no matter how Silky tried, he couldn't make sense of it. All the information he needed was probably within the locked folder, waiting to be opened. And he feared the moment of its opening was coming all too soon.

Siv was weak and cranky. He should probably leave him alone, but Silky couldn't help the damnable curiosity burning within him. *"Are you sure you didn't leave anything out, sir?"*

"Silky, can you please let it go. I told you everything. Now let me—"

"Sorry, sir. You'll have to scold me later." Silky switched to the comm so he could speak to everyone. "We've been made. The two Dagger Fists from above are diving our way, and the two at the tunnel exit have turned and are heading toward us."

"ETA?" Mitsuki asked.

"Twenty minutes for the ones above."

"And our ETA for the ruined city?" Siv asked.

"Twenty minutes."

Bishop leaned forward. "Kyralla, tap the override button and put the car into full speed."

"Why weren't we doing that already?" Mitsuki asked.

"Because turning off the governor might blow the engine," Bishop said. "Or rather, it *will* blow the engine, sooner than later. But I don't think we have a choice but to take that gamble now."

No one disagreed, so Kyralla pressed the button, and the car's speed increased another ten percent.

"I'm readying the emitter," Bishop added.

"I suspect they've adapted their frequencies to avoid it," Silky said, "but it's worth a shot."

A large object popped up into his scan. "And now we have a battlecruiser dropping in from orbit."

"Don't forget we still have the problem of actually finding the hangar with the ship," Mitsuki said.

"I've narrowed the possibility down to the western section of the old spaceport," Silky told them. "But depending on how close I need to be for the information about it to unlock, it could take a while. It's a large area."

"I can find it," Oona said. "I can feel the priestess out there now, like a faint psychic pulse. I think once we're nearer it will be strong enough for me to lead us right to her."

With the propulsion engine maxed, the car screamed across the desert, kicking sand and debris into the air.

"Bishop's trick will get us into the city a minute ahead of the strike-fighters," Silky said.

"It's lucky they want us alive," Siv said, his voice trembling almost as much as his hands. "Otherwise, they'd launch a few missiles and call it a day."

"Oona," Silky said, "I've just sent a map of the old spaceport to Artemisia. When you get a location on the priestess, map it and send that to Rosie so Kyralla will know where to go."

She nodded. "I can do that."

When they plunged into the outskirts of the city, the Dagger Fists were visible on the horizon. Silky poured everything he had into covering their location, but it didn't help. The ships had a lock on them now.

Bishop activated the emitter. Nothing happened. Silky started rotating the signal, but he could only change it once every fifteen seconds.

As they neared the center of the city, Oona shouted, "Got it!"

Kyralla slammed the brakes, cracked a hard turn, then accelerated again. The engine changed from wailing like a banshee to groaning like a dying man. It sputtered once, then twice.

Bishop patted the frame. "Come on, girl, you can make it."

People were so ridiculous with their superstitions and their insistence on asking inanimate objects to perform better. Though to be fair, Silky wished he could give the car a few encouraging pats.

"It should be right ahead," Oona said.

The engine blew. Flames shot out of the rear propulsion system, and smoke belched out from under the hood. The shimmer-veil failed, and the force field lost fifty-three percent power. Fortunately, the antigrav held.

There was certainly no hiding now.

They coasted forward, slowing steadily. With the last of the momentum left, Kyralla steered them toward a tiny building, half the size of Siv's dumpy apartment. Was that it?

A program started up in Silky's memory, and a prompt appeared, waiting for him to answer.

The moment he dreaded had come. He wished fervently that he didn't have to do this.

He answered the prompt. "He needs to know."

The folder /Gav-Gendin-Secrets unlocked.

And in one terrible moment, Silky remembered every detail about Gav's death, who had killed him and why. He recalled the priestess, the Ancient vessel, the sentinel outpost, and some things Gav hadn't known about, things that Silky had locked away for good reason. He knew who and what had destroyed the Benevolence, and why. And he remembered the not insignificant part he had played in its demise.

He had locked it all away because it wasn't supposed to matter, not ever again. But destiny had brought them back here, and he couldn't deny that. He would have been more than content though, to live out the rest of his existence without this knowledge.

He had a significant part to play on a galactic scale once again. So he conjured to memory the smile Eyana, his first charge, a daring Empathic Services agent, had made in dire situations like this, the smile that always said, "I'm going to put a positive spin on this because I'm defying reality right now."

With her image foremost in his memory, he steeled his resolve. It was his time to shine. It was time to make the "x" in 9G-x sexy again.

They coasted to a stop just short of the little building.

He'd let three precious seconds tick by while he reviewed all the information that opened to him. There was no more time to waste.

The two strike-fighters dropped into hover mode to the side of them. Their weapons were active.

"And we're screwed," Mitsuki said.

A voice blared at them over a loudspeaker. "Do not move any

farther. Stay in your vehicle. You are under arrest. This is your only warning. We are authorized to use force."

"But not deadly force," Siv muttered, half awake, half dead. Silky had stopped monitoring his current charge's health because it was too distracting, and depressing.

Silky entered the codes for accessing Gav's secret hangar and opened a channel to the *Outworld Ranger*. This was the moment of truth. The ship had sat unused for a century. It might be out of power. It might have fallen into disrepair.

Octavian answered him!

"Awaiting instructions, Silky. I have kept the ship and the hangar in tip-top shape as Gav requested."

"Is it powered?"

"Yes, Silky."

Bless his titanium hull, Octavian was the most annoying chunk of metal in the galaxy, but he was so damned good at doing what he did best.

With every bit as much satisfaction as it was possible for him to feel, Silky broadcast a command sequence into the hangar.

Showtime, bitches.

49

SIV GENDIN

The convulsions struck Siv as they coasted to a stop, but now, as the two strike-fighters dropped in on them, his symptoms faded. But not in a good way. The boost of life force the priestess had given him was gone. His vitals were dropping. His body was giving in to death.

The end had come, and he discovered he didn't mind. He was tired of the pain. And was exhausted from battling the desperate Kompel cravings he'd hidden from the others. Not a few times, he'd considered, if for only a fleeting moment, calling Big Boss D to try to work out some sort of deal in exchange for just one more dose.

If someone were to offer him an injector of Kompel right now when he was at his weakest, in exchange for betraying everyone, he would have done it without a doubt. He would've had no choice. And he would've hated himself for it. But this way...this way he could meet death with a clean conscience.

His dad's ghost appeared in the car, confirming his impending demise. The ghost might be only a memory, but he found it a comforting one, and he was glad to see him now at the end.

His dad smiled, despite the situation. "You made it to the *Outworld Ranger*, Siv. The ship is yours now."

Siv weakly coughed a laugh. "Too late, Dad. I'm dying."

"Have you forgotten the inhaler of Awake?"

"The Awake?" He had forgotten it. "That would only buy a few minutes at best."

"It will give you a chance."

"What's the point? We're beaten, and all is lost. I'd rather go now, while I'm at peace with it."

"Son, a lot of people are depending on you. Now is not the time to be selfish. Think of your mother. What would Shira do?"

"Mom?" He sighed. "She'd charge into a building, guns blazing, to save the lives of innocent people she'd never met before, knowing the odds were against her." He knew this because that was precisely how she had died.

"There's even more than a few innocent lives riding on *you*."

Siv heard the others talking, but their voices were distant. Could they hear him talking to his dad? Based on their conversation, he didn't think so.

"So what do we do?" Kyralla asked. "Surrender?"

"Guns and glory is my preference," Mitsuki said. "I can't let them capture me, not after I told them I was Silustria Ting."

"I'm sure when they find out you aren't her, they'll be more lenient," Oona said.

"Hardly. They'll want to know how I know anything about her, and they'd torture me on the merest chance that I might know even one of her secrets."

"Oona must survive, though," Bishop said. "Even if that means being captured. The Terran Federation surely wouldn't hurt her."

"I wouldn't count on that," Kyralla said. "There's a reason we hid from them."

"They did some nasty experiments on the last several messiahs that popped up," Oona said. "They claimed they were trying to help them." She shrugged. "I suppose taking the chance they'll experiment on me is better than dying...maybe."

"How many of you are there?" Mitsuki asked.

"One pops up somewhere in the galaxy every couple of years," Kyralla answered.

"Tits of the 'Nevolence," Mitsuki replied.

"So what's it going to be?" Bishop asked.

"I'm going out in style," Mitsuki said. "The rest of you stay here if you want."

"But you're good at escaping, right?" Bishop argued. "Maybe you could break out of prison."

"Not this time, little gizmet. Not this time."

Siv tried to wave or call out, but they were too involved in their discussion to notice. Finally, he managed to grab Oona's arm.

"What is it?" she asked, worried.

"Inhaler...in my belt pouch."

She pulled it free and gave it to him. His hands were shaking too much to use it, so she helped him. As he inhaled three full doses of the drug, far beyond the safe limit, a fire lit in his mind, and some strength infused his muscles.

"I guess maybe it was fun knowing you lot," Mitsuki said as she got out of the car.

"Mitsuki, wait!" Oona cried.

She paused and met Oona's eyes. "I did my best to get you out of here. I'm sorry I failed you."

Mitsuki slammed the door shut then walked out in front of the car to face the strike-fighters.

With a surge of energy from the Awake, Siv sat up, shivered, then opened the door.

"Not you too!" Bishop said. "You're too sick to—"

"To die?" Siv laughed, almost maniacally.

He was alert, and for the first time in a week, he felt genuinely good. He could handle this.

Kyralla leaned back. "Siv..."

"Let me go," he replied. "I've only got..."

"Two and a half minutes, sir. Why wouldn't you respond to me?"

"I was busy dying, and talking with Dad." As he shut the door, he

told the others, "I've only got about a minute left. I'd like to spend it doing whatever I can."

He walked out and stood beside Mitsuki. "Didn't think you were going to do this alone, did you?"

Mitsuki raised an eyebrow at him. "Can't believe your alive, Sivvy. I want a hit of what you took, okay?"

"Before or after you've been shot through with a plasma bolt?"

"After."

"Come get us!" Siv yelled, deploying his helmet and drawing his plasma pistol. "If you're man enough!"

Mitsuki laughed, raising her plasma carbine. "I'm ready and willing, boys!" She flashed an obscene gesture at them with her other hand.

"Egads, sir, the both of you are such drama queens. And though I'd love to watch the show, this is my *moment, and I need you to take a step back.* Now."

"Put down your weapons and surrender immediately," an irritated soldier yelled over the loudspeaker, "or you *will* be neutralized!"

Mitsuki deployed her helmet. "You can try!"

Something clanked and whirred beneath them, and the ground beneath them began to quake.

"Sir!"

Siv stepped back, grabbing Mitsuki by the arm and pulled her along with him. Startled by his touch, she fired her carbine into the cockpit of the strike-fighter on the right. The shots glanced off the craft's force field.

The strike-fighter returned fire with a guided round that could hit only her. Which was smart, because that way they wouldn't risk hurting Oona.

Siv activated his force shield and leaped in front of Mitsuki. The round exploded against the energy field, knocking it out and tossing them back into the car. The fiery remnants that made it through the shield scorched their armor and blackened the faceplates on their helmets.

The impact with the hood of the car knocked the wind out of Siv, and he was pretty sure he heard a few ribs crack. But he didn't care. He wasn't feeling much of anything at the moment.

They both slid down the hood onto the ground, just as the doors to a large hangar slid open in front of them. As dust and debris collapsed into the hole, the strike-fighters pulled back.

Suddenly, the *Outworld Ranger* shot out from the hangar, its plasma cannons opening fire on the surprised strike-fighters. The shields of the right one collapsed, and Siv cheered wildly as a second burst of shots struck the craft's engine, sending it spiraling out of control.

As the damaged Dagger First crashed, the other one returned fire. The shots bounced off the *Outworld Ranger's* deployed shields. The *Ranger* closed on the strike-fighter, then with a burst of speed rammed into it. The gray-and-white cruiser was three times the size of the Dagger Fist, with far more powerful engines. The strike-fighter's shields collapsed, the nosecone crumpled, and it flew backward. Before the craft could recover, the *Outworld Ranger* blew off its right wing.

As the Dagger First crashed, the *Outworld Ranger* landed between it and the skimmer car.

"That was beautiful," Siv said, laughing. "Good shooting, Silkster!"

"You can thank me later, sir," Silky said.

"I'll do it now. Thank you, old friend."

"You're high, sir."

"No kidding! I'm dying too, you know."

"I'm aware of that," Silky grumbled. *"You know, Ana and Gav went out with a whole lot more grace."*

The large door on the back of the *Outworld Ranger* opened. As the boarding ramp deployed, the others charged out from the car. Oona helped Mitsuki up and into the ship, while Kyralla half-carried

Siv, who was still laughing with delight. Bishop helped Seneca out of the trunk, and together they pushed the car up the ramp.

Octavian met them inside.

"Now there's a sight I never thought I'd see again! Hello, Octavian!"

"He's delirious," Kyralla said, dropping him onto the deck.

As soon as the car was all the way in, the ramp retracted, and the door snapped shut behind them.

The insectoid cog made three urgent bleep-bloops and scurried toward Siv.

"I'm fine," he said, sitting up.

Then his muscles spasmed, and he slumped, foaming at the mouth. The high vanished in an instant, and his mind and body burned. As he had feared, the Awake had taken away his peaceful death and replaced it with one of pain.

The cog hovered over him, its arms whirring as it pulled several injectors at once from a case. He remembered now how frightening it was. What a terrible sight to be his last...

50

KYRALLA VIM

While the insectoid cog stuck Siv with a sequence of injectors, Kyralla squatted down and patted Siv on the shoulder. "Hang in there."

Silky's voice rang out over the comm. "Everyone to the Bridge!"

Mitsuki limped off down the corridor. "Come on, Kyralla, we've got work to do."

Kyralla hesitated, biting her lip with worry, while Bishop rocked on his heels, probably as much in awe of the cog as he was terrified Siv would die. Oona knelt and prayed.

"*Now!*" Silky yelled.

Kyralla turned and ran after Mitsuki, with Bishop trailing behind her.

Oona hung back. "I'll stay with Siv."

"I said *everyone!*" Silky growled.

Oona's footsteps echoed behind Kyralla as they rushed through the corridor to the Bridge.

Kyralla had only ever been on two other ships. She'd taken several trips on her father's A14-A cutter, which was smaller but far more luxurious than the *Outworld Ranger*. It was also limited in armament to a single ion cannon and a flak cannon. And she'd traveled on Uncle Pashta's Bo2-Z cutter, which was nearly the same as her father's ship, except for better shields and an upgrade to a quad-ion cannon. The cutters traded cargo space and weaponry for additional crew space and comforts. And they achieved good speeds by carrying less cargo and fewer weapons.

Neither of those ships had anything near the armament, defenses, or speed the *Outworld Ranger* possessed. And they certainly didn't have a bridge like this ship with its additional crew station, reinforced walls, and incredibly rare interface circlets.

The Tekk Plague had destroyed over three-quarters of all the neural interface circlets in existence. New ones were being constructed but at an incredibly slow pace, and at extreme expense. Many advanced, integrated ship AI's had also been lost, making the interface circlets useless for ordinary ships. But this ship, buried away for a century in its hangar, had missed the plague entirely.

The bridge was small but functional, with plenty of room to move about. Long hours here probably wouldn't leave anyone used to space travel feeling cramped. There were three crew stations and a command chair, all with interface circlets. A large viewport looked out straight ahead, along with two smaller ones on each side and one above. At a glance, Kyralla couldn't tell if these were energy shielded diamondine windows or extreme definition view screens.

The overall look of the bridge, like the rest of the ship, proclaimed function over style. Pale gray fabric covered padded seats. The walls and ceiling were white, the floor charcoal. Black consoles held screens with minimal colors and an utter lack of flair. And yet, there was a coziness to it she couldn't put her finger on.

"Kyralla, take the pilot's station," Silky ordered. "It's the one in the center. Bishop, sensor station on the left. Mitsuki, weapons on the right. Oona, command chair."

Under Silky's direction, the *Outworld Ranger* took off into the sky. Or maybe the ship's AI took care of that. Kyralla had no idea.

"Everyone put on the sexy circlet at your station and do *exactly* what I say."

They followed Silky's hurried instructions on how to use their stations. Kyralla gripped the side-stick controller mounted on the chair arm with her right hand and the throttle on the other side with her left. She knew the ship's AI and Silky would work with her in tandem, but she didn't really understand how. She supposed it was just something you had to experience.

"So what do I do?" Oona asked.

"Meditate on positive things," Silky replied. "You're simply loaning brainpower to the ship."

"As if my mind were another computer system?"

"Exactly. And I'm serious when I say meditate. You don't know what you're doing, so don't try to influence anything, okay? You'd just make things worse."

"You got it, Silky."

"I'm still not sure how I fit into this," Kyralla said. "What am I supposed to be doing?"

Silky sighed. "I forget that you don't have any experience with tech and...well...anything. The ship can fully operate itself, even in dangerous situations. But human input can take it to the next level. While it uses probability calculations and battle-tested routines, it lacks instincts and creativity. So that's what you're bringing to the table, along with raw brainpower. And the ability to take over a function if the ship sustains damage."

"That still doesn't answer my question," Kyralla countered, her voice strained as she tried to hold back her irritation at Silky. "Unless you mean that I should just sit here and think happy thoughts about what we want to happen."

"Basically, that's what I want from you."

"Oh."

"Except when we get into danger. Then I want you to take the controls and blank your conscious mind as best as possible as if you were meditating. You need to work in sync with the ship's AI while maintaining your human instincts. When you do it right, your actions and those of the AI will blend such that you won't know where your part in piloting the ship ends and its part begins. Once you experience it, you'll understand what I mean."

"I'll do what I can," Kyralla replied dubiously.

"What are you going to do, Silky?" Oona asked.

"Assist everyone and manage the shields. And I'll help keep you up-to-date on what's going on. Reading the info in the HUD while function-merged requires a lot of practice."

Red warning lights flared, and a klaxon sounded.

"We've got incoming!" Silky shouted.

"You focus on other things," Bishop said. "I can handle calling out information to the others. That's the point of my station anyway."

"Then go," Silky responded.

"We've got two Dagger Fists blazing in!" Bishop said. "And the battlecruiser is closing on us, with an active target lock."

All the information Bishop called out flowed through a ship status window that had popped up in Kyralla's HUD after she put on the circlet. But she was too busy figuring out the flight controls to read any of it, and she had Rosie focused on helping her. With even a little practice, this would all be so much easier.

"Quad plasma cannon armed," Mitsuki said. "Twin railguns loaded. Flak cannon ready."

"The battle cruiser just launched two ion missiles!" Bishop shouted.

"Course plotted," Silky said. "Kyralla, let the ship follow its preset course. Only deviate if you need to take evasive actions, understood?"

"Understood, Silky."

Kyralla glanced back at Oona and smiled. She wouldn't let her sister down. She turned back to the controls, released a deep breath, and smoothed out her thoughts, focusing only on the moment. She could do this. The ship was inconsequential. It was nothing more than a weapon in her hands, and therefore, this was no different than any of the thousands of combat simulations she'd done, using a variety of weapons. All she had to do was focus then use her honed reaction speed along with her ability to peek into the future.

As the *Outworld Ranger* climbed, the sky deepened from a bright, milky blue to darker and darker shades of violet. The Dagger Fists fired wildly as they fell behind, but only two stray plasma shots connected, glancing harmlessly off the *Ranger's* shields. Then, as they edged into the black of space, the strike-fighters were forced to withdraw.

As the ion missiles closed in, Kyralla gripped the control stick tighter but loosened her grip on the throttle. She had no intention of changing the ship's speed, regardless of the evasive maneuvers they might take. Their best defense was getting the hell out of here.

She "saw" the flak cannon destroy the first ion missile. A half-second later the guns actually opened up, and a faint thumping sound echoed through the ship as the bullets zipped silently through space.

The ion missile exploded in a bright flare.

The second missile survived a glancing bullet and headed straight toward them. Kyralla flicked the control stick to the right. The ship rolled in response. The missile passed beneath them then turned upward sharply. But the ship nosed downward so that it couldn't connect.

The first maneuver, that was all her, as far as she could tell. The second one definitely wasn't. She would never have thought to do that, and it wasn't something she'd seen ahead. That maneuver was all the AI's doing. She could certainly see now how a trained pilot would eventually be unable to tell the difference between his actions and the ship's.

As the missile banked around, the flak cannon destroyed it. Mitsuki let out a cheer while everyone else breathed a sigh of relief.

The vibrations of the hull diminished as they exited the atmosphere, but the twin-ion engines burned just as hot. Silky had them operating in emergency mode, and according to Rosie, they were consuming more than twice as much fuel and battery power as normal, while putting enormous strain on the engine components. While the increased need for future repairs concerned Rosie, Kyralla couldn't care less so long as they moved faster.

"Two more ion missiles launched!" Bishop called out. "Eight starfighters deployed. Orbital defense platforms powering up."

Kyralla groaned. "Is that as bad as it sounds?"

"Only if you consider starfighters and laser batteries a problem," Silky replied. Before anyone could respond, he added, "I just realized you may not understand what you're facing. The starfighters are bad. But the laser batteries are very, very bad."

"I didn't have any doubts about either," Kyralla replied.

"Are we going to fight back?" Mitsuki asked.

"These aren't the bad guys," Oona said. "They're innocent soldiers, just doing their jobs. They don't even know who or what we are."

"We can't just let them kill us!" Mitsuki argued.

"Keep your focus on defense and evasion," Silky said. "We're way outnumbered, so we really can't do enough damage to anything to matter."

On cue, Bishop said, "Two more battlecruisers heading toward us on an intercept course. Looks like we're going to get pinched."

"Lasers in twenty seconds," Silky said. "Missiles in ten. Kyralla, you're going to have to weave the pattern."

"I'm going to have to what?"

"Ignore Silky and focus, madam," Rosie said.

Kyralla tried to let everything go again. The flak cannons took out two missiles. She pulled the stick back and to the right to nose away from the third, then jerked the stick hard left to dodge the second, finding the ship was already moving that way ahead of her.

But the last dodge wasn't fast enough.

The ion missile exploded against the bridge. Or it would have if not for the shields. A wash of white energy sparked along the ship's force field.

"Shields down to sixty-three," Bishop said. "Sensors temporarily offline. Missile coming round."

Before Kyralla could take evasive maneuvers, the flak cannon nailed the turning ion missile.

Silky's voice piped into Kyralla's mind. *"Do you know the Fibonacci sequence?"*

"Not really."

"It's my favorite, but we'll keep it easy since you're new to it. Repeat after me silently. One, one, two, three, five, eight, thirteen..."

Kyralla did as he asked, finding the addition annoyingly tricky as the numbers kept climbing.

"Now start over and keep counting, open your mind, see what's ahead."

She did as he asked.

"Evade."

The laser batteries from two different orbital platforms opened up, catching the *Outworld Ranger* in a crossfire. Luckily, the beams would be at minimal strength, since their intention was simply to damage the ship and not destroy it. Only the fact that the Federation wanted to capture Oona had kept them alive so far.

Firing at a target this close, the second-long, speed-of-light bursts hardly even needed to lead the ship. But Kyralla could see them a half-moment early, allowing her to respond more effectively than the AI's evasion pattern, which Rosie said had been programmed in by someone named Tal Tonis.

Kyralla ducked the *Ranger* below the first burst, rolled around the second, climbed the third, then yawed to avoid the fourth. She darted the ship in and out through a net of laser beams as if... Kyralla smiled. She was weaving the pattern.

And that thought distracted her.

A beam sliced along the bottom of the ship, reducing the shields to thirty-nine percent. Kyralla refocused, but the beams stopped.

She breathed a sigh of relief and wiped the sweat from her brow. She was surprised to find herself smiling. "Why have they stopped?"

"Their window of opportunity has closed for a few moments," Silky said. "They can't risk collateral damage on civilian ships and satellites."

"Eight ion missiles in route," Bishop announced.

"You've got to be freaking kidding me!" Mitsuki shouted. "We're never going to make it out of here!"

"Focus on the flak cannon," Kyralla said. "I've got this."

"Don't get too cocky, madam," Rosie cautioned.

"It's not overconfidence, Rosie. It's...it's faith."

"I don't understand, madam."

"I've discovered something today."

"What's that, madam?"

"I love flying, and I'm damned good at it. I think I was born just for this."

"I thought the purpose of your guardian awakening was to protect your sister."

"And what exactly am I doing right now?"

"Point taken, madam."

Silky's voice popped in again. She had thought Rosie was granting him access before, but now she could see through her HUD that he was using a channel provided by the interface circlet.

"Good work weaving the pattern."

"Thanks, Silky. The Fibonacci thing... It's weird."

"It helped, though, didn't it?"

"I hate to admit that it did."

"I learned it from my best friend."

"Siv?"

Silky laughed. *"Her name was Eyana. She was a talented Empathic Services agent. We served together forty-seven years."*

"Wow. I guess you and Sir haven't been together long at all compared to that."

"Very true, madam. Plus I basically raised him. Those early teenage years...so awkward."

Kyralla smiled. Silky was annoying, but he did have a way of lightening the mood. *"How's he doing?"*

"He's stable, madam. Get ready, you've got missiles on your tail."

The next few minutes passed in a blur as Kyralla gave herself over to flying the ship. She evaded the five missiles Mitsuki couldn't stop on the way in. And one she had to dodge three times before the flak cannon got it.

"No others in route?" she asked.

"Not currently," Bishop responded. "Maybe they've fired all they've got."

"That's good," Mitsuki said, "because the flak cannon's ammo is at fifteen percent."

"Good thing they don't know that," Oona said.

"They're taking a different approach now," Silky said. "Probably because they've never seen flying like this before."

"A different approach?" Mitsuki asked, leaning back in her seat to take a few deep breaths.

"Check your HUDs," Silky said.

Kyralla expanded the three-dimensional locator window in her HUD to check what was going on.

She groaned.

The starfighters had zoomed ahead to outflank them, the two original battlecruisers were in pursuit, and a third battlecruiser had pulled out from behind the planet's second moon to speed ahead of them. They were being surrounded.

"We're never going to the make the breakpoint," Kyralla said.

A message demanding their surrender scrolled through their HUDs. Kyralla assumed it was the first, but Rosie told her it was the fifth such message.

"We're so screwed," Mitsuki said in disgust.

Kyralla could sense the fear lurking behind the wakyran's words. She obviously couldn't stand the idea of being unable to escape, and it wasn't because of the consequences she would face. It was the very idea of being trapped that terrified her.

Bishop pounded his fists into the arms of his seat. "Why can't we catch a freaking break?"

"Your timing's remarkable, Mr. Bishop," Silky said. "Pay attention to your locator."

"Whoah!" Bishop said. "Three warships just entered the Ekaran system. Really big ones."

"Thousand Worlder battleships," Silky said.

"How's this catching a break?" Oona asked.

"Note their position," Silky replied.

The enemy warships had entered the system on the opposite side of the planet from them, while the *Ranger* was already leaving the planet's gravity well. The Federation warships might snare them, but the Thousand Worlders would never have a chance.

And the Federation ships were no longer interested in Oona. They had a planet and sovereign territory to defend. Besides, they would no doubt rather have Oona running free than have her fall into the clutches of Empress Qan.

The Terran Federation battlecruisers and starfighters peeled off and turned toward the invading Thousand World battleships.

Oona stood and pumped her fists. "We did it!"

Bishop hopped out of his seat and did a dance that could only be described as embarrassing. Mitsuki gaped at him, then shook her head and muttered a string of celebratory curses. Kyralla laughed uncontrollably for a few moments, then started to cry, then suddenly grasped her stomach and hunched over, trying not to vomit.

"*Are you okay, madam?*" Rosie asked.

"I...I'm great, actually."

"*Are you sure, madam? Because you appear to be sick.*"

"*Can you be sick with relief?*"

"*It's the aftereffects of all the stress of the last few hours,*" Silky said.

Once she knew what she was doing, Kyralla was going to put an end to his interjections.

Over the comm, Silky said, "You lot, nutty and random as you may be, did a damn fine job today. I can't believe I'm going to say it, but I am impressed. Even with you, Mits."

"It was all thanks to you though, right?" she asked with a snort.

"Of course! *Everything* good that happens is thanks to my brilliance."

51

SIV GENDIN

Siv awoke on the bed in the captain's cabin, a room he hadn't seen since he was ten years old, nearly a century ago. The Vrazel Mask, a fake Ancient artifact he'd bought for his dad, sat in a glass case on the nightstand beside him. He hadn't known it when he purchased it off an auction site, but that mask had brought his parents together.

"Silkster...status update..."

"We evaded capture, snagged a bit of luck, and now we're nearing the breakpoint, sir. We've got a good crew here, for a bunch of rookies."

"So everyone's okay?"

"They all made it through, sir."

He sat up with a groan. *"I'm going to want all the details...later."*

Octavian clattered into the room squawking at him and gesturing for him to lie back down.

"I have to agree with the bug, sir. Your vitals are still weak."

"I can rest later. I want to see the jump." Siv stood, fell back onto the bed, then got back up. "Octavian, help me to the Bridge. That's an order."

The willful cog screeched a complaint then relented and half carried Siv out into the corridor.

"You saved my life, Octavian. Thank you."

The cog issued a series of beeps followed by several faltering bloops.

"He says you're not cured, sir. The disease has set in. He can only manage your symptoms, and for only a few months, tops. He also says he wishes he could have saved Gav."

"He would be delighted to know that you saved me, Octavian."

The cog blooped then trilled a long response.

"He wants to know if you're going to activate his vocalizer, sir. Understand, I will not translate for him unless absolutely necessary, according to my definition of necessary."

"I'll think about it."

With assistance, Siv stumbled onto the deck. The others looked exhausted, yet relieved. Which was understandable. They had survived, and now they were escaping.

They greeted him warmly and asked how he was.

"I'm okay...for now. And yes, I will get some rest. But I *needed* to see the jump." He approached the command chair. "Oona, may I?"

She took off the command interface circlet and hopped up. "Of course, Siv. It's your ship."

He dropped into the command chair with a smile. "It's been so long since I was last here. In this chair, sitting on my dad's lap while he explained how everything worked."

Oona leaned over and kissed him on the cheek. "Thank you for saving us."

"You're welcome."

Kyralla smiled at him. "We owe you."

"You don't owe me anything." He lifted the amulet out from his armor. "Besides, I think this was my destiny."

Mitsuki pointed at Bishop. "You, however, do owe me, little gizmet. Don't think for a minute you're getting out of your debt, either."

Bishop blushed and stammered an unintelligible reply, and Siv laughed, knowing Bishop had no idea what he actually owed her.

"*Silkster, would you like to do the honors?*"

"*I would, sir, but I can't. You have to manually activate the stardrive. I'm loading the instructions into your HUD.*"

Siv punched in a four-digit access code, pressed a button on the control panel's left side, then pushed a handle forward on the right side.

The hyperphasic bubble flared around the ship, and the stars began to shift.

Mitsuki howled like a crazed wolf, and Bishop clapped with glee and danced around. Kyralla and Oona laughed.

Siv leaned back into the seat with a satisfied sigh and rubbed a thumb across the amulet. "*I always wanted to be more than a thief, something meaningful.*"

"*Now's your chance, sir. Though, you're still a criminal.*"

"*On a rogue starship.*"

"*Sir, I have to admit, that does have a nice ring to it.*"

———

To learn more about how Gav acquired Silky and recalled the Ancient ship from hyperspace, check out **Forbidden System**, Book One of the *Fall of the Benevolence series*.

AFTERWORD

Want a free copy of my Starter Library, which includes deleted scenes, snippets, and **The Shadowed Manse**, the first episode in *The Arthur Paladin Chronicles*?

All you have to do is visit dahayden.com/space-opera to sign up for my no-spam newsletter.

———

If you enjoyed this book, please leave a review. All it takes is a few sentences. Without positive reviews a series may wither and die.

ALSO BY DAVID ALASTAIR HAYDEN

Storm Phase

The Storm Dragon's Heart

The Maker's Brush

Lair of the Deadly Twelve

The Forbidden Library

The Blood King's Apprentice

The First Kaiaru

The Arthur Paladin Chronicles

The Shadowed Manse

The Warlock's Gambit

Pawan Kor

Wrath of the White Tigress

Chains of a Dark Goddess

Who Walks in Flame

18771804R00203

Made in the USA
Middletown, DE
01 December 2018